William Dalton

Lost in Ceylon

William Dalton

Lost in Ceylon

ISBN/EAN: 9783337321406

Printed in Europe, USA, Canada, Australia, Japan

Cover: Foto ©Andreas Hilbeck / pixelio.de

More available books at **www.hansebooks.com**

LOST IN CEYLON:

THE STORY OF

A Boy and Girl's Adventures

IN

THE WOODS AND THE WILDS OF THE LION KING OF KANDY.

BY

WILLIAM DALTON,

AUTHOR OF

"THE WHITE ELEPHANT," "THE WAR TIGER," ETC.

With Illustrations by Harrison Weir.

LONDON:

GRIFFITH AND FARRAN,

(SUCCESSORS TO NEWBERY AND HARRIS),

CORNER OF ST. PAUL'S CHURCHYARD.

MDCCCLXI

TO MY READERS.

MY dear friends, should you perchance *read* this preface, it must be satisfactory for you to know that while the characters, (and story so far as there be one), in the following narrative are of the Author's creation, it contains not a single incident that has not fact for its basis.

For the truthfulness of the descriptions of the natural history and productions of Ceylon, it is not necessary to vouch in this place, inasmuch as the names of my authorities will be found quoted in the text.

WILLIAM DALTON.

London, November, 1860.

TO

THOMAS DALTON, Esq.,

THIS BOOK

Is Affectionately Inscribed

BY HIS SON,

THE AUTHOR.

CONTENTS.

LOST IN CEYLON.

CHAPTER I.

I AM INTRODUCED TO MAY FORD, WITH WHOM I
GO TO SEA, AND MAKE ACQUAINTANCE WITH
TWO QUEER PEOPLE—BOB CHASE AND FOSFORUS.

So lively is my disposition, so buoyant my spirits,
and so elastic in general my gait, that at times I
am inclined to think the original intention of
nature was to keep me a boy the whole of my
days, even at this present writing, an it were not
for a semi-girdle of lumbago, and the by no
means light weight of some eighty years piled
upon my shoulders, I should feel game for a
match at cricket, leap-frog, or fly-the-garter. As,
however, I think it quite possible that at eighty
I might not be a match for twenty-eight, eighteen, or even eight, I shall instead take up my
pen and perform a solo—for your amusement I
believe, and for your instruction I hope. Do not
let the latter word frighten you; for the experience of the old should always be for the benefit

L.I.C.   B

of the young; but at the outset let me impress upon your minds that in the following narrative I shall put forth no incident or adventure that has not fact for its basis.

The two chief events which led to my after adventures in the island of Ceylon, were, first, the appointment of one Thomas Elton (namesake and father of mine) to the command of a ship belonging to a very old person, recently deceased, one John Coompany—better, however, known as the Honourable East India Company—in whose service my father had spent the greater portion of his life. That appointment was my first heart's rejoicing; for I heard him tell my mother that he had at length obtained that which would not only enable him to place me in a position in the world, but which, under Providence, must in a few years give them both the means of passing the evening of their lives in comfort and repose.

Event number two was the return of my father from his first voyage in command. Having embraced my mother and me, he said—

"I have a present for thee, wife, and for thee also, son Tom."

"A present!" repeated my mother; "surely it is the parrot you have so often promised me."

"No, no, mother; it is the monkey father promised me," said I, with a thrill of delight at the fun I should have with the animal.

"Nay, neither parrot nor monkey exactly, though mayhap a little of each; but rest patient, and you shall judge for yourselves."

So saying my father ran back to the hackney coach which had brought him from the docks, and then stood waiting at our door.

During his short absence my brain was strangely puzzled: "Part parrot, part monkey! What animal is this my father has brought us from those wonderful Indies?" I muttered to myself. But guess my astonishment when in another minute he returned, bringing a little girl about two years younger than myself, with light olive complexion, smiling face, features as beautifully chiselled as the statue of a Greek goddess, lithe fairy figure, and an abundance of very dark brown hair, which hung around her fair brow, and, falling over her shoulders, almost reached her waist.

"Lord a mercy, Tom! why, what a little beauty!" said my mother, starting with surprise.

"Is it parrot or monkey?" said my father, laughing.

"Fie, fie, Tom," replied my mother, snatching the child up in her arms and kissing her.

"What a pretty girl. How jolly! wont she do for a sister?" said I, running up to her and taking both her hands in mine; adding, "You will be my sister, little girl, wont you?"

But although she smiled very prettily, and seemed

B 2

greatly pleased, I was both pained and surprised
to hear her reply in a language that was strange
to me, and, indeed, to my mother, who said—

"From what heathenish land comes the lass,
my husband, that she speaks not English?"

"Tut, tut!" said my father; "thou hast heard
but one side of her tongue yet. She is a little
scared at present, and has lost the use of the
other; but take her to thy heart, dear wife, for
that will understand the language of misfortune,
however strange to thine ear may be mere lip-
words."

And, obeying, my mother clasped the little
stranger to her bosom, when I knew that their
hearts had spoken to each other through their
eyes, for in both gleamed affection; and thus was
I first introduced to one who will play no un-
important part in the following narrative.

Now, young people become friends much sooner
than their seniors; so, before we had been an hour
together, the little girl found the use of the *other*
side of her tongue, which was a kind of foreign
English. Strange, however, as it was, I soon
learned from her that the language she had first
spoken, and which neither my mother nor myself
could understand, was Dutch, and that her name
was May Ford, and that she was the child of an
Englishman and a Dutch lady; but, as I at once
made up my mind she was an orphan, I inquired

no more, for fear of tearing open old wounds, that night—however, as I lay awake thinking of my new companion—and that, too, with the head of my bedstead next a thin wooden partition which divided my bedchamber from my parents' sitting-room—I heard my father give my mother the following account of May's history:—

"Mayhap, dear Lotty," said he, "you may remember an old shipmate of mine, one Mat Ford."

"Truly; he sailed with you in the *Martha* as third officer," said my mother.

"Aye, the same; but thou dost not know that, having been long promised the command of a ship, and getting tired of waiting, he at length took service with the Dutch East India Company; when, after making several successful voyages, he settled for life in the Indian seas—that is, he married a Dutchwoman, of Bantam, in Java—and from that day to this has been employed in trading trips among the islands in the Pacific and Indian oceans.

"Now, as, you know, we were bound for Madras. Well, having discharged our cargo there, the agent sent us on a trip to the coast of New Guinea. The run there was pretty smart, and we discharged our cargo and shipped another; but, on our return to Fort St. George, it so happened we fell in with such a hurricane in the Straits of Sunda, that we were obliged to cut the mainmast by the board. Accordingly I put into Bantam to refit; when, bethinking me of my old shipmate Ford, I searched him out, and found him in great distress, for his wife had recently died, leaving him with this little girl, his only daughter."

" Poor dear child," interposed my mother, with a deep sigh.

" Aye, aye, maybe, wife; and poor Ford, too, I say; for it is hard fate for a seaman to be left with such like gear as a girl to look after, and he all the while obliged to be with but a board or two between him and the sharks. But that is neither here nor there; so, to go on with the yarn, you see I tried to cheer Mat up under his trouble; and knowing he had an old aunt in this country, I persuaded him to send the girl to her, to be educated like an Englishman."

" An Englishwoman, you mean," said my mother, interrupting him, for the dear soul liked to be precise in all things.

" Tut, tut, Lotty; you *know* what I mean. Of course, like an Englishwoman, and not like the Indian Hollanders, who, at the best, are but a mixture of the worst parts of both races, without any of the good of either; and so you see Mat jumped at the notion. As for the little girl, although at first she whimpered a little at the idea of leaving her father for an old grand-aunt whom she had never seen, when we had made her comprehend that, anyhow, her father would be away from her, with the exception of short intervals, till his fortunes over-balanced the necessity of his keeping afloat, she dried her eyes, and from that moment has not shed a tear."

"The darling!" said my mother; "but," she added, sorrowfully, "surely you do not intend looking after this old aunt now, who, take my word for it, Tom, wont love her as I shall."

"Tut, tut; thou art impatient, wife of mine," said my father. "When the ship, on arriving, put in at Plymouth, I at once set out in search of the old lady; for Mat told me she lived about five miles t'other side of the town. I soon found the house, but also, to my disappointment, that the old lady had left it some twelve months before for her last home; so, as the girl was adrift and lonely, I brought her to thee, that she might be brought up like a Christian and an Englishwoman; and mayhap be a daughter to thee till it shall please God to restore her to her father."

"Aye, husband; and as I am a true woman, thy wish shall be carried out," said my mother.

And I listened no longer; for, having heard it arranged that she was to remain with us, I fell asleep, to dream of the merry life I should have now that I had a new companion; but, as it is not the history of my whole career, or even of my boyhood, that I am about to narrate, but only an account of my adventures in the island of Ceylon, I will pass in rapid review the early events of my life.

The coming to our home of May Ford gave me a delight the like of which I had never before known; for not only was she pretty and clever, but so good-humoured and lively, that the three following years, during the whole of which my father was at sea, passed away as quickly almost as if they had been but so many months.

At the end, however, of that happy three years, when my father returned, he grieved us, but especially my mother, by telling us that May's father had retired from the sea service, and settled as a merchant in Bantam; and as he longed to have his daughter with him, it had been arranged that upon my father's next voyage May should accompany him to Madras, at which place she would remain until a passage could be taken for her in some ship that would touch at Batavia on her homeward voyage.

Now, to lose May was grief enough for my poor mother; but, alas! she had more to bear; for, having long resolved upon following the sea for my livelihood, and being fifteen years of age, I was so restless to begin, that I persuaded my father to take me with him that next voyage; and thus I entered into that profession which it is pro-

verbial most boys hanker after, and of which most
men tire when too late in life to turn to other
means of obtaining a living; and that they should
so tire of the sea is not to be wondered at, for so
monotonous, so wearisome is the life, that in time
the dangers which seem so charming, so romantic
to the youthful imagination lose their relish, and
become hated for their dull frequency.

Apart from being separated from my mother, to
whom I was passionately attached, and with whose
grief at parting for a very indefinite period with
those so dear to her affectionate heart, I could not
but sympathize, the day I first touched the deck
of my father's ship was the happiest I had ever
known. A new world, a fresh life, seemed opening
up to me. It was, or seemed to be, the sudden
transition from boyhood to manhood; nay, from
that very moment I became as impatient to com-
mence my duties as a race-horse to run the course
stretched before him. But such was not to be; for
but a few hours after the ship left the river, sea-
sickness laid me by the heels, and there kept me
for a good three weeks; but what was more galling
to me was, upon my recovery, to find that while
I, the boy, had succumbed, my little sister—as I
always called May—had had the use of her sea legs
from the outset; an advantage over me at which the
little rogue laughed so often, that—well, I must
own, I only wished she had been a boy for a few

hours, that I could have quarrelled with her. But when, bless her heart! she saw I was really pained by her innocent banter, she begged my pardon, and from that moment never repeated the offence. Of our voyage out I have little to tell that could interest you; for, like most voyages, we had the usual share of calms and storms. The event of chiefest importance to me was the making the acquaintance—indeed, I may say friendship—of one Bob Chase, an old man-of-war's man, but then coxswain, boatswain, and almost confidential friend of my father. Now, this Bob was a rough, honest, hearty old fellow who had spent the greater portion of his life at sea, and, like all old sailors, loved the society of young people; and so, when we got into warm latitudes, he would employ his spare hours in spinning long yarns about his former service and experiences, greatly to the delight of May and myself, who, sitting upon a coil of rope, would listen as earnestly to his stories as if every word had been gospel truth: but of Bob more anon, when he will speak for himself. Suffice it to say that the old man's yarns did much to shorten the tediousness of the voyage after we had passed the Line.

About seven months after leaving the Downs we arrived in the Madras roads, and for the first time I saw the continent of India, the wonderful India of which I had heard so much; and greatly

was I disappointed to find that, in consequence of
want of anchorage, and a surf so strong that the
largest ships can never approach the town, and
sometimes even boats cannot live, our landing
must be indefinitely postponed. In a week, however, we were able to land our cargo; and this
was no sooner done than the Company's agent at
Fort St. George ordered us to ship a fresh cargo
for, and make a quick run to, Ceylon, where, if
possible, we were to open up a trade with the
natives, in spite of the avaricious Hollanders,
who at that time were the only Europeans who
openly traded with that "pearl hanging from the
brow of India," as the island has been charmingly
called.

Here let me remark, for the benefit of those
of my readers not versed in the history of the
East, that although so large a portion of Asia is
now under the dominion of England, the Portuguese and Spaniards were the first Europeans
who, by force of arms or fraud, established themselves in India, the Indian islands, China, and
Japan. But these people, although brave, were so
cruel and treacherous, and consequently so hated
by the Asiatic races among whom they endeavoured to establish themselves, that they were
without great difficulty driven from their chief
settlements by the Dutch, who for a long time
were the real Lords of the East (even now they

hold vast and valuable possessions); but if the Portuguese and Spaniards had been hated and feared, the Hollanders, by their selfish love of mere money-making and grovelling habits, earned so deservedly the utter contempt of the natives, and were, moreover, so feeble in the military art, that they had in their turn to succumb to the English, who, it is to be hoped, may be found to deserve the conquests they have made, and recently fought so hard to retain, by building an empire of love, gratitude, and respect in the hearts of the conquered.

Well, in obedience to orders, we had shipped our cargo, and were ready to stand out to sea; but what was to be done with May? for it was probable that months might elapse, and no ship bound for Batavia touch at Madras. This was a great trouble to my father, till the agent, coming to his relief, kindly offered to take charge of her till our return. Kind, however, as was this offer, May would not listen to it—no, she would sail with us; and so earnestly did she plead for my father's permission, that he could not find it in his heart to refuse, and thus it was that she became a fellow-wanderer with me in the woods and the wilds of Ceylon.

Now, the true reason of our being so hurried was, that two Malabar merchants, who had had dealings with the agent, had for some time been waiting for a ship in which they might obtain a passage to Trincomalee, from whence they intended proceeding to Kandy, the capital of the island. The agent, therefore, deeming it an opportunity of opening up a trade with the natives, agreed to give the merchants a free passage, on the condition that they should make such a representation to the chiefs of the Siughalese of the wishes of the English, that any attempts the jealous, avaricious Hollanders might make to foil us (for it was certain they would make such attempts) would be fruitless.

Now, notwithstanding our hurry-scurry in freighting the ship, and getting her fit for sea, to accommodate these Malabar merchants, they kept us waiting two days, greatly to the vexation of all, but to the especial annoyance, I may add fear, of Bob Chase, who, to use his own language, "could see not no reason whatsomdever why decent Christian white people should be kept skulking about just to oblige a pair of lazy heathen lubbers;" but the old man's ire rose to boiling point when, upon the morning of the day they were to have arrived, the agent sent a message telling us that they would come on board early the following morning. "For, look you, Cap'n," said he to my father, "to-morrow is Friday, and no good ever came of a ship that sailed on that day; and of that I'm sartin sure, for three times in my life have I been cast away, and it all came of sailing on Fridays. I tell 'e, it's playing your cards right into 'Davy Jones's' own hand;" and, although I laughed incredulously, and my father pooh-poohed and pshaw-pshawed, it was of no use. Bob was in a fit of the doldrums, and in it he would be sure to remain until we had weighed anchor, and the active business of the ship occupied his mind.

Well, night came, and with it a delicious land breeze, that repaid us for the choking, sickly heat of the day. May and I, as was our wont, were sitting upon the half-deck, near my father's cabin, talking of England, my mother, and regrettingly of the time when she would quit the ship to re-join her father; and delightfully the minutes seemed to pass—the elements were calm, the sea unruffled, and nought but the bright moon shining upon the ship, which sat upon the waters like a slumbering swan. My father and the crew were at rest—all, indeed, save one man, who was to the fore, and Bob Chase, who had the first watch, and who kept pacing to and fro with the surly restlessness of an ill-conditioned bear, growling and grumbling at the two "niggers" who were the cause of our being at anchor in those roads.

For a time he soliloquized his discontent, but at length, coming to where May and I sat, he said, "Now, look you, Master Tom, and you too, Miss

May, old Bob isn't the man to croak, but it's my hope that these pleasant overhaulings of your memory mayn't come to split upon a reef of misfortune."

" Oh, Bob, you disagreeable, spiteful creature ; you are envious," said May, skipping towards the old man, and playfully patting his weatherbeaten cheek.

" Lor' bless your pretty little face, Miss May, old Bob isn't the man to show spite, no, nor envy either; but when a man has been afloat nigh upon forty years, and has kept his weather eye open, so as always to see what comes of sailing on a Friday, and that, too, to please a couple of niggers, who, being black, you see, must be more akin, and on friendly terms with the old un, why, you see——"

" Fie, fie, Bob, I thought you were a Christian," said May.

" Aye, aye, Miss ; that's where the wind lies ; for don't you see these niggers aint; but, Lor' love you, as for that, niggers though they be, I'd do 'em any good turn in my power; that is, at least, if so be it didn't go for to injure the Cap'n, the owners, or the passengers ; but, as for this sailing on a Friday, I tell 'e no good 'll come of it."

" Come, Bob, clear out of these doldrums; for, remember, if these forebodings of thine should come true, thou wilt deserve being burned for a witch," said I.

"Come, come, Bob, if you do not soon forget these fancies, I shall really think you are afraid of putting to sea," said May.

"Afraid," he replied, "Lor' bless you, it's little old Bob's afraid of; but then I am only a man, and a Christian, and so, you see, can't no how stand up agin a dead head wind like Fate, any more than I could expect to keep my head upon my shoulders if I claps it atwixt the jaws of an alligator; but if so be you think I'm afraid—and perhaps I am a little—it's because, d'ye see, a little while after I heard we were to sail to-morrow (Friday) I fell into a kind of dog-sleep, and dreamt that I was a-keeping the mid-watch, and walking to and fro, when all of a sudden there jump'd over the ship's side a"—but the old man stopped as if at a loss for a word—" but——"

"In the name of Goodness what?" asked May.

"Why," replied he, scratching the back of his head, "axing your pardon, miss—a devil."

"Fie, fie, Bob," said May.

"Then, maybe, a friend of his'n, miss."

"But, pray, master Bob, how did you know it was the Evil One?" I asked.

"'Cos, d'ye see, he was black, with great goggling eyes."

"Nonsense, Bob; besides, the colours of demons

are more varied than the natives who believe in them—white, red, blue, and black," said I.

"That may be, Master Tom; howsomdever, all I ever see wor black uns."

" All you have SEEN," repeated May and I, laughing.

" Well, well; all I have heard on, I mean," he replied; adding, " but, at first, the sight of this unearthly shark as I wor tellin' you on, took me a little by surprise : and, before I could speak, he winked his eye at me, and said, says he, ' Mind, Bob, if *you* sails on a Friday, *I* sails on a Friday ; and if we both goes together, you'll know what'll happen ;' and then——"

"What? Bob; what?" asked May and I together.

" Why, you see, I'd overcome my fright, and was so enraged at his cool imperdence, that I snatched up a marlinspike, and——"

" Struck him," said I.

" Lor' bless you, no ; but brought my knuckles so heavily alongside the bulwarks, that it skinned 'em ; and that just woke me up, when of course I didn't see him, because, d'y' see, that kind o' varmint never lets you see 'em with your eyes open."

" Tut, tut, Bob !" said I, laughing at him. " This demon of thine was conjured up by the last meal of salt junk, which, sitting heavily on thy chest, caused nightmare ; but, really, old friend, thou shouldst have been an old wife to believe in such things."

"I tell 'e what, Master Tom," he replied; "I've been in the world some forty years longer than you, and so may have got a little rusty in salt water; but what I believe I believe; an' as for a heap o' years upon your head, if they do nothing better, they teach you not to laugh at things you don't understand," he replied, walking away from us much angered.

"Beg his pardon, dear brother," said May.

I did not, however, want pressing to do that; and so, jumping from my seat, I caught him by the hand, saying—

"Forgive me, Bob; for, although I may be young and thoughtless, it would grieve me to offend you."

"Lor' love the young skipper, I'm not offended; for, d'ye see, I believe there are old fools in the world as well as young ones, and I may be one on 'em."

And, uncomplimentary as was this reply, it satisfied me that the old sailor held no malice; to prove which, he there and then sat down upon a water-cask and began to spin one of his long yarns; but, stopping suddenly, he held up his hand, and in whispering tones said—

"Hush! there is some one in the stern chains."

I listened, and sure enough heard a noise as of

some person (not a seaman) climbing up the side
of the ship.

" That fish aint in his own water, I can tell, by
the flapping of his fins; but follow, and maybe
we'll put him right," said Bob.

I followed Bob to the side, when, having cautiously looked over, he said—

" It is some land shark from the shore ; let us
see the object of his cruise."

And the next instant we were crouching down
behind a heap of packages, but so that we could
easily watch the movements of the thief, for we
had little doubt that it was some rogue who, taking
advantage of the night and the calm, was about
attempting some petty pilferings ; an occurrence,
by the way, not uncommon in those latitudes.
Well, the man, whoever he might be, at length
fell upon the deck as softly, as noiselessly as a
cat upon all fours. For a moment he crouched
down, and looked cautiously around. As he did
so, the pale light of the moon shone upon his
face.

" It is, it is the very demon I saw in my dream ;
but this time he shan't escape," exclaimed
Bob.

And as he spoke, he darted forward, and snatching up a pike from the deck, would at once have
slain him, had I not caught his arm; when the
new comer, a poor, half-starved black boy, fell upon

his knees, and turning upward his great, brilliant eyes, said—

"Sar Excellency, I no debil; I Fosforus."

"Come, come, Bob, don't look so furious; for, after all, your devil is but a rogue of a black boy, whose turn may be served at most by a good rope's-ending."

"Sar, I no steal. I no debil. I no tief. I no black boy. I white boy Fosforus. I 'ropean," said the boy.

"Devil or no devil, you go to the sharks," said the angry Bob, taking the boy up in his arms, and in another instant the poor fellow would have been tossed into the sea without further ceremony, but for May, who, little angel as she was, caught hold of Bob's arm, crying—

"Fie! shame upon you, Bob! Would you be guilty of murder? Indeed," she added, catching hold of the old sailor's arm, "you shall not hurt the boy."

"Lor' bless you, miss," he said, for Bob was softened; "murder! Why, you might as well try to kill a fish by throwing it into the sea as to drown this imp."

"Imp? What dat, sar," asked the boy, gaining courage. "I not imp. I white boy Fosforus, and 'ropean like sar hisself."

"Well, well, white boy," replied Bob, who had now recovered his temper, but who, wishing to frighten the thief, as he believed him to be, added,

as he held him by the neck, " These good young
people are harder with you than old Bob; for,
instead of giving you a washing, they save you
for a skinning to-morrow with the rope's-end;"
and so saying, Bob lashed him to our great bow-
gun, there to remain during the night, notwithstanding the entreaties both of May and myself.

The next morning, when our captive was
arraigned before my father, I could not help
laughing at the pertinacity with which he insisted
upon his being a white boy and a 'ropean (European). In height he was a little more than four
feet; his limbs were thin, and so loosely adjusted
at the joints that they might have been sticks
held together by wire; for an Asiatic, his shoulders were broad, and his chest rather prominent;
his head was quite round; his features in shape a
mixture of European and Asiatic; his face, indeed
his whole skin, nearly black, though far from the
shining blackness of the negro, from whom he
again differed by his thin lips and long black
hair; moreover, his forehead was higher and
squarer, while his eyes, if not larger and more
brilliant, were certainly fuller of intelligence.
His dress was comical in the extreme, and evidently got together by instalments: upon his
head he wore a red cotton handkerchief, adjusted
turban fashion; his neck was bare, but the upper
part of his body was encased in the tattered, well-

worn, left-off uniform red coat of an English
soldier, and which fitted him as gracefully as a
purser's shirt upon a marlinspike; his nether
garments were of a light-blue calico; and, while
without stockings, which he had evidently not
been fortunate enough to pick up, his legs were
immersed in a pair of what had been cavalry
boots, and the upper leather or leggings of which
reached up to the knees; and of all this dress he
seemed immensely proud, for whenever he spoke
of his being a white boy, and a 'ropean like us,
he would let a glance of satisfaction fall from his
red coat down his blue trowsers into his great boots.

Now, my father, who, although a kind, was a
stern man, and moreover with a great horror of
thieving, no sooner heard how the boy had made
his appearance on board the ship, than he ordered
him at once to receive a rope's-ending, and be
sent adrift in his little boat; and as old Bob was
greatly prejudiced against the boy, and the latter
could not speak sufficient English to give weight,
or rather impress upon my father the real motive
of his coming on board, he most assuredly would
have been at once dismissed, in accordance with
the sentence, but for May, who herself being proficient in Dutch, and finding the boy knew more
of that than any other language that she could
understand, questioned him, when he told her—

That he was born in Kandy, was of Portuguese

descent, and that some two years before he had been persuaded by a Dutch skipper to enter on board his vessel as a kind of cook-boy. On board the Dutchman he served till within a few months of that time; but the skipper so fearfully and brutally ill-treated him, that he sought every opportunity to escape. That opportunity occurring, he swam ashore on to the Malabar coast; had made his way to Madras; there he had served an English merchant, always, however, with the hope of getting back to Ceylon; when, finding that we were bound for that island, he had taken a boat from its moorings, and boarded us, with the hope of hiding until we had got too far out to sea to put him ashore.

When May had told us this story, she added to my father, "And now, dear sir, he is very sorry for having come on board without your leave, but will serve you as a faithful slave if you will take him to his native island."

"As soon believe the old un as such a yarn," growled Bob.

"Silence, Bob," said my father; adding to the boy, "Here, thou rascal—what is thy name?"

"Sar Excellency, I not rascal—I white boy, 'ropean, like Excellency, and called Fosforus."

"Fosforus!" repeated my father.

"A proper name, too, for such an imp, as I take it he is, Cap'n," said Bob.

" Sar, I no imp, I Fosforus.   Look, Excellency
say so; because I quick foot, quick eye, quick
tongue, quick eberting; see in the dark, run in
the dark, like cat, Excellency—boy useful servant."

My father having meditated for a minute—he
always thought more than he spoke—then said,

" Take him below; feed the poor wretch; let
him make himself useful to the cook; moreover,
he speaks the tongue of the heathen Singhalese,
and will serve us as interpreter."

Thus the matter ended, and Fosforus (which I
suppose meant Phosphorus) became known and
attached to us; indeed, no more than May and I
did to the boy himself, before we had known
him many months.

Later in the day, the two Malabar merchants
came on board, and we sailed—sailed, too, on a
Friday; and although I do not believe in the
seaman's superstitious objection to that day, still
old Bob's predictions came true. We did sail on
a Friday, and were unfortunate, most unfortunate:
but I will not anticipate.

CHAPTER II.

WE ESCAPE THE JAWS OF A SHARK, AND LAND
IN CEYLON, BUT EASILY FALL INTO A TRAP.

FROM the time of our rounding Cape Comorin
and losing sight of the great continent of India,
till we came in view of the dark mountain chain
of the beautiful island of Ceylon, notwithstanding
Bob's forebodings, all went well; and although
to most on board the voyage was tedious, by
reason of an almost dead calm, the whole of the
passage gave much pleasure to May and myself;
for we whiled away the time in watching the
sporting of the smaller members of the deep, the
swarms of flying fish, and the gambolling of the
huge whales which infest those seas, but which
we then saw for the first time.

Fosforus, who on our voyage had shown, by
his liveliness and willingness to serve every person on board, how well he merited the character
he had given of himself, was the first who made
out the island.

"There, there," said he, pointing to a dark
speck in the distance, "is Lanka-Lanka Dwipa."

"Lanker-Wiper! Who's he? you black dog; for

though, man and boy, I've been in the seas well
nigh half a century, this is the first I ever heard
on him," said Bob.

" No, sar, not him; but what *you* call Cee-lon,"
replied the boy, who had called the island by its
Singhalese name. And Fos was not mistaken; for
there before us, as it were in the midst of the
ocean, a very universe of hills, tipped with the
rays of the evening sun, sat the island reposing—
hiding, as it were, from the orb of day amidst its
thick clothing of cocoa woods and palm-trees.
Lanka the resplendent, one of the most ancient
of the world's kingdoms; the Ceylon of modern
Europeans; the Taprobane of the Greeks and
Romans; but the Lanka Dwipa of the natives,
who in a portion of the island yet show an im-
print which Brahmins declare to have been left
by the foot of Brahma; the Buddhists, of their
deity, Buddha; and the Mahometans, the foot-
step of our first parent Adam, who, being expelled
from Paradise, sought rest for the soles of his feet
in Ceylon. But apart from such fables, the
island is regarded as sacred by the antiquary and
the philosopher as the undoubted tomb of a lost
but once vast civilization and of an energetic
race; remnants of whose vast works still exist to
mock the puny efforts of the effeminate people
who now inhabit the island, and who, if descendants of the former race (which, by the way, is

most questionable), have miserably degenerated, but who, miserable as they are, can yet show a veritable record of a monarchy consisting of a hundred and seventy kings, the first of whom reigned 543 years before Christ—that is, remember, before the time of King Ahasuerus, Haman, and Esther, of holy writ; prior to the battle of Marathon, and about two hundred years only after the supposed founding of Rome,—and the last of whom the monarch who occupied the throne at the time of which I write, was deposed by the British in 1815. So you see, in point of antiquity, which by nations no less than families is made a greater boast than virtue, the Singhalese have reason to be proud; that is, if any race have anything to be proud of, whose long line of ancestors have left no benefits to their descendants, and, like the beasts of the field, have only been born, fed, and died. For my part, I think the beasts have the best of the comparison, for they at least cannot be reproached with having misused God's noblest gift—reason.

But to resume my narrative. When we arrived at the great bay of Trincomalee—a bay, by the way, said to be sufficiently large to float the whole of the navy of England—we put the Indian merchants ashore at a native town called Cottiar, desiring them to inform the authorities of our arrival and wish to trade with the people. We cast anchor in the bay, there to await the result of our application to trade, but, for fear of treachery, did not venture to send a boat ashore, and well was our patience tested, for more than a week elapsed ere we received the slightest sign from the land that the merchants had even made known our wishes.

At length, when tired of lying at anchor, and my father was debating within his own mind whether he should send a boat party ashore, we observed, skimming through the water at the rate of some ten miles an hour, a queer-looking little craft, or rather double canoe, made of two trees lashed together by yarn, and hollowed out about two feet in depth; moreover, so frail that a single capful of wind would have upset it, but for an outrigger made of two long elastic poles, at the end of which was fastened another, which falling in the wake upon the windward side, steadied her; a contrivance, by the way, which was in fashion among the same people some eighteen hundred years ago. This boat was manned by four rowers, who manfully toiled at their long paddles to the tune of some native air, and who, with the exception of a band of cloth around their heads, and a loose linen cloth around their waists, were quite nude. As soon as she came alongside the ship, we saw she brought an individual who, from the superior texture and greater length of the cloth around his waist, the addition of a broad silk band, a shirt, a waistcoat, and a loose jacket worked with silver thread and ornamented with buttons of the same material, we imagined to be an officer of some rank. And so it proved; for when he came over the side, we found from Fosforus, who acted as interpreter, that he was a messenger from the King of Kandy, who, having heard from the Malabar merchants of our arrival in his kingdom, had at once sent down to the coast a dissuava (*i. e.*, general) and some troops to welcome us. Whereupon my father, stopping all conversation between the king's messenger and the boy, at once ordered a royal salute to be fired. This piece of politeness and respect, however, by its noise, much terrified the poor man, who seemed very far from thinking that, by shaking his body and almost stunning him with the thundering of cannon, we meant peace and amity. His alarm, however, only continued till Fosforus had explained to him the meaning, when he appeared greatly pleased at the compliment.

When the salute was over, he told us, through the boy, that Dishondrew the Dissuava (his Excellency the General) was the bearer of a letter from the king; but as his Excellency was commanded by his Majesty to give it only into the Captain's own hands, he begged that he would there and then come ashore and receive it. And so straightforward did this appear, that I verily believe my father would instantly have manned a boat and proceeded to an interview with the great man, had not I, fearing for his safety, said—

"It is impossible, my father, that you can leave the ship, and trust yourself among perhaps a whole army of men, who, if treachery be intended, may be even now hidden in yonder forest, within gun-shot, and awaiting to get you in their power. Let me therefore represent you; for, as your son, they will not be offended at the rank of the messenger, while it is scarcely likely it can serve any purpose of this chief to harm a mere boy, especially if he really intend mischief. It can be nothing less than to get the whole ship and her cargo into his power."

At this my father became thoughtful, when Bob Chase said,

"The young skipper is right, Cap'n; for if this nigger fellow wants the old bird and his nest, he wont be contented to harm the chicken; and so be as you let him go and fetch this letter, Bob Chase 'll keep alongside, and convoy him safe in and out of the enemy's port."

"Thou art right, Bob, yet the risk is great," said my father; "but, Tom," he said to me, "dost thou not fear to trust thyself among these savages?"

" Fear !—not I, even if without Bob, for they'll not harm a boy like me; and if they do, it is better they should, than you, my father."

" Did I really fear that it was their *interest* to harm you, my son, you should not venture among them for the whole cargo, aye, and the island to boot; but," he added, " go, and whatever may happen, be guided by Bob, whose experience may aid thee; and take with you this black fellow, who will serve as an interpreter."   Then taking some half-dozen silver dollars from his pocket, and showing them to Fosforus, who stood near with open ears and gaping mouth, he said,

" What say you, boy? will you serve us well and honestly, and so earn these and some like them ?"

" Sar Excellency," began the boy—but he was suddenly interrupted by a fit of sneezing; upon recovering from which he drew a long, melancholy visage, and continued, " Sar Excellency, Fosforus will be good servant to white man, and 'ropean, for Fosforus is white boy, and 'ropean too; but, sar———"

" But?   Give me no buts, boy; go at once, or I'll have you rope's-ended," said my father.

" Sar Excellency, Fosforus white boy, and 'ropean, and so no tell lies; but, sar, it is what white man call not possible to go now, for gods send message not go now—so;" and as he spoke he imitated a sneeze.

This speech astonished me, for at the time I did not know that, however important may be the business upon which a Singhalese is about setting out, a fit of sneezing—which he regards as an omen or warning from the gods of evil, if that business be carried out at that time—will cause him to forego it till a fitter opportunity. My father, however, being aware of this superstition, but yet not in a temper to humour the boy, at once ordered Bob to launch the long-boat, and if he would not go without, throw him into it; but finding my father firm, Fos got into the boat, but not without exhibiting much disgust and muttering some prayer which he believed might induce the gods to avert the misfortune which they had threatened. Bob was scarcely less contumacious; for, being given to superstitious fancies, he rather regarded the boy's omen as a confirmation of his own doubt of the happy result of an expedition commenced upon a Friday—

"For, look you, Master Tom," said he, as we were pulling towards the shore, "though it may not be given to these niggers to understand the religion of us Christians, still they have a kind of understanding when something wrong's a-going to happen, as maybe the birds and the animals have of a storm afore a drop of rain or a gust of wind has come."

"Pooh, pooh, Bob. What! an old salt, and fainthearted?" said I.

"No, no, Master Tom, not exactly fainthearted, but you see I don't like to go a-tempting fate: it aint Christian-like. Howsomdever, once shipped, it's no good kicking against the articles, and so we'll just see if we can't come yardarm and yardarm with this misfortune, whatever it be," replied Bob.

And it was not long before his resolution was put to the test; for, when we were about midway between the ship and the shore, Fosforus, giving a sharp, short cry, jumped up in the stern sheets of the boat, holding in his hand his long, gleaming knife.

"What! a new omen?" said I, laughing.

"Sar Excellency, 'um shark!"

"By Neptune! the rascal is right. There he is," said Bob, pointing to a large shark, which seemed not swimming, but darting after the boat.

"Pull for your lives!" said Bob to the men.

"Why need we fear? The brute will not board us," said I.

"Don't know that, Master Tom; at any rate, it's best to be prepared," said Bob, drawing his cutlass, which, fortunately, he had brought with him, as well as myself, to make a formidable appearance before the Dissuava.

"Sar Excellency, keep look!" said the boy, who had become excited, and evidently feared the savage fish might make an attempt upon the boat;

for it had now passed us—aye, and kept swimming, or rather darting, through the water, backwards, forwards, and around the boat, with its hideously great goggle eyes fixed upon our crew.

"It looks as if it were making choice of one among us," said I.

"Aye, aye," said Bob; "the black boy in course; the brutes 'll never take white flesh while they can get black."

So Fosforus seemed to think, for he trembled terribly as the fish darted around the boat; but with a strange courage, probably arising from intense fear, he hung half way over the stern, with his long, gleaming knife in his hand, as if ready for an encounter.

"Bah! it is useless to provoke the brute," said I; but before I could finish the sentence the monster made a dart out of the water in the direction of Fosforus, but, fortunately, with more force than calculation, passed the boy, and fell into the bottom of the boat. Again, fortunately, the latter had been prepared by experience for such a feat, and in an instant the stunned fish lay writhing and plunging, lashing its tail, but with fifty knife-wounds in its stomach and under its fins; for, the moment it had alighted in the boat, the boy had commenced striking it with his knife, and had so often repeated his blows that, although it flounced terribly, there was but little to be

The Shark following the Boat.—Page 34.

feared save from the lashing of its tail, which
Bob, who had often seen sharks taken, hacked off
with a hatchet which luckily happened to be in
the boat. After which Fosforus, as if he had no
doubt that the fish had been solely bent upon
making a meal of him, shook his knife at it,
saying—

"He! he! debel ob shark, neber again mistake a white boy and a 'ropean for a black man."

"Truly you have had a lucky escape, boy.
But, come, let us heave the carcass overboard,"
said I.

"Sar Excellency; no. Debel want makee
meal of Fosforus, so Fosforus take him shore and
makee 'um into dollar, den makee dollar into
meal," was the reply.

"Aye, aye; the boy's right, Master Tom. We
will take the carcass ashore; for it's only fair the
boy should sell it to the natives, who will make
oil of his liver, dry and prepare his fins, and sell
them again to the Chinamen, who will make
them into shagreen."

"So be it. But let's pull ashore with all
speed, and in the meantime keep a look-out fore
and aft, for another such an adventure may not
prove so fortunate," said I, gazing at the brute,
which was some twelve feet long, and so heavy
that it required three or four men to lift it.

Then, as they pulled lustily at the oars, and

we kept a look-out for any of the shark's family who might be tempted to come and fetch his carcass, Bob said—

" Look you, Master Tom : one of us was nearly losing the number of his mess. It might have been me, it might have been you, in which case it would have been owing to sailing on a Friday."

" I don't see that, Bob," said I, laughing ; " for, if there had been any truth in your superstitious nonsense, we should undoubtedly . have been the victims, but which we certainly are not."

" But look you, Master Tom, though you are misbelieving in such things, you can't go for to deny that there was something in the black boy's omen ; or how is it, d'ye see, that he was so near being at this very time in that shark's stomach?" said Bob.

" Tut, tut ! It *is* this very *near*, and not *quite*, that proves you both wrong; but bother such nonsense," said I, adding, " Now tell me, Bob, do you really believe that sharks, when they have the choice, prefer black to white men?"

" Sartain sure. Do ye see, the brute is always cunning enough to know black from white ; and this is how I came to know it. It is now about thirty-five years agone, when I was little more than a youngster on board a King's ship, a cruising in the West Indies. Well, our cook was a nigger called Cæsar, and very fond of him we all were; for, though only a nigger, he was as big-hearted, brave, and good-natured as if he had been a Christian. Well, one day the cap'n, just to keep the men from thinking too much about Yellow Jack (the yellow fever), which was then ashore, killing blacks and whites by thousands, ordered the boatswain to pipe all hands to mis-chief. About twenty took it into their heads to bathe, and among them was Cæsar. Well, while they were swimming and plunging about, like so many overheated porpoises a trying to cool them-selves, I and a sort of a hobbydehoy—that is, something between a man and a boy (axing your pardon, Master Tom, as you might be, d'ye see) —named Dick Bones, were stationed together to look out for sharks, which swim in shoals in them seas. Now, we had been on the look-out may-hap about ten minutes. The men were swimming a sort of game like a hoop—that is, round a circle, in the middle of which wor our black cook Cæsar. Well, all at once Dick turns pale in the face, and calls out to 'em at the top of his voice to clear away from a great white shark whose goggle eyes and big tail I could see as it came darting for'ard. Well, the men in the water swam towards the ship; and we on board threw out ropes and scrambled up the sides sooner than you would say Jack Robinson—at least, that is, all but one, and he was the poor nigger Cæsar.

Howsomdever, even he managed to get hold of a rope; when, giving a cheer, we hauled him on deck—that is, d'ye see, all that was left of him, which was not more than a half; for the shark had bitten the poor fellow right clean in two, just about the middle.

"Now, in course, this set our bloods biling, though, so scared were the crew, that, while some ran for pikes to revenge his death, others—the greater number—stood stupid-like, not knowing what to do; but as for Dick Bones, no sooner did he see what had happened, than he snatched up a long knife, and, afore one could whistle, jumped into the sea, and swam towards the shark. Then, Lord, how all our hearts came into our mouths; for the hungry brute, thinking he had a new meal before him, opened his great jaws in readiness, and made one great plunge towards Dick; but, finding he disappeared, we prepared to lower a boat and harpoon the brute, for we made no manner of doubt he had swallowed our messmate, when all of a sudden we saw the shark plunging and writhing, and lashing his tail.

"'Hurrah!' cries one, 'Dick has killed him.' And so it was; for the brave heart had plunged beneath the shark, and, after the fashion of the pearl-divers, had struck his knife again and again and again into its stomach, all the while keeping hold of its fins, so that the brute could neither get away nor hurt him. Well, for some minutes the struggle went on; but the shark, getting weaker and weaker, made towards the shore. That was fortunate for Dick; for, once feeling his feet touch the ground, yet still keeping his hold of the fins, he forced the brute on shore, when he finished him by ripping him up; and sure enough there was the other half of the body of poor Cæsar. The end was, that we gave the poor fellow's two parts Christian burial in the sands. And I tell you, Master Tom, although he was only a nigger, I don't think there was a dry eye in the ship during that cruise; at least not when the fate of black Cæsar was talked over," said Bob; adding, very illogically, "and so you see that was a proof these sharks prefer black men to white; or why did he choose the only black man out of twenty-one or so?"

I did not answer Bob, for I was too busy contemplating the fate that one of us had escaped; for, although the monster was not so large as some I had seen—hitherto I had only viewed them from a distance, and with every sense of security around—a close examination of one of these savage and voracious fishes, with its large, flat head, long mouth, goggle eyes, mouth and throat large enough to swallow a man, made me thankful for our escape. If you would realize the ease with which it can snap a man into two halves, just think for a moment of its six rows of hard, sharp-pointed, wedge-like shaped teeth, amounting to about one hundred and forty-four in the whole, and which, curiously enough, the animal has the power of erecting or depressing at pleasure: for, when it is at rest, these teeth lie quite flat in the mouth; but when he prepares to seize his prey, he erects all of them by the help of a set of muscles which join them to the jaw, so that the man or animal he seizes dies pierced with a hundred wounds almost instantly. Then its terrible eyes are so arranged in its head by nature that it can turn them so as to see behind as well as in front; moreover, formidable as it is in appearance, it is no less so in courage and activity, for no other fish can swim so fast, or is so fearless in attacking. Now, as it is evident that, possessing such terrible powers of destruction, the shark tribe might soon have cleared the ocean of other fish, Nature has shown her wisdom by at the same time having so formed the shark's mouth—that is, made the upper jaw project so far beyond the lower—that the fish is obliged to turn on one side to seize its prey; an operation which takes so long to perform that it affords an opportunity for the escape of its intended victims.

Now, as this adventure with the shark had delayed us for at least half-an-hour, when we reached the shore we found the Dissuava's messenger, who had quitted the ship simultaneously with us, so urgent in his request that we should proceed to meet his master, that poor Fosforus was compelled to make a very hasty sale of the shark's carcass—to take, indeed, the first offer, namely, a small box of betel-nut and a long hunting knife. The latter we found truly useful hereafter; but the first was to me, at least for some time, a source of much annoyance, for the nasty fellow's mouth was for ever running over with a bright-red saliva, caused by chewing the preparation of betel. But, mind you, in this he was no worse than the rest of the natives, who, from king to peasant, are for ever munching this nut; but of this practice and its uses more anon.

The boat had touched the ground. I was about stepping out when Bob, catching hold of my arm, said—

"Steady, steady, Master Tom; don't let us make ourselves bait for land-sharks; to my thinking, it aint all fair and above board."

"Nonsense, Bob," said I, impatiently.

"Well, well, Master Tom; you're skipper here: but, if all's fair and straightfor'ard, where's the General, if so be he aint one of these niggers?" replied Tom; and I saw at once that he was alarmed that, instead of the Dissuava being there in person, there was only the officer who had boarded us, and some thirty black-skinned more-than-half-naked natives, armed with bows, arrows, and long knives.

"Right, Bob, right," said I, retreating back-wards into the boat; adding, to Fosforus, "Put the question, boy—ask this chief where he in-tends taking us."

"Aye, aye; let's find out where this General lies at anchor," said Bob; and, leaping from the boat, the boy made a low obeisance to the chief, put the question, and having returned, said, as he pointed to a magnificent wood of cocoa-nut trees,

"Sar Excellency, Dissuava at village half a gow through cocoa-nut trees."

"Half a *cow!* that's a queer measure," said Bob, who mistook the sound of the *g* for *c*.

"How far is that?" said I; and Fosforus, pondering for a minute to think how he should make me comprehend him, held before me six of his fingers, saying—

"Sar Excellency, Dissuava not many what you call dog's talk—bow-wow-bow—dat is, 'bout as far as can hear."

"Bah! what's the fellow mean?" said Bob. "Just now it was half a cow, now it's six bow-wow. Don't go, Master Tom, don't go; he may mean a hundred knots."

"Sar, no; not one knot," said the boy, who understood that sea phrase; and then I compre-

hended the distance. It was some time, however, before I learned that a Singhalese gow
means about three miles, and that the natives
calculate distances by the sound of the voice.
For instance, if they mean to express a distance
of a quarter of a mile, they call it a dog's cry;
by which is signified the distance they believe the
cry of that animal can be heard.

"Don't half like it, Master Tom. If the nigger
General has a letter for the Cap'n, can't see no
how why he shouldn't have been here hisself,"
said Bob.

"Nonsense, Bob; the General cannot intend
harm to you or me—it could answer no purpose:
so forward at once, or the fellows will think we
are afraid of them," said I, stepping ashore, to
put a stop to further argument.

"Aye, aye, sir," replied Bob, obeying orders;
and the next minute we were by the side of the
officer, who, by motion, signified to us that a
couple of horses which stood near were for our
use. Before mounting, however, I stepped back
near enough to get within hearing of the crew,
and told them to await our return, just keeping
far enough out from the shore to prevent a
treacherous surprise, yet near enough in-shore to
come to our aid, should we find it necessary and
possible to beat a retreat.

Having given this order, Bob and I mounted

the horses, which were bridled with ropes, and getting as near as possible to the officer of the party, the only other person mounted, I bade Fosforus jump up behind Bob; and so, at the head of a long line in single file, we proceeded on our embassy.

Then, leaving this small collection of huts, which I have dignified by the name of village, we proceeded on our march through a vast plantation of cocoa-nut-trees. The path was new, having but recently been hewn through the branches and dense underwood; therefore not penetrated without great difficulty, no little toil, and some danger: for every now and then we disturbed a family of monkeys, who, in return, pelted us with cocoa-nuts; or fell in with the lair of a leopard or bear, who in alarm would scamper across our path. At length, after about two hours sheer pushing, we came upon an open plain covered with tall lemon groves, to the great disgust of a herd of wild elephants, who, alarmed, scampered off at a pace which I thought could alone have been achieved by much more slender animals. It was a comfort to find the plain; but imagine our surprise, in passing through the opening which led to it, to see that at least one half of the men, who at starting had been behind, were now spread before us in crescent form.

"Treachery, Bob, treachery. These fellows

must have gradually fallen off to the right and left; and so, by other and shorter paths than the one we have just quitted, met and formed here to surround us," said I.

" Can't be no manner of doubt about it. It's what I expected, d'ye see," replied Bob, with provoking coolness, but with a gusto that plainly showed his predictions of mischief were likely to be verified.

" Comes ob neber minding omen," said Fosforus.

" Silence, you black dog," I cried, in a rage.

" Sar Excellency, Fosforus white man; 'ropean," replied the boy, indignantly opening his mouth, and showing a set of teeth encrimsoned with the juice of the betel.

" The boy's right, Master Tom. Never knew no good, d'ye see, of sailing on a Friday."

" Silence, Bob," I said angrily; adding to Fosforus, " Ask the chief if we are near the place of our destination; and tell him we wont advance a step further."

" To my thinking, Master Tom, it would be a foolish fish that'd wait till he got into the net afore he'd say he wouldn't be caught," said Bob.

" Tut, tut, Bob; let us hear what the chief says," I answered, too angry with myself to notice Bob's impertinence, for such I then considered it.

" Sar Excellency say, no fear ; he is your friend. The great General is only one gow further."

"Three miles; probably more. Why, we shall not get back to the ship to-night," I muttered, angrily.

" No, sar ; not back to-night," said Fosforus.

" What do you mean, you rascal ? Are you laughing at me ? Did you tell the chief we would go no further ?" said I.

" Sar, no ; 'cos it no good. Excellency mean to take you to General, and it's no good say no ; 'cos why ? 'cos he got 'um in net, and he hold strings tight."

" Very sensible that for a black fellow, Master Tom. And so we had better make the best we can of our position ; for, d'ye see, I have always remarked through life that the best way to meet a difficulty is to drive your bow into it 'midships ; when ten to one you cut it in two and run atwixt the pieces," said Bob.

" Sar, bo'sen is wise man. Speak good ; for what use elephant kick when all him legs in hunter's rope," said Fosforus, who on board the ship had frequently appended what he assumed to be Bob's rank to his title of courtesy.

Although sorely vexed, having no alternative, I resolved to make the best of my error in having placed myself so entirely in the power of the Singhalese chief ; and so, without another word, I submitted to be conducted across this plain, through jungle, then through the forest again, until we came to a park-like space of at least five hundred acres in extent. These openings, which occur chiefly in the lowlands, or forests upon the sea-coasts, in addition to the relief they afford from the dense woods and jungle, have an especial beauty in themselves; for it is in such vast meadows, belted as they are by trees, and dotted here and there with a single tamarind or banyan of magnificent size, and, to Europeans, most rare foliage, that herds of wild deer, buffaloes, and elephants seek sportive relief from the monotony of the forest, which, by the way, these wild animals seldom quit before nightfall.

It was in the midst of one of these *talwas*—as the natives term these openings—that we found the Dissuava and his party encamped beneath tents formed of the leaves of the talipat palm-tree. That it was the encampment of the great man we were soon assured; for, when within a few hundred yards of the tents, the chief of our party drew his men in a circle around us, and proceeded at once to report our arrival. During the officer's absence I had the first opportunity of examining that extraordinary member of the vegetable world the talipat-tree, one of which stood near at hand. It is a straight tree, and grows from eighty to one hundred feet in height, with a huge tuft of leaves at the top, each of gigantic size. As this tree,

however, is not only singular in appearance, but
to the natives one of the most valuable in the
island, it is deserving of an especial description.

The wood is seldom used except for rafters
of buildings. Near the root it is black, very
hard, and veined with yellow; but the inside is
nothing more than pith, for the sake of which
the natives sometimes cut it down for food, rendering it eatable by beating it in a mortar till it
becomes like flour, when they mix it with
water for dough, and bake it. Singularly,
this tree bears no fruit until the last year of its
life. When the flower—which is encased in a
sheath like that of the cocoa-nut—is ripe, the
sheath bursts with a loud noise, and emits a smell
so disagreeable that the people sometimes cut it
down, not being able to live near it. The fruit
is round, and about the size of an apple. It
contains two nuts. I have said that the tents of
the Dissuava were made of the leaves of this tree.
Indeed, the latter are a wonderful curiosity of
natural history; they hang down from the top,
and are nearly circular, and so large that a single
one is sufficient to cover fifteen or twenty men.
The size, form, strength, and elasticity of these
leaves render them of the greatest service to
the natives, who, as they will fold up in
plaits like a fan, use them as umbrellas against
the sun. Indeed, any person of any con-

sequence has a talipat-bearer to keep off the rain
or sun.   People upon long journeys carry with
them large quantities of these leaves already prepared and cut into the requisite shape; so that
the labour of erecting a tent is but small, and very
quickly effected.   Then, in addition to its uses as
a covering for houses, carts, and palankeens, it is
used for the manufacture of a paper, which, as well
as for ordinary purposes, is used for books; when,
however, required for the latter, which are called
olàs, the leaves are taken when young, cut into
strips, and boiled in water; first dried in the shade,
and then in the sun; after which they are made
into rolls, and stored for sale or use.

We had not long to wait; for, a few minutes
after our conductor had entered the tent, the Dissuava, accompanied by six attendants, one of
whom walked behind holding a large talipat
umbrella over his head, walked forward to meet
us.   He was a short, slim man, with a very disagreeable, forbidding-looking countenance, grey
hair parted in the middle, and at the back, towards
the neck, rolled up in a coil called a kondè; a
white calico hat, shaped like a saucer; a long
grizzly grey beard, which fell upon a vest of trans-
parent cloth partly hidden by a jacket em-
broidered with gold.   Then his legs, in addition
to the long white cloth, or comboy, as it is called,
which is fastened round the waist, were encased

in loose white cloth trousers; but the little man, as if ashamed of his natural spareness, or what the Chinese call "short measure," had several folds of cloth around his legs, and so much more around his stomach, he could scarcely waddle; and his attempts to support a dignified carriage under such disadvantageous circumstances were so ridiculous, that I could scarcely refrain from laughing outright.

Our interview with this personage was short; and his disappointment at finding only a boy and a common sailor, instead of the commander of the ship, was plainly visible; indeed, so much so, that he found a difficulty in suppressing his indignation.   However, having by way of form first asked who we were, and what we wanted in Ceylon, he condescended to inform us that the King, his master, having heard of our arrival and wishes, desired that we should remain and trade as long as we chose; but at the same time he gave us to understand that he could place his Majesty's letter in no other hands but the Captain's, and therefore urged that one of us should immediately return to the ship and desire my father to come to him.

"Tell him," said Bob to Fosforus, "that that's agin the ship's articles; and it aint to be expected, nohow, that the Cap'n 'll come all this distance."

"Silence, Bob!" said I; adding to the boy, "Tell his Excellency, also, that, if he will proceed to the sea-side, the Captain will come ashore, pay his respects, and receive the letter."

"And if the old gentleman wont do that, he may as well keep his letters to make curl-papers for that hair of his, which, to my thinking, ought to be his wife's," added Bob.

When Fosforus had translated my words to the General, the great man seemed much vexed; but having pondered for a minute, and talked aside with the chief who had conducted us to him, he told the boy to tell us that he was sorry the Captain could not come to him, but, as it was so, it could not be helped, and therefore the next day he would do as we wished, namely, go down to the sea-shore; but that he prayed we would accept his hospitality and one of the tents for the night, and return with him the next day. To which I should have given an instantaneous refusal, had not Fosforus intimated that, although couched in courteous terms, the General's invitation was a command which it would be worse than useless to dispute; so, with no little chagrin, I permitted myself to be led to a tent, where, in company with Bob, I passed the night. As for Fosforus, he was berthed among the native soldiers and attendants.

The last words Bob said, before going to sleep, were—

" That black skipper means mischief—there can't be no manner of doubt of it; but it all comes of sailing on a Friday !"

CHAPTER III.

I AM SURPRISED AT THE CONTENTS OF A CASK, AND MY FATHER IS KIDNAPPED.

Bob's surmises were correct; for, under pretence that the General was much engaged, and that we could not be permitted to depart till we had had another audience, we were detained until late in the afternoon of the next day. Then we were conducted to the great man's tent, when, lo and behold ! there before us stood my father and six of the ship's crew, unarmed, and surrounded by a multitude of natives armed to the teeth.

"Thou rascal !" I exclaimed ;

"You black land-shark !" cried Bob; at the same time shaking our fists in the face of the General ; but it was a foolish proceeding, for the next minute we were both pinioned.

"It is no use repining—we are in the hands of Providence; but thank Heaven thou art safe, my son, for I feared they had killed you."

"Excellency no mean kill; say he mean good to Sar Captain," said Fosforus, who was standing by the side of the Dissuava, ready to interpret his wishes or commands.

"Ask him wherefore he has caused this violence towards me, and why he has thus made us prisoners?" said my father; who then told me that, finding I did not return, he and his men had come ashore early in the morning, and proceeding a short distance into the woods, they found themselves suddenly surrounded by the natives, who then secured their arms and legs with ropes of cocoa-nut fibre, and brought them upon their backs to the Dissuava.

Fosforus having interpreted the Captain's question, said—

"Excellency say, Sar Captain no prisoner, but good friend of Excellency's."

"Then tell him to give me the King's letter," said my father. And this being interpreted, the reply was—

"Excellency good friends of English; has got in village the letter from King of Kandy, and presents to send to King of England; but Captain must come and be his friend, and live with Excellency till presents are got ready."

And this was all the satisfaction my father could get; for the General then, saluting him, left the tent, taking care, however, to leave it so guarded and hemmed in by his soldiers, that we could not escape. An hour after, the tents were struck, and we were conducted about five miles to a native village, consisting of some thirty or forty huts. To one of these, the largest, we were taken; and the reception we met with, by the beating of tomtoms, the bowings and bendings of the native head people of the place—the doctor, the schoolmaster, the barber, and the washerman—as well as the fact that the hut appropriated to our use was hung with white cloth (a mark of honour to visitors), made us believe that the Dissuava really intended treating us as friends, although his mode of proceeding had hitherto been, to say the least, very doubtful.

Upon our arrival at this hut we found a plentiful meal of fish and rice prepared for us; after partaking of which, we received a visit from the Dissuava. Now, thought I, the letter will be forthcoming; and again my father, through Fosforus, desired to have the document given to him. But the Dissuava again evaded it, saying that it could not be delivered till the presents were ready, and that would be some days first. And Fosforus added—

" Excellency say, the Captain has big ship at sea, and that the Dutch people will burn it; so Captain had better send his son to ship, to tell his next officer to bring her up the river, out of way of Dutch."

" The rascal!—then he intends treachery, after all," said my father; adding, "Tell him, boy, that he is a rogue, and that, although he kills me, I will not do this thing."

"Sar Cap'n must not tell Excellency this; better tell him will do it; then little Cap'n [meaning me] can go to ship, and tell officer to take him ship away."

The Dissuava was growing impatient for a reply; so my father said—

"Your advice is good, boy; so tell the rogue I will send my son with orders." And then to me my father said, "And if the rascal permits you to leave here, let those orders be that the ship runs back to Madras, and tell the Governor we are prisoners, but that we may yet be saved, if he at once sends to this King of Kandy."

The reply having been interpreted to the Dissuava, he appeared mightily pleased, and left the hut, chuckling with delight that he should soon have the whole ship in his power. As for Fosforus, who was evidently our friend, he said—

"Excellency big rogue, like crane; hope, like crane, he too get choked."

"Like crane, you rascal; more like a sick monkey, with a bit of the jackal, the black-looking land-shark!" said Bob.

"No, sar; like crane," said the boy.

"What mean you, boy?" said my father.

"Sar Captain neber hear old crane. Well, Forforus tell him," and he began—

"Sar, once a crane very hungry, so he look in a pond at fishes. He frighten fishes, because

he tell 'em he know a great big fish was coming
to eat 'em; but if they would trust him, he would
get 'em out of danger. Well, fishes ask him
home: then crane say, there is another pond not
far off, where you had better go; but fish say,
don't know how get from one pond to other; so
crane say he be delighted to carry 'em one at a
time; and stupid fish believe him. So crane gobble
one, gobble two, gobble three, and would gobble
all; till a friend of theirs, a crab, who believe
crane a rogue, ask him to carry him too. Crane
didn't like, but tinking fish might find him out
rogue, he say yes. So crab get in his mouth, and
choke rogue crane. So, Sar Excellency is de
crane, and he tink English all foolish fish what
he can swallow little at a time."

Well, early the following morning Fosforus
conducted us to a native whom, he said, the
General had ordered to lead me through the
woods to the sea-side; and, further, that his Excellency had given permission for Bob to accompany
me. As for my father, after he had given me
instructions what to tell the officer in command
of the ship, with tears in his eyes he took leave
of me as if we had been parting for ever; nay,
that he must have believed, for he said—

" Get thee to the Governor at Madras, my son,
with all speed, and tell him, that although, by my
imprudence, I have probably sacrificed my life and

that of several brave fellows, it is some consolation to me that I am enabled to save the remainder, with the ship and cargo; and, moreover, let him know our plight."

"Surely, my father, shall this message be given; but it will be by another mouth than mine; for can it be possible you, my father, can believe me such a coward as to remain behind while my parent is in danger? No, no."

" By the piper that played before Moses, if I didn't expect this. Hurrah, Master Tom, you're a lad after my own heart," said Bob, taking my hand, and giving it a hearty grasp.

Then my father grew serious indeed, and commanded me, as I loved him, to save myself by remaining on board; and what shall I say? Well, I fairly mutinied, and at length, by begging and praying, got him to say that, as my sense of duty would not permit me to obey him in that instance, he would forgive me; and then, when he called me his brave, noble-hearted boy, and wished me " God speed" and a happy deliverance from the hands of our enemies, I went upon my task with a light heart and bounding footsteps. As for Bob, he jumped about like a playful kitten, so pleased was he that the " black-looking old land-shark," as he called the Dissuava, had permitted him to accompany me.

As we had a horse each, and a guide, who

ran before us, hatchet in hand, to cut, where necessary, a pathway through the jungle, we were not long in making the journey to the ship; and much delighted were our people, for they had given us up for lost. But great was their rage upon being told the manner of my father's capture; indeed, one and all, as they stood around, volunteered to attempt his rescue.

"Nay, nay, my lads; the effort would be madness: my father is too far in the interior, and too well guarded," said I.

"Aye, aye, it would be moonstruck nonsense; you might as well march into the belly of a shark to fetch back a messmate who had just been swallowed; moreover, it's agin orders, as the young skipper here 'll tell ye," said Bob.

Then I delivered my father's orders, insisting they should be carried out immediately. But how? what of May? says my reader. Well, I will tell you. I was both surprised and disappointed at her behaviour; for she heard the news of my father's capture, and how that I and Bob were returning to place ourselves again in the hands of the enemy, with dry eyes; aye, not a single tear—no, nought at parting but a warm shake of the hand. Indeed, so indignant was I, that when Bob returned from the cabin, to which I had sent him for a couple of rifles (one double-barrelled), and several flasks of powder and a small store of shot, I gladly bade her farewell, and hastened over the side into the boat. But seeing Bob loitering behind, I cried up from the boat, "Come, look alive, Bob, or I will pull ashore without you."

"Aye, aye, Master Tom; but just you hold on there till I fetch a few things as may be useful;" and so he disappeared below, and kept me waiting so long that I grew impatient. At length, however, he came over the side into the boat; and having, by the aid of a messmate, helped into the stern-sheets a large cask apparently filled with clothing, such as jackets, Guernsey shirts, and trowsers—

"Why on earth have you brought those things?" said I.

"Because they are my own, and mayhap will be useful; and if they aint, d'ye see, Master Tom, we may change them for something that will, for all these niggers likes barter."

"But why bring that big cask?"

"D'ye see? The things happened to be in it, and so, besides, it'll sell for something better," replied Bob; adding, "but look out for sharks, Master Tom. One of the relations of t'other animal that jumped into the boat after the black boy may be cruising about in these waters."

And feeling at once the necessity of the caution, I put no more questions to the old man,

who then pulled might and main at his oar till we
reached the shore, where our guide stood awaiting
with the horses.

"Now, Bob," said I, leaping from the boat
with a rifle in each hand, "just hand out the
ammunition, and then capsize that precious cask
of yours, and we'll lash the clothes athwart the
animals."

"Aye, aye, sir!" said Bob; "here's the ammunition; but flog me if I land these clothes
without the cask, seeing as how this cask is useful;
so just lend us a hand, mates."

And taking no further notice of my order, Bob,
by the help of one of his shipmates, brought the
cask ashore.

"Zounds, Bob, this is rank mutiny!" said I,
sadly vexed; for if, as I thought, he intended to remain until he could barter away the cask with the
natives, it might delay us some hours; for, with
the exception of our guide, there were no natives
nearer than a village about a mile along
shore.

"Ax your pardon, Master Tom; but, d'ye see,
when you comes to know the value of this cask,
you'll forgive me," said Bob. Then turning to
the people in the boat, he said—

"Three cheers and a quick deliverance for the
Captain!" and so hearty were the cheers that I
forgot the cask; and having bid the men farewell,

they pulled off from the shore. But then, again, thinking of this troublesome cask, I said—

"Come, Bob, capsize this cask, and let's lash the things to the horses."

"Aye, aye, sir; just you look after the horses, and I'll 'tend to the cask."

And as I saw the obstinate old fellow was bent upon having his own way, I complied. Well, I had lashed some things I had brought with me from the ship—that is, the two rifles, the shot and powder, and the books—to the animals; indeed, was busily engaged, when Bob, taking two large pea-jackets and a blanket, brought them to his horse, and by means of some cord he had with them, lashed the things across the animal's back, but after such a fashion that they formed a soft saddle—

"Why, Bob, you'll never be able to straddle that," said I, laughing.

"D'ye see, it's a kind of quarter-deck I'm rigging out, Master Tom. Hilloah!" he added, looking out to sea, "the people are alongside the ship?"

Now, the native guide, who could neither speak nor comprehend a single word of our language, had been standing holding the rope bridles of the horses in his hand, and staring out to sea; but, as Bob spoke, he fixed his eyes upon the cask, then suddenly he fell upon all fours, with his face to the ground, muttering what I took to be some short prayer. And well he might; for, as Bob spoke, some clothes jumped out of the cask of their own accord, and after them the figure of a boy with a loose pea-jacket and a large slouched hat.

"What means this?" said I.

"Why, d'ye see, it is the officer as is going to walk this quarter-deck," said Bob.

"It means, dear Tom, that I wont be left behind while my father and brother are in danger," said the sailor boy; who, having extricated himself from the cask, now held both my hands, adding, "You'll forgive me now; wont you, Tom?"

"Shall I capsize the cask now, Master Tom?" said Bob, maliciously.

"May, dear May! this is imprudent; this must not be. It will endanger thy life; it will anger my father. Should anything happen to you, it will make me miserable for life. May! you must return to the ship."

"Tom, dear Tom! it is useless to ask me, for I *will not*," she replied, firmly.

"Shall we put her in the cask again, and set it afloat; because, d'ye see, we can't send her no other way?" said Bob.

"Silence, Bob! You should at least have known better than to have suffered this," said I.

"Lord bless you, Master Tom! I only did it

because I couldn't help it; for, d'ye see, when we were aboard, and while you wor a-talking to the hands, Miss May called me to her cabin and begged that I would smuggle her into the boat, saying she knew you would not, and that the chief mate he wouldn't; and if so be *I* didn't help her, she would swim ashore!"

" May, dear May," said I, taking her hand in mine, "you are a brave, noble girl. Still, this must not be. You must return to the ship."

" What Bob has told you is true. Had he not helped me, I would have jumped overboard, and at all risks have swum ashore; therefore, think you I will return now? No, indeed, not I. So, Master Tom, just make up your mind to have me for a comrade; and, mind, I shall not make such a bad one; for, if you are a sailor, and a sailor's son, I am as great a sailor, and also a sailor's daughter," she replied.

" Hurrah! Master Tom. What a skipper Miss May would have made, had she only been a man," said Bob; adding, " Now, look you, we can't help what's done; so we had better make up our minds to sail together. And, my life on't, she shan't come to a ha'porth of harm while old Bob keeps upon this world's books; or, at least, while he can show a clean bill of health."

" Well, well," said I; " I would rather it had been otherwise; but what must be, must be. So let us mount and away, or we shall never reach the village by nightfall."

And, so saying, I helped May to her saddle; and mounting the other horse, with Bob behind, we followed the guide's lead through the dense belt of cocoa-trees which line the plains near the sea : indeed, it is only near the sea, great towns, or villages that this tree will grow; and the natives superstitiously believe it will not thrive out of the sound of the human voice. A superstition, however, that in all probability grew out of their affection and pride for this member of the vegetable world ; a pride, by the way, not only excusable, but commendable, for it is as dear to them as the Nile to the Egyptians, or the bamboo to the Chinese ; and that it is thus valuable you will easily believe, when I tell you that the trunk of this tree—which most boys only know from its agreeable fruit—supplies the natives with timber for building, making furniture, ships, farming implements, fences, and firewood ; the leaves with thatch, matting, fodder-baskets, and minor utensils; its web for strainers and flambeaux ; its blossoms for pickles and preserves; its fruit-sap for spirits, sugar, and vinegar ; its nut and its juices for food, and for drinking, for oil, curries, cakes, and cosmetics; its shell for cups, lamps, spoons, bottles, and tooth-powder ; its fibre for beds, cushions, carpets, brushes, nets, ropes,

cordage, and cables; "and," says Sir J. E.
Tennent, who has published the most elaborate
history and description of this interesting island,
"it acts as a conductor in protecting houses from
lightning. All that has ever been told of the
bread-fruit, or any other plant contributing to the
welfare of men," adds Sir James, is as nothing
compared with the blessings conferred on Ceylon
by this inestimable plant. The Singhalese, in the
warmth of their affection for their favourite tree,
avow their belief that it pines when beyond the
reach of the human voice; and recount with ani-
mation the hundred uses for which its products
are available. Houses are timbered with its wood,
and roofed with its plaited fronds, which, under
the name of cajans, are likewise employed for
partitions and fences. The fruit, in all its varieties
of form and colour, is ripened around the natives'
dwellings; and the women may be seen at their
doors, rasping its white flesh to powder, in order
to extract from it the milky emulsion which con-
stitutes the essential excellence of a Singhalese
curry. In pits by the roadside the husks of the
nut are steeped, to convert the fibre into coir
(cords made from cocoa-nut), by decomposing the
interstitial pith; its flesh is dried in the sun pre-
paratory to expressing the oil; vessels are attached to collect the juice of the unexpanded
flowers, to be converted into sugar; and from

early morn the toddy drawers are to be seen ascending the trees in quest of the sap drawn from the spathes of the unopened flowers, to be distilled into arrack, the only pernicious purpose to which the gifts of this bounteous tree are perverted." Indeed, so precious an inheritance does the Singhalese deem his ancestral garden of cocoa-nuts, that when, in the year 1797, an attempt was made to impose a tax upon them, the population arose almost *en masse* in rebellion.

Now, although mounted, we made less progress than if we had been a-foot; for so dense were the trees, that we often had to halt while the native guide cut a pathway for the horses; and by these frequent delays, the shades of evening surprised us before we had made any great headway; and, as the day grew towards its close, we began to look out for wild animals. Then, again, we were terribly annoyed by the great multitude of bats which, commencing their nocturnal gambols in search of food, filled the air with their din, and compelled us to keep bobbing our heads in every direction; but, with all our efforts, every now and then one or the other would receive a blow from their wings.

"Look ahead, Master Tom; for, if that big beast be a bat, I'm a Dutchman," cried Bob, as a roussette, or flying-fox, which must have measured at least five feet from wing to wing,

launched itself through the air from the branch
of a tree, and struck my horse's head so violently
that the animal reared upon its hind legs.

" Keep a better look-out, Bob, for the future
—this time you were too late," said I; adding,
" but let us stop here and load the guns."

"Aye, aye, sir; for I take it there are worse
things at night in these latitudes than even such
flying varmint," replied Bob; so we dismounted
beneath the branches of a magnificent satin-wood
tree.

" Now, Master Tom, for the rest of the voyage
I'll just ease these here two legs of mine, and
this nigger may get aboard the animal, for, d'ye
see, he must want to bring his legs to an anchor,"
said Bob, as he dismounted.

" Aye, aye, Bob; we will both tramp the rest,
and let the man have the horse all to himself," I
replied, beckoning to the guide to mount. The
man complied with a grin, and we set to work to
unfasten the guns, which were secured to the
sides of May's saddle; but, as we were loading
the weapons, a sound rang through my ears so
strange, wild, and terrible, that I can compare it
only to the shrieks for assistance of a half-
strangled man.

" Haloo! that's onnatural-like," said Bob,
grasping the barrel of the rifle, and poising the
weapon, so that he could bring, if necessary, the

stock to bear upon the head of a sudden assailant. What I said I know not; but, as May
shrieked, I clutched her arm, saying—

"May, fear not, dear May;" but, shaking my
hand off, she replied—

"Pooh, pooh, nonsense, Tom—I am not
frightened, only a little startled; but look to the
guide—see, he is running away."

Which was the most frightened of the two,
man or horse, it was difficult to judge; for at
the strange sound the animal lifted its ears,
snorted, and started forward at a terrified galop,
while the man crouched down upon its back,
with his arms around the neck, and in a minute
they were out of sight. Immediately afterwards
there was a movement, a rustling of the underwood.

"Haloo! keep your weather eye open, Master
Tom; the enemy is within gunshot," said Bob,
who, not having had time to load his rifle, held
it, as I have said, by the barrel, and so poised
that the stock might give something worse than
a headache to the animal, man, or whatever it
might be.

"All right, Bob," said I, jumping in front of
May's horse, and levelling my piece.

"For Heaven's sake, Tom, don't fire—it's a
man," cried May, who, being mounted, was the
first to sight the cause of our alarm.

"Crocodiles and caterpillars! to think we should a-cleared the decks only to fight this young nigger," said Bob, as Fosforus thrust his head and shoulders forth from the underwood.

"Hush! hush! Sar Bosen; Fos got news not good for Excellency," said he, looking cautiously around.

"What mean you, boy? Has aught happened to my father, the Captain?"

"Hist! Fos tell," replied he; adding, "when young Excellency go to big ship, the Captain very foolish: he tell Excellency the Dissuava what message he had sent; then Dissuava find he cannot get all the sailors into his hands, like crane did fishes; so he get angry, break up his camp, and go, Captain and all, to Kandy."

"To Kandy!" I repeated, in stupified surprise.

"'Cos Kandy right in middle of the island, that's where take Sar Captain; but young Excellency need not fear—will do him no harm—only keep him. King keeps all white people he can catch," replied the boy; adding, "but when Excellency Dissuava go, he leave many soldiers behind at village; so, when young Excellency and Sar Bosen come back, they catch 'em, and take 'em to Kandy; so Fos know this, and he come away from village, and hide under here; and when he see the guide coming, he frighten him and his horse away by making a noise just like devil-bird."

This devil-bird, which the boy had so cleverly imitated, is a large brown owl, common in the forests of Ceylon, and is so named because of its screech; which the superstitious natives never hear without a sensation of horror, for they regard it as the harbinger of certain terrible calamities.

"It wor you, wor it, that made that queer noise?" said Bob, with an incredulous stare; "then, hark ye, youngster, it's my belief you must be near akin to the gentleman you have named."

"Sar Bosen, Fos know what um knows—um know um frighten guide; so he go one way, while young Excellency go another, and not get umself into net, and be caught like a fish," was the reply.

"Harkee, boy; this looks all fair, and as if you had done us a good turn; but if so be as you means all square and above board, just you show us how we may get back to the sea without falling in with any of these black land-sharks," said Bob.

"For shame, Bob, to talk of returning to the sea, and deserting our good father," said May, as it were almost taking the words out of my mouth.

"Ask your pardon, Miss May; but old Bob

aint the man to forget his duty. I only mean
that we had better clear out of this into some
harbour. So that, should the nigger return, he
will think we have proceeded onwards to the village without him."

"Right, Bob, right. We will clear out of this.
But," said I to the boy, "can you show us a
hiding-place?"

"Sar Excellency, Fos knows all 'bout forest
here. So, if follow 'um, will show place where
can hide."

The boy led; and for more than half an hour
we followed, beating our way as best we could
through a small pathway made in the jungle by
a bear or a leopard, till we came to an opening
of about one hundred feet in diameter. This
opening was formed by a circle of trees—the ebony,
the tamarind, and the satin-wood; but in the middle was a hillock, upon which stood the most mar-
vellously-shaped member of the vegetable world I
had then seen. It was a banyan-tree, evidently
of great age; for the main trunk was hollow, and
large enough to hold at least three men. I say
the main trunk; for from the top, or crest, from
among the foliage, the branches had grown downwards; and in long slender, but tough poles, had
taken root in the ground, giving the appearance
of a large canopy supported by about fifty pillars,
all placed at regular intervals.

"It is a marvellous tree," said I, looking with astonishment upon its strange formation.

"Aye, aye; and will afford us a place to hang our hammocks," said Bob. "But still, d'ye see, this tree is a kind of vegetable shark, or at least bear, amongst other trees; for it never grows but by strangling some other tree, and this is how it is :—D'ye see, a bird, perhaps, carries some of the seed of one of these banyans into the leaves of a palm-tree. There it takes root, branching out as it descends; in fact, growing downwards and around the trunk of the palm, till it reaches the ground, when it takes root like a stem. But, you see, it isn't like other stems; for it throws out no buds, leaves, nor flowers. No; the real stem, with its branches, its foliage, and fruit—very queerly, as you see—springs upwards from the top of the tree wherever the root grows down, and so, in time, forms these pillars. But the process entirely strangles, or hugs to death, the tree around which this banyan originally entwined itself, as this is."

So saying, Bob pointed to what had been the trunk of the original palm, but which now formed only a hollow cylinder interlaced with branches and roots of the fig.

"Very wonderful; and, as we must pass the night in this forest, we could not have found a better fortress against the beasts; for the hollow of the tree will do for May's state-cabin; while you and I, Bob, having first lighted a circle of fire around these stems, will bivouac in the middle."

"Aye, aye. Well thought of, Master Tom," said Bob. Then addressing Fosforus, he added, "Now, mate, just put us in the way of getting some fuel."

"Ess, Sar Bosen. But s'pose all help, or we neber get 'nuff."

"The boy is right. You and I must help, Bob, or we shall never get sufficient fuel. But you, May——"

"Will take care of myself, brother," replied she; and, before I could say another word, she had dismounted, and was fastening her bridle-rein to the branch of a tree.

"Nay, May!——"

"Tut, tut, brother! Say no more; for, once for all, it is my intention to share in all the labours for our common good."

Then, as opposition was useless, I accepted May's aid; and we at once began cutting and pulling the driest underwood to be found; and so earnestly did we work, that before night quite closed in, we had collected so much fuel that we were enabled to surround our leafy tent with a ring fence of fire, which we regulated and caused to burn slowly by the addition of damp grass, small heaps of which we placed within the circle, ready for use.

Then, taking the clothing which had formed May's saddle, and having placed it within the hollow of the tree, so as to form a sleeping mat or bed, we sat down within the circle to a supper of sliced cocoa-nuts and milk. During this rough but welcome meal we consulted as to our plans for the future. There were but two courses open. One was, to endeavour to make our way through the woods to the nearest Dutch settlement, and throw ourselves upon the mercy of the Hollanders, who might also be induced to intercede with the King of Kandy for my father's release. The other, to proceed at once to the presence of the King himself. To the first proposition Fosforus at once put a stop, by telling us that not only were the Dutch at that time at open war with the king, but that several of their officers and men were then, like my father, prisoners in the capital. The course, then, that we resolved upon was to beard the lion in his den; or, in other words, make our way to Kandy.

The conference being over, we retired to rest after the following fashion: May within the tree, which I slightly barricaded with twigs; myself, with my rifle by my side, before the entrance to the tree; and Bob and Fosforus, who arranged by turns to keep watch and the fire alive, as nearly as possible in the middle of the circle.

Then, fatigued, I laid down; but "Nature's sweet restorer, balmy sleep," was long delayed by the screeching of the owl or devil-bird, the humming of numerous insects, the roaring of prowling beasts. At length, however, it did visit me; but as, save Providence and the guardianship of Bob or Fosforus, I felt conscious of being at the mercy of the first beast who might pass in search of its nocturnal meal, my sleep was fitful; for every now and then I would put forth my hand to feel for my rifle, or sit up to see whether the fire was kept alive, and listen if May were stirring or making any signs of terror, although, bless her brave heart! I believe she was as bold as either of us.

CHAPTER IV.

I FIND A BEAR IN DIFFICULTIES, AND FOSFORUS VERY USEFUL.

VERY restless must have been my sleep; for, being awakened about daybreak by a deep groan, and putting forth my hand to my rifle, I found it was not there. Starting up with alarm, however, I saw that, although I had moved, the rifle was still where I had laid it, near the tree; but, with his hind feet upon the weapon, stood a huge bear, busily engaged at a crevice in the tree, searching for honey, I at first thought. His amusement, however, I soon found, was much less satisfactory to himself. The brute had fallen in with a nest of red ants, which he was busily engaged in cramming into his mouth with one paw, while with the other he tried hard to brush away those insects which adhered to and were stinging and biting his eyelids and lips.

Terrible as was my situation (for I could neither advance nor recede, for fear of calling his attention), the battle was amusing, although the bear seemed to be getting the worst of the contest; indeed, the truth was, he had "caught a" large family of "tartars."

After the instincts of his tribe in those parts, the bear had been hunting for honey, which is commonly found in the holes of the trees, where the bees build their nests; and having, as he believed, discovered a comb, he had thrust into it his paw, and filled his mouth, alas! not with sweet, but bitter insects, who, in their great rage at the treatment, commenced such a furious attack upon their new lodgment, that the disappointed beast became maddened with rage; yet, as if senseless of the real cause, he still continued to thrust pawful after pawful of the supposed honey into his mouth.

My fears, however, for the safety of May were greater than my satisfaction at the unexpected punishment of the angry thief: but what could I do? to withdraw would bring the brute upon me. A moment's thought, a desperate resolution followed, and, lifting myself gently upwards, I made one spring at my rifle; my foot slipped, and I fell at the feet of the brute, who, instantly turning from his attack upon the ants' nest, had his huge paw upon my breast. The thought flashed through my mind, was such to be the end of my efforts to save my father? No; for, almost simultaneously with the paw touching my breast, a ball passed through the animal's brain. It was a scene for

The Bear turns upon Tom.—Page 79.

an artist. Picture it to yourself: day just dawning, the bear upon his side at his last gasp, with its glassy eye in impotent rage fixed upon me, who, although upon my feet, so tottered with fear, that a feather almost would have capsized me. May, with the paleness of death upon every feature, just stepping forth from the tree, where for some time she must have been watching the beast's movements in terrible suspense. Fosforus, running towards me, followed by Bob, who, as he ran, shook his fist, exclaiming, " By my grandmother's toe, and a little gouty it was, but I would have had you up at the yard-arm, you little baboon, if that ball hadn't found its billet."

" Thank Heaven ! God bless you, boy !" said May, wiping the sweat of terror from her brow; " but you are hurt, dear Tom ?"

" Nay, May, not so ; but a little frightened : which was natural, seeing it was my first fight with a bear, and might have been my last."

" Every man's frightened when he first goes into action ; but, d'ye see, danger's a thing you gets used to, as eels do to being skinned," said Bob ; adding, " howsomdever, although I forgives the young varmint for taking such a responsibility upon him (which is agin all orders), as to save your life, Master Tom, that trigger ought to have been pulled by old Bob."

" Tut, tut, old friend, you are jealous ! but if

you love me, shake hands with the boy; for ' Bis dat qui cito dat.' "

" Why, what on airth's that?" said Bob, scratching his head; adding, " if it isn't one of them perscriptions as tells the doctors ashore how to make their physic."

" Prescriptions, Bob? Well, it is a kind of receipt for the benefit of charity, and means that ' he gives twice who gives in time,' " said I.

" Aye, aye, Master Tom, and a very good one; for, d'ye see, if you can do a messmate a good turn, doing it in time is a kind of physic that'll save a sight of doctor's stuff; so give us your hand, boy." And so saying, Bob shook the hand of Fosforus till he made wry faces at the pain.

" Sar Bosen couldn't watch and sleep same time," said the boy.

" That's it, d'ye see, Master Tom; it was this fellow's watch, and so he came in for the luck. Howsomdever, it's no good talking, so let's pipe to breakfast."

" A meal would be a godsend, Bob; but where is it to come from?" said I.

" Sar Excellency, many meal up there," said Fosforus, pointing to a kittul-tree; that is, a tree nearly as large as the cocoa-nut, from the stalk of which the natives express a coarse sugar called jaggory, and the pith of which, when dried and granulated, becomes the favourite pudding material, sago.

"Monkeys!" said I, perceiving some twenty or thirty of the little animals called wanderoos busily engaged with their morning meal, the seeds of the tree.

" 'Es, sar; good for eat," said the boy; and before I could reply he had snatched up my rifle. There was a chattering and screaming as the little animals, with their young ones in arms and regardless of height or width, leaped from branch to branch with astonishing accuracy of aim, and a mother and her young one fell dead at the feet of May; who, shocked at the sight (for it was a sad one), exclaimed—

"You cruel boy, how could you kill the poor things?"

"Never mind, Miss May, it's only the fortune of war," replied Bob, laughing.

"Shame upon you, Bob; for what purpose can this cruel slaughter answer?" said I, with indignation.

"The young varmint has done only after his nature; for, d'ye see, you can't expect a nigger to act like a Christian. They eats 'em in these parts, I suppose."

" 'Es, sar, little'n berry good to eat; like young pig, if roast him," said Fosforus, fully con-

vinced that what May and I had deemed a useless slaughter was a meritorious act.

"Pah! they are cannibals," said I.

"Let us move from here, and look for cocoa-
nuts, Tom," said May, with disgust at the sight of
the slaughtered animals.

"Aye, aye, cocoa-nut's better than monkey;
so, look you, boy, get us some nuts and a little
water, if you can find it," said Bob.

"'Es, sar."

"Then why don't you go?" said I, seeing he
did not move.

"'Cos, I think, if Excellency don't like monkey,
he like bear's-paw better than nuts."

"That's good, Master Tom; why, the fellow is
fit to cater for a man-of-war," said Bob.

"'Es, Sar Bosen," said Fosforus, and, delighted that he had suggested something that
pleased us, he pulled out his knife, and manfully
and skilfully set to work amputating the paws.

In the meanwhile Bob and I endeavoured
to prepare the fire, in order to make the meal
as dainty. as possible, and so we left the ill-
fated monkeys where they had fallen; but, as
I afterwards found, to the great terror of the
first Singhalee who passed that way — for,
inasmuch as in England there is a kind of
vulgar proverb that dead donkeys are rare, the

natives of Ceylon believe that the remains of a
monkey are never found in the forests; which
accounts for their proverb, that "He who has
seen a white crow, the nest of a paddy-bird, a
straight cocoa-nut tree, or a dead monkey will live
for ever." And in this belief they are not less
superstitious than the people of India, where it is
believed that if a man takes up his residence
upon a spot where a hoonuman monkey has been
killed, he will certainly soon die; hence, before
building a house, they use every means to discover
whether there are monkeys' bones in the ground.
With regard, however, to the eating of monkey
flesh, I must admit, that although I for one should
not prefer it to beef or mutton,—for the animal
bears too great a resemblance to man to be an
agreeable sight upon a dinner-table,—it is only
custom; for roast monkey is in many countries a
favourite dish, and I am told is really a delicacy
much resembling sucking-pig, while in China
monkey-soup is frequently used by the doctors as
a restorative. Thus you see there is much truth
in the vulgar adage, that "What is one man's
meat is another man's poison."

Well, we dressed the bear's paws; and our
breakfast-service, which, by the way, consisted of
cocoa-nut shells for plates and cups, splints of
wood for forks, and our pocket-knives, being

ready, we began our meal; but lo! we were famishing for water. Fosforus offered to go in search of some stream.

"But, d'ye see, you have nothing to bring it in," said Bob.

"Sar Bosen will see," said the boy, running off; and in about half-an-hour returned, bringing a quantity of water in a vessel which he had improvised by shaping a talipat leaf into the form of a basin.

"Pah! boy, you don't mean us to drink this filthy stuff," said I, sickening with disgust at seeing the muddy fluid.

"No better can get; but Sar Bosen hold leaf, and water soon get well."

"It's very bad now; get better out of the cook's slush tub," said Bob, holding the leaf; when the boy purified it by the following process.

Taking from his pocket two horny seeds, about the size of coffee-beans, and holding them in the water, or rather mud, he rubbed them vigorously together for some minutes, until the seeds became reduced to one quarter their original size, when the effect was apparent; for the ground seed, now mixing with the water, seized upon the impure particles, and carried them all to the bottom, forming a thick, glutinous sediment, leaving the water above comparatively pure; at all events, quite drinkable.

"Water quite well now; Missee try," said he,

dipping a cocoa-nut shell into the water and handing it to May. .

" Fosforus, you are a jewel," said May, after drinking the water with great relish.

" Aye, aye, boy, you are too clever for this land of niggers. Why, do ye see, if you were in old England, you'd make a fortune," said Bob.

" A fortune! what's dat, sar; Fosforus not know how make dat; he neber eat such ting," replied the boy.

" It is not anything to eat, you rascal," said Bob.

" Den Fosforus no care what it am ; for, if not eat, it am no good."

" But what berries are those," I asked.

" Call 'em Goda-Kadru, sar;" and with that answer I was compelled to rest satisfied. I should not, however, have relished the water so much, had I known, as I afterwards learned, that they were the seed of the deadly poison strychnia. The *Strychnos nux-vomica* is very common in the forests of Ceylon, and grows near the banks of rivers or tanks. Its fruit is about the size and colour of a small orange ; within which, in a pulpy substance, is held the nux-vomica, from which the poison strychnia is extracted. Of this *Strychnos nux-vomica* Tennent says, " In this genus there are two plants—the seeds of one being not only harmless but wholesome, and that of the other

the most formidable of known poisons. Amongst
the Malabars there is a belief that the seeds, if
habitually taken, will act as a preventive of ill
effects from the venom of the cobra di capello;
and thus they accustom themselves to eat a single
seed per day, in order to acquire the desired protection from the effects of the serpent's bite."

Thus having made a tolerable meal, we began
to think about making the best of our way on the
road to Kandy; but a formidable difficulty stood
before us—which, by the way, was pointed out
by the boy—who, having partaken of a bear's paw,
said—

" Sar Excellency, Sar Bosen, and Missee,
s'pose all stop here while Fosforus goes to village
and get tent and axe; 'cos s'pose got no tent,
can't get away from sun; s'pose got no axe, can't
make path."

" Very good; but s'pose don't know how to get
'em," said Bob, laughing.

" S'pose Fosforus tell Massa Bob Bosen."

" Well, let us hear," said I.

" S'pose Sar Excellency and Sar Bosen help
pull bear-skin off, den s'pose Excellency got some
dollar, when Fosforus take dollar and skin to
village, and get all ting wantee to go to Kandy."

" Good, again; but will it not bring the people
down upon us?" said I.

" No; 'cos people be pleased to find bear

killed and get dollar, and wont say noting to Fosforus, but gib what 'um want."

Now, this suggestion was so reasonable, and the boy had already shown his willingness as well as capability of serving us, that we at once complied; and, setting to work under the direction of Fos, who seemed to be a proficient in the hunter's art, we speedily divested it of its skin. This done, with the skin around the horse's neck, and a couple of dollars in his hand, he started upon his expedition; and we, having loaded our two rifles, took up our position beneath the most shady portion of the tree, and, while awaiting the return of our messenger, we were sufficiently employed in studying nature as she exhibits herself during the first few hours of day in Ceylon.

When I had been so suddenly awakened the dawn was first breaking; the bats, owls, and other birds of night were hastening to their haunts; elephants and elks from the open pastures and pool sides to the shade of the forest; but now the sun had burst forth in all its splendour, melting the dewdrops from the foliage of the trees, sparkling like hanging clusters of diamonds; the flowers, trees, and shrubs were crowded with butterflies; bees were hastening forth in all directions. Then, as the morn grew older—but the scene has been described by the eloquent writer I have before named, and this is his picture :—

" The earliest bird upon the wing is the crow, which leaves his perch almost with the first peep of dawn, cawing and flapping his wings in the sky. The paroquets follow in vast companies, chattering and screaming in exuberant excitement; next the cranes and waders, which fly inland to the breeding-places at sunset, rise from the branches on which they had passed the night, waving their wings to disencumber them of the dew; and, stretching their awkward legs behind, they soar away in the direction of the rivers and the far seashore.

" The songster that first pours forth his salutation to the morning is the dial-bird (*Copsychus saularis*), and the yellow oriole, whose mellow flute-like voice is heard far through the stillness of the dawn. The jungle-cock, unseen in the dense cover, shouts his *réveille*. As light increases, the grass-warbler and maynach add their notes; and the bronze-winged pigeons make the woods murmur with their plaintive cry, which resembles the distant lowing of cattle. The swifts and swallows sally forth as soon as there is sufficient warmth to tempt the minor insects abroad; the bulbul lights on the forest trees; and the little gem-like sun-birds (the humming-birds of the East) quiver on their fulgent wings above the opening flowers.

" At length the fervid morn approaches, the

sun mounts high, and all animated nature begins to yield to the oppression of his beams. The green-enamelled dragon-flies still flash above every pool in pursuit of their tiny prey; but almost every other winged insect instinctively seeks the shade of the foliage. The hawks and falcons now sweep through the sky, to mark the smaller birds which may be abroad in search of seeds and larvæ. The squirrels dart from bough to bough, uttering their shrill, quick cry; and the cicada, on the stem of the palm-tree, raises the deafening sound whose tone and volubility have won for him the expressive title of the 'knife-grinder.' It is during the first five hours of daylight that nature seems literally to teem with life and motion, the air melodious with the voice of birds, the woods resound with the simmering hum of insects, and the earth replete with every form of living nature."

How charming, how delightful, to spend one's life in such a place, says the reader. True, it would, if only there were no pestilential fevers; no land leeches, which, despite all effort, cling to your legs, and bleed you nigh to the weakness of death; no mosquitoes, which are an ever-present plague; no snakes, the bites from which are death; no savage leopards, bears, wild pigs, maniac elephants, which render the traveller's life worth a small purchase; or, if such a climate would permit any race to live without deteriorating into

listless savages, whose greatest pleasures are acts of
cruelty and the love of jewels ; no, such climates
have ever enervated and effeminatized humanity.
For it would seem impossible for man to be energetic and industrious where nature is so bountiful;
and no country in the world gives greater proof of
this; for the very numerous ruins of beautiful cities
and stupendous works which exist in the island,
which it would be impossible for the existing race
of natives either to imagine or build, prove that a
great race or races have lived, and died, or in their
descendants have become sadly deteriorated.

The same pen which has so eloquently pictured
the first five hours of the day, tells also how, " as
the sun ascends to the meridian, the scene is singularly changed, and nothing is more striking than
the almost painful stillness that surrounds the
vivacity of the early morning.　Every animal disappears, escaping under the thick cover of the
woods ; the birds retire into the shade ; the butterflies, if they flutter for a moment in the blazing
sun, hurry back into the damp shelter of the trees,
as though their filmy bodies had been parched by
the brief exposure ; and, at last, silence reigns so
profound that the ticking of a watch is sensibly
heard, and even the pulsations of the heart become
audible.　The buffalo now steals to the tanks and
watercourses, concealing all but his gloomy head
and shining horns in the mud and sedges ; the

elephant fans himself languidly with leaves to
drive away the flies that perplex him; and the
deer come in groups under the overarching jungle.
Rustling from under the dry leaves, the bright-
green lizard springs up the rough stems of the
trees, and pauses between each dart to look inquiringly around. The woodpecker makes the
forest re-echo with the restless blows of his beak
on the decaying bark; and the tortoise drops awkwardly into the still water, which reflects the
bright plumage of the kingfisher as he keeps his
lonely watch above it. So long as the sun is
above the meridian every living creature seems
to fly his beams and linger in the closest shade.
Man himself, as if baffled in all desires to escape
the exhausting glare, suspends his toil; and the
traveller, abroad since dawn, reposes till mid-day
heat has passed. The cattle pant in their stifling
sheds, and the dogs lie prone upon the ground,
their legs extended far in front and behind, as if
to bring the utmost portion of their body into
contact with the cool earth."

Our position now was critical, for, as the sun was
ascending the meridian, we should have sought
the shade of the forest; but if we did, the boy,
upon his return, might not discover our whereabouts; yet to remain beneath that burning sun
was to risk sunstroke; providentially, however,
near us stood a great talipat-palm, up which Bob

clambered; and having secured some leaves, we erected a temporary tent beneath the banyan; but even under that covering the heat was so intense, our thirst was so great, that we seemed consuming; yet we bore it patiently till the sun's decline and the birds, once more upon the wing, betokened that the cool hours had again returned.

"Look out, Bob; there is some beast upon us," said I, hearing a rustling in the jungle.

"Aye, aye, Master Tom; but you reserve fire while I give it first welcome," replied Bob, bringing his rifle to shoulder.

"Golly, no! If shoot, kill Fos; and he no beast," exclaimed that personage as he forced his horse through the thicket.

"And sarve you right, too; for, d'ye take us for salamanders, that you have kept us all this time in this broiling sun?" said Bob.

"Lion am bery quick; but 'um turtle more clever. Fos, like turtle, gone bery long time, but got all ting. See, Sar Excellency," and as he spoke he threw a large bundle upon the grass.

"Bravo, Fos; you are indeed a jewel of a fellow," said I, when, opening the parcel, I saw an equipment before me worth its weight in gold; namely, two portable tents made of talipat leaves, three axes, small but sharp, a deer skin, two good-sized jars for water, a bag of rice, pepper, salt, and an iron vessel to boil food in, some jaggory (coarse sugar), a tinder-box, some betel, and, though last, in the eyes of Bob not by any means the least, two bamboo-pipes and a quantity of tobacco; for, seeing the latter, he caught hold of the boy's hand, saying—

"I ax your pardon, youngster; but, d'ye see, it was enough to vex an admiral to look at yon cool forest, and yet, for fear of parting company with you, to be kept in the sun till our skins have become like a porker's after a roast—crackling."

"'Um had to wait; but so 'um good come at last, it no matter, sar," replied Fos.

"That's philosophy; but where did you get that gun, Fos?" said I, catching sight of a rusty-looking, old-fashioned rifle fastened to the horse's side.

"'Um buy it with bear-skin and dollars, like de rest; s'pose it belong to some Dutch pig; but it little, so just do for Missee," replied the boy, handing the weapon to May.

"Belonged to a Dutch pig; what mean you?" asked May.

"Yes, 'um Dutch pig; not 'um four legs, but 'um two legs; 'um Dutch not good; 'um all pigs —beef-eating rascals."

"Then am I a pig? for, my mother being a Dutch woman, I am half Hollander," said May, laughing. At which reply Fos seemed greatly vexed; but having paused for an instant, he said—

" 'Es ; but dat half make de difference. Fos himself only half white ; but dat half de best, 'cos it was 'um fader's half."

" But did you hear of our father the Captain ? " asked May.

" 'Um know de way. Dissuava rogue's gone ; so Missee, and Excellency, and Sar Bosen go anoder, what Fos take 'em ; but now better make tent, make meal ; so 'um go on journey to-morrow before sun wakes."

" Very good advice, Fos ; so get you in search of water while we prepare the pot," said I ; and the boy, fastening the horse to a tree, was out of sight in an instant. Then, while Bob and I erected the tents ; one for ourselves and another near the hollow-tree for May, she set womanfully about her duties as our *al fresco* housewife, clearing away the long grass, cleaning out the cooking-pot, and kindling a fire. By the time these things were done Fos made his appearance with a calabash of water and the carcass of a flying fox, which he insisted upon our eating. After some objections, we conquered our repugnance. Fos skinned the little animal, and while May roasted it, the boy purified the water, so that in a short time we sat down to a rough meal of flying-fox meat, and boiled rice ; the only one who would not be prevailed upon to partake of the meat being May.

Then, when we had finished, Bob smoked his pipe, and with no little relish, for he had not seen such a thing since our first leaving the ship; as for myself, my mind was fixed so entirely upon my father's captivity, that I employed myself by questioning Fosforus as to his knowledge of the country between the coast and Kandy, and as to the chance of our being able to rescue him; but to all of which he replied so explicitly, that any doubt I might have had as to his fitness for a guide vanished.

" To my thinking, d'ye see, Master Tom, if so be we are going to walk into the lion's den, we ought to keep our weather eye open," said Bob, thoughtfully.

" 'Um lion very strong; but 'um not clever, like tortoise," said Fosforus.

" Hark ye, boy; you *have* a head on them shoulders o' yours, though it's only a black un; so why can't you open fire in plain English, instead of going cruising about in them fables ?"

" Fable? Fos not know what fable is; nebber put his eyeballs on him; but Fos means he like tortoise."

" Hark ye, boy; bring your tongue to an anchor."

" Nay, nay, Bob; let Fos tell his story in his own way," said I. Whereupon Fos said—

" Well, 'um great lion make angry 'um tortoise

by jumping over river four yodun [sixty-four miles] across, and so tortoise told lion 'um could swim across under water quicker than he could jump. Well, lion laugh, but 'um say he try. So tortoise get 'um friend bery like himself, so lion not know difference, to swim to oder side. So when day come to try, tortoise go in water, and lion jump; but when he came toder side, he find tortoise dere, who look at him fierce, and say, 'Why you come so late? I been wait here some time;' and dat so frighten lion, he tumble in water, and get killed."

"And, to my thinking, it's all a lie," said Bob, very seriously; "because, d'ye see, the beast could as well jump up and sit astride the moon as jump all them miles; and if so be the yarn *is* true, d'ye see, the turtle was a lubber, and ought to have been made into soup, for a rogue of a land-shark, as he was."

"So Dissuava am lion, and Fos am turtle," said the boy, disregarding Bob's interruption; adding, as he took his knife, and a small packet containing some needles and thin string, from his pocket, "but night coming; so, if Missee and Excellency give Fos 'um legs——"

"Give what?" May and I exclaimed, with astonishment.

"'Um legs; and Fos cut up deer-skin, and

make shoes, so legs no get pricked, and land-leeches can't bite 'um."

"Why, the fellow adds cobbling to his other trades," said Bob.

"'Es; Fos berry poor boy, so he do a little ob eb'ry ting."

"Bravo, Fos! all right, here is my foot," said I; and, having taken our measures, he sat down upon the spot where, with loaded rifle by his side, he intended taking up his first watch and position for the night; then, loading the other guns, and placing the lightest in May's hand, I said—

"Now, May, in the event of a necessity, do you think you could fire?"

"We none of us know what we can do without trying; but if I had had it in my hand when the bear attacked you, I think I should have saved Fos the trouble of firing: at all events, I shall feel safer with, than without it," said she, taking the weapon in her hand, aye, and handling it, too, after the fashion of a sportsman, as if she knew what she was about. Then, wishing us good night, she retired within her tent; and Bob and I, having drawn a circle of fuel so as to enclose both tents, we retired within our own, leaving Fos at the entrance to watch, keep up the fire, and make deer-skin boots at the same time.

CHAPTER V.

MAY HAS AN ADVENTURE WITH A LEOPARD, AND
BOB HEARS THE GHOST OF A SHIPMATE.

AT early dawn I awoke, and finding Bob still
sleeping soundly, I was about to awake him;
but at the moment hearing the crack of a gun,
and fearing it to be a signal from May that she
was in danger, nay, perhaps even at that moment
being set upon by some beast, I caught up my
rifle and ran out of the tent, when, lo! I met
May running to my tent upon a similar errand,
for she had been alarmed at the same report.
The cause, however, was soon apparent.

Fosforus came running towards us with his
discharged rifle in one hand and a large jungle
fowl in the other. Throwing the bird at our feet,
he said—

"Sar Excellency, dat for Missee; it not like
monkey, for it good for all people to eat."

"You are a jewel, Fos; it will make a breakfast for us all," replied May, taking up the bird,
and at once commencing to pluck its feathers.

And while the meal was preparing Fos finished
the deer-skin shoes, or mocassins; with which

we were delighted, for they did indeed seem capable of protecting us from the prickly shrubs, and even reptiles of the jungle.

Having made a hearty breakfast, we packed the stores into the smallest possible parcel, and fastened them upon the horse behind May; then, each with ammunition in a pouch hastily made by ourselves, and fastened around our waists, loaded rifles in our hands or thrown across our backs, and sharp little axes in our belts, we commenced our march to—where? Well, just where chance or the boy's knowledge of the pathless forests and jungles would take us; but, as we were about to start, Fosforus cried out, " Neber do go yet; no chule to frighten 'way pigs, bears, or elephants."

" Chule! what's chule?" I asked.

" Sar Excellency see!" he replied, running to a cocoa-tree, and choosing the driest of a vast quantity of leaves upon the ground, with some fibre which served for string, he bound them together in bundles of about six feet long and three inches in diameter; then, giving each person two, one for the hand and the other for the belt, he secured several bundles to the package upon the horse; then placing three in his own belt, by way of showing their utility he lighted one, and I saw that, although rudely made, they were yet very good torches. Afterwards I found that they were in common use for forest travelling.

"You are a smart imp, you are, mate; but what's the use of hanging out a lantern at the masthead by daylight?" said Bob.

"Sar Bosen's got head well as Fos; can't 'um tell chule good to drive away elephants and leopards, so we get through jungle?" replied the boy.

"Right again, Fos," said I.

"To my thinking, d'ye see, Master Tom, the young varmint's too clever for his size," said Bob, rather surlily; but not wishing to anger the old man, I made no reply.

We then commenced our march; but so thick was the thorny jungle, and such the employment for our axes, that our progress might have been equal to that of a mole working its passage through a mound. By the way, this jungle, through which we had to hew our way inch by inch, is said to have been caused by the wretched character of the soil, which is so bad, that the natives, by felling the forest, and burning the timber upon the ground, can only produce one crop of some poor grain; the land is then exhausted, and upon its consequent desertion it gives birth to an impenetrable mass of low jungle, comprising every thorn that can be conceived. This deserted land, fallen again into the hand of nature, forms the jungle of Ceylon; and as native cultivation has continued after this fashion for some thousand years, the immense tract of country now in this impenetrable state is easily accounted for; but the fatigue was terrible, not alone from the toil, but from the heat of the sun, which, in about three hours after we had set out, became unbearable; and of such a temperature had the ground become, that Bob cried out—

"The sooner we get off this gridiron, the better it will be for our health, Master Tom."

"You are both of you fatigued; let me take my turn with an axe," said May, bravely offering to dismount.

"Bless your pretty heart, but you wont, though, while I've got arms left," replied Bob. Then turning to Fosforus: "But hark'ee, boy, art quite sure you aint out in your reckoning, and that you've got a correct chart in your head of these waters; for it's such a queer cruise, that hang me if I can make out whether we are stem or starn for'ard."

"Throw palm-cat off cocoa-tree, and 'um fall on its feet, so Fos," replied the boy; adding, as he pulled aside some very tall jungle to the right, and exposing a long pathway, "See, Sar Bosen, 'um work all over; path ready made."

"Good, Fos; this is the first piece of luck we have had to-day; but will it lead directly to yon forest?" said I, pointing to a mass of immense

trees which appeared to me within a very short
distance.

" S'pose walkee fast, 'um come dere berry
soon ; s'pose walkee slow, 'um berry long time
fust."

" That's clever ; but look here, boy," said
Bob, " aint these here latitudes populated with
wild creatures—tigers, and sich like ?"

" 'Es, sar, many, so it good for all take gun
in hand, 'cos may meet bear and leopard going
to forest to get out ob sun," he replied ; and
thinking the boy's advice but reasonable, I looked
to the charge of my piece, telling Bob and May
to do likewise.   May, however, putting her hand
down to the side of the horse where her rifle had
been placed, found it missing.

" It's broken away from its moorings," said Bob.

" Fallen among the high grass, I have no doubt.
But what's to be done ? " said she.

" What be done berry easy ; Fos 'umself go
back and look for it," said the boy.

" Tut, boy, you will never find it," said I.

" Sar Excellency, Fos don't know 'um nebber ; so 'um go back, while all oder ob you go
on, and find gun 'gain, so not go out ob path."

" Well, that's plucky, too, for a black fellow ;
but no palaver, get you back at once," said Bob.

" Fos white man, 'ropean, not black feller,"
he replied, surlily.

"Fos, you are a jewel of a fellow, and shall have the horse," said May, slipping from the saddle ; at which I remonstrated, but—

"Nay, dear Tom," said she, "let me have my way, please, for it is but fair ; moreover, by helping him we shall help ourselves."

"Lor bless your pretty little heart ; it's ventur'some-like ; but I don't see as how you could do otherwise," said Bob. Then going up to the horse, and untying the pack from the animal's back, he added, "Look you, Master Tom, as we may be parting company with the boy till we don't know exactly when, we had better take our stores with us ; so just help to fix this pack upon my back."

"Nonsense, Bob ; we will divide it between us."

"Nay, nay, Master Tom ; can't hear of no such thing ; so just fix it behind, so that I have my rifle at hand," said he : and as to remonstrate would have been wasting time, I did as he desired ; and there was the brave old fellow ready to trudge through the jungle or forest as if he was some pedlar bent upon transacting business with the wild animals.

Then bidding the boy God-speed, we—that is, May, in her loose sailor dress, slouched hat, thick deer-skin leggings, and rifle in hand, looking every inch a hunter, and Bob and I, with weapons loaded, ready for any emergency—went on our way. Thus, with our eyes alternately to the right or left of the forest, and often to the rear, we tramped onwards, in momentary fear of an attack from one of the savage denizens of the wilds. Some time, however, elapsing without meeting with any animal more terrible than ourselves, Bob, by way of whiling away the time, began a yarn about an old shipmate in whose company he had been shipwrecked upon one of the South-Sea isles.

" D'ye see, Master Tom," said he, " we found ourselves in just such a latitude as this ; but, as we were without arms or ammunition, and therefore obliged to live for three weeks upon herbs and nuts, George—for that was my mate's name— took sick with jungle-fever and died, and with these here hands I buried him beneath a tamarind-tree, when, by way of making a tombstone of the trunk, I set to work, and with my knife carved in big letters——Good Lord, what's that?" exclaimed he, suddenly, in great terror.

" It's a human voice," said May.

" Tut, tut, May; it is the screeching of some animal," said I ; but the words, " George Joyce — George Joyce — George Joyce," rang through the welkin ; aye, and as distinctly to my ears as the words are to your eyes upon this page.

"What cheer! shipmate; don't you lie easy?" said Bob, mournfully.

Still the cry was "George Joyce—George Joyce—George Joyce."

"Why, what folly is this, Bob?" said I.

"Don't you hear the poor soul answering for himself; it's the very name I was going to tell you I cut upon the trunk of the tree."

"George Joyce—George Joyce," again echoed through the air.

"Aye, aye—there he is again. What on airth can the poor ghost mean?"

"Stuff, Bob; ghosts don't speak. Moreover, they can't be shot;" and as I spoke I fired my rifle into the jungle, and the next instant a number of beautiful jungle fowls arose; and as the terrified birds flapped their wings, the cry was taken up by the whole—some twenty.

"See, Bob, there are twenty George Joyces; are they all ghosts of your shipmate?" said I, laughing.

"Well, well, Master Tom; there can't be no manner of doubt that I am an old fool; but still it's very astonishing-like that these here creatures should call out the poor fellow's name just at that identical moment."

"It is a curious coincidence, truly; but still you are wickedly superstitious. — You, Bob, who have been all over the world, and so much in the Indies, too, and not know the cry of the jungle fowl."

"Now, look you, Miss May; you can't persuade me that it isn't onnat'ral-like that these creaturs should have the name of my old shipmate all by heart; because, d'ye see, they couldn't know it if they hadn't been taught. So I tell you, I believe there *is* more in it than is in our reck'ning; howsomdever, be it as it may, they shan't make a fool of me for nothing," replied Bob; and as he spoke he fired and brought down one of the birds in the middle of the path, about ten yards in front. May ran forward to pick it up, but suddenly stopped, uttering a scream, as well she might; for a huge leopard had with a single bound leaped from the jungle into the path, and in an instant was crouching upon its hind legs, with one paw upon the fowl, and its great eyes flashing in her face.

It was a terrible moment; one blow from the beast's paw would kill her. Yet how rescue her, for our pieces were discharged?

Well, there was no time for meditation. I had my axe; but, as I was about to rush forward upon the animal, May, without moving backward or forward, and with her eyes steadily fixed upon those of the leopard, said—

"For your lives—for my life—move not."

Then it suddenly occurred to me that such

The Leopard leaps on the Fowl.—Page 106.

beasts had sometimes been cowed by a resolute
eye, especially if not attacked; and, to our relief,
so it proved in this case, for in less than a minute
the animal arose, dropped its tail, and, with a low
growl, ran back again into the jungle.

"Thank Heaven, we have escaped this time!
but, once warned, it is our own faults if we are not
prepared next time. So, Bob, let us load," said I.

"Aye, aye; that's true enough," said Bob.
"But look you, Miss May, if you were a boy,
you'd live to be an admiral; for hang me if you
didn't fight your ship like a man. It was your
own brave heart that saved you."

"Not my bravery alone, Bob; for, see, I tremble
even now. God alone saved me," said May;
who, although cool while the peril lasted, was now
trembling with fear at the danger passed.

"Aye, aye, May; but, next to Heaven, it was thy
bold heart alone that saved you," said I.

" Nay, Tom, I deserve no such credit, for it
was but a trick learned from my father when but
a little child in the woods near Bantam; moreover, it is only the exaggerated stories of travellers
that have given rise to the belief that the leopard
will attack without being attacked, except it be a
horse or deer," said May.

" Then so far we are fortunate that you happened to be dismounted, May."

" It *was* fortunate; for nought would have prevented that magnificent creature from attacking the horse: but let us thank Providence that no such mischance occurred, and, moreover, that we can at length seek shelter under yon tree from this intolerable heat," said May, as we approached an opening of the jungle, through which we could see a large hilly space covered with tall lemon-grass and shaded by the branches and foliage of several enormous trees. The largest of the latter was a Bo-gaha, that is, a god-tree; so called because the natives believe their god Buddha, when upon earth, used to sit and preach beneath one of these trees, and that he died leaning against one of them; hence it is so sacred in their eyes, that any place where it grows is believed to be holy. One of these Bo-trees is always found growing near their wihâras, or temples, and is generally en-closed with stones to the height of three or four feet, the roots carefully covered with earth, and the space around swept clean; indeed, the Sin-ghalese carry their veneration for this tree so far as to erect an altar or place a table under it, and burn lamps near it, offering up daily sacrifices of flowers: moreover, they esteem the planting of these trees a work of such great merit, that he who does so is sure to go to heaven.

Now, although there are very many of these sacred trees in the island, they are all said to have sprung from *one*, and that one the great Bo-tree of the ruined city of Anarajapoora, which, by the way, is the oldest tree in the world. It lives and flourishes at the present time, yet it was planted 288 years before the birth of our Saviour; that is, two thousand one hundred and forty-seven years ago. Of this venerable tree Sir Emerson Tennent, in his great and excellent book, tells us—

" The degree of sanctity with which this extraordinary tree has been invested in the imagination of the Buddhists, may be compared to the feeling of veneration with which Christians would regard the *attested* wood of the cross. To it kings have even dedicated their dominions, in testimony of their belief that it is a branch of the identical fig-tree under which Gotama Buddha reclined when he underwent his apotheosis. When the King of Magadha, in compliance with the request of the sovereign of Ceylon, was willing to send him a portion of that sanctified tree to be planted at Anarajapoora, he was determined by the reflection that ' *it cannot* be meet *to lop it with any weapon;*' but, under the instruction of the high priest, using vermilion in a golden pencil, he made a streak on the branch, which ' severing itself,' hovered over the mouth of a vase filled with scented oil, into which it struck its roots and descended."

Taking this legend as a sacred law, the Buddhist priests to the present day object reli-

giously to "lop it with a weapon," and are contented to collect any leaves which, *severing themselves*, may chance to fall to the ground. These
are regarded as treasures by the pilgrims, who
carry them away to the remotest part of the
island. It is even suspected that, rather than
strip the branches, the importunities of an impatient devotee are sometimes silenced by the pious
fraud of substituting the foliage of some other
.fig for that of the exalted Bo-tree. Nor is this
superstitious anxiety a feeling of recent growth.
It can be traced to the remotest period of Buddhism; and the same homage which is paid to the
tree at the present day was wont to be manifested
two thousand years ago. Age after age the sacred
annals record the work which successive sovereigns erected for the preservation of the Bo-tree
—the walls which they built around it, the carv-
ings with which they adorned them, and the
stone steps which they constructed to lead to the
sacred enclosure.

Now, the most positive proof of the intense veneration that all Buddhists have ever had for this
tree is, that although the Malabars of the neighbouring coast have several times invaded the
island, deposed its kings, seating their own in the
capital, destroyed temples, and carried away the
most precious relics, the Bo-tree has ever stood
where it now stands unmolested: nay, were any

harm to happen to this tree, it would cause a consternation throughout the vast populations of China, Tartary, Siam, Burmah, and the other Buddhist countries that those people have never known, even in their turbulent chronicles. But to return to my narrative.

The Bo-tree beneath which we determined to pitch our tent had evidently been deserted for some length of time; for, although enclosed by a stone wall some four feet high, it was in a sadly dilapidated state, for the inner space was half filled with fallen leaves and rubbish. This, however, Bob and I soon cleared away; and then, by disuniting the pieces of talipat which formed one of the tents, we refixed them around the trunk, so that it not only proved a comfortable cover from the sun, but would, by reason of the stone enclosure, form a little fortress for May at night against beasts.

Having thus erected our tent, we sat down to rest our wearied limbs, and to await patiently the return of Fos; but, oh! the burning thirst that was consuming us, and that, too, without the prospect of relief for some hours; for until the cool time came we did not dare venture in search of water—*but* for the misfortune of dropping the rifle, Fos would have been with us to have procured water. Oh, how we longed for his return! but in vain; the temperate hours came first.

"It is strange the boy does not return; I begin to be alarmed for his safety," said May.

"Mayhap he's skulking. Anyhow, Miss May, we wont wait any longer for water," said Bob.

"But what can we do?" said I.

"I'll just take one of these vessels, and hunt about for a stream."

"No, Bob; you shall not go alone."

"Must, Master Tom, d'ye see; for we cannot leave Miss May by herself."

"Nonsense, Bob; leave me a rifle and I will protect myself," said May.

"Can't hear of such a thing, nohow," said Bob.

"Then you remain here to watch for the boy, while Tom and I together go in search of water," said May.

"That's better, though I don't half like that; but, as we must have water, and one must remain behind, it's no good circumlocuting."

Whereupon, knowing that it was of little use to dispute with May when she had once made up her mind, I agreed. With rifles in hand, and two large empty vessels, we sallied in search of water. Well, we waded with some difficulty through the lemon-grass, which was so far above our heads that we were compelled to keep very near each other, until we came to what we had in the distance taken to be a forest; but which proved to be a long, narrow belt, or vanguard, of trees, between which and the forest there was another plain covered with grass.

"This is indeed fortunate. See, they are mangoes," said May, when we reached the trees.

"Bravo! Be yours the honour of the discovery," said I; and the next moment I had plucked some of this delicious fruit. Its juice revived us, and we pursued our journey through the grass, expecting to find some stream at hand; but, alas! an hour's search left us hopeless; and we began to think of returning, when a few low but deep growls, loud almost as thunder-claps when heard in the distance, fell upon our ears.

"What is it? We are lost, Tom!" said May, clutching my arm.

"Let us remain quiet," said I, almost with as much terror. Then came sounds like those from a shrill trumpet.

"It is a herd of elephants. No other animals could produce such sounds," said May.

Then came a noise like the rushing waters of a mountain torrent; and a few yards before us the grass was beaten down as some six or seven of these animals ran past us.

"This is fortunate; for, like us, these beasts are famishing with thirst, and in search of water. Let us follow in their trail," said I, advancing into the pathway which they had beaten through the grass.

Then we saw the animals stop at a distance of about five hundred yards.

"It is a river, and has been hidden from us by the long grass, May."

"Then it is dried up; for, see, they are moving further onwards," said May.

And as the elephants moved forwards, we ran towards the spot they had vacated; when, lo! we saw nought but the nearly dried-up muddy bed of a narrow stream. Water there was here and there, but it was filthy, and in the holes made by the animals' feet.

"But look, Tom; we need not despair yet. The elephants have found water," said May, pointing to the animals, who appeared to have discovered a pool, in which they were bathing and drinking.

"Stay; I will give them notice to quit; then we may take possession," said I, bringing my rifle to my shoulder; but before I could fire, May clutched me by the arm, saying—

"Don't fire, Tom; there is something at hand. Listen!"

And I heard a rustling among the grass. We both crouched down, with fingers upon our triggers, expecting to see some beast or reptile approaching; but, as a great bird with a large bill and a pouch beneath its under-chap, flew down, May said, laughing—

"It is a friend, not an enemy. It is a pelican or cormorant."

"Good; for there must be fish and water at hand," said I; adding, "Let us rest quiet, and watch."

Then we crept softly through the grass, and held the tall blades apart, so that we could watch the creature's movements.

The bird took up his position upon the edge of a small creek which ran out of the river,—but, with the exception of mud in little rills, it was free from water,—and at once became earnestly engaged.

"He is fishing," said May.

"Nonsense, May. How can there be fish where there is no water?"

But, pressing forward, to my surprise I saw a great number of fish, like perch, struggling upwards from the bed of the river. There must have been hundreds; but, as they passed near the bird, he picked them up, sometimes three or four at a time, and kept dropping them into his pouch, as if laying in a store for self and family for some time. Still, notwithstanding this wholesale destruction, numbers of the fish struggled past him on to the sandy bank, and then in something like order marched or wriggled themselves along and through the grass.

Wonderful as this appeared to me, these fish are commonly met with in Ceylon; sometimes even pursuing their march along gravelly or sandy roads; but, more wonderful still, nature, to enable these creatures to escape from the consequences of the drought, and seek water where they may, has provided them with an apparatus in the head, which holds a sufficient supply of water to keep their gills damp during their land journeys.

"Now," said I, after watching the winged fisherman for nearly half-an-hour, "I'll see if I can't kill one bird and frighten a herd of elephants with one shot."

As I spoke I fired: the poor bird fell over; the leader of the herd threw up his trunk with surprise, and, blowing his trumpet—I suppose as a signal for retreat—ran forward, followed by his companions.

"It was cruel to kill the poor bird. We could have made him disgorge the fish," said May.

"True, May; but we should have had to have caught him first. Let us secure him now," said I, running forward.

And, to my delight, I found him a capital prize; for, from the dimensions of his pouch, he must have had in store at least a hundred fish. The size of this you may imagine, when I tell you that, by opening the bill to its widest extent, you might have put your head comfortably within it. This pouch the bird uses simply as a fishing-basket, which he first fills, and then digests at leisure. Many extraordinary stories are told of the pelican. One writer, Ruyset, declares that a man has been seen to hide his whole leg, boot and all, in the monstrous jaws of one of them. At first appearance this would seem impossible, as the sides of the under-chap, from which the bag depends, are not above an inch asunder when the bird's bill is first opened; but then they are capable of great separation; and it must necessarily be so, as the bird preys upon the largest fishes, and packs them by dozens in its pouch. Indeed, it is asserted that it can store in this receptacle with which it has been provided by nature, as many fish as would serve for a meal for sixty hungry men.

"Now, Tom," said May, picking up her water-vessel, and placing it upon her head after the fashion of an Oriental maiden, "I think I can see a pool."

So saying, she went on in advance; and I, snatching up the fisher, which, by the way, being larger than a swan, was no light weight, I threw it across my shoulder, and followed at a distance of some half-dozen yards. But scarcely had May reached what she believed to be the pool, than she uttered a sudden scream; and no wonder, for, as she stepped down the muddy bank, she ran nearly into the jaws of a large crocodile. In an instant my rifle was to my shoulder. Such, however, was my fear for May, that the bullet missed. For an instant I thought all was over; when, singularly—at least, I thought it so then—the reptile, evidently the most terrified of the three, made a dart forward, and coming to a hillock of mud, thrust its head and shoulders therein; as if, like the ostrich, it thought that, not to see, was not *to be* seen by its pursuer. Such I afterwards found really to be the habit of this species of crocodile, which inhabits the tanks and small rivers of the island.

" The monster is a great coward, after all, Tom," said May.

" It may be; but, as the brute, perhaps, is only making a feint, in order to attack us with vigour, we had better leave him plenty of sea room," said I.

And May being of the same opinion, had no sooner filled her water-jar with the muddy fluid, than we endeavoured to retrace our steps, taking the direction of a wreath of curling smoke which we saw rising above the trees, and which we had little doubt came from Bob's fire.

CHAPTER VI.

BOB MEETS WITH AN ACCIDENT—FOS RELATES
THE HISTORY OF TWO DEVILS AND A LITTLE
BOY—AND I FIGHT WITH A WILD BOAR.

" Namo Bud-dhaya [Buddha be praised], Missee
and Sar Excellency's come back," said Fos, meeting us at a short distance from the tent, or rather
tents; for during our absence Bob had erected
the other.

" Aye, aye, boy; and with a store of fish and
water," I replied, throwing the bird upon the
ground.

" Dat good; but Missee no must carry water,"
said the boy, relieving May of her load.

" Hilloa, Master Tom, lend us a hand," cried
Bob from within the tent.

And from the fact that the old sailor had not
come forward to meet us, both May and I ran
forward into the tent.

" Why, what's the matter, Bob?" said I, seeing
him lying upon one side, apparently helpless, as
far as the use of his legs, for the right calf was
bound round with handkerchiefs; moreover, there
was blood about the ground.

" Dear Bob, what has happened ?" cried May, running up to him.

" Bless your heart," said he, raising himself with one hand; "you need not alarm yourself, for it is not much, though enough` to bring me to an anchor; and this is how it happened.   D'ye see, shortly after you and Master Tom started upon your cruise, I thought I might as well kindle a fire; that the smoke would serve as a signal as to these latitudes : and so thinking that, if the wood was a little green-like, the smoke would be all the darker, and, therefore, the plainer to be seen, I clambered up a tree, struck off a branch ; but, somehow or other, d'ye see, I was cutting away at the very branch upon which I was sitting, and only found it out when it gave way, and dropped me right athwart my axe, and split my leg nearly in two just about midships.   Well, of course it bled pretty freely ; so much, that at first I made up my mind that I had lost my moorings in this world, when at that identical minute back comes the boy, who ought to be a born Christian ; for, before I could say Jack Robinson, he had plucked some leaves, plastered them upon the wound, and bound the leg up, as you see, with these han'kerchiefs.   But I take it," he added, " that it's a kind of punishment, d'ye see, for being such a foolish old porpoise as to cut away the very deck upon which I was standing. But just lend me a hand, and I'll try what I can do upon one leg."

"No, Bob, you will not; you shall remain where you are till your wound is healed. Moreover, I intend to be your nurse."

"Bless your pretty heart, but——"

"There, now, no more talking; it is a bad affair, and we must just get you well as soon as possible. But now for our evening meal, for you all look half starved."

So saying, May skipped out of the tent to boil the fish which Fosforus had taken from the pelican's pouch.

"But, Lord love ye, Master Tom, this here accident of mine, d'ye see, is just the very least of our misfortunes," said Bob.

"Why, what's in the wind now, Bob?"

"Well, here's the boy, and he can spin his own yarn," said Bob, as Fos at that moment entered the tent, bringing Bob half a dozen juicy mangoes, each as large as a goose-egg.

"Did Sar Bosen tell Excellency how 'um lost horse?" said the boy.

"Lost the horse!" I repeated, greatly shocked at such a calamity; though chiefly for May's sake.

"'Es, sar, lost horse. Not long after 'um go look for gun, 'um big cheetah [leopard] smell horse, jump out of jungle, knock Fos off, and, before 'um could get on back again, dragged 'um into jungle. Fos did not follow, so lost horse altogether; but 'um keep on with no horse till find gun where him fall, and so why gone so long time."

"Well, it can't be helped; but it's a sad loss," said I, really grieved; for I knew not how we should carry our baggage for the future; or, indeed, how May would be able to tramp through the woods; although, for the latter, I need not have cared, as she proved to be as capable of fatigue as any of us. As, however, our straits were too serious to admit of repining, we soon cast aside all regrets, and sat down to a large dish of boiled fish and rice. After which, May, who had taken upon herself the nursing of Bob, rebandaged his wound, promising at the same time that, if he would remain patient, he should recover in a week.

" Moored here for a week, like an unseaworthy old hulk; it is too bad," moaned the impatient sailor.

" Fos tell how quite cure by time sun gets up," said the boy, confidently.

" If so be you can manage that, boy, old Bob 'll make over the pay due to him since he left old England," said Bob.

" S'pose 'um, Sar Bosen, say ' Namo Buddhaya.' "

"Well, s'pose I do," said Bob, repeating the words.

"Den s'pose 'um say 'Namo Bud-dhaya' again."

"Well, boy, s'pose 'um do, again," said Bob, mimicking the boy.

"Den 'um must keep say it 'gain, 'gain, 'gain, all night; so 'um say it 'sleep, say it wake; den in morning all wound gone."

"Avaunt, you young imp of Satan; do ye think I'm going to forget I'm a Christian?" said Bob.

"'Um berry good ting to say; for 'um drive bad debel away from little boy," said Fos, stoutly.

"Why, you black lubber," said Bob, sitting upwards; then, suppressing his passion, he said to me, "Now, look you, Master Tom, if you've any regard for old Bob, you'll just pitch that rascally young heathen into the jungle."

"Nay, Bob; Fos has some story to tell. Let us hear it," said I, rather curious to hear the legend from which this superstitious belief in these words arose.

"Well, if so be it's only a black fellow's yarn, I'll just bring my tongue to an auchor," said Bob.

Whereupon Fos repeated the following legend from one of the native books—

"There once lived in the same street a follower of Buddha and a follower of Brâma. Each had a son, and the two boys used to play dice together;

but as the son of the Buddhist always won, the
other boy said to him one day—

"'Friend, how is it that you gain, and I lose,
every day? What is it you say when you cast
the dice? Is there any charm that you know and
make use of?'

"'No,' said the other; 'I know of no charm;
but whenever I throw the dice, I say, "Namo
Bud-dhaya" (Let Buddha be praised).'

"From that time the son of the follower of
Brâma used the same words, and therefore their
gains became equal. Some time after this, the
son of the heathen—*i.e.*, the follower of Brâma—
went with his father to gather firewood in the
jungle, and having filled their waggon, they were
returning to the city. As they were at the city
gate, they let loose the oxen to the grass; but they
[the oxen] went to the city with the other cattle,
which caused the father to go in search of them.
As, however, the city gates were shut for the
night, the father was left inside; and the poor
boy could do nothing but lie down to sleep beneath
the waggon.

"Now, as two devils, the one a Buddhist, and
the other a heathen, who were rambling in search
of prey, came up to the sleeping boy, the
heathen devil said—

"'Let me devour this child.' But the other
objected, saying—

" ' That must not be; for, by having said the words " Namo Bud-dhaya," he is devoted to Buddha.'

" But the heathen devil, taking no heed of this, caught hold of the child's legs, intending to gnaw him like a root; but, lo! the child happening to mutter the very words, the devil became alarmed; the hair of his body stood on end, and he took his hands off the child as if he had caught a serpent thinking it was a pearl.

"Then the Buddhist devil, seeing that the heathen was disappointed in his evil designs by the influence of Buddha, said—

" ' Friend, it is my duty, being a friend of yours, to show you what to do. You are guilty of a great crime, and deserve to be'punished for attempting aught against one who is devoted to Buddha.'

" These words were fearful to the devil as the noise of flies that settle' on the dead bodies in the field of battle is fearful to the warrior who has lost the victory, and he asked his friend what was to be done. The Buddhist devil then commanded him to bring some food to the poor boy, who had fasted since morning; and he immediately made himself invisible, and went to the king's palace, and brought therefrom a golden dish of sweetmeats, which (having first taken the form of the boy's father) he commanded him to eat. After which the devil engraved the history of the whole transaction upon the golden dish, and went his way.

"In the morning, when the breakfast was to be prepared for the King, his Majesty's attendants, not finding the dish, went about seeking it; and when they found it with the boy near the waggon, they carried him and his father with the dish to the King, who, as soon as he had read the engraving, was so much pleased with the boy, that he said—

"'If such a devil, who knows nothing of the power of Buddha—a devil so fierce and cruel—would do so great a kindness even to a boy when the name of Buddha is mentioned, it is, therefore, my duty, who am a believer, and know the depths of the power of Buddha, to show him favour to the utmost.'

"And, accordingly, the King conferred on him the same day rank, power, and wealth, and made him one of the nobles of his kingdom."

"D'ye see, I don't believe a word of it. Such a yarn isn't fit even for the marines. And, if so be it were true, to my thinking, that boy got his promotion without deserving it," said Bob.

"Nonsense, Bob. It is a parable; which, if the name of Our Saviour were substituted for that of Buddha, and it were divested of its superstitious phraseology, might stand side by side with those to be found in our own holy writings; which teach that in all, aye, in any difficulty, there can be no greater reliance than in the name of God," said May.

"D'ye see, I didn't see it with those head-lights. So, mayhap you are right, Miss May," said Bob, thoughtfully, scratching his head.

And May was right. The story wanted but the substitution of the *real* for that of the Buddhist God. The Buddhist religion, however, false as it is, is yet the noblest of *heathen* creeds ; for do but note the following passage, which is meant to impress upon the heart the all-sufficiency of faith in God—

"Oh ! the supernatural power of Buddha. A person not offering his life as a gift, but by merely saying 'Namo Bud-dhaya,' shall have no fear or horror. He who takes refuge in Buddha till his life's end shall fear nothing. As the voice of the peacock causes dread to the serpent, so the word Buddha is a fear to devils and demons ; for they flee at its sound. As the poison of serpents is destroyed by the power of charms, and as wax melts before the fire, so devils and demons flee from those who have taken refuge in Buddha. Such is the influence of this one word. It is, indeed, a fortified, lofty, and strong line of defence to them that believe ; a palace of gold, a cave of glass kept by a noble lion, a cave of gold, a great ship to carry them through the ocean of transmigratory existence. It is a golden crown upon the head of believers, a pair of spectacles for the eyes, a pair of earrings for the ears, a golden chain for the neck, a string of pearls, a sword to destroy the enemy, a banner to those who believe, frontlets between the eyes, a staff to destroy the adversary, a coat of mail to defend the body, a mighty wind to drive away the dust of sorrow. Therefore, those wise persons who take refuge in this gracious word Buddha, the name of that omniscient one who is the eye to guide the world, shall be great in the world to come."

Convincing, however, as this story might be to Fos of the efficacy of muttering such words, it had a different effect upon Bob; who, soon after it was finished, fell into a profound sleep. May then retired to her own tent, leaving myself and Fos to divide the night's watch between us. I chose the latter half; and thus, as in that dread wilderness, with rifle in hand, I sat, with ears open to every sound, and my eyes fixed upon the fire, I pondered upon the difficulties of our position. Bob maimed, so that perhaps for weeks he might not be able to walk; the horse upon which he might have ridden, killed. We had three good rifles, it was true; but, then, our ammunition would be insufficient for any lengthened stay in the woods; for, apart from the necessity of keeping sufficient to protect us from the sudden inroads of wild animals, in a climate where meat killed in the morning becomes by night so decomposed that it is unfit for the use of man, every meal, at least of animal food, would cost us one, if not more charges. So very gloomy were my thoughts and ponderings till the dawn of day brought May to my side.

"Why look so gloomy, dear Tom, seeing Heaven has been kind to us as yet; for, 'd'ye see,' as poor Bob would say, it must be a dense forest that has no opening."

"Is it not enough to make one gloomy, May? Bob an invalid; our horse killed; and, save herbs and fruits, Heaven only knows how we are to obtain food."

"Why, with the rifle, to be sure, Tom," said she, laughing.

"Nay; that is not possible, without the game will come here purposely to be killed; for Bob cannot, and Fos *must* not, go in search, for fear we lose our guide; while I dare not leave you."

"Not leave me! Why, Tom, I shall soon begin to believe that it is I who dare not leave you," she replied, good humouredly.

Which, however, I confess, so vexed me, that I said, angrily,

"Tut, tut, May."

"Tut, tut, again, Tom; don't be angry; it is of no use tut-tutting; we are in a difficulty, and must make the best of our way out of it; but, for the present, I have resolved that, while one

L.I.C. K

remains to nurse Bob and act as housekeeper, the other two shall go in search of a good fat elk and a calabash of water. Now, you know, of the two that hunt, Fos must be one; the other must be either nurse and housewife, or hunter," she replied, archly adding, "Which shall it be, Tom, you or I ?"

"But, May——"

"There, but me no buts, for the matter is settled," she replied, placing her finger upon my mouth. "You will be the hunter, of course; and I, housewife. As for danger, there is the same heaven above me, whether with or without you; besides, shan't Bob and I have a rifle and an axe or two between us?"

"Well, well, May, I see it is of no use for me to object; you are an obstinate puss; and if you will, you will, and there's an end on't."

"Yes; and if I wont, I *wont*, you may depend on't. But, come," she added, taking my arm, "let's to the tent, for both Bob and Fos are stirring; and in this climate it behoves us to make our hay *before* the sun shines."

"Sar Bosen's leg good as new," said the boy, who was busily engaged preparing rice for breakfast.

"Belay there, you imp; d'ye think my jaw tackle's out of order, that I can't speak for myself?" said Bob; adding, as he sat upright and shook his leg at me, "Look you, Master Tom, I shall be able to sail as well as any craft afloat, upon two legs soon."

Then, while we made our scant and hasty morning meal, I told him of the arrangement May and I had made. Whereupon he caught up his rifle, looked to the charge, and having placed it near at hand, declared that neither man nor beast should hurt her while she kept under its cover : and thus, feeling satisfied of my sister's safety, Fos and I departed upon our foraging expedition ; and that, too, tolerably well armed ; for, in addition to axes, knives, and Fos's rifle, I carried a double-barrelled piece.

"Now, Fos," said I, as we started, "we have no dogs to start the game ; but you must hunt up a buck, and I will bring him down."

"Excellency no find big deer in low country ; all up in hills : but, if make legs go quick, shall catch little moose as 'um come home to forest."

"On, then," said I.

And away we scampered, Fos leading through jungle and tall lemon-grass, till, by quite a different direction from that in which May and I had taken the day before, we entered a forest of ebony, satin-wood, tulip, and tamarind trees. Once there, we were enabled to increase our speed twofold, for the ground was hard, smooth, and free from grass or jungle ; and with as little

hesitation as a London street-boy would guide a
stranger through the intricacies of our huge
metropolis, did the boy lead, till we came to a
spot where the trees were fewer and wider apart,
and through which we could see an open plain;
then stopping, he said—

" Now, Excellency, keep 'um eyes open all sides.
Fos get up tree, and look for deer."

And the next instant he was running up the
trunk of a tamarind-tree with the rapidity of a
wild cat. A few minutes of observation, and
down he came again.

" 'Um very good deer at river, Excellency; see."

And he pointed to some rising ground, where,
sure enough, I could see a group of animals;
of what description, however, the distance, but
more especially the tall grass around them, would
not permit me to distinguish. Not doubting, however, that Fos was correct, I brought my gun to
my shoulder, and would have fired; but the boy,
catching hold of the barrel, said—

" No, not shoot. Frighten, not kill. Excellency must go on knees, so not be seen. Fos go
forward; like dog, start deer, then Excellency
catch 'um."

Then, falling upon his hands and toes, the boy
ran through the grass; but in a circuitous direction, so that he could get to the other side of the
animals, and drive them towards me.

According to the boy's direction, I crept forward through the grass in a straight direction for about fifty yards, till I came to a clearing. I then stood upright, looking for Fos. He was not to be seen. I was sufficiently near now to the animals to distinguish the forms of deer— the small moose-deer. So far so good. I would await the re-appearance of the boy, who I expected every instant would drive the animals on to the muzzle of my rifle. The clearing to my left seemed to extend for many a mile; while to my right hand the grass grew to a great height. And from the rifle, which every now and then appeared above, I could see that it was through that tall grass Fos was creeping towards the deer. It was my first essay in real sporting; consequently, I stood in breathless anxiety, but fully determined that the animal should not escape my rifle, when suddenly there was a rush in the grass to my right. Now, having kept my eyes to the front, I was taken by surprise. Still I turned. My gun was at my shoulder. But guess my consternation; instead of a poor little moose-deer, I found myself confronted by a huge wild boar! The animal, as if no less surprised than myself, stood stock still, as if to weigh in its mind whether I was friend or enemy. I did not, I would not fire. My life depended upon the success of the shot. A minute, a full minute, we stood gazing

at each other; each, like Macbeth, letting "I dare
not wait upon I would." I was the first to move,
and that, too, in a backward direction; but still
with my rifle to my shoulder. For an instant I
glanced behind to examine my chance of a good
run and a speedy cover; nay, or a tree up which
I might clamber. Alas! it was a wilderness.
In that glance, however, I had seen a heap of
sweet potatoes at a little distance in my rear; and
at once it occurred to me it was to them the brute
was making his way. Then I thought, if I can
but slowly retreat past the potatoes without firing,
the animal may prefer the vegetables to your
humble servant. Of course all this passed very
rapidly through my mind; but as I moved backwards, the brute sniffed the ground, and gave a
grunt, much more significant of war than peace.
Still I moved backwards. Then down went his
head to the ground. Heaven alone can save me
by directing the shot, for he is taking aim. And
seeing clearly that there was no choice between
my having his tusks in my body, or his having
my ball, I fired one barrel. The ball told—it
struck his shoulder, and fairly knocked him over.
Here was a chance for my legs. I turned, ran
forward. There was a solitary tree in the distance.
I would make for that; when, if followed, I could
either clamber or fight behind cover. I had cleared
a few yards, but behind me I could hear the savage

grunting, and almost howling with rage. I turned to look. He was within a few feet of me. The sight of the brute gave elasticity to my limbs. One leap; the heap of sweet potatoes was before me, and into the midst of them I alighted. But the ground gave way beneath me. My head was bumped forward; my rifle was out of my hand; my hands and face were cut; my chest and back tightly compressed between two opposing forces. For a minute or two I was stunned. Recovering my senses, I found I had fallen into a staked pit some six feet deep; and that, too, between the stakes. My first thought was my rifle: it was by my side, and not discharged. Above me, with his great snout stirring up the earth, the brute kept walking backwards and forwards, grunting with rage that he had been balked of his prey. Well, I forced some of the stakes aside, so that I could crouch down upon my knees; and then, with my finger upon the trigger, I remained gazing at the enraged pig, who kept pacing backwards and forwards, in a state of indecision as to whether he should leap in after me. It was well, however, for both of us that he had too much sagacity for that; for, not only should I have been gored to death, but he would have been taken; as, indeed, the natives, who had set that trap on purpose for him or some of his family, had intended. But, in the meantime, what should I do? Fire? Yes;

a lucky aim might dispatch him. But, even then, in his anger he might tumble in upon me, and between his tusks and the weight of his huge body, finish me. So, come what would, come what might, I determined to reserve my fire.

It was not an agreeable position; for, as the brute walked round and round the edges of the pit, as if examining for a means of safely reaching me, I turned round; and so, with pointed rifle, and eyes fixed upon his snout, I turned, and he walked round and round. And this must have lasted half an hour—to me it seemed hours. At length, with a loud growl, the boar turned his head from the pit. " He is tired now," thought I. No, not he; for the sound of footsteps told me the brute saw a new enemy in the field; and, as I had no doubt as to who the new comer was, I placed my cap upon the muzzle of my rifle, and, holding it up above my head, shouted—

" Fos! Fos!"

There was a reply, though what it was I could not hear; for the boar at that moment gave a savage grunt, and left the pit. In an instant I clambered to the top. There was the gallant boy standing at bay, with his hunting-knife lashed to the point of a long pole, awaiting to receive the boar, which was charging at him. I'll weaken his charge at least, I thought. And the next instant I sent a ball through his hind quarters. So noble, however, are these brutes in their warfare, that even dying they turn not aside; and so by sheer force he ran the lance through his body. And, desperately wounded with shot, and the spear in his body, I believe he would still have had strength sufficient to have gored Fos with his tusks, had I not rushed forward, and with one blow of my axe struck him to the earth.

"Namo Bud-dhaya! [Buddha be praised] pig dead," said Fos.

"You are a brave fellow, Fos. Still, it was foolhardy to trust to that flimsy knife while you had a charge in your rifle," said I.

"Excellency, Fos not fool. S'pose 'um fired gun, and not kill pig, pig kill Fos. With knife pig run and kill 'umself. So got rifle spare, if not quite dead."

"Well, well, Fos—*Finis coronat opus.*"

"What dat?" asked the boy, quickly.

"Why, Fos, it means the end crowns the work; that is, that your plan must have been good, or it would not have been successful," I replied, laughing to myself at the idea of using a Latin proverb to such a personage.

CHAPTER VII.

I WITNESS A DUEL BETWEEN TWO SERPENTS—FIGHT
ONE MYSELF WITH A BUFFALO, AND AM ROBBED
BY SOME JACKALS, WHO ARE PLUNDERED BY A
LEOPARD.

Now, although by killing the boar we had
frightened away our game, the discovery of the
trap, with which I had fallen, was somewhat of a
recompence; for, in the first place, it had saved
my life; and, in the second, betokened a village
to be not far distant. Fos, however, was sadly
disappointed at losing the deer; and gazing at
the carcass before him, said—

" Pig dead; but 'um no good. It too big to
carry to missee."

" True, boy; the whole of this carcass may be
too heavy to carry. Nevertheless, we must not
return to the tent without something in the shape
of game."

" No, dat nebber do; 'cos Sar Bosen laugh, and
say Fos bad guide; Excellency not good hunter."

" Yet," said I, thoughtfully, " we cannot help
ourselves; for we cannot remain beneath this
burning sun till nightfall, when the deer are likely

to return. Therefore, boy, let us lop off one of this fellow's hind quarters."

"Nebber do eat pig. Better wait in wood till sun down; den, if can catchee, shoot deer or jungle fowl," said he.

"Aye, aye; that notion will do. So lead the way," I replied; but, observing that we were taking a path different from that by which we had quitted the forest, I hesitated to proceed; seeing which, Fos said—

"Dis better path. Near river. Plenty water."

And, to my joy, in a few minutes we stood by the bank of a wide river, whose running waters divided us from a dense forest. Oh! how refreshing was the sight of that delicious stream, clear as crystal, but so shallow (not more than four feet deep) that the bottom was plainly visible. I delighted in bathing, and I could not resist the opportunity; although, from the indents in the banks and in the bed, it was certain that large animals, elephants or buffaloes, frequented the water. So, stripping off my clothes, I said—

"Now, Fos, I shall swim across. You wade, though, taking care not to get our ammunition or arms wet."

"'Es; but, Excellency, look see no crocodile," said the boy, as he packed the arms and clothes into a convenient parcel.

I looked to the right and to the left, but

seeing nought but a log of wood floating down the stream, I jumped in; and so delicious was the coolness after the sultry heat, I made no haste to cross, but floated at leisure with the stream. Fortunately, however, turning round to see if the boy was following, I found the object I had taken for a log of wood, and which was now within twelve yards of me, to be in reality a large shark, who, like myself, was floating at his ease, now with one of his huge fins out of the water. The sight lent wings to my movements; for, shouting to the boy to beware, I plunged my body forward, struck out my arms, and in a few minutes had scrambled up the opposite bank, in my great fright not quite certain that I had been permitted by the monster to bring both my legs with me; but, looking back, to my horror I saw Fos, with the arms and clothes above his head, wading as leisurely across as if he had been on terms of the greatest affection with the finny brute, who was absolutely within a yard or two of him.

"The shark, boy; the shark!" I cried out; but Fos only laughed, and kept on his way, as if in not the least danger. "You stupid fellow; what are you grinning at?" said I, angrily, when he came ashore.

"Nebber care 'bout shark in river dis time ob year; dey only eat man in river at 'tic'lar season."

"Oh, oh," said I, amazed at the queer whim

of such monsters being as particular in their man-sporting as sportsmen in England, who may not kill a partridge till the first of September; "but suppose the shark had been troubled with a short memory, and had forgotten that man was out of season; for he certainly might have made such an exception to his rule, Fos?"

"Shark nebber make no 'ception," replied he.

Whether this be true or not I cannot vouch. It is, however, a belief current among the natives; and the self-denial of the fish in the instance related would seem confirmatory; for both Fos and myself had been completely within reach of its jaws, had it honoured us with its regard. For my part, I thought my escape so fortunate—that, alive to the dangers around, chiefly from the beasts, who were doubtless at that moment seeking the shade of the forest—that, as soon as we had gathered a few juicy mangoes, and broken the shells of a couple of cocoa-nuts which we found upon the ground, I ascended one of the trees, followed by Fos, greatly to the disgust of a Mr. and Mrs. Monkey, and some three or four Master and Miss Monkeys, who, screaming and chattering, hastened from branch to branch, and ulti- mately leaped into a neighbouring tree.

Well, in this position we continued for about three hours; when, believing the most intense heat of the day had subsided, we resumed our journey homewards. As, however, I descended the trunk, there came upon my ear a curious hissing noise; still, not thinking it business of mine, in another instant I should have alighted, but for Fos, who cried out—

" Sar Excellency not go; noya-polonga!"

At this warning I rested upon the lowest branch, about five feet from the ground, and there saw two serpents: one, a polonga, of reddish grey, about five feet long; the other, a noya, or cobra, about four feet in length; but both engaged in deadly contest with each other.

It was a curious scene. The polonga lay upon its belly, every now and then lifting its head, hissing, and darting forth its fangs at the somewhat lordly-looking cobra; who the whole time waited to receive and ward off the attacks of its enemy, with one half its body quite perpendicular; but with its fierce, fiery eyes darting from its spectacled head like balls of living fire. In my anxiety to witness as much as possible of this contest, I bent forward my body; unfortunately, too forward; for, from the combined weight of my body and rifle, the branch snapped, pitching me down, head foremost, between the two reptiles. For a moment I was stunned; after which, my first sensation was a sharp tingling in my left leg. Great Heaven! I had been bitten by the cobra. In an instant

I was upon my feet, and the next, the head of
the reptile would have been beaten into a jelly
with the butt-end of my rifle, but for Fos, who,
having alighted almost as soon as myself, seized
my arm, and having dragged me a distance, of
some dozen yards, said—

"Excellency no kill noya; fader, moder, broder
all die."

"What mean you, idiot," I cried, amazed
at his coming between me and my vengeance.

"Excellency stop—sit down; for, if don't
want to die, must cure bite first, tellee what
mean after."

And as a painful, darting, shooting sensation
up my arm, as far as the shoulder, had set in,
I complied; when, unfastening his vest, Fos
brought forth a small, black, highly-polished
stone; which, having placed over the bleeding
wound, it affixed itself immediately with all the
tenacity of a leech; then, finding it would not
easily come off, he rubbed my arm for about
one minute with a violence that made me wince
again. After this, he took from his vest a small
piece of white wood, or root, which he passed
over my arm to and fro, till the black stone
relinquished its grasp; when I at once felt relieved from the pain.

This wonderful stone is called pamboo-kaloo,
or snake-stone; and from time immemorial has

been regarded by the Asiatics as a certain cure for the bites of the most venomous reptiles. Of what it is composed is not positively known, for it is kept a secret; science, however, and chemistry in particular, is a terrible foe to secrets, and so thought Sir James Tennent, who, being very desirous to find out the secret, tells us, " I submitted a snake-stone which had been used to Mr. Faraday; who, having analysed it, said, he believed it to be a piece of charred bone which has been filled with blood, perhaps several times, and then carefully charred again. Evidence of this is offered as well by the apertures of cells or tubes on its surface, as by the fact that it yields and breaks under pressure, and exhibits an organic structure within. When heated slightly, water rises from it, and also a little ammonia; and if heated still more highly in the air, the carbon burns away, and a bulky white ash is left, retaining the shape and size of the stone."

Whatever may be its composition, there can be no doubt that it cures; for, being porous, when instantly applied, it acts as an absorbent to extract the venom from the recent wound, together with a portion of the blood, before it has time to be carried into the system. As for the piece of white wood, which Fos passed backwards and forwards over my wound, it was a cutting from the root of a plant which, as the ichneumon, who often fights with venomous serpents, when bitten, hastens to eat and be cured of the bite, the natives believe to be of equal service either to cure a wound or charm a serpent itself. As observation, however, has not raised this belief into ascertained fact, we must regard it as one of the tricks of the snake-charmers.

Finding myself relieved from all pain, and even nervousness, as to consequences from the bite of the terrible snake, we proceeded onwards to the tents; but as we walked I could not resist reproaching Fos for standing between me and my vengeance upon the reptile; and his excuse, if not quite satisfactory, was both instructive and amusing, for it enlightened me as to another superstition among the people, namely, that the cobra was called noy-rogerati, *i.e.*, the king's snake, because it would do no harm if not provoked; but that, if one happened to be killed, all the other snakes of the same kind would avenge its death upon the family of the killer, and devour his wife, brethren, and children. Therefore, when one of these serpents have bitten a man, the custom is for his friends to enchant it, and thus having cited it before them, give it a sharp reproof; after which it is believed the reptile will do no more harm.

As for the battle between the two snakes, I also

learned that the polonga and the noya never meet
without fighting, till one is killed and devoured
by the other ; and, by way of accounting for this
mutual feud between these reptiles, the Singhalese
say that once, during a great drought, a noya,
meeting a thirsty polonga, told the latter that he
knew where there was a bowl containing water,
but that by its side sat a child, which, although
it kicked him while he was drinking, in con-
sideration of the great benefit he derived from the
water, he put up with the affront. Well, the
polonga, being introduced by his friend the noya
to the bowl, drank heartily; but being kicked by
the child, he turned and devoured it : whereupon
the noya became so much enraged at his friend's
ungrateful behaviour, that he at once slew and
devoured him. Since which such a mutual hatred
has existed between the two reptiles, that of
irreconcileable enemies the natives have a saying
that "they are like the noya and polonga."

"Not cross here, but higher up," said Fos,
when we came to that point where the shark had
exhibited so much contempt or forbearance that
he would not eat me.

"Nay, lad; it will make our journey at least a
mile longer."

"'Es, Excellency ; but den get water clear—de
riber much more wide, less deep; so den go dere wash
and drink," replied Fos; and admitting the reason

to be good, I followed his lead along the bank for
about a mile, the last quarter of which was passed
in toiling through a dense jungle, which reached
nearly to the water's edge; but it appeared I
should be well rewarded for my trouble, for,
pushing aside the thorny wood, there in the
stream, but near the opposite side, in advance of a
herd of some half dozen, stood a fine moose buck.
At length game was before me, my rifle was at my
shoulder; but that imp of a boy, again catching
my arm, cried—

"Sar Excellency not shoot little buffalo, large
one not far off." But the warning came too late,
and worse, the action changed my line of fire from
the buck to the animal he had named, which was
wallowing in the water close to the bank.

"Confound you, Fos; you have made me waste
my last charge but one."

"Dat bad, berry, 'cos Fos got none shot left."

"Worse and worse; but follow on, we may
get the calf before the old one finds out its loss."

"No, no, Excellency; run back, ole buffalo,"
replied the boy, and at the same time a large cow
came forward from behind a large thicket of rushes
or water-plants, grunting, groaning, and bellowing
with rage. The novelty, the danger of the situation, deprived me of my self-possession. The animal
was within a few yards of me. Summoning all
my coolness, my rifle was again at my shoulder,

and I made over to her the contents of the second barrel. She received them in the shoulder. Her onward career was stayed; but fancy my horror when, instead of falling, I found she stood with her fore-legs stretched forward, with her savage eye glancing in my face, as if conscious that I was now in her power, and that she intended to prolong my torture by keeping me in suspense. Yes, there she stood in front of me, within two yards. I dared not advance, still less retreat, for the instant I had taken my eyes off her I knew she would be after me. What was to be done? I had powder, rifle, but no bullet. What should I—what could I do? Take an oblique direction, and run for it? An instant's thought told me the absurdity of such a proceeding. No, I had but one course; that I would risk, keeping my eyes still fixed upon the animal. I cried to Fos to keep in my rear with his hunting-knife ready; then, still fixing my eyes upon the enemy, I put a double charge of powder in my rifle, and taking off a piece of my handkerchief, I cut off the six round brass buttons from my waistcoat; but scarcely had I rammed this novel charge down the barrel, before the brute sprang forward. In an instant my gun was upon a level with her head; the action again stayed her, for she stood still bellowing and pawing the bottom of the river. It was a good opportunity; but yet I would not fire, for it was my only charge, and so for nearly five minutes we stood staring at each other. The cow, however, got tired first. I saw she intended business, for she lashed her tail, brought down her head so that her horns were at goring position, and started forward, and for an instant my life depended upon my waistcoat buttons; it was, however, only for an instant, for at the next the charge of buttons pierced her head, and over she rolled. We did not stop to see if she were dead, or only stunned, but scampering through the water, reached the opposite bank, and then, as fast as legs would carry us, made the best of our way to a tree about half a mile ahead; and well it was that we did, for when, at a distance of some two hundred yards, we turned to look back, we saw that she was once more upon her legs, aye, and giving chase at a pace which, considering the quantity and quality of the charge in her head, somewhat surprised me. Her efforts, however, were impotent, for long before she could reach the tree she fell, but then lifeless from exhaustion.

What a proof, I thought, that, but for the brain which makes man lord of the creation, he would be one of the most impotent of animals—a poor, defenceless wretch, whose legs would serve him neither for pursuit or escape, if compelled to trust to his own speed, and whose weakness of body would render him the easy victim of a host of enemies now his slaves, notwithstanding they possess a hundred times his strength.

Now that our enemy was really dead, we returned to the river, and dragging the buffalo calf out of the water where it had fallen, made an effort to carry it with us in lieu of the buck I had lost. Finding, however, that the weight, but more especially the bulk, was too much, by dint of our axes and hunting-knives we managed to hew off the fore-quarters; then when, porter-fashion, Fos had adjusted our prize upon his neck and shoulders, that he might carry it with the greater ease, we set out upon our homeward march for the tents, not a little pleased that we had at last something to show for our day's absence.

For some time we passed on our way without molestation or fright from any living creature; indeed, we had reached that portion of jungle which I believed to be not very far distant from our tents, when through the night air (it was moonlight) there arose a fearful noise, compounded of a scream, a howl, and a bark. I started, and looked around anxiously, for the dismal howling pierced my very soul. I believe I had never heard any sounds so fearful. Neither, from the sound, could the animal from whom it had arisen be far distant. No, that was certain; for, as if it had been but the signal for a hideous concert, the whole welkin became filled with howlings, barkings, yelling, and screaming.

" Dat 'um debel, 'um scent calf, Excellency; use 'um legs," said Fos, starting into a trot.

I followed his example, bitterly regretting my want of ammunition. However, to make up for its loss, I held my axe in one hand, and my rifle by the barrel so poised that its stock would serve as a very good club, should we come to close quarters. Well, the howling continued; we changed our trot into a run; but the faster we ran, the nearer sounded the howling. Then for an instant it ceased; but, instead, there was a sound among the lemon-grass and jungle like the downward rushing of an avalanche, and we were completely surrounded by some fifty jackals, who, seeing us at bay, recommenced their howling. What was to be done? Defend ourselves? The best way to do that was to toss the calf, which had drawn these vultures of the animal world, among them. Fos, however, did not want telling; he knew their natures too well: so, throwing down the quarters of the calf, he cried—

" Golly, 'um debels got Missee supper."

The effect was instantaneous; the brutes discontinued their howling, and fell at once upon the meal.

" Golly, but 'um hab dat what's better den calf," said Fos; and as he spoke the axe flew from his hand into the brain of one of the animals.

"Are you mad, boy?" said I, thinking that the animals would revenge upon us the fall of their companion; but, before he could reply, the jungle was dashed aside, and out sprang a huge leopard, at the sight of which I ran forward; but Fos, catching hold of my arm, cried—

"Excellency, not go; 'um chetah do no harm; no eat man; 'um like buffalo better."

And so it appeared, for the sight of the leopard drove away the jackals, who now howled more dismally than ever. The beast coolly took the quarters of the calf in his mouth, and throwing them across his back, vanished in the jungle. Thus, because of my thoughtlessness in bringing too small a quantity of ammunition, did we lose our hard-earned game. Bitter, however, as was the loss, it was some consolation that the original thieves had themselves been robbed of their ill-gotten plunder.

Now, I dare say you have heard the jackal greatly abused; nevertheless, in some respects, he is more noble than the lion, the panther, or the leopard, all of which habitually await till the call and screaming of the jackal proclaim it in search of prey; then following the pack, till they have hunted it down, the lion and his large brethren rush in, and take it from the unfortunate providers, but invariably at the time when they are about to share the fruits of perhaps an entire night's hunt.

Fos, instead of being dispirited at the loss of

our prospective meal, seemed delighted; for no sooner had the leopard, or chetah, as he called it, disappeared, than he drew his long knife, and commenced cutting from the head of the slain jackal a small cone-shaped horn about half an inch in length, muttering, as he performed the operation, "Namo Bud-dhaya" (Buddha be praised), which thanksgiving, while I was smarting under my loss, vexed me so much that I exclaimed, "At what are you rejoicing, you idiot?"

"Fos not what you call eediot, *Namo Bud-dhaya.* He has found Narri-combo, and Narri-combo better den one, two, tree buffalo, 'cos it make 'um good luck all time 'um live."

The meaning of which was, that the horn he had taken from the jackal's head, and which he called Narri-combo, is believed by the natives to be a charm which will protect its possessor from the ills of life, but especially against thieves, and, moreover, so adhesive to its discoverer, that even if lost or stolen, it will invariably return of its own accord.

"Well, well, Fos, secure this precious treasure in thy vest, so that we may hasten to the tents, for I am well-nigh wearied out with our day's adventure," said I.

Fos obeyed, saying, "Excellency, 'es. But see, tent not far. See Sar Bosen's fire."

And as he spoke he pointed to a distance of

about a mile, where, beneath the clear, brilliant moonlight, I saw a column of dark smoke wending its way skywards.

"Hurrah ! It *is* the tents. Let's onwards, boy," I exclaimed, joyfully.

And, tired as I was, I put my best foot forwards ; and away we trudged through the jungle, then through the skirt of a forest. Scarcely, however, had we entered, than Fos, falling upon his knees, and placing his ear to the ground, cried—

"Ah ! what dat ?"

But the noise that had arrested his attention was too plain to admit of a doubt.

"For the love of Heaven, quick, Fos ! It is the cry of a woman. It may be that my sister is in some danger," said I, thinking at once of May.

"No ; not missee," said Fos.

And he was right ; for as the screaming grew louder, I could hear the sounds of footsteps. We had passed from the woods, and were entering a wide, open plain. The moon shone upon the grass, which had been trampled down apparently by a herd of elephants or a party of human beings. A woman was before me, screaming and running towards us with the fleetness of a hunted deer. As, indeed, hunted she was ; for, not twenty yards behind, followed, in full pursuit, a scantily-attired individual, whose dark skin, long, black, shaggy hair, and savagely-exulting eyes, gave him more the appearance of a demon than a man. But taken, even as I was, by surprise, my mode of action required no thought. It was clear that a woman was being hunted, perhaps to death, by a man. I ran forward. She advanced; but, mistaking me for a new enemy, she stood aghast for a minute; then, as if resigned to her fate, whatever it might be, fell at my feet, clutched my knees, and looked up into my face most piteously, as if appealing for protection. This appeal I answered by at once holding my rifle club fashion; and the pursuer, perceiving the attitude, came to a dead halt, and for an instant stood as if undecided whether to advance or retreat. A little reflection, however, led him to adopt the latter course. So, turning upon his heels, he fled as if for his life; and the woman, finding I could not understand her language, turned to Fos.

CHAPTER VIII.

WE SAVE THE DAUGHTER OF OUR ENEMY—FOS
SHOWS HIS ANTIPATHIES—AND BOB IS CURED BY
THE SAVAGES.

FLUTTERING with fear, like a fresh-caught bird,
the poor girl—for girl she was—related her story
in a few words; but so agitated was Fos with
indignation, that it was with some difficulty he
performed his office of interpreter.   He stamped
his feet—he spluttered—and shaking his fist at
the retreating man, said—

"Dat 'um dirt.   'Um pig's son.   *Namo Bud-
dhaya!* he not touch Excellency."

"Come, come, Fos," said I, endeavouring to
calm him, "what has the poor girl to say for
herself?"

"'Um dirt; 'um pig's son; 'um Rodiyas," he
repeated, still shaking his fist; then adding, "Lady
am de chile ob great man, friend ob King ob
Kandy, who send farder down to Minery; but
while 'um wid daughter, two bad man, enemy,
tell King big lie about de fader, which make King
send soldier after 'um, wid order to kill fader,
and give daughter to pigs, to dirt, to filth."

" Give her to the pigs !" I repeated.

" Excellency, 'es. Worse den de pigs ; to de Rodiyas," he replied. " But," he continued, " soldier long time before find pigs ; but, when 'um did, and dat pig's son what ran away was going to put de betel in lady's mouth, she went off dead."

" Dead ?" I repeated, interrogatively.

" 'Es, Excellency ; dead till 'um come to life again," he said, endeavouring thereby to explain that the lady had fainted ; then he continued, " When lady dead, pig's son take her to his fader, moder, broder, and sister pigs. But, when 'um lady come out ob dead, she find 'umself in tent wid a white lady."

" A *white* lady, Fos ?"

" Excellency, 'es. Must be good missee. Den good missee help her to run 'way ; but, when run, pig find out, and run too, till Excellency frighten him away."

Here the poor lady caught hold of the boy's knees, and was evidently begging some favour of him.

" What is she saying now, Fos ?" I asked.

" She beg, she pray, Excellency be good man, and kill her, or let her go and jump in water."

" Nay, she is mad. Hold her arm, Fos. Let us take the poor thing to the tents," I said, myself taking hold of her, for fear she should escape.

" Excellency, let poor lady go," said Fos, greatly to my astonishment.

" You rascal! would you let the poor creature destroy herself," I said, indignantly.

" Excellency, 'es. 'Um no good live; for if pig touch 'um, make 'um pig too."

" Silence, idiot! Take hold of her arm. Tell her we will take her to the good white woman, who will treat her as her sister. But, hark ye, Fos," I added, sternly, for I believed he had a strong inclination to let her go, " if you permit her to escape, I will thrash you within an inch of your life."

And thus, with Fos and the poor girl half dead with fright a few paces in my rear, I advanced. In about half an hour we entered the jungle which skirted the open space where our tents were pitched. Speedily I caught sight of them. The fires were burning, and dear little May was standing, rifle in hand, at the door of the one which we made our common day abode, no doubt anxiously expecting my return. But what meant those other tents, or, rather, hurdles, against the trees, some little distance beyond our fire circle? A moment's thought, and it flashed through my mind it was, it must be, the main party from which that cowardly savage had pursued the girl.

" Stay, Fos, yonder coverings may hide the

girl's enemies; guard her for a minute or two; but, as you value a whole skin, do not let her escape."

Having so said, I ran forward.

"Thank Heaven you have returned safe, Tom," said she.

"Stay, dear May; tell me who are the occupants of yonder tents."

"Oh, don't be frightened; they are only a few harmless savages. But, come, come, you are wearied; another time I have a story of adventure to tell you anent them."

"Nay, nay, May; answer me one question more—Are they the savages from whom, not long since, a girl fled for her life?"

"You have heard the sad tale, then. You have met the poor creature; but tell me, Tom, is she safe?"

"Aye, May; for she is at this moment with Fos; but if we would save her from these men, she must be hidden for a time."

"Good, Tom, good; and as the savages are asleep, all save one, who is with Bob, bring her at once to my sleeping tent, for there she will be safe till they have departed."

This satisfying me, I returned, and told Fos to inform the girl we would lead her to the white lady who had befriended her; but the encampment of the Rodiyas frightened her so that she

trembled violently. A few words, however, from
Fos reassuring her, she fell upon her hands and
knees; when, with Fos and I walking between
her and the Rodiyas, she crawled till we reached
May, with whom we left her. Then, going to
our own tent, we saw Bob, stretched at full length
upon the ground between two torches, by the
light of which a swarthy, half-naked being was
binding some herb around the old sailor's leg.

"Hurrah! the young skipper is safe," said
Bob, lifting up his leg so suddenly that it capsized
the native.

Bob, however, could now stand; for he jumped
up, and clutched both my hands more warmly
than agreeably. Fos, however, seemed to have
become suddenly mad; for, taking up May's
rifle, he pointed it at the savage; who, now upon
his hands and knees, was looking pitifully and
imploringly in the boy's face; at the same time
he seemed to be begging his life. The boy kept
pointing with one hand to the door; and as the
abject savage obeyed the hint, Fos keeping at a
respectful distance, but still advancing, with a
countenance upon which was depicted every feeling of loathing, horror, and contempt. The
savage had got half out of the tent, the boy's
passions had reached their culminating point,
and verily I believe he would have sent the
contents of the piece into the poor wretch's body,

had not Bob dashed the rifle from his hand,
and, throwing him upon the ground, said—

"Thou imp of Satan! Art stark, staring mad?"

"Rodiya's pig's son; Sar Bosen mad, not Fos.
Sar Bosen, Excellency, Missee, Fos, all lose caste,
neber lib with moder, broder again."

And although we pacified the boy, no entreaties,
no threats, would prevail upon him to remain
within that tent that night. It had been defiled
by a Rodiya.

"But, these Rodiyas, what, who are they," asks
the reader, " that their touch should be held so foul
that the girl we had rescued should prefer death
to life, after having come in contact with one of
that hated race?" Well, I will tell you the miserable history ; for, not only is every fact relating
to mankind, in its various phases, interesting, but
it is a history that will give you a fair notion of
the terrible power wielded by Asiatic tyrants, and
the real misery of that system of caste which has
prevailed in India from all time.

The ancestors of these Rodiyas (Rodiya means
filth) were a tribe called Daddah Vedahs—*i. e.*,
hunters—whose business it was to furnish the
King's tables with venison; but, instead of venison,
they brought him man's flesh ; which the king
well liking, commanded them to bring him more
of the same sort. But it being discovered by the
king's barber, his Majesty was so enraged, that

he thought death too good for them, and to punish their persons not a sufficient recompence for the injury done him. Whereupon he established a decree that all the tribe should be expelled from dwelling among the inhabitants of the land, and not be permitted to use any means or calling to provide themselves sustenance; but they should beg from door to door, through the kingdom, for ever, and be looked upon as the most base and odious of all people. Hence it is that they are obliged to give such titles to all people as are due to kings and princes only. They are not permitted to fetch water out of the wells, as other people are; but fetch it from holes and rivers. None will touch them, lest they be defiled. They are not permitted to cross a ferry, to enter a village, nor even to build houses with two walls or a double roof; but, instead, houses formed by merely placing a hurdle slantingly against a single wall. Begging is their chief means of living, but they receive gifts for protecting fields from wild beasts or burying dead cattle; yet they are not permitted to come within a fenced field even to beg. Another means of existence is, by converting the hides of animals into ropes, and preparing monkey-skin for tom-toms and drums, which they barter for food. They are prohibited from wearing a cloth on their heads; and neither men nor women are allowed to cover their bodies above the waist or below the knee. If benighted, they dare not lie down in a shed appropriated to other travellers, but hide themselves in caves or deserted watch-huts. They may not enter a court of justice; but, if wronged, have to utter their complaints from a distance; and, although nominally Buddhists, they are not allowed to go into a temple, but are compelled to pray "standing afar off." Indeed, so vile and valueless have they ever been held by the people, that once, when it was represented to the king that the Rodiyas had so multiplied as to be a nuisance to the villagers, an order was given to reduce their numbers, by shooting a certain proportion in each of *their* villages. Thus, it may be easily seen, that the most dreadful of all punishments was to hand over the lady of a high-caste offender to the Rodiyas; and the mode of her adoption was, by the Rodiya taking the betel from his own mouth and placing it in hers; after which ceremony her degradation was complete.

In the order of creation, how great, but how low, is man; for, among what tribe of animals or reptiles, however savage, can be found such fearful, such blasphemous tyranny as this degradation of a vast number of beings created after God's own image, and, singularly to say, these outcasts are remarkable for their beauty? At the time at which I write,

the island was under native rule; but now, even
now, beneath the rule of our gentle Queen, the
status of these poor people is but little improved;
for Sir James Tennent, writing in 1859, says :—
" Under the rule of the British, which recog-
nises no distinction of caste, the status of the
Rodiyas has been nominally, and even materially,
improved.   Their disqualification for labour no
longer exists; but, after centuries of mendicancy
and idleness, they evince no inclination for work.
Their pursuits and habits are still the same, but
their bearing is a shade less servile, and they pay
a profounder homage to a high than a low caste
Kandyan, and manifest some desire to shake off
the opprobrious epithet of Rodiyas.   Their houses
are better built, and contain a few articles of furniture; and in some places they have acquired
patches of land and possess cattle.   Even the
cattle share the odium of their owners; and,
to distinguish them from the herds of the Kandyans, their masters are obliged to suspend a
cocoa-nutshell from their necks by a leathern
cord.

   " Socially their hereditary stigma remains un-
altered; their contact is still shunned by the
Kandyans as pollution, and instinctively the
Rodiyas crouch to their own degradation.   In
carrying a burden they still load the pingo (yoke)
at one end only, instead of both, like other natives.

They fall on their knees, with uplifted hands, to address a man of the lowest recognised caste; and they shout, on the approach of a traveller, to warn him to stop till they can get off the road, and allow him to pass without the risk of too close a proximity to their persons. Their habits are filthy, and their appetites omnivorous. Carrion is as acceptable to them as the flesh of monkeys, squirrels, the civet cat, mangoos, and tortoises; and they hover near ceremonies and feasts, in hope of obtaining the fragments. The men are employed occasionally on the coffee estates and in making roads; but they are generally stigmatized as imbecile, and shunned as reputed thieves. The character of the women is still more disreputable. They wander as jugglers, and at feasts perform dances, during which they keep two polished brass plates rotating, one on the top of each forefinger."

But, degraded as are these miserable creatures, there are others yet more wretched; for, as if to demonstrate that within the lowest depths of degradation there may exist a lower still, there are two races of outcasts in Ceylon who are abhorred and avoided even by the Rodiyas. These are the barbers and the betel-box makers of Oovah, who are looked upon as so vile that no human being would touch rice that had been cooked in their house. And the Rodiyas, on the occasion of festivals, tie up their dogs to prevent their

prowling in search of food to the dwellings of
these wretches.

Now, reader, that thou hast read this most sickening account of the poor degraded Rodiyas, canst
longer wonder at the terror of the lady, or the
apparantly insane loathing of Fos?   However, to
continue the thread of my story, when the boy
had left the tent, Bob, who had been in the Indies
before, and knew much respecting the revolting
system of castes, said—

"Look you, Master Tom, these niggers are
onnat'rals.   Only to think that anything upon
two legs, and with a tongue as can talk Christian-
like, should go and have all this spite agin one
another; 'specially as they are the same colour.
Then, d'ye see, Master Tom, these pigs, as that
young heathen calls 'em—at least, the one as has
been kicked out of here—has been as good as a
mother to me and Miss May in your absence;
for though, when they first hailed us, we took
'em for savages, and they shook like, upon their
legs, as if we had been a-going to eat 'em, when
Miss May, with her bright, pretty face, made a
lot of dumb motions, to show 'em they were welcome, they pitched their tent alongside where you
saw 'em.   And she and the one the boy kicked out,
came to us with some fresh-caught jungle-fowl,
water, and rice, which he gave to us free gratis for
nothing-like.   Moreover, I believe the poor fellow

must have been educated for a doctor; for, clapping his eyes upon my game leg, he made a lot of dumb notions for me to let him examine the wound. At first I refused; but then, thinking better of it, lifted up the limb, when the nigger had the bandage off before I could say Jack Robinson. Then, when he had made faces at it for about a minute, he put it down, gave an onnat'ral scream, left the tent for a few minutes, when he came back again with some leaves. These he clapped athwart the wound, and they have nearly given me the use of my sea-legs agin." Then, stopping for a moment to recover breath, Bob added, "But, Lord love you, Master Tom, I have been talking here as if you didn't look as hungry as a scarecrow, and as worn-out as if the ship had sprung a leak, and you had been at the pumps for a week without rest or rations."

As Bob spoke he limped across the tent, and, lifting a cloth, exhibited a single fowl, a bowl of water, and some rice.

"Bravo! old friend. This is kind to have prepared this meal," said I, falling cross-legged before the viands.

"Me kind! Why, Lord love ye, it's the doings of Miss May, who, it warnt likely, could think of cooking this here fowl without leaving sufficient rations for you. For, somehow, d'ye see, we thought you mightn't have a prosperous cruise."

"Indeed you are right," said I.

And while I was eating the meal, I told him, in the fewest possible words, our day's adventures; concluding with the meeting with the fugitive lady.

"Aye, aye. Miss May told me all about that woman. That is, d'ye see, as much as she could find out, seeing that she couldn't speak heathen, and the woman couldn't speak Christian English. Howsomdever, she will tell you all about their meeting herself," said he; adding, "But now, Master Tom, if wouldst get underweigh in the cool of the morning, thou hadst better betake thee to the land of Morfus [Morpheus], and dream of better luck than thou hast had to-day."

"Aye, aye, Bob, thou art right," said I; and in a few minutes I was cradled in the arms of the gods of sleep and dreams.

When I awoke the next morning I found Bob up, and busily preparing our morning meal.

"Is it possible, my friend, that the savage can have performed so wonderful a cure?" said I, at seeing him, who the day before could with difficulty put his foot to the ground, now running to and fro without even a limp.

"Aye, aye, Master Tom, thanks to that mahogany chap, it's a leg fit for a Christian agin; and

a good job it is, d'ye see; for, though I've been trying ever so much, I can't get that Fos to come in
here, for he says the place has been defiled by the
Rodiyas. Moreover, it's my opinion that just now,
for the twist of a rope yarn, the imp 'd slip his
cable, and leave us to ourselves, for having eaten
food brought to us by the chap, God bless him,
as cured my leg."

"Well, well, Bob, never care. Upon the whole,
he is a good and useful lad, and we must humour
his prejudices," I replied; adding, to turn the
conversation, "But how about those Rodiyas, are
they still where we left them last night?"

"Lord love you, not a bit of it. They have
been scared away; for when I awoke and found
my leg all taut and seaworthy, I went, as in duty
bound, to shake hands with the mahogany chap
as cured it, but found him and all the rest of 'em
clean gone, tents and all."

"Slipped their cable in the night; eh, Bob?"

"Aye, aye, sir. No doubt, as I said afore,
scared nearly out of their lives by the young imp."

At that moment, however, our conversation was
arrested by the entrance of the fugitive lady and
May.

"Oh, Tom," said the latter, with sparkling
eyes, "the Rodiyas have decamped, and the poor
creature is safe."

"Aye, aye, Miss May; so far it's all fair, square,

and shipshape; but what we are to do with her bothers me," said Bob, scratching his head.

"To begin, give her a hearty breakfast; for I do not think the poor girl has tasted food these two days."

"Aye, aye, that's plain sailing, and all right enough; but as that young varmint wont show himself inside this tent, I should like to know how we are to make this young woman understand us."

As, however, Bob at the same time set about the arrangements for our primitive breakfast, the difficulty was soon solved; for as the native did not happen to eat in our language, she managed to make a very good meal without the aid of our tongue.

Before we again set out, May related how she obtained her introduction to the girl.

"You must know, Tom," said she, "that yesterday, when the greatest heat of the sun had subsided, I ventured, rifle in hand, in search of some refreshing fruits; or indeed, had any game crossed my path, I should have bagged it. Scarcely, however, had I left the tent, when, advancing in front of me, I saw a party of savages. Alarmed at the sight, I clutched the rifle, determining to sell my life or protect my liberty to the last; but for such a resolve there was really no necessity, for, observing me, the poor creatures,

to my great surprise, fell upon their hands and
knees. Well knowing by that that their intentions
must be anything but warlike, I made an advance
of some yards towards them ; but, as if horrified
at my approach, they waved their hands and
otherwise gesticulated, as if to warn me off. As,
however, I saw that two of the men were carrying
what appeared to be a lifeless girl in their arms,
I at once went up to them, when, seeing that the
girl was in a fainting fit, I gesticulated till I made
them comprehend it was my wish for them to take
her to my tent. Well, having complied with my
wish, they left her under my care, and at once
set about erecting their little huts. About half
an hour after they had quitted my tent, the girl
recovered her senses, but for some minutes gazed
about her as if in dread of some approaching
calamity. By manner and dumb motions, however, I soon dispelled her terror, and so she remained till the approach of dark, just indeed
before the moon had arisen. Then every now
and then she would go to the opening and peep
forth ; and thinking she was anxious for the company of the people who had been carrying her, I
succeeded in making her understand that I would
go and fetch them ; but at this she gave a sup-
pressed scream, and falling upon her knees, said
something which, by her face and uplifted hands,
I understood as plainly as if she had spoken in

English, to mean, that she implored my protection from the party with whom I had found her.   But what could I do?—Bob was unable to walk."

"But he could handle a rifle," said I.

"True, Tom; so could and so did I, with a firm resolve not to permit one of the savages to again come into my tent.   Then, thinking she must be sadly in want of refreshment, I left her to fetch some rice and water; but scarcely had I entered this tent for the purpose than, hearing a scream and the trampling of feet, I ran out again, when lo! I saw she had taken advantage of my temporary absence to make her escape.   One of the savages, however, seeing her leave the tent, ran in pursuit; and well for him it was that I did not happen to have the rifle in my hand, for such an impression had the girl's terror made upon me when I had offered to fetch to her one of those whom I had believed to be her friends, that I believe I should have shot the pursuer.   Thank Heaven, however, I was saved from that."

"Bravo! little girl May.   You behaved like a heroine," said I.

"Aye, aye; or the skipper of a seventy-four alongside a parley-vous; and she is worth her weight in gold," interposed Bob.

When May had concluded her story, I repeated to her all Fos had told me; whereupon, having pondered for a minute, she said—

" How wonderful, Tom, if this great man, the lady's parent, should be the Dissuava who betrayed your father !"

"Aye, aye; maybe, maybe," said Bob; adding, however, vindictively, " but if it be so, the hussy deserves all she's met with; and no doubt Providence means it as a punishment for that old rascal's treachery to the skipper."

" Fie, Bob ! and you call yourself a Christian, too," said May.

" Shame upon you, Bob ! How can the poor girl help the faults of her father?" said I; adding, " But come, it is time we set out again."

" Yes, we have no time to lose," said May. " But mind, Bob, this poor girl goes with us as my friend and companion—at least, until she thinks fit to leave us; therefore she must be treated in all respects as myself."

" Aye, aye, Miss May, that's like your good heart; but still there's a big sea difference in my mind betwixt your father's daughter and the daughter of that mahogany-coloured old hulk who played foul with the skipper," said Bob, surlily; adding, as he shook his fist, " And may be, old Bob wouldn't like to get the lubber within reach of his grappling-irons."

CHAPTER IX.

BOB HAS A QUEER ADVENTURE WITH A TOUCAN—
WE FALL IN WITH SOME TIMBER CUTTERS, AND
MAKE A BEDCHAMBER OF A TANK.

IT was not until we had left the place of our
last encampment some distance behind, that Fos
recovered from the shock given to his prejudices
by having come in such close contact with the
Rodiyas. Then, however, he entered into conversation with the lady. But observing the
humility of his carriage while addressing her, and
also that, while speaking, she frequently pointed to
me, I asked Fos the subject of their discourse.

"'Um lady daughter of Dissuava who run
away with Captain."

"That is good news. Ask her if she knows
where they have taken my father," said I.

"'Um lady not know. The Dissuava was taking
Excellency Captain to Kandy; but he stop at
'um own village on de way, and den de King's
soldiers met 'um, kill fader, and after take
daughter to give to pigs of Rodiyas; and now
lady pray of Excellency to take her back to village, where she hab plenty friends, who will give

Excellency and Missee plenty ob eat and drink,"
replied he.

Then, finding that the village of which the
Dissuava had been lord and proprietor was some
five days further onwards, and on the way to
Kaudy, I complied, though bitterly disappointed
at hearing no certain news of my parent.

" Keep up thy spirits, dear Tom; remember,
if it be God's will that we meet him again, it
will happen in good time," said May.

" Thou art right, May; thou art right; so no
more desponding, for fear it may retard our
hopes. And so we kept onwards. Onwards, I say,
truly, but at a snail's pace; for the jungle and
underwood were so dense, we were compelled to
hew our path almost step by step; and by the
time the sun had ascended to the meridian, we
had arrived at a large, shady forest, where we
pitched our tents beneath the huge foliage of two
india-rubber or snake-trees.

This tree is remarkable for the pink leathery
covering which envelopes the leaves before expan-
sion, and for the delicate tracing of the nerves,
which run in equidistant rows at right angles
from the midrib. But its most striking feature
is the exposure of its roots, masses of which appear above the ground, extending on all sides
from the base, and writhing over the surface in
undulations. So strong, indeed, is the resem-

blance, that the natives give it the name of the snake-tree.

Having found so favourable a spot for a halt, we—*i. e.*, Fos, Bob, and myself—set to work manfully in the erecting of our tents; beginning, first of all, with that for the ladies. But at the outset an incident happened that made us laugh. Bob had stripped to the waist, and stood with his back against the trunk of the tree, repairing the talipat leaves which had become broken. Upon the other side of the trunk Fos was engaged, knocking some nails into the bark with a stone, which served for a hammer. We were all busy; May, upon the ground, picking up some rice which had fallen; Fos, knocking his nails in; Bob, sewing the broken parts of the talipat leaves; myself, upon the ground, spreading out the remaining leaves; when suddenly Bob dropped the leaf he held in his hand, and quickly running round the tree, caught hold of the boy with one hand, exclaiming, as he cuffed his ears with the other—

"Thou young imp, dost not know a man's shoulder from a tree trunk, that thou shouldst drive nails into him?"

The boy cried out with astonishment, endeavouring to get away from the angry sailor. I went to the rescue; and having seen the real cause of his anger, said—

"For shame, Bob, it is thou that art ignorant of the difference between the beak of a bird and an iron nail."

Bob let the boy go; but, looking at the tree against which he had been standing, stood aghast at seeing peering from a hole the cause of his anger; namely, the bill, and what appeared to him, to be the double head of a bird. Having gazed for a minute, he turned to Fos, saying—

"Ax your pardon, messmate; but, d'ye see, it isn't a joke to have a porthole bored in your shoulder."

"Tut, tut, Bob, you are not hurt," said I; although the bill had certainly left a deep impression in his skin.

"Howsomdever, this double-headed warmint shan't have the laugh of me," he replied, about to strike at the bird.

"Nonsense, Bob; recover your temper; it would be a shame to injure the bird," said I, holding his arm.

And this was sufficient, for he soon became restored to his good humour.

"What a brave seaman, to fight a little bird," said May, laughing.

"Little bird, Miss May! Why, look you, it is a small demon; first, because it has two heads; and, secondly, because it has carved its name so deep into my shoulder as to become a memory for some time to come."

" Ho, ho! hi, hi! Massa Bob Bosen don't know 'um bird from 'um boy, and 'um bird didn't know difference between Sar Bosen and monkey," said Fos.

" Would you laugh at me, you imp?" said Bob, angrily; adding, "It's lucky for ye that I thrashed you by mistake just now; for if I hadn't, I'd just give you a rope's-ending for this here mutiny—don't know a man-of-war's man from a monkey! Pretty state of discipline that is, I take it."

Fos was quite right; it was a toucan, a bird whose habit it is to build its nest in a hole in a tree, where it sits upon its eggs, with its great beak protruding a little distance out, in readiness for its greatest torment, the monkeys, who are for ever seeking to rob the nest of its eggs. So, you see, it is very likely the toucan had really mistaken Bob for a larger kind of monkey.

This toucan, or hornbill, was about the size and shape of a jackdaw, with a great head, and a large excrescence at the top of its great bill which gives it the appearance of having two heads. Indeed, early travellers believed such to be the fact. The toucan preys chiefly upon tiny reptiles and smaller birds; which, when it seizes, it tosses into the air, catching it as it falls. This bird is also what naturalists term frugivorous, *i.e.*, it feeds upon vegetables and fruits; and when endeavouring to detach a fruit, if the stem is too tough to be severed by its mandibles, it flings itself off the branch, so as to add the weight of its body to the pressure of its bill.   With regard to its building in the hollow of trees, I must tell you, that when incubation has fairly commenced, the female takes her seat on the eggs, and the male bird carefully closes up the orifice by which she entered, leaving only a small aperture, through which he feeds his partner; whilst she, generally successfully, guards her treasure from the roving monkeys, who stand in fear of the formidable bill which so raised the anger of Bob.

Our temporary resting-place being erected, we remained till the cool of the day, when we again set out upon the march; pitching the tents at night, but always, when possible, in the neighbourhood of a pool or a small stream; for although we were sometimes a whole day without finding anything better than a thin mud, Fos's process of purifying remedied to a certain extent that evil.   Thus, for five days, marching only in the cool of the morning or evening, we kept on our course, living as best we could upon herbs, fruits, jungle-fowl, or teal; indeed, anything that fortune threw in our way.   Upon the sixth day, however, having a shrewd suspicion that Master

N 2

Fos, who was acting as our guide, knew but little more of the locality than myself, I said—

"Come, Fos; tell the truth. Do you, or do you not, know where we are?"

"'Es, Excellency; by side of great river," he replied, pointing to a stream, upon the banks of which we had encamped.

"That's sart'in fact; at least, if so be our eyes *is* eyes. But if that's *all* you knows, mate, I take it, d'ye see, you've been steering us all this time without ere a compass in your head; and as that's agin all reg'lations, you'll just get flogged if you run us on a reef," said Bob.

"Fos know 'xactly. Dat river near big lake Minnery; and big lake Minnery near village, where Excellency want take lady," replied the boy.

But as this river might in all probability be one or two hundred miles in length, this reply was not altogether satisfactory. Still, it was the only one we could get, and so we rested contented under his guidance; and soon I found my suspicions unfounded; for, about an hour after, we fell in with a party of timber cutters, with their bullock-carts, axes, cooking utensils, and assistants. For a time I was undetermined whether to hail them or not, fearing they might betray us into the hands of the King's people; seeing, however, they were a jolly, reckless-looking

party—laughing, singing, and, I supposed, joking—
I hailed them; and then, through Fos, found that,
after three months of successful timber-felling in
the forests near the river, they were returning to
Minnery, the very village for which we were in
search. And right glad was I that I had hailed
them; for their chief hearing of our many days'
toil, and that we were proceeding to Minnery,
good-naturedly offered to turn his people out of
one of the bullock-carts, and place it at the service of the ladies; an offer, I need not tell you,
I gladly accepted.

To hold this conference, Fos and I had advanced
a considerable distance in front of our party; and
luckily we had done so; for, upon returning, we
found the native lady in great distress of mind,
for fear these timber-cutters should recognise her.
Our difficulty, then, was to smuggle her into the
cart so that her features might not be seen. A
moment's thought, however, and, untwisting a
large scarf, which reached from her shoulders to
her feet, she dexterously readjusted it; so that,
after the fashion of the women of Persia, nought
but her eyes could be seen. We then helped her
and May into the cart; and Fos having represented to the chief of the timber-cutters that she
was a lady who desired not to be gazed upon by
strangers, took his place at the head of the bullock-cart, muttering to me as he did so—

" Namo Bud-dhaya [Budda be praised], Sar Excellency ; but dis be fortunate day, now we find cart."

Then, Bob and I falling into the rear, we continued our journey, now made less toilsome because we were relieved from anxiety for the comfort of the ladies, but more especially May's, who for the last few days had begun to exhibit symptoms of ill health from over-fatigue. But, reader, a few words with you anent our new friends. Well, these timber-cutters are a merry, care-scorning class, whose whole lives are spent in their occupation. The trees chiefly hewn by them are those the woods of which are of great esteem in our own England : ebony, coromandel or calamander, iron and satin woods, all of which are of such density, and, consequently, so heavy, that the labour of cutting and carrying away is very great. Ebony, the most valuable of them all, they are compelled to hew into short logs. That which in England is know as ebony is, in reality, but the centre of the trunk, and is encased, as it were, in a surrounding of much whiter wood, out of which they have to hew it before it is ready for the market. But all of these trees when felled are of such great weight, and the roads in Ceylon are so few and far between, that all, at least of those intended for foreign commerce, are, by dint of vast exertions, first drawn to the nearest river, and being launched, are left to float by themselves down to the sea.

Well, for three days we journeyed with these jolly woodmen across plain, through forest and underwood, most agreeably and with tolerable ease, bivouacking during the heat of the day and by night beneath our tents, with a cordon of fire around to frighten away the animals; but upon the fourth, we entered upon a jungle so dense that it was with the utmost difficulty we could make our way through. Having, however, surmounted this difficulty, we were rewarded for our toil by finding what at first appeared to me to be a vast plain, that, by comparison with the country through which we had passed, was scantily wooded, and, as regards man or his habitations, very lonely, yet beautiful as the heavens at sunset. It proved, however, to be no plain, but the bed of an artificial lake of at least twenty miles in circumference. This lake is formed by the confluence of numerous valleys, separated by low promontories, which, by the way, so obscured my view of the whole, that it was not until we had advanced some considerable distance I saw that the greater part of the bed, which in the wet season would be one vast expanse of water, then consisted but of much dry land and many small valleys, which, although left by the sun only half filled with water, were yet teeming with teal, wild fowl, and other aquatic birds.

It was early evening when we approached this lake; the time when the beasts of the forest hasten to revel in the pools; and then fell upon our ears the trampling and bellowing of herds of buffaloes, the trumpets of elephants, and the horrible screaming of jackals; while, at the same time, we could see herds of deer browsing upon the wooded promontories which divided the valleys. Now, for want of a better choice, we pitched our tents in one of these valleys, of course the driest we could find; and that, too, without a thought of danger; for we knew that while water was to be found in other parts of the lake, neither elephant, buffalo, nor leopard would molest us.

The bed of this valley, and which was to be our couch that night, was so soft that it gave way to our feet, at which we were greatly surprised; for, during the burning heat that for weeks precedes the rainy season, the beds of tanks or rivers, dried up by the sun, are almost invariably as hard as stone, and nearly as hot as furnaces; this, however, Fos explained by pointing to a recent break in the earthy division that separated our compartment— if I may so call it—from another and very deep pool, from which a large body of water had escaped, so moistening the otherwise hardened soil.

"But why has the chief of these timber-cutters chosen such a damp spot?" said I to Fos.

"'Cos long way from buffalo and elephant, 'cos

can't get better if go furder, and 'cos get tent-poles in ground soon."

"Three very good reasons, too," said Bob; " but, d'ye see, Master Tom, I've seen watercress-beds, and I've seen oyster-beds, but this here's the first time I've seen rheumatiz and ague almost sprouting up in my face. It makes one shiver to look at it. Howsomdever, we can't help it; and there's one blessing, if we spread the talipat leaves over the ground, and some pea-jackets over them, we shall have as soft a bed as if it were filled with feathers."

Bob was right. We had no choice; and so, having given to May and her companion much more than a fair share of such bedding material as Bob had named, we prepared our own couch. Before, however, trying its virtues, Fos and I went out, rifles in hand, in search of a deer for the morning meal.

It was a bright moonlit night. So far so good for us; but it was also good for the animals, for if we could see them, they could see us. The chief of the timber-cutters, however, lent us one of his buffaloes, a tame, domesticated creature, that had been trained to appear to be browsing, and with his body in such a position that the hunter might keep hidden till within a fair shot of his game. Now Fos, having, like most natives, practised this ruse, I sent him forth to choose and bring down a good fat buck—a task he speedily performed; for not half an hour after, while I was standing near the timber-cutter's tent, he returned with a fine young buck hanging across his shoulders, when, as a return for the loan of the buffalo, I offered one half the game to the chief. To my surprise, however, he refused it, telling Fos he would shoot one for himself.

"Bravo! Master Tom; this is better sporting than your last," said Bob, as we entered our tent, alluding to the day's trip Fos and I had made by ourselves.

"You may laugh at that trip, Master Bob," said I; "but let me tell you, that if we had our game taken from us, we saved a poor girl from death, or worse—the hands of the Rodiyas; and that would count in any Christian country as a good day's sport."

"Ax your pardon, Master Tom"—but as Bob spoke we heard footsteps, and not knowing whether it might be friend or enemy, I clutched my rifle; but Fos, pulling aside the door of the tent, the chief of the timber-cutters stepped inside, made a polite obeisance to us all, and then began a conversation with Fos.

"Oh, oh," said I, laughing; "so he has thought better of my offer, and come for the half of the deer."

"Aye, aye, all square and shipshape too; he

deserves it for his safe convoy," said Bob; adding, "Ask him what he wants, boy."

Fos put the question.

"Nicamara," replied the chief.

"What's that, boy?" asked Bob.

"Nicamara—what you call noting," replied Fos.

"Noting—you mean nothing," said I.

"'Es, Excellency; nothing."

"Hilloa, mate, what outlandish nonsense is this? d'ye mean to say he's come for nothing?" said Bob.

"'Es, Excellency; he come for nothing."

"Bah! then let him take it and be off," said Bob, who objected to all roundabout questions and answers.

"Tut, tut, Bob; are you mad that you would offend this man?" said I; adding, "What does he want—what does he come for—is it for his promised share of the deer?"

"Excellency, no; he say he come for noting; but 'um want Excellency give him gun for little while, so 'um shoot deer for self."

This request rather raised Bob's suspicions, for he said—

"Now, look ye, Master Tom; when he asked for nothing, he put himself out of the way, for he asked for what he could have taken himself; but this affair of the rifle is another task altogether;

and if I tell you my mind, it is, that we shouldn't
by no manner of means put firearms in the hands
of the niggers; for look you, if they don't play
foul, and use 'em agin us, they'll go and shoot
themselves."

"Nonsense, Bob; the man is a good fellow,
and shall have the loan of my rifle," and so saying, I placed it in his hands, telling Fos to make
him understand it was to be returned in the
morning, the which the chief promised, and left
the tent much pleased.

Then Bob, choosing the first watch, left to post
himself between our two tents, and Fos and I
threw ourselves upon our primitive couches—
rheumatiz and ague beds, as Bob had termed
them. Before, however, I closed my eyes, the
boy explained to me the meaning of the timber-
cutter's roundabout method of borrowing. It
was as follows :—

The Singhalese, whenever they go to beg a
favour of another man, wait until the question,
"What do you want?" is put to them, however
desirous they may be to obtain any given object.
It is considered but politeness for them to answer,
"Nothing," the origin of which item in their code
of civility is the following fable :

A certain god came down upon the earth one
day, and summoned all living creatures to come
before him, promising to give them whatever they

might demand. Some desired strength, or legs, and others wings, &c., all of which were bestowed. Then came the white men, and the god asked them what they came for; and they said, they desired beauty, valour, and riches, which were also granted. At last came the Singhalese, and the god inquired of them what they came for. They answered, Nicamara—*i.e.*, they came for nothing; to which the god replied, "Do you come for nothing? then go away with nothing;" and the Singhalese, for their compliment, fared worse than the others. And to such an extent has this custom grown in the island, that when one Singhalese proffers a gift to another, although it be a thing he greatly desires, he will say, "Eeppa quienda"—"No, I thank you. How can I be so chargeable to you?" Yet while the words are in his mouth, he will reach forth his hand to receive it. This is curious, but only as showing how very much these semi-savages of Ceylon are like their civilized conquerors.

CHAPTER X.

BOB IS ASTONISHED AT THE BEHAVIOUR OF HIS
BEDSTEAD—FOS IS NEARLY KILLED BY BEE
HUNTING—AND I WITNESS A QUEER CEREMONY.

I MUST have slept for about three hours, when,
being suddenly awakened, I heard Bob (who
having been relieved from the watch by Fos,
whose bed he then occupied) grumbling aloud to
himself. Irritated at being disturbed, I called
out—

" Hilloa, friend, can't you sleep ?"

" Sleep ! Why, I have been trying for this
two hours ; but I can't do it, d'ye see."

" It is the mosquitoes, Bob," said I.

" Is it ? Then they must be the biggest and
strongest I ever came alongside of, for it seems
as if a whole army of 'em was under this bed,
trying to run away with me on their shoulders."

" Nonsense ; it is all fancy. · You are over-
fatigued. Go to sleep, Bob, like a good fellow."

" Fancy, do ye call it ? I tell ye, Master
Tom, this bed keeps moving every now and
then, as if something was beneath a-bumping it
upwards."

"Tut, tut; you're dreaming. Go to sleep, man."

"Dreaming, am I? Now, I tell you, Master Tom, it's my opinion that we are just going to sleep atop of an earthquake."

What else Bob said I know not, for I fell asleep, and I suppose he must have done the same, for when I again awoke it was bright morning, and I could hear the bustle of the timber-cutters outside the tent.

"Hilloa, Bob, it's late!" I cried.

Bob, who had been between sleeping and awaking, jumped upright in his bed; then, moving backwards, got upon his feet, crying—

"Good Lord! it's a mercy I've a leg left."

At the same time I jumped up, and shouted to Fos; for there, at the foot of Bob's bed, crawling from out of the soil, were the head, shoulders, and fore-paws of a crocodile, and we had no rifle at hand.

Fos entered. We were standing aghast; but the boy, seeing the cause of our alarm, said—

"'Um crocodile no hurt man; no fear." But, as if to satisfy us, he discharged the contents of the weapon into the reptile's brain; and thus died the object of our present terror, and the cause of Bob's uncomfortable night.

Now, remarkable as this adventure may appear to you, it is one of no uncommon occurrence in

Ceylon; for this reason, that this species of crocodile, during the droughts, when unable to provide their ordinary food from the drying up of the waters, bury themselves in the mud, and there remain in a state of torpor, till the ground becomes again softened by the heavy rains. Bob's crocodile, however, had evidently mistaken the water which had forced its way from the break I have before mentioned for the regular rains; and so, like many another hasty personage, by being too premature, lost not only his opportunity but his life. By way, however, of verifying the statement of the crocodile's habit of burying itself in the ground, I will repeat a story told by a notable governor of Ceylon, who says—

"In 1833, during the progress of the pearl fishery, Sir R. W. Horton employed men to drag for crocodiles in a pond which was *infested* with them, in the immediate vicinity of Aripo. The pool was about fifty yards in length, by ten or twelve wide, shallowing gradually to the edge, and not exceeding four or five feet in the deepest part. As the party approached the brink, from twenty to thirty reptiles, which had been basking in the sun, rose and fled to the water. A net, specially weighted, so as to sink its lower edge to the bottom, was then stretched from bank to bank, and swept to the further end of the pond, followed by a line of men with poles to drive the

crocodiles forward. So complete was the arrangement, that no individual could evade the net ;
yet, to the astonishment of the governor's party,
not one was to be found when it was drawn on
shore, and no means of escape was apparent, or
possible, *except descending into the mud at the
bottom of the pond.*"

To resume my narrative. When Bob had
dressed the deer, and we had made a hasty meal
—the more hastily as we wished to reach the
village before the greatest heat of the day had set
in—we started again ; and although with difficulty making our way through the lofty trees
with which it was overgrown, we continued along
the great embankment of the tank till we reached
a rest house, near a small temple, originally built
to the memory of King Maha-Ten, who, in the
third century before Christ, formed this mighty
and wonderful among mighty and wonderful
works. So vast, indeed, was the work, that the
natives have a tradition that it was made by the
conjoint labour of men and demons ; and of such
immense benefit did the people consider this work
to themselves, that they raised its creator to the
rank of a god ; the temple, indeed, near which
we rested, being dedicated to him as to the god
of the lake, and is said still to contain, as a relic,
the bow with which his antique majesty used to
hunt. But a word or two with you, reader,

about these tanks, which are very numerous, and although for the greater part in ruins, are most noteworthy among the world's antiquities.

Well, once, when the island contained a dense population, all of whom subsisted upon rice, a vegetable that will only grow in marshes or swamps, the greatest merit of a king was to cause a plentiful supply of that grain. Now, as that could only be done by a vast and extensive system of irrigation, these tanks were formed. But what are they? asks the reader. Well, imagine a space of ground as large as an English county, situated say in the midst of a polygon of hills, the interstices being filled up with massive stones, and the whole regularly embanked, and fitted with dams and sluices; imagine the whole reservoir to be some twenty or thirty miles in circumference, and you will have some notion, not only of the tanks of Ceylon, but at the same time what stupendous works they are. But, in addition to these vast reservoirs, there are between five hundred and seven hundred smaller tanks scattered over the country, the majority in ruins, but many still serviceable.

Of one of the largest of these monuments of a race whose remaining works prove how much greater they must have been than the races which now inhabit the island, Sir J. Tennent says :—

" What, too, must have been the advancement

of engineering power at the time when this immense work was undertaken? It is true that it exhibits no traces of science or superior ingenuity; and, in fact, the absence of these is one of the causes to which the destruction of the tanks of Ceylon has been very reasonably ascribed, as there had been no arrangement for regulating their own contents, and no provision for allowing the superfluous water to escape during violent inundations. But, irrespective of this, what must have been the command of labour at the time when such a construction was achieved? The Government engineer calculates that, taking the length of the bank at 6 miles, its height at 60 feet, and its breadth at 200 at the base, tapering to 20 at the top, it would contain 7,744,000 cubic yards, and at 1s. 6d. per yard, with the addition of one half that sum for facing it with stone, and constructing the sluices and other works, it would cost £870,000 sterling to construct the front embankment alone. What must have been the numbers of the population employed upon a work of such surprising magnitude? and what the population to be fed, and for whose use not only this gigantic reservoir was designed, but some thirty others of nearly similar magnitude, which are still in existence, but more or less in ruin, throughout a district 150 miles in length from north to south, and about 90 from sea to sea? Another mysterious

o 2

question is still behind and unanswered. What was the calamity, or series of calamities, which succeeded in exterminating this multitude? which reduced their noble monuments to ruin, which silenced their peaceful industry, and converted their beautiful and fertile region into an unproductive wilderness, tenanted by the buffalo and the elephant, and only now and then visited by the unclad savage, who raises a little rice in its deserted solitudes, or disturbs its silent jungles to chase the deer, or rob the wild bee of its honey?"

These are all unsatisfied speculations, nor do even the few inquiries I have suggested serve to open up the full extent of interest which attaches to this singular district. I have mentioned the existence of numerous other tanks as large as that of Pathavie; some are of even greater dimensions; and one, known as the Giant's Tank, the main embankment of which is fifteen miles in length, was calculated to enclose an expanse of water equal in extent to the Lake of Geneva. It was to have been supplied by directing into it the largest river which now flows into the Gulf of Manaar; and the causeway commenced for this stupendous purpose, composed of blocks of stone of almost Cyclopean measurement, has been completed for a great portion of the way. But, from some unknown cause, the work appears to have been suddenly abandoned, and never resumed. The vast area of the Giant's Tank is now the site of some thirty prosperous villages, each with a smaller tank, sufficient for its own rice-grounds, and all enclosed within the boundary of the original tank.

Having left this artificial lake at least three miles in our rear, we entered upon a chain of paddy-fields, through which ran a small river, which irrigated the surrounding country; and great was our delight; for, by the fields, and a belt of cocoa-trees upon their furthermost side, we knew that some village was at hand. Indeed, Bob, seeing some smoke ascending above the trees of a forest to our left, exclaimed—

" Let's thank our stars that we are once more near two legged creatures like ourselves, for if so be they are only heathen niggers, it's a comfort, after such a cruise among unchristian beasts and reptiles."

" Dat smoke not come from huts ; dat bee-hunters catch honey," observed Fos, authoritatively.

" Catching honey, are they ? Then, maybe, young powder-monkey, you can show us how to catch a little," replied Bob ; adding, to me, " For, d'ye see, Master Tom, it's just the thing Miss May would like ; bless her heart."

At that moment, however, the chief came up to

Fos, and after a few words had passed between them, the boy said—

" If Excellency like get honey, he can go wid head-man of timber-cutters ; for he going catch honey for take home wid 'um."

" Aye, aye, that will I; but you, Bob, remain here with May till I return," I replied.

Fos having then told the chief that I would accompany him on his visit to the bee-hunters, our party was brought to a halt by the side of the river.

The chief and one of his men were soon ready. Indeed, their equipment consisted of nothing more than some torches, similar to those Fos had made at the outset of our journey ; and as the part of the forest from which we could see the smoke arising was but a few hundred yards' distance, we—that is, Fos, the two timber-cutters, and myself—soon reached the bee-hunters, whom we found in the midst of a dense underwood, called the " nillho."

This nillho, by the way, consists of trees of straight stems, each from twelve to twenty feet high, and about an inch and a half in diameter, having no branches, except a few small arms at the top, which are covered with small leaves. This nillho blossoms but once in seven years; the flower is purple and white ; but the perfume is so delicious, that the bees swarm from all parts of the island to the spot where the nillho is in flower. With regard to the honey, as the nests hang in clusters from the lofty boughs of trees, it is taken by a simple process; for, the hunter ascending, torch in hand, drives away the insects by means of the dense smoke, and then takes the comb, which consists of a beautiful circular mass of honey and wax, about eighteen inches in diameter and six inches in thickness. Simple, however, as this process may be to professionals, to amateurs it is sometimes attended with considerable annoyance, if not danger; as I will show you.

When we had beaten our way through the nillho underwood to the presence of one party of bee-hunters, I found that the timber-cutters preferred begging honey of the professionals, to hunting for themselves. As, however, they met with a flat refusal, we proceeded some distance further, till we came in sight of a tree the branches of which were absolutely laden with hanging nests: we might have been twenty yards from the tree, when the two men and Fos lighted their torches; then Fos, placing his finger upon his lips, said—

"Excellency hush, talkee berry little, berry low, else bees hear."

And away they went, I following. As they neared the tree, the three waved their torches

above their heads, causing so great a smoke that
my eyes ached, and my mouth became filled
almost to choking; still we crept forward, the
three muttering some native incantation, I suppose, for they advanced by slow and measured
steps till they reached the foot of the tree. Then
Fos, who had been deputed to ascend the tree,
with the torch between his teeth, clambered up
the trunk, almost with the rapidity of a cat.
Too quickly, however, for he reached a branch
from which hung a cluster of nests before he had
calculated, and clutching hold of it to assist his
ascent, the branch, which was young and slender,
snapped, and down fell the boy, accompanied in
his tumble by no less than three different insect
colonies.

The chief and his men fled with the speed of
deer. I stood bewildered in the midst of count-
less thousands of enraged insects; but, curiously
enough, they seemed so bent upon wreaking vengeance upon the destroyer of their hives, that
they heeded me not.

"Excellency, oh, golly! hundred tousand
debels!" exclaimed the boy, jumping to his feet;
when, seeing he was blinded, I said, as I took
him by the hand—

"The river, the river! run for your life!"

The stream was soon reached, and the boy
plunged in, taking down with him thousands of

the bees. Many, however, becoming detached by
the water, bestowed their favours upon me; when
I believe I should have been punished as much
as the boy, had not the timber-cutters come to my
rescue with lighted torches, by means of the
smoke from which they drove away the bees.

But where was Fos? Yonder, about the middle of the stream, with the insects swarming above
him. To escape them he would bob his head
beneath the water; it was, however, of little use,
for thousands went down with him, regardless of
all but their revenge. And when, to take breath,
he put his head above water again, the rest of the
swarm attacked him. There seemed to be no
tiring them out; and I believe the boy would
have been drowned through sheer exhaustion, had
not the wood-cutters and myself, by plunging into
the river with fresh torches, driven off the insects,
and dragged the boy ashore.

We carried him to one of the bullock-carts,
when, the chief having collected from his men all
they could muster among them of white chuuam
(a substance made from lime obtained from burnt
sea-shells, and which the natives use with the
betel-nut), and with it he sprinkled the boy's face
and body, at least those parts where he had been
most stung.

"Now, look you, Master Tom," said Bob, who
had been impatiently watching this process, "this

here savage doctoring may be all very well for a few flea-bites; but it's my opinion, d'ye see, that if so be we don't get this poor fellow into hospital pretty quickly, he'll lose the number of his mess. So I'll just take him up on my back, if so be you'll make one of these niggers go with me as a guide."

Fos, hearing this suggestion, spoke a few words to the chief; then by a great effort turning upon his side, he said—

" Sar Bosen bery good man if take Fos on his back. Tamil man (one of the wood-cutters, who, by the way, were all of the Tamil race) will go to village, and take Fos to headman."

" Aye, aye, mate," said Bob, taking up the boy in his muscular arms, and adjusting him gently across his shoulders as if he had been a pet lamb, " I'll carry you as carefully as I have afore this many a messmate down to the cockpit to have a leg or a arm off." Then adding to the guide, " Now, mate, shove off, and don't let go your anchor till we get safe ashore in some inhabited port."

But as they started, Fos cried out to me—

" Excellency not let Tamil men see de lady 'long missee. And when get to village, bring bullock-cart up to headman's house. So lady get in no man see 'um."

" All right, Fos," said I.

And signalizing to Bob to hasten onwards, he went at what equestrians would call a gentle canter. And thus my mind was relieved; for so exhausted was the poor boy, that had even a bullock-cart been placed at his service, what with the heavy, lumbering, springless vehicle, and the roughness of the road, he would have stood a fair chance of having had the breath jolted out of his body.

"But," asks the reader, "where was May all this time?" I will tell you: in the covered cart, from which she dared not stir, for fear of any intrusion upon the native lady's privacy. When, however, as we went onwards to the village, and I walked at the back of the cart, I related to her the boy's misadventure, she was much vexed that, at all risks, I had not summoned her to his aid.

"For," said the conceited minx, "a woman can sometimes save a life while men creatures are considering whether there is anything the matter. Since, however," she added, "you have thought fit to send the poor boy on first, let us make as much haste as possible to join him. But, for goodness' sake, dear Tom! keep where you are (she meant close to the cart) the whole way."

And for two reasons I readily obeyed this order; first, for her protection; secondly, because now that Bob and Fos had left, there was no other person with whom I could converse; and I was not sufficiently accomplished in the art of making dumb-motions and telegraphic signals to feel comfortable.

In about an hour's time we came to a large collection of huts—the village, I supposed—and we rejoined.   But, passing a ridge of cocoa-trees, guess our annoyance to find our pathway obstructed by a congregation of something like a hundred semi-nude people witnessing the fantastic tricks of two parties.   At the time I believed it to be some mountebank performance.   It was, however, a religious ceremony, called the "pulling of horns," and was being performed for the purpose of ridding the village of an epidemic disease then prevailing.   I will describe it to the best of my memory.   There was a large hole about three feet deep, from the centre of which, root upwards, arose a cocoa-nut-tree, about ten or twelve feet high.   Upon each side of the tree were some thirty or forty people, each party having a large branch of a tree, with the bark peeled off, notched in the middle; and another piece of wood, very strong, fastened tight across it, so as to resemble a hook.   The two parties having linked together their branches, and fastened them to the cocoa-tree with strong ropes, at a given signal they began to pull with all their strength in opposite directions, shouting, dancing, and bellowing all

the time, in the midst of the beating of tomtoms;
and this pulling, dancing, and bellowing continued
for about half an hour, till, one of the branches
snapping, the other party fell head over heels backwards with the pieces in their hands.

After this, the broken branch was placed in a
small hut at hand, built purposely for its reception, and the other was carried in procession, on
a man's shoulder, wrapped in white cloth, together
with the rope, with which it was fastened round
the cocoa-tree about a dozen times, under a
canopy supported by four men; and thus they
carried the victorious branch, until they came to
a tree, before which stood a cocoa-nut shell lamp;
into this they placed the branch; and then, by
way of invoking one of the goddesses (Pattinis)
to take away the epidemic disease, they repeated
a number of verses; after which they worshipped
the branch, by raising their clasped hands to
their foreheads, and then danced round the cocoa-
tree, singing, blowing a kind of trumpet, and
beating tom-toms. Then the conquered party
(the one who had broken their horn, or branch)
sat upon the ground, and being separated from
the other by a rope, patiently listened to volleys
of abuse which were showered upon them by the
party of the *un*broken branch.

Now, as I have said, at the time of witnessing
the ceremony I knew not its meaning; but ob-

serving the earnestness of the men engaged, and, believing it to be a national amusement, I had approached very nearly to the performers. For a time, so deeply were they engaged, that they did not notice me; when, however, the ceremony was over, and they saw me, they one and all gave a shriek, which did not a little alarm me; for at the time I thought it a kind of overture to a tragedy, in which my massacre was to be the chief incident. Of course this notion alarmed me, and knowing it was of no use to attempt a fight, I retreated to the cart. May, seeing my fright, arose, and was going to alight; but gently pushing her back, I said that which I did not then believe, namely—

" Nay, dear May, keep hidden; these brutes mean no harm, they are only paying me some compliment."

May fell back within the covering; fortunately she did so, for the next minute the whole mob, headed by one who, from the yellow cloth around him, I knew to be the priest, came forward; first, all paying me the native obeisance of lifting their hands up to their foreheads, with the palm outward, and a bending of the body. This was so far so good, for I could see no harm was meant, and I bowed and smiled; indeed, I knew not what else to do. But I believe my bow was very stiff, and my smile about as natural as an attempt to be funny with the toothache, or the smile which I sometimes try between twitches of rheumatism.

This smile, however, seemed to satisfy my tormentors, for they gathered about, hustling me, till they had placed me in such a position that I was compelled to move backwards or forwards at their will; and in this fashion they succeeded with me, as did the Scotchman in the world, by "booing and booing," for, bowing all the time, they propelled me to the very doors of a small temple, just at the entrance to the village.   Then suddenly I remembered to have read of temples and of altars among savages, whereat human sacrifices were offered, and a cold shudder seized upon my frame; but again their gestures and voices reassured me, and the real fact crossed my mind, *viz.*, that they were inviting me to take part in some ceremony; which, indeed, proved to be the case; for when we reached a small temple near the village, I was ushered into the presence of the figure of a god, before whom several of the party played many antics, the chief being those performed by what they call a Devil-charmer, *i. e.*, one who feeling himself possessed, twisted his body into all kinds of unnatural contortions, before and around the image; whilst several others made hideous noises with their voices and tom-toms.

This ceremony may have lasted about an hour, after which they escorted me back to the bullock-cart; where, as the ground was more clear of the branch-pulling gentry, we proceeded on our way, and shortly after entered the village.

CHAPTER XI.

WE ALL FIND A FRIEND—FOS IS UPON AND OFF THE SICK LIST — WE ARE INVITED TO A MARRIAGE.

THE inhabitants of the village were Tamils, one of the many races who people Ceylon, and who are celebrated for their industry and cleanliness, and, by consequence, handsome appearance. The village itself was placed in a high and airy situation, being bounded upon the side by which we entered by extensive paddy fields, and, upon the opposite side, by large pasture grounds for sheep and tame buffaloes, while upon the left was a small tank, a miniature imitation of those I have hitherto described. As for the houses, each was well built, and stood alone in a well-fenced enclosure, without grass or weeds, but the ground covered with sand so white, so well and regularly raked, that it looked as if paved. Moreover, these dwellings, which were but one story in height, were raised upon platforms, and roofed with palm leaves; but each had its luxuriant garden of cocoa and teak-trees, mangoes, orange, lime, and other tropical fruits.

As we entered this village, being stared at by numbers of swarthy, naked little children, with glossy black hair and graceful limbs, decorated more or less with armlets, anklets, and rings, and barked and yelped at by dozens of pariah or out-cast dogs, May popped her head from the cart, saying—

"Thank heaven, we have reached this village! But, oh! Tom, how are we to find the house of the headman?" And the difficulty startled me; for, as you know, I could not speak one word of the native tongue.

"Oh! Tom, what is to be done? How foolish were we not to tell Fos to make it known to the timber-cutters where we wished to go," said May.

"It is of little use repining, May;" but while speaking, I heard the voice of Bob hailing the chief, and telling him to bring his carts to an anchor. Yes, there, at the opening of the en-closure which surrounded the largest house in the village, stood the old sailor, who, seeing me, said—

"Why, Master Tom, you have been so long running this little distance, that I thought you had been wrecked upon the coast, as it might be, d'ye see; and I was just making up my mind to set out on a cruise after ye;" adding, "Did you fall in with a pirate?"

Not, however, waiting for a reply, Bob ran

into the house; but by the time the bullock cart
which held May and her companion had drawn
up in front of the fence, he returned, attended by
an elderly native of rank, and some ten or a dozen
slaves. The latter drew up on either side, so as
to form a lane. Then, coming to the cart, and
handing May down, Bob said—

" All right, Miss May ; this respectable-looking
old skipper is to be trusted ; for though I don't
understand one word of his unchristian lingo, the
boy Fos has jist opened my eyes ; for, d'ye see,
he says this here skipper is the young woman's
uncle, and jist because we've behaved like Christians to her, he's going to give us good berths as
long as we like ; but on no account must those
outside niggers clap their eyes upon the young
woman, seeing she's under a bit of a cloud. And
that's why all these black lubbers are drawn
up."

This caution was very necessary, for my white
skin had drawn around us a host of naked, curious-
minded little urchins. However, they were foiled;
for the headman (*i. e.*, the lady's uncle), bringing
with him two long shawls, precisely alike, and
throwing one over each lady's head, they passed
through to the house in such guise that even I
could scarcely distinguish one from the other.

The lady safely housed, Bob and I expressed,
as best we could, by dumb motions, our thanks

to the chief timber-cutter for his safe convoy, and
followed the headman—for such the slavish bearing of all around proclaimed him—to the house,
at the doorstep of which he turned, and with his
body bent nearly double, and walking backwards,
conducted us into his state-room, a large square,
but low apartment, hung with cloths of snowy
whiteness, a circumstance that occurred to both
Bob and me as remarkable, for our interview with
the Dissuava had taught us that these cloths were
placed there to do honour to some expected guest.
Surely, it could not be for us; that it was, however, we could no longer doubt, when the little
great man led us to two stools, signalling to us
to be seated, while he himself squatted down upon
the carpet; for to offer a stool to a visitor in
Ceylon, is to do him the utmost honour. Bob,
however, thinking but little of the honour, and,
moreover, forgetting that the great man understood not one word of English, said—

"Look you, mate, can't you get the young
skipper here a chair with a back to it?"

But the old man stared in vacant ignorance.
Indeed, had he comprehended Bob, he would
have been horrified at such a request; for in
Ceylon, in those days none but the king himself
dared to sit upon a chair with a back.

"Nonsense, Bob; the old gentleman is evidently making much of us, so let us be contented;

though what the meaning of all this is, I can't make out."

" I tell 'ee, Master Tom, perhaps he takes you to be Prince of Wales, and me to be your—what d'ye call 'em who convoys him?"

" Equerry, Bob ; well, maybe he does, but how are we to make him understand that I don't mean to be parted from May ?"

" I'll try," said Bob ; who at once arose, and began to gesticulate very comically, but finding his gesticulations not comprehended, he raised the pitch of his voice, as if it had been from deafness instead of ignorance of English that the old gentleman was suffering, and pointing to the door, ejaculated slowly, but sonorously—

"Miss May— white lady — Miss May— not black lady."

To do the old gentleman justice, he paid every attention ; and, I believe, must have much strained his understanding powers by endeavouring to comprehend him. Then suddenly, as lively as a kitten, he jumped upon his legs, and left the room, crab-like, inclining, bowing, and laughing as he went.

" I've done it. The foolish old lump of mahogany, not to understand Christian English. Howsomdever, I thought old Bob hadn't travelled all round the world without knowing how to make himself understood."

" Stuff—nonsense—Bob; he did not understand you."

" We'll see, Master Tom."

And we did see; for just then the old gentleman returned, accompanied by two black slaves carrying brass basins, china bowls, and a water-jar, and placing them upon stools before us, he sat down again upon the carpet, looking up to us with a smile upon his face, expressive of the satisfaction he felt in having so well understood our wishes, which he very reasonably translated to be a desire for refreshments.

But Bob, angry with chagrin, after the bold assertion he had hazarded, said to our host,

" Now, look you, Cap'n; I aint no objection to these here rations, but d'ye see, it's the young lady—*white* lady, not black lady, that I want," and the old gentleman now looked the very picture of distress.

" Stuff, Bob; you may call out *white* and black till you deafen him, and then he wont understand you," said I.

" I tell'ee, Master Tom, I'd rather have a hundred deaf and dumb Englishmen to deal with than one of these heathen niggers as can't understand a decent white man when he speaks," said Bob, quite at random ; " but," he added, " I tell'ee what, if so be Miss May don't come alongside soon, I'll just overhaul the whole ship till I find her."

"Nonsense, Bob; no violence. But where is Fos? We can't get along without him."

"Aye, aye; the poor lad's in dry dock, laid by the heels. But, d'ye see, I've a notion," he replied, and greatly to my surprise he quitted the room, leaving our host and me grimacing at each other like a couple of tongueless monkeys. We had been alone half an hour, when I heard the rolling of some heavy object along the ground, and a moment after in came Bob with a large barrow, in which lay poor Fos, who was wrapped closely round in a white cloth.

"Fetched him from the hospital; for though, d'ye see, we've all got tongues in our heads, the boy's is the only one of any use."

"Well, Fos, my poor fellow, how are you now?" said I, taking his hand.

"Excellency berry good. Fos all over bite; little holes, big holes, berry sore; but 'um tongue berry good now, if Excellency want talkee to headman."

"My sister, Fos, where is she?"

"Missee long ob lady; she berry well. But 'spose Excellency wantee Missee, can hab Missee."

"Then tell his Excellency the headman that I want her here now."

And Fos having interpreted my request, the headman left the room, and in a few minutes returned with May, who told us that, although pleased with the manner and bearing of her companion, and delighted that she had been of service to the poor girl, she rejoiced to escape from one with whom she could hold no converse.

"But, dear Tom," she added, "I am burning with curiosity to know her relationship to this benevolent gentleman. Surely, he can't be the Dissuava, her father."

"Now, look you, Miss May; I bears no enmity agin women; but if so be this old skipper had been that old shark that run foul of the Cap'n (God bless him), he wouldn't a been all taut long after my eyes had rested upon him," said Bob.

"Well, well, we shall hear all about it in good time; but now, May, restrain your curiosity while we partake of this good man's hospitality," said I, as another slave made his appearance, bringing an addition to the repast, of which, from the countenance and movements of our host, I could see he was anxious that we should partake.

The meal, however, being finished, Fos told us that our host was the only brother of the Dissuava, at whose death he had been sadly grieved, though less so than at the disgrace of his niece, who having, as he believed, been given into the hands of the Rodiyas, he had never expected to see again; moreover, that when he (Fos) had informed him that his niece had escaped, the old gentleman, instead of rejoicing, had fallen into a terrible rage, threatening to kill the boy for having brought back to his family one who had suffered that which, in the eyes of the natives, is the last disgrace; but when told that the poor girl had been rescued from the Rodiyas *before* the ceremony of the betel-nut being placed in her mouth, the old man's joy became as great and unreasonable as had hitherto been his rage. Further, hearing that none save Fos and his three white companions knew of her existence, and that she was now on her way to his house under the charge of a white lady, he capered about with delight, till remembering that if by his joy he made it known that his niece had escaped, some one of his slaves might again betray her into the hands of the soldiers of the king, he became thoughtful; and after promising the boy all care, and the attendance of astrologers and devil-dancers, during his illness, with large rewards upon his recovery, he at once set about making great preparations for our reception, giving out among his servants that we were a party of distinguished white Christians about to pay him a visit, and that it behoved him to do us all honour. At the same time, he did not fail to prepare his only daughter to receive her cousin into the bosom of his family, where she might remain hidden till the tyrant king's wrath had passed away.

"But my father, the captain; know ye aught of him?" I asked, anxiously.

And Fos, having first held converse with our host, replied—

"Excellency, headman say captain taken to Kandy; but tink no harm happen to 'um, except keep in city 'long wid Hollander people; all prisoners, but not tied up."

"Now, Fos, ask his Excellency if he really considers we deserve well of him for having rescued his niece from the Rodiyas."

And the boy must have interpreted the question literally; for, rising from the carpet, the old gentleman came towards May and me, and throwing himself upon his knees, caught hold of our feet, and in plaintive but lively tones murmured forth his gratitude; concluding by a declaration that his life was at our service.

"Which, seeing that we aint onchristian cannibals, would be no manner of sarvice, dy'e see, boy; and so tell the old skipper," said Bob.

"Then tell him, Fos, that the love he has for his niece is but a tithe of that which I have for my father; consequently, that his gratitude to her preservers is but small to what mine will be to him who helps to rescue my parent from the hands of this King of Kandy."

Fos having repeated these words, the old gentle-

man pondered for some minutes, then replied to
the following effect :—

That if he were discovered interfering with a
king's prisoner, he should be rewarded by being
crushed to death beneath the feet of the royal
elephant retained at Court as the executioner of
State criminals; yet *that*, and even more, would
be done for those who had saved his family from
so great a disgrace. " Fortunately," he added, "the
next day his only daughter was to be married to
one of the King's officers, who immediately after
the ceremony would, with his new wife, set out for
Kandy; where, upon his arrival, he would leave
no stone unturned to find out the captain, and
give him an opportunity of escaping. And that his
son-in-law would do all this, he could not doubt ;
for it was but natural that he should feel great
gratitude towards those who had saved from disgrace the family with which he had been allied.
The old gentleman concluded by begging we
would take up our residence in the village as his
guests until we heard from the capital.

At this proposition we all looked blank, neither
liking to give an opinion. Bob was the first to
break silence ; for having scratched his head by
way of enlivening his ideas, he said—

" Now, d'ye see, the old skipper here may mean
fair, but he may mean foul; 'cos, d'ye see, I haven't
nohow any good notions of these here niggers;

for I b'lieve, for the most part, they look upon white Christians as cats do upon mice!"

" Nonsense, Bob; this is uncharitable. But what think you, Tom ?" said May.

" That we must either remain here, and await the result of the endeavours of our host's son-in-law; or do as we first determined—go seek my father at the capital," said I.

"That's it, d'ye see. We must decide one way or t'other. And for my part, I don't think it's all fair and above board to leave the cap'en to the mercy of a set of niggers, while his own bosen and his flesh and blood like, squat down awaiting for what turns up. Look you, Master Tom," he added, " if I had my choice, it would be to take a couple of boats' crews right up to this here Kandy, and just haul down their flag and get the cap'en at the same time."

" Sar Bosen talkee 'bout what *like* to do, not what *can* do : dat just like little chile, not big man," said Fos.

"Mutiny agin, you imp," exclaimed Bob, fiercely ; but instantly recovering his temper, he replied, " The boy is right, Master Tom. It is no good shillyshallying. So, d'ye see, it's my opinion we had better accept the old skipper's offer, and wait here till his son-in-law, on his return to Kandy, may find an opportunity of helping the cap'en to slip his cable, and come here to us."

And as Bob's opinion coincided with mine, the matter was thus settled, to the infinite satisfaction of the headman, who for that night resigned to us the largest apartment in his house. As for May, she took up her quarters with the old gentleman's niece and daughter. The next day we were provided with a house to ourselves; and a very neat little residence it was, situated in the midst of a large garden plentifully supplied with cocoa and tamarind-trees.

This marriage, however, upon which, as regarded ourselves, so much depended, was postponed for three days, during which interim vast preparations were made. The headman's house was decorated with the leaves of the young cocoa-tree, and temporary houses were erected for the accommodation of the friends and relations of the young people.

Upon the arrival of the bridegroom, guess our surprise to find that he brought with him a Christian (native) priest, and that our host was also of our own faith.

" Gadzooks, Master Tom, isn't it out of your reckoning to find Christians among these niggers ?" said Bob.

" What is there surprising, Bob? Do you not know that throughout Asia there are many thousands of Christians, the descendants of converts made by the Portuguese and Dutch ?"

Of the Christianity of the natives, May might

have added, that it was then (whatever change may have since been wrought in the hearts of the Singhalese by our most indefatigable missionaries) but a wretched mockery of the true faith, both painful to the mind and heart—a hybrid between the *forms* of Buddhism and Christianity. Let us, however, hope that the time is not far distant when the good seed so long scattered among these people shall yield in their hearts a bountiful harvest.

To return to the marriage ceremony. First let me tell you the gentleman had as yet never seen the lady. On the wedding-day, the bridegroom, the priest, and the friends arrived in fourteen palankeens, accompanied by a retinue of nearly two hundred horses. This party were preceded by dancers in comic masks, with small bells tied around their ankles and wrists, a man upon lofty stilts stalking along at a good pace, but as awkwardly as might an ostrich with rickety legs, followed by tom-tom beaters, and performers upon other and even more discordant instruments. The path from the main road to the house was ornamented upon each side with leaves. A little further on, and near the house, the village washermen (of whom more anon) had spread white cloths upon the ground, upon which the bridegroom, with his friends, alighted, and together walked to the house.

The first sight the young couple had of each

other, was in the room wherein the ceremony was to be performed. After the marriage, the bride's father, and some near relations, sprinkled her head with rose-water, and the bridesmaids and others took handfuls of silver paper, cut into very small pieces of the shape of diamonds, and threw over her in showers. After this, the bride sat down, and they put upon her head a garland of pearls, and in that seat she remained till the time arrived for the bridal repast.

The company sat down upon stools covered with white cloth, when two native musicians began—one, to beat a tom-tom, and the other to blow a wind instrument, the sounds from which made one's blood curdle in the veins; but now, instead of dancing, as might have been the case in this country, the company one and all commenced a furious onslaught upon a preparation of betel, which was handed round. The bride—and you must not feel angry with her, for it is the custom of her people—had a silver vessel placed by her side to spit in. Indeed, similar vessels, but of polished brass, were placed round the apartment, one to every other person.

The mastication of betel occupied the assemblage until tea was announced; then the young couple, taking hold of each other's hands, led the way to another apartment, plentifully supplied with cakes, plantains, oranges, pine-apples, and other fruits. After this meal, the company returned to the first room ; when, as soon as all were seated as before, the tom-tom beaters and other musicians began to play, and the men in masks to dance. This being concluded, the man on stilts went through a series of very dexterous performances, upon one and upon two legs ; the latter was really very surprising, for the stilts were six feet high. After this, came a man made up like a large crane, who danced about with his mouth wide open, in which temporary beak the company, as he passed, placed pieces of money. Lastly, the entertainment concluded with a great display of fire-works. After which, the bride and bridegroom entered their palankeens, and preceded by tom-tom beaters, set out upon their journey to Kandy.

CHAPTER XII.

WE ASK A CHIEF TO DINE WITH US, AND HE IS
HORRIFIED AT THE BEHAVIOR OF A COUPLE OF
CROWS, WHO HAVING ROBBED BOB, ASTONISH
ALL.

"HABIT is second nature," says the proverb,
but I do not believe it ; for so flexible is the mind
of man—of youth especially—that he can with
little difficulty adapt himself to circumstances as
they arise.   No, I do not believe in this proverb ;
but rather, that nature is ever prompting us
"when at Rome, to do as Rome does ;" for
at school the much-stared-at, much-bewildered
"new" boy gets the rough edge of his awk-
wardness smoothed down, and becomes as much
at home as the oldest, in a very few days.

Thus, in less than a week, May, Bob, and I
felt ourselves almost as comfortable in that village in the wilderness, as if it had been our native
home.   The truth was, that, in the first place,
we were happy within ourselves ; and, secondly,
having accepted our position, we determined to
make the best of it.

In a week, the health of Fos had become so

L.I.C.   Q

much improved, that he was enabled to accompany us upon our visits to the headman, and
these visits were made daily, sometimes of a
morning, when, in his magisterial capacity, he was
engaged in settling disputes among his people; at
others, in the evening, to partake of his hospitality.

Now, as a magistrate I believe the old gentleman was just, *i. e.*, just for a Singhalese; but of
his wisdom I will not say much; for to make a
silk purse out of a sow's ear, is not a harder feat
than to make just and wise judges under bad
laws, and cruel, despotic sovereigns. Of the wisdom
of these laws we had a specimen upon our first
visit to the judgment hall.

Scarcely had the headman taken his seat, when
who should we see enter but our old friend,
the chief of the timber-cutters, and not alone,
for he dragged with him a slave, whom he charged
with having entered his house in the night, and
robbing him of a portion of the money he had
received for his recent labours.

" What witnesses hast thou of these things ?"
asked the judge.

" None, oh Excellency, limb of a dog that
I am, none but my base self, whose eyes saw
this son of a pig taking the money."

" Then get thee to the temple and swear this
charge," replied the judge.

And an officer took both men to the temple; but when he brought them back, we found that both had sworn hard and fast, one against the other. This was a dilemma for the judge; but his Excellency got over it by saying—

"Since each slave swears against the other, who shall decide but heaven? Therefore let both depart hence, and await patiently the judgment of the gods, who doubtlessly, by exhibiting their wrath upon the real criminal, will point out to us he whom we are to punish." And both obeyed; the slave with delighted alacrity, but the poor timber-cutter with sullen slowness, and much chapfallen. Oh! Solomon, what wouldst thou have thought of such a decision?

"Now, look you, Master Tom," said Bob, as the men left, " if old Bob were yonder timber-cutter, he'd just ropes-end that rogue till he disgorged the plunder; for that he *is* the thief, there can't be no doubt, because, d'ye see, ' hang-dog' is written on his face, all up one side and down t'other."

The Singhalese, however, have another method of ending more important disputes when there are no witnesses upon either side, which, by the way, will remind you of the custom in European countries during the middle ages. It is by swearing in hot oil. First, each party must procure a license from the government, then they wash their hands and bodies, which is a religious ceremony, and the same night they are confined in a house over which a guard is set, and a cloth tied over each of their right hands, and sealed, lest they should make use of any charm to harden the skin.　The following morning, both litigants are brought out, washed, and put on clean clothes.　They are brought into the presence of the image of Buddha.　Then to their wrists are tied the pieces of talipat leaf, upon which the governor's license is written, and they are taken before a bo, or god tree.　Great numbers of people are present.　Cocoa-nuts are brought forward, and the oil extracted before all present, that no deceit may be practised.　A pan of cow-dung and boiling-water is at hand, and when they have made the oil boil, one, either the accuser or accused, says—"The God of heaven and earth is witness that I did not do this that I am accused of;" or, "The four sorts of gods be witness that this land in controversy is mine;" the other, of course, making oath directly the reverse.　This being done, the trial begins.　The cloths are unsealed and removed from their right hands; each slips two fingers first into the hot oil, and then as often into the cow-dung.　After this, their hands are again tied up, and they are kept prisoners till the following day, when their hands are examined, and their fingers are rubbed with a cloth, to see if the skin will come off; and he from whom it does, is judged forsworn, and is severely punished. Of this ceremony, the quaint old writer, Robert Knox, who lived in the island twenty years, and who had witnessed the trial by hot oil, says—"It is certain that the fingers of some that have been thus sworn have remained whole from any scald after the use of hot oil; *but* whether it be by their innocence, or art, that this comes to pass, is ·hard to judge, though they judge 'tis always the first, because so much care is taken to prevent the last."

I have told you how soon we felt quite at home in our new residence. At that, however, you would not have wondered, had you seen our neatly arranged apartments, and known how capital a housewife May was. Now, she was just the kind of girl who would have made an admirable wife for a man who was not over abundantly rich, for not only was she an economist of domestic *materiel*, but also in taste; in fact, a person who adapted everything to advantage, and could make you feel as happy in a scantily furnished apartment as in an elaborately fitted drawing-room; but mind, I will not say that her sweet temper, laughing eyes, and pretty face had not a great deal to do with it. May was also proud—proud of her arrangements and her abilities as a cook, and therefore ambitious to have our friend, the headman, to dine

with us, if only to show him the difference
between a semi-savage repast and an English meal.
Accordingly we sent his Excellency an invitation.

Well, to do honour to our guest, Bob and I
shot a hare, a buck, and a jungle fowl, which,
with the addition of the rice, fish, and fruits of
the country, would not only afford a handsome
dinner, but leave us with dressed provisions for a
week to come.   But unfortunately his Excellency
arrived a couple of hours before we expected him ;
indeed, while we were all engaged in the business
of preparation in a small building at the back of
the house, which we had turned into a kitchen, so
that May, Fos, and myself were obliged to stay
with him in our state apartment, leaving Bob to
superintend the cooking.

This state apartment had but two sides, for the
places where the other two should have been were
left open for the sake of coolness.   Well, there
we sat, patiently awaiting for the dinner, and, by
means of Fos, conversing with our guest, when, as
ill luck would have it, an incident happened which,
although very comical to us, not only deprived the
headman of his appetite, but left his nerves un-
strung for a considerable time afterwards.

Our guest was seated upon the stool of honour,
May and I by his side, while Fos stood sufficiently
near to all to interpret easily, when, lo ! there fell
upon our ears the sounds of flapping wings and a

loud caw, cawing. The old gentleman arose, and (albeit a Christian) exclaimed simultaneously with Fos — "Namo Bud-dhaya!"—magic words to frighten away bad spirits and impending mis- fortune. I laughed outright; for two great crows, flying one after the other, darted through the room, in at one window and out at the other, cawing as they went.

"Namo Bud-dhaya!" again muttered the head- man.

"Golly! golly! Excellency, Massa Tom!" cried Fos, with trembling limbs.

"Why, what is the matter, you stupid fellow?" said I.

"O golly, golly! dreffil trouble cum soon when crows come and *caw, caw* so," the boy replied, imi- tating the unusually *hoarse* croaking of the birds.

At that moment their fright became still greater, for the two birds flew back into the room as before, one being chased by the other; the reason of which being, that the chased bird held in its beak a something that the pursuer was en- deavouring to seize. But, oh! the horror upon the countenances of the old man and boy when, as passing over our heads, a small black-handled, long-bladed knife, reeking with blood, fell upon the floor between the headman and myself.

"Namo Bud-dhaya."

"Golly, golly! Massa Tom!" were the cries of

the two; but the countenances, the aspenlike movement of their limbs, are indescribable. But to add to the comicality of the scene, Bob, in cooking uniform, a small apron before him, and with tucked-up shirtsleeves, just at the moment ran into the room, crying aloud that some rascally thief had stolen his knife.

The secret was out. I could not speak for laughing, but pointed to the knife upon the floor.

"Mother of Neptune! how on airth did it get there? Sure*ly*, you young imp, you can't have been playing any tricks while I left the kitchen for a minute," said Bob; but turning to the boy, and perceiving his scared looks, the old sailor scratched the back of his head, and with a look of astonishment exclaimed, "art crazed, boy; art crazed? and this old skipper here, too!"

By this time Fos had divined that, following up their thievish propensities, the birds, taking advantage of Bob's temporary absence, had entered the kitchen, and, mistaking the knife for a titbit, had flown away with it; so, endeavouring to hide his real feeling that the incident was intended as an omen of impending evil, he laughed—

"Hi, hi! ho, ho! Massa Bob Bosen. Fos not frightened! it am Excellency headman."

"If ye aint, mate, your looks aint a behaving honestly towards you, that's all!" said Bob. "But look you; just explain all this to the old gentleman, so that he may get his head-tackle in shape agin."

So saying, Bob, bethinking himself of his cooking, returned to the kitchen. As for our guest, although after the boy's explanation he became somewhat appeased, and even affected a laugh at the notion of the crow running away with a knife, he continued very uneasy during the remainder of the time he was with us, every now and then maintaining it as his belief that it was an omen, and that something terrible must happen shortly. While, however, Bob is preparing the dinner, I will repeat to you an incident or two told by a recent Governor of Ceylon, which will prove that crows are at the present day neither less numerous nor less mischievously intelligent than they were in the days of which I am writing. Moreover, it will perhaps make you think better of the "lone" couples which you may see of an evening in country-places, returning to their nests after their day's foraging. So accustomed are the natives to its presence and exploits, that, like the Greeks and Romans, they have made the movements of the crow the basis of their auguries; and there is no end to the vicissitudes of good and evil fortune which may not be predicted from the direction of their flight, the hoarse or mellow notes of their croaking, the variety of trees on which they rest, and the numbers in which they are seen to assemble. All day long they are engaged in watching either the offal of the offices or the preparation for meals in the dining-room; and as door and windows are necessarily opened to relieve the heat, nothing is more common than the passage of crows across the room, lifting on the wing some ill-guarded morsel from the dinner-table.

No article, however unpromising its quality, provided only it be portable, can with safety be left unguarded in any apartment accessible to them. The contents of ladies' workboxes, kid gloves, and pocket-handkerchiefs, vanish instantly if exposed near a window or open door. They open paper parcels to ascertain the contents; they will undo the knot on a napkin if it encloses anything eatable; and I have known a crow to extract the peg which fastened the lid of a basket, in order to plunder the provender within.

One of these ingenious marauders, after vainly attitudinizing in front of a chained watchdog which was lazily gnawing a bone, and after fruitlessly endeavouring to divert his attention by dancing before him, with head awry and eye askance, at length flew away for a moment, and returned bringing with it a companion, who perched itself on a branch a few yards in the rear.

The crow's grimaces were now actively renewed, but with no better result, till its confederate, poising himself on his wings, descended with the utmost velocity, striking the dog upon the spine with all the force of his beak. The *ruse* was successful. The dog started with surprise and pain, but not quickly enough to seize his assailant, whilst the bone he had been gnawing disappeared the instant his head was turned. Two well-authenticated instances of the recurrence of this device came within my knowledge at Colombo, and attest the sagacious powers of communication and combination possessed by these astute and courageous birds.

But to return to our guest. So deeply was it impressed upon his mind that the incident of the crows was an omen of evil fortune, that he sat silent with his chin resting upon his breast, and it was some time before we could raise his spirits. At length, however—perhaps in consequence of copious draughts of the native spirit which he took—his tongue became loosened, and he explained to Fos the form in which he expected the threatened evil would come.

Now, you probably know that Ceylon abounds with elephants, and must also have heard and read much of the intelligence and kindliness of those animals. You may not, however, be aware that there are among them a few so savage, fierce, and destructive, that they are more dreaded by the natives than any other beast or reptile of the forests. These animals are termed hora, or rogues, but so remarkable are they that I will give Sir J. Tennent's admirable description :—

"An elephant if by any accident he becomes hopelessly separated from his own herd, is not permitted to attach himself to any other. He may browse in the vicinity, or frequent the same place to drink and to bathe ; but the intercourse is only on a distant and conventional footing, and no familiarity or intimate association is under any circumstances permitted. To such a height is this exclusiveness carried, that, even amidst the terror and stupefaction of an elephant corral, when an individual detached from his own party in the *mêlée* and confusion has been driven into the enclosure with an unbroken herd, I have seen him repulsed in every attempt to take refuge among them, and driven off by heavy blows with their trunks as often as he attempted to insinuate himself within the circle which they had formed for common security. There can be no reasonable doubt that this jealous and exclusive policy not only contributes to produce, but mainly serves to perpetuate, the class of solitary elephants which are known by the terms *goondahs* in India, and from their vicious propensities and predatory habits are called *hora*, or *rogues*, in Ceylon.

"These are believed by the Singhalese to be either individuals who by accident have lost their former associates, and become morose and savage from rage and solitude, or else that, being naturally vicious, they have become daring from the yielding habits of their milder companions, and eventually separated themselves from the rest of the herd which had refused to associate with them. Another conjecture is, that being almost universally males, the death or capture of particular females may have detached them from their former companions in search of fresh alliances. It is also believed that a tame elephant escaping from captivity, unable to rejoin its former herd, and excluded from any other, becomes a " rogue" from necessity. In Ceylon it is generally believed that the *rogues* are all males (but of this I am not certain), and so sullen in their disposition that, although two may be in the same vicinity, there is no known instance of their associating, or of a *rogue* being seen in company with another elephant.

" They spend their nights in marauding, chiefly about the dwellings of men, destroying their plantations, trampling down their gardens, and committing serious ravages in rice grounds and young cocoa-nut plantations. Hence, from their closer contact with man and his dwellings, these outcasts become disabused of many of the terrors which render the ordinary elephant timid and needlessly cautious : they break through fences

without fear; and even in the daylight a *rogue*
has been known, near Ambo-gammoa, to watch a
field of labourers at work in reaping rice, and
boldly to walk in amongst them, seize a sheaf
from the heap, and retire leisurely to the jungle.
By day they seek concealment, but are to be
met with prowling about the by-roads and jungle-
paths, where travellers are exposed to the utmost
risk from their savage assaults.   It is probable
that this hostility to man is the result of the
enmity engendered by those measures which the
natives, who have a constant dread of their visits,
adopt for the protection of their growing crops."

But to return to our guest.   He believed the
coming of the crows portended a visit from one
of these rogues.   Thus you may no longer wonder
at his terror; but that his fears had a more reasonable basis was more apparent when Fos told us
that some eight months before, a ferocious rogue,
distinguishable from all others of his species by
a light-coloured or nearly white ring upon his
forehead, terrified the villagers by frequent raids
in the neighbourhood, when not only had he
trampled down their paddy-fields, destroyed the
watch-houses, and set at nought the great fires
which were kept alive during the night to frighten
away more reasonable beasts, but had taken possession of a certain pass, from which he had at
different times slain some twenty persons; and

although the neighbouring villages combined to attack the beast, he still continued his ravages until some three mouths before, when his sudden disappearance and long absence gave people room to hope and rejoice that he had died from the effects of one of the hundreds of poisoned arrows which had been shot at him.

"Dat elephant was mad, bery mad; for, though rogue, 'um not be so bad if not mad," said Fos, by way of concluding the story. And Bob, who had listened very intently, said—

"But lookye, mate, seeing the big warmint is dead, what need has the skipper yonder to be so downhearted?"

"But, Sar Bosen," said the boy, slowly and seriously, "'spose rogue not dead, ony hide, and come back again: dat what Excellency tiuk two crows come tell 'um."

"D'ye see, boy, it's my opinion that the skipper and you are scaring yourselves without any airthly reason, for if so be this elephant has stopped away so long, it isn't likely that he'll come now just because an hungry thief of a crow flew away with a knife, thinking it was meat," said Bob.

And his opinion coincided with my own. True, however, as it is, that facts are often more strange than fiction, and coincidences sometimes pass for the work of what superstitious persons term fate —as if, indeed, there were any fate except that wrought under Providence by man's own acts—as the headman arose to take his departure we heard a great uproar in the village, shrieks of women and children, angry cries of men, and loud sounds of wailing and lamentations.

"Great Heaven! Tom, what can these fearful sounds portend?"

"Is it a mutiny or an earthquake?"

"The village is attacked by beasts or savages," exclaimed May.

That was sufficient. Bob and I ran out of the house, followed by the headman and Fos, both crying—

"Hora! hora!"

CHAPTER XIII.

TERRIBLE ALARM CAUSED BY A GREAT ROGUE, WHOM WE VOLUNTEER TO HUNT, BUT FIRST VISIT A COMICAL SMITH, AND ATTEND TO GIVE EVIDENCE AT A REMARKABLE TRIAL.

WHAT a sight presented itself. At least two hundred persons were in the road, shouting, madly gesticulating, and all with countenances disturbed by terror and rage. But who is the man, the old woman, the two girls, who step forth from the crowd, and, throwing themselves at the feet of the headman, seem to be imploring his aid under some terrible calamity? But patience; we shall soon discover. For the present, it is enough that the headman has addressed the people. All but the kneeling party become somewhat pacified, and retire to their homes.

Fos accompanied the headman, and May, Bob, and I sought our own house, there to await patiently for the solution of all that we had seen until the boy returned, which happened in about an hour; when he told us that early in the morning a party of mat-makers, consisting of about fifty women, had sought the vicinity of the

R

great tank, for the purpose of gathering from its
grassy border the chief material for their trade.
They had been busily engaged the whole day, and
towards evening began to gather together, sort,
and tie in bundles the rushes; they were indeed
upon the very point of returning homewards,
when their attention was aroused by the sound of
an elephant's trumpet, and a minute after to their
horror they saw running towards them, at a mad
pace, a great rogue elephant. But, horror of horrors!
it was *the* rogue who had caused the villagers so
much misery. They could not mistake him; for
upon his forehead was the white spot. The ground
around was open; no trees near where they might
have sought shelter—no, nought but the jungle
from which the animal was emerging. Up in an
instant, and helter-skelter away; they rather flew
than run, for it was for dear life's sake. One,
however, must be hindermost;—she, the youngest,
fairest, most valued among her companions, and
moreover the newly-made wife of the young man
who had fallen at the headman's feet, the daughter
of the old, the sister of the young, women who
were with him. For this poor creature there was
no escape. The savage monster seized her in his
trunk, and held her aloft as if in triumph. Her
companions stood as if petrified, gazing at the
poor victim suspended in mid-air, and shrieking
to them for aid; but, alas! what could those poor

helpless women do? Nothing; and fearing for themselves a similar fate, they fled homewards, leaving the helpless being to be crushed to death beneath the brute's huge feet. Upon reaching the village, their cries and screams rent the air; but their tale told, one and all arose, and, led by the bereaved husband, had sought out the head-man, of whom they craved permission to go in search of the assassin.

"When do they start, boy?" said I, my blood being fired with a fierce desire to revenge this poor girl.

"Not day, not morrow day—day after dat, when get quite ready," was the reply.

"We muster three good rifles; let us join them, Bob," said I.

"Dat what headman tell Fos to ask Excellency, Massa Tom," said the boy.

"Aye, aye, Master Tom. Old Bob is as ready for a fight as an Irishman for a row; but, d'ye see, to my thinking it isn't fair, it's a kind of taking advantage of the animal, for a whole village to go agin him," replied the old sailor; adding, "Now, look you, it's my opinion that you and I, and our two rifles, 'd be a good deal more fair and English like."

"Nonsense, Bob; you are too venturesome. The number can scarcely be too great to encounter this terrible beast. So you, Tom, and Fos march first with your rifles, while I will follow in the rear, as the soldiers call it, ready to attend the wounded," said May.

" Tut, tut, May ; you are mad to propose this. You must remain here with the women," said I.

" Dear Tom," said she, placing her hand upon my shoulder, and fixing her full dark eyes upon me resolutely, " I am *resolved* to accompany you. It is of no use your objecting. Remember, a mouse once saved a lion ; and although I am not quite so small as the one, nor you so large or fierce as the other, I may yet be of some use to you, if only to attend the wounded, should there be any so unfortunate."

" Bless her brave heart ! it is no manner of use to refuse," said Bob ; and believing he uttered no more than the truth I gave up the contest, and shortly afterwards we all retired to rest, perchance to dream of our anticipated campaign.

The next morning the villagers began preparations for the expedition ; some set to work preparing talipat leaves for tents, some making arrows or repairing bows, others sharpening their axes, knives, or spear-heads, while the women were busily engaged in making cakes and other portable food of rice, believing that the campaign might possibly last many days.

Then, as regards our own party, May made rice cakes, Bob and I cleaned the rifles, and Fos set

about looking after our hunting knives and axes.
Of the latter, however, Fos declared that his was
lost, and Bob's so notched as to be useless. We
were therefore necessitated to search for a smith.
Was there such an artisan in the village? Fos
declared in the affirmative, and moreover undertook to lead us to his shop. But our negotiation
with this worthy worker in iron required to be
managed with great caution, for a reason that I
have no doubt will cause you to smile—no less,
indeed, than his pride of rank ; for you must know
that goldsmiths, blacksmiths, carpenters, and
painters were at that time held to be next in rank
to the Hondrews, or inferior nobility, and like them,
allowed to sit upon stools, which was permitted
to no person of lower rank. "Once upon a time,"
as the story books say, these smiths were held to
be of almost equal rank with the Hondrews, who
would eat with them. How they came to be
degraded, I will tell you.

Some Hondrews taking their tools to a smith's
shop to be repaired just about dinner time, the
hungry artificer left them in the shop, and moreover very rudely slammed the door as he went
out ; which piece of rudeness was taken as such
a great affront, that the little noblemen (morally,
they must have been very little indeed) procured
a decree from the king that for ever after all
people of the rank of smiths should be deprived

of the honour of having Hondrews eating in their houses; but although that decree has ever since been observed, these smiths take a great deal upon themselves. And no wonder either, for they are monopolists; that is, each smith has the work of several towns given to him, and should any other man undertake any job from the inhabitants of either of these preserves, he is severely punished.

Well, having been informed by Fos of the great consequence of the personage we were about to visit, we went prepared with presents—for instance, a fowl, some rice, and a bottle of native spirits; and upon reaching his shop we were greatly amused to find the illustrious descendant of old Tubal Cain sitting upon his stool of state before his anvil. Just before us some villagers had arrived in quest of spear-heads. Then, having propitiated his highness by a fee of corn, produced the material (iron), and even fuel for the fire, which having kindled themselves, one of the party blew the bellows, while another, taking up a great hammer, fashioned the spear-head. All the while, it must be remarked, the smith remained staring at the process; when, however, the work for which he had been paid was really finished, his highness caught up a tiny hammer, and having pretended to work at the implement for a minute, handed it over to his customers, who thereupon took their departure, apparently well pleased at the great man's condescension.

But, par parenthesis, there is one race in Ceylon of whom even these proud smiths stand in awe. They are the Veddahs, a wild tribe who live by hunting, of whom it is said that when they require spear-heads, they go to the smith's shop during the night, and hang up to the door patterns made of leaves of the implements they require, and by their side the cocoa-nuts or other fruits they intend as payment. This these wild people hold to be giving due notice both of their wants and the payment; therefore, if the smith neglects to make the implements exactly to pattern and number wanted (the latter, by the way, is indicated by the quantity of separate patterns), and leave them at the door the following night, they take the first opportunity of slaying the contumacious worker in iron and steel.

Bob, however, who had watched with great impatience the haughty airs of the artisan, could not help exclaiming to me—

"Now, look you, Master Tom, it's my opinion that a tough rope-yarn 'd mend the manners of that lubber."

"Tut, tut—hush, Bob," said I, fearing that if we were wanting in the expected humility we should be compelled to go without our axe. So the first customer having, after a given fashion, been served, Fos delivered the presents, and at the same time made our wish known to have the axe ground and sharpened. The smith smiled, and bid the boy take the axe to a large stone at hand and grind it himself. Fos obeyed; and having ground it sufficiently, placed it in the hands of the smith, who having passed a small hand-stone two or three times up and down the edge, returned it to the boy.

"Top-sails and sheet-blocks! if that isn't the impudentest lubber I ever clap'd eyes on," said Bob, when we had left the smithy. "Yet," he added, thoughtfully, "it's pleasant to see working people free and independent sometimes, if so be it's only among a wilderness of niggers."

To which philosophising I made no reply, for my attention was just then arrested by a more than usually neat-looking cottage, the garden of which was larger, in better order, the mangoes and cocoa-trees more plentiful and luxuriant, than in any other house, not even excepting that belonging to the headman. Fos observing that I stopped to gaze at this house, said—

"Dat house bery good; it belong to chief of timber-cutters."

"Aye, aye, I shouldn't wonder, for it's the best cabin in the whole ship; and, d'ye see, it's my opinion that the nigger has a heart in his bosom, although his tongue and figure aint

English," said Bob: adding, "But suppose we
give him a hail, Master Tom, if it's only to find
out whether he has discovered the fellow who
stole his money?" and as Bob spoke he led
the way into the garden; but arriving at the
house, we found it closed and evidently then un-
tenanted.

"Sar, timber-cutter gone; get ready to meet
rogue elephant," said Fos.

"Hilloah, what's afloat here?" cried Bob,
stumbling over some impediment as we passed
through a thick bush.

"It am leg," said Fos, with amazement.

"Aye, aye," said Bob, who had seen the limb
at the same time; "it's a land-shark, no doubt.
Yo hoy, let's look at your figure-head;" and as
he spoke, cheering at the same time, as if he had
been hauling a ship's rope, he dragged forth from
his hiding-place a trembling native.

"Hilloah, what port do *you* hail from?" said
he.

Bob, however, letting go his hold for an instant,
the fellow improvised a summersault on to his
legs, and was out of sight in a minute.

"It's my opinion that that shark had no
business in these here waters," said Bob.

"It am slave man, what timber chief 'cuse of
robbing him," said Fos.

"Then I'm as good as a witch," replied Bob,

"for that was just my opinion. Suppose we give chase, and just overhaul the rascal's intentions."

Now, although my inclination was not dissimilar, I did not think it prudent for us to take part in native disputes; so moving forward more briskly, I replied—

"Tut, tut, Bob; it is no business of ours."

"Aye, aye, Master Tom!" was the surly reply. "Of course I'm not going agin orders; still, it's my opinion that rascal-catching is everybody's business; for the less of them kind of sharks is in the sea, why the better it is, d'ye see, for plain sailors."

Fortunately, however, his grumbling was stayed by the headman, who, meeting us at that moment, begged that we would go with him to his house, to confer together and arrange preliminaries for the attack upon the rogue elephant. After this council, which lasted till nearly dusk, the result of which was, that all things being ready, the whole party was to start upon the third morning, we wended our way homewards.

Now, about three hundred yards from our house, and in the midst of a grove of the cocoanut, palm, and tamarind-trees, was a large well. It was barely dusk, the hour when, from all time, it has been the custom of the women of the East to fetch the water; and some twenty girls, whose

shawl-cloths gracefully draped, and their sym-
metrical arms uplifted to sustain upon their
heads the vases or jars, made them resemble
statues of the classic East, were approaching the
water, singing a song, the refrain of which rang
sweet music in the air. Their faces being towards the well, they could not perceive us, and
for fear of disturbing them, we stood still, to
watch their singularly elegant forms and graceful
movements. But, getting within a yard of the
well, they started, as if with surprise—it was at
another figure, who, with vase upon head, as if
in imitation of themselves, was approaching the
same reservoir from behind a cluster of large
trees.

That figure startled us no less—do you wonder?
—it was May!

"Bless her brave heart, she has been preparing for our return, even to fetching the water,"
said Bob; adding, "Howsomdever, this sha'n't
be, for she's no more fit to do like these nigger
girls, than I am to act the court lady, and play
the pianner."

And Bob hastened forward to relieve her of
the jar; but at the same moment a monkey,
either from love of mischief, or fear that he was
about to be molested by one of us, threw down a
small, thick branch, which, striking the vase from
her head, so startled May, that, losing her pre-

sence of mind, she ran forward—missed her footing—the native girls screamed.

"Great heaven! she has fallen into the well," I exclaimed, running to her aid.

"Get rope, Excellency," said Fos, making towards the house.

Simultaneously with her fall, a low, savage growl fell upon my ears. What could that mean? In an instant, however, the meaning was too apparent, for reaching the edge of the well, I saw therein a bear, one of the largest of its kind. May had fallen upon his back, and so perhaps saved herself from being crushed to death. But the situation was terrible; there was May, dear May, crouching near the wall, with the great beast sniffing and growling, and, I thought at the moment, prepared to close with her. My brain was in a whirl with excitement. What could I do to save her?

"A branch, tear down a branch, Bob," I cried.

But the old sailor had gone—where? to fetch a rifle—a rope, perhaps; and the thought gave me hope; but May, dear girl, though pale with terror, no sooner saw me, than with great presence of mind she said—

"It is you, Tom, thank God! Make a feint of attacking him."

And comprehending her meaning, I made grimaces, shouted, and shook my clenched fist at

Tom discovers May with the Bear.—Page 252.

the brute. The *ruse* answered, for the animal turned, and stood up upon his hind legs, with his front paws against the masonry of the well; this gave May more room, but oh! how terrible the suspense of that moment: May, in fear the brute might turn again, yet with hands clasped, and eyes uplifted to Heaven, as if praying for aid; me, howling, shouting, to keep the bear's attention fixed to myself. Oh! it seemed as if Bob, Fos, would never return; but at length, though I dared not turn to look, there was a murmur of applause from the native girls, and the sound of approaching footsteps; then Bob and Fos appeared upon the opposite side of the well, and behind the animal. Bob held in his hand a looped rope; as he lowered it to May, I shouted and shook my fist in the face of the brute, who kept growling with rage. The rope fell over May, she fastened it round her waist, grasped it firmly above her head, so as to prevent the noose from tightening too much; the ascent was made—the dear girl's feet touched the ground! I gave a shriek of delight, ran round the well to her side; but now her courage failed her, the reaction was too great.

"God is good," she exclaimed, and fainted in my arms.

Can I describe my feelings at that moment? No, they were indescribable; exuberant joy at her escape, yet a fear that the shock might kill her. Of course she had but swooned; she soon became restored, when, offering up a prayer of thanks for her most miraculous escape, she ran off to the house. To get to her own chamber was necessary, for although, in consequence of the long drought, there happened to be but little water in the well, it had been quite sufficient to saturate nearly the whole of her dress.

"Namo Bud-dhaya, missee get away," said Fos, earnestly.

"Aye, aye, boy; thanks be to God, without whose aid we should pretty often get cast away; and may the Lord forgive me if it be wicked to say it, but I b'lieve he sends angels on earth to look after us when we can't look after ourselves, or how so be could Miss May, bless her, have 'scaped that frizzly brute? But," he added, as he wiped away the tears of joy which were rolling down his weather-beaten face, "old Bob's a woman or a baby, else he wouldn't stand blubbering here while yon savage is alive."

"Bob," said I, placing my hand upon the rifle which he had turned upon the bear, who was now pawing the walls, and growling as if in rage at having been so cheated out of his prey, "I am more than half inclined to spare the brute, out of gratitude."

"What! and leave him to be the terror of all

the native girls, and so maybe make 'em famish
for water? No, no, Master Tom, that be mawk-
ish ; beside, to give him a rifle ball will be doing
him a merciful turn, for, d'ye see, it 'll save him
dying of starvation ;" and before I could reply the
old sailor sent a ball through its brain, and if
angry at this disobedience of orders, I could not
but rejoice at witnessing the delight of the native
girls at the destruction of their enemy—and the
bear is a terrible enemy to the Singhalese girls.
Remarkable as perhaps you who have never
travelled may deem May's adventure with the
bear, I can assure you that so common is it in
time of great droughts to find these animals in
wells, down which they slip in their desire to
quench their burning thirst, that the custom of
women resorting to them for water is entirely
suspended. Apropos of these wells, as they are
among the phenomena of the island, I must tell
you something about them.

The one into which May had fallen was of the
ordinary kind, being large in diameter, but not
above twelve feet deep. There are, however,
wells at other portions of the island of so extraordinary a description, that the water is of three
different kinds—*i.e.*, fresh at the surface, brackish
lower down, but intensely salt below. Sir Emerson Tennent, writing of one of these, says—

" Near Potoor, in a bed of stratified limestone,

so hollow that in passing over it the footsteps of our horses sounded as though they were striking on an arch, there is a well about thirty feet in diameter and twenty-four fathoms deep. On the surface it is fresh, but lower down it is brackish and salt, and on plunging a bottle to the extreme depth the water came up highly fœtid, and giving off bubbles of sulphuretted hydrogen gas. But the most remarkable fact connected with this well is, that its surface rises and falls a few inches once in every twelve hours, but it never overflows its banks, and is never reduced below a certain fixed point, even by the extraction of large quantities of water. In 1824, the Governor of Ceylon conceived the idea of using this apparently inexhaustible spring for maintaining a perpetual irrigation of the surrounding districts. With this view, he caused a steam engine with three pumps to be erected at the well of Potoor, when it was found that, though the pumps were worked incessantly for forty-eight hours, and drawing off a prodigious quantity of water, it had in no degree reduced the apparent contents of the well, which rose each day precisely one inch and a-half between the hours of seven in the morning and one o'clock in the afternoon, and again between eight o'clock and twelve at night, falling to an equivalent extent in the intervals. According to the universal belief of the inhabitants, it is an underground pool, which communicates with the sea by a subterranean channel, bubbling out in the shore about seven miles to the north-west." But to resume the thread of my narrative.

Now, when the native girls had done dancing around the well which contained their defunct enemy, several ran home to summon their male relatives with ropes to get up the carcass. To aid them in their labour, we left Fosforus. When Bob and I reached our little house, we were delighted to find May had not only changed her wet clothing, but had recovered from her fright, and was bustling about getting ready our evening meal.

"Bless thee! thou art the bravest little craft I ever saw weather a storm; and such a storm as a deep well, and a beast for a companion who is fond of hugging, and whose hugs are death, would make many a stout old salt shiver from his keel to his masthead," said Bob aloud, taking her in his arms, and kissing her cheek as affectionately as if she had been his own child.

"Nonsense, Bob; if it had not been for God's providence, brave dear Tom here, and thyself, you would have eaten this evening's meal by yourselves," she replied.

"Come, come, May, thou hast a brave English heart, and cannot deny it," said I.

"But it is only half English," she said, with an arch smile.

" Aye, aye, dear May ; but that half is so much the better, that the other counts for nothing," said I.

" Nonsense, Tom, you are illiberal. The Hollanders are as brave and as great as the English."

" Now, there, Miss May, I ax your pardon, for you might as well go and compare a lumbering old lugger alongside with a frigate, as compare a Dutchman with an Englishman."

" Nay, Bob, that was not a civil speech of thine," said May. " But," she added, " come and let us partake of our evening meal; it will be better than quarrelling."

" Quarrel ! Why, Lord love your dear heart, I'd sooner eat my old head off !"

" A feat that, with all your bravery and a good appetite to boot, you would find rather difficult," replied May, laughing ; and as Bob was puzzled for a reply, he merely made a comical kind of grin at May's very literal reply, and we all sat down to the meal, after which May retired to her room, leaving Bob and myself waiting for Fos, upon whose return we stretched ourselves upon our sleeping mats.

How long my sleep lasted I know not, but I was dreaming of old England, of my mother, my father, when a din like the distant murmur of the sea or the clamour of a multitude, an uneasy sensation in the throat, awakened me. All was dark around, but the sensation in my throat became unbearable. Then my eyes smarted, and my nostrils were filled with the unmistakeable scent of fire. All was explained. The room was filled with smoke. I jumped up from my mat, and putting aside the board which served for a shutter, saw lurid flames ascending to the sky, and heard the hum of many voices.

"Aye, ho! Bob," and I pulled the old gentleman almost upon his legs. Fos awakened at the same time.

"Golly! golly! what am de mischief?" cried he.

"Hilloa, the ship's on fire! Pipe to the pumps, to the buckets," cried Bob, not yet more than half awakened.

"Aye, aye; quickly, Bob. The village is in flames," said I.

And the next minute we were all three on our way to the conflagration; but we arrived too late. The house (for, notwithstanding all the smoke there was but little fire) was burned to the ground; and although the villagers were dancing and howling, they were giving but little aid; that, however, was scarcely a fault of theirs; for so long had the drought continued, that the wells were nearly dry, and the river too far away to be of much use. The most melancholy sight was a man, who, with his wife and a little girl, stood as if stricken

dumb by the misfortune, gazing upon the ruins.
It was the hopelessly ruined owner, but it was,
alas! our friend the timber-cutter, and so I said
to Fos—

"Beg of him to come with us, boy. Tell him
my sister will share her portion of the house
with his wife and daughter."

The boy obeyed; and need I tell how readily
or with what delight the poor fellow accepted the
invitation.

"Ask him," said I, as we returned, "how this
misfortune happened."

"'Xpect dat 'um enemy de tief made big fire,"
said Fos.

"Aye, aye, boy, there can't be no doubt about
it. It is the work of that foul-weather bird we
caught skulking in the bushes," said Bob, adding,
reproachfully, "which comes, d'ye see, Master
Tom, of your dislike to rascal-catching."

But as I bitterly repented having interfered
with Bob in that matter, and we had, moreover,
arrived at the door of our house, I evaded a reply
by telling May what had happened, and consigning
the wife and daughter to her charge; after which we
threw ourselves upon our mats to finish our sleep.

The next morning we related to the timber-
cutter our adventure with the slave whom we
had seen loitering about his grounds, who, it
must be remembered, was the same who had been

accused of stealing before the headman; and as the latter felt convinced that the thief was also the incendiary, he resolved at once to charge the slave with the crime. So, as soon as we thought it likely the headman would be visible for purposes of justice, we proceeded together before that dignitary, when the timber-cutter, throwing himself upon his knees, at once accused the slave of setting fire to his house.

The man charged, who, as will be seen hereafter, was in court for another purpose, at first seemed much astonished, and of course took terrible oaths as to his innocence. The cross-swearing again much puzzled the worthy judge. How was he to decide? for, although it was evident some one had perjured himself, it might be either. The artful slave seeing this indecision, threw himself at his feet, saying—

"Let not thy great ears be defiled with the words of this pig's son, who would charge the smallest of thy slaves with a misfortune which the gods, in compliance with the request of the magnificent Lord himself, have brought upon his house, to prove that he alone is the dog who perjured himself before thy greatness. And," he added, "it was to demand punishment of him whom the gods have declared guilty of false swearing, that the most miserable of thy slaves dared to appear before thee, oh! great judge."

"May the earth, oh, Excellency, open and swallow thy slave and his relatives, if, to answer his own wicked purpose, this pig's son has not burned thy servant's house," said the timber-cutter.

But as the slave had suggested to the slow intellect of the headman a possibility of solving the difficulty by declaring that the gods, having decided the former trial by the visitation of fire, had therefore also proved the falsity of the present charge, I believe the robbed and burnt-out timber-cutter would there and then have been sentenced, had I not come forward, and through Fos, declared my positive belief in the truth of the charge of incendiarism, inasmuch that I had seen the slave prowling around the house some short time previous to the fire ; and the firmness with which I delivered this testimony had so much weight, that, although irritated with an interference that increased his trouble, the head-man, having pondered for a time, said—

" Now, although the white Excellency's evidence casts suspicion upon the slave, it is yet no proof that the dog fired the house ; therefore it is but justice that the first charge, that of thieving, should be tried again. So shall it be, but this time by the ordeal of the charmed cocoa-nut."

Now, as thief-catching by means of a cocoa-nut detective is both curious and novel, I will repeat to you the description of the process given by one Robert Knox, who lived in the island upwards of twenty years :—

" When a robbery is committed," says he, " to find out the thief they charm a cocoa-nut, which is done by certain words which anyone may utter, and thrusting a stick into it, set it at the door or hole where the thief went out, and it will lead him who holds it by the stick the way the thief went, and bring him to the house or place where the thief is, if they continue charming it all the way, and throw betel-flowers upon it, and run upon his feet; but this is not enough to find the thief guilty, unless the charmer will swear point blank that he is the thief, as sometimes he will do upon the goodness of his charm, and then the supposed thief must swear or be condemned. Oftentimes men of courage and metal will get clubs and beat away the charmer and all his company, and then all is at an end ; or if the thief has the wit to charm the cocoa-nut, it will suddenly stop, run round and round, but go no further."

This same old author, who, by the way, must have had *some* faith in such superstitious practises, very quaintly adds—" I, doubting of the truth hereof, took the stick once, and held it myself when they were charming thus, but it would not move with me, though they used all their art to provoke it ; but when another took it, it went forward, and he assured me it guided his hand."

Now at this decision the slave quaked with fear, for he had no doubt that the timber-cutter would so manage that the cocoa-nut would stop at his feet. Honesty, however, in this case saved the rogue; for the accuser being a simple and upright man, moreover, one who had faith in the charm he was practising, held the nut in the ring of people, and patiently awaited to see it quit him, and of its own accord travel round the people and stop only when it reached the feet of the person it meant to indicate as the thief. But you will not be surprised at my telling you that in this instance, notwithstanding the ceremonies and many mystic words used, the nut was obstinate and contumacious; in truth, after the fashion of all other nuts that I have seen, it would neither roll nor move without a kick, and as this could not be permitted, the poor man, with a bitter sigh, was compelled to admit that he could not prove the charge against the slave; whereupon the headman, delighted that the affair was settled at last, sentenced him to pay a large fine to the king for having caused so much trouble, and a sum equal in amount to that of which he alleged he had been robbed to the slave, against whom it had now been proved by the gods he had brought a false charge.

Upon hearing the sentence, the poor fellow fell

upon his knees, and declared that he could pay no fine, for he was now hopelessly ruined. Then the magistrate, with a burst of indignation unworthy his position, combined with a dash of ironic generosity, arose and said—

"Then let the son of a mean pig hide his unworthy head, even as the crocodile in the sands ; for though he is forgiven the fine to the great king, if after sundown he is found within ten miles of this village, we grant permission to the calumniated slave to do his will either upon him or his family, wherever he or they may be found, and for which none shall call him to account."

The result of this great trial is soon told. The sentenced man, accompanied by his wife and daughter, fled the village, not however without being narrowly watched by the slave ; but of that, more anon. So for a time—but for a time only, even in that savage land—guilt, roguery was successful.

CHAPTER XIV.

IN WHICH THERE IS MUCH SMOKE BUT VERY LITTLE FIRE, YET CONSIDERABLE ALARM.

FOR several days the preparation for the expedition continued, and it was well that there was this delay, for it gave time for the dissemination among the neighbouring villages of the news of the terrible death of the poor girl ; and such terror did it excite, such anger did it arouse, that each village at once armed and sent forth its contingent to aid in the destruction of the common enemy.

At length the day arrived for the marching of our army of hunters, under the command of the headman ; but such an army did we form, that to a stranger it would have seemed that we were setting forth for the conquest of a province rather than the destruction of a single animal. This formidable troop consisted of about one hundred natives, all picked elephant-hunters, slight, active, but athletic fellows, all bone and muscle, without an atom of superfluous flesh about them ; moreover, as accustomed to danger and difficulties (perhaps more so) as to their daily food. Some were armed with axes sharpened to the keenest edge; some with long spears; while others of lower caste carried elephant ropes made of twisted thongs of raw deer hide. The march was arranged so that upon reaching the jungle, and the trackers (who were sent in advance) having discovered the hiding-place of the elephant, they could at a given signal easily form into a square, the spearmen in front, the axemen upon either flank, and the ropemen in the rear.

"Oddsbobs! what a fuss about nothing. A hundred men to one beast. Why, hang me, if it don't beat bombarding a doll's house with a broadside of sixty-four pounders," said Bob, who had been silently watching the marshalling of this warlike array.

"Massa Bob Bosen laugh, 'cos 'um neber see rogue elephant; but Fos tell 'um dat rogue, 'specially bull rogue, berry, berry drefful," said the boy, seriously.

"Bull! what d'ye mean by a bull, boy? It's an elephant they are going to make love to, isn't it?" replied Bob.

"Ah! ah! Massa Bob heard of man-child, woman-child; but s'pose 'um neber hear ob bull-elephant, cow-elephant. Dat berry queer," replied the boy, with a laugh, but at the same time getting out of Bob's reach.

However, leaving the two to settle the dispute

as best they might, I returned to our house with the hope of persuading May to remain with the women in the village.

"Nay, nay, Tom; for however I might fear accompanying you, I should still more dread remaining here while both you and Bob were away."

"Tut, tut, dear May, this is foolish; for what have you to dread in this village?"

"Tom," she said, very seriously, "my suspicions may be groundless—I hope they are—but the truth is, I doubt the honesty of the headman."

"Nonsense, May. But even so, the headman goes and returns with the party."

"Poh, poh! dear brother; think you he does not leave those behind capable of doing his will?" adding, "I tell you, Tom, it is my belief that he is a rogue; and moreover, that during your absence it is his intention to have me seized and sent up to Kandy as a slave present to the king; so, brother, once for all, I *will* go with you."

And—but not to prolong my narrative—she did accompany us upon a small horse the head-man had provided for the conveyance of our tents, provisions, and extra ammunition, and, like Bob and I, armed with a rifle, hunting-knife, and small axe.

Well, all being ready, the order was given to march. At that moment, however, we were sur-

prised and annoyed by a fearful yelling and howling ; and the order was rescinded, while a party
was detached to drive back the whole community
of dogs of the village, which animals, either
desirous of volunteering for the expedition, or,
which was more probable, sadly hungered by the
long-continued drought, which kept them more
than half starved, followed in the rear.

Now, of the annoyance of these dogs in a
tropical climate you can have no conception ; for
although pets in this country, in Asia, but in
Ceylon especially, they are a pest, or rather *were*
at that time. What they are even now we may
learn from the pages of Tennent, who writes :—

"There is no native wild dog in Ceylon, but
every village and town is haunted by mongrels of
European descent, which are known by the generic
description of Pariahs. They are a miserable
race, ackowledged by no owners, living on the
garbage of the streets and sewers ; lean, wretched,
and mangy, and if spoken to unexpectedly, shrink-
ing with an almost involuntary cry. Yet in these
persecuted outcasts there survives that germ of
instinctive affection which binds the dog to the
human race, and a gentle word, even a look of
kindness, is sufficient foundation for a lasting
attachment. The Singhalese, from their religious
aversion to taking away life in any form, permit
the increase of these desolate creatures, till, in the

hot season, they become so numerous as to be a
nuisance ; and the only expedient hitherto devised
by the civil government to reduce their number
is once a year to offer a reward for their destruction, when the Tamils and Malays pursue them
in the streets with clubs (guns being forbidden by
the police for fear of accidents), and the unre-
sisting dogs are beaten to death on the side-paths
and door-steps, where they had been taught to
resort for food.　Lord Torrington, while Governor
of Ceylon, attempted the more civilised experi-
ment of putting some check on their numbers by
imposing a dog-tax, the effect of which would
have been to have led to the drowning of puppies;
whereas there is reason to believe that dogs are at
present *bred* by the horse-keepers to be killed for
sake of the reward."

Well, having at length by great exertions
driven these dogs back to the village, we resumed
our march, and upon our way heard from some
villagers who had joined that morning, that the
King of Kandy, having been informed of the
ravages which for so long a time had been committed by this terrible rogue, and, moreover, of
the murder of the woman, had given his royal
permission for the beast to be killed (for in those
days no elephant, however terrible, might be slain
without a royal license) ; also his best wishes for
our success, and a promise of his royal favour to

the person or persons by whose hand or hands the
animal might be destroyed.

At this message the hopes of May, Bob, and
myself arose high.

"For who can doubt," said I, "that it will
be our rifles that will at one and the same time
bring down the beast and earn my father's
liberty?"

"That is, if so be a decent white man may
trust a nigger. For my part, d'ye see, Master
Tom (then pr'aps it's because I am older and more
unbelieving than you), I'd sooner trust the word
of one of them Bartlemy-fair kings."

"S'pose, Massa Bosen, country berry big, berry
great?" said Fos, inquiringly.

"Why, as for that," replied Bob, who never
let an opportunity pass of exalting his own country at the expense of another, "though this
Ceylon, d'ye see, might pr'aps be a little too large
for one of the King of England's flower-pots, I
can't say as it 'd be too big for one of his gardens.
But what makes you *s'pose* at all about it?"

"'Cos 'um say one of dem, and dat mean one,
two, tree, four, or eber so many kings."

"Oh, aye; all right. It's the Bartlemy-fair
kings you mean; but then they be more for
ornament-like than use; for, d'ye see, they be
never used except when his real Majesty (God
bless him!) be ill."

"Tut, tut; don't tell the boy this nonsense," said I, for I could see that Fos really believed all Bob said.

". Pr'aps it's mutiny, Master Tom, but I couldn't help it; for, d'ye see, if he hadn't asked any questions, he wouldn't have heard any stories."

By this time we had reached the river in which I had encountered the polite shark, and having forded it, we proceeded along the bank for about five miles, when, turning in a north-westerly direction, we entered upon a forest, amid the cool shades of which we rested and sought shelter till the great heat of the mid-day sun had subsided, when, the party being re-formed in precisely the same order as at first starting, so that we might be ready to act upon the instant that the trackers should bring news of the rogue, we resumed our march.

As we advanced nearer and nearer to the scene of the rogue's misdeeds, it is worthy of remark that the headman—hitherto so valorous in his professions and so conspicuous in heading the party —fell step by step rearward, till, indeed, Fos, Bob, May, and myself, found ourselves in the front rank, observing which, I said—

"The old skipper's a wise man after his generation. He's skulking under cover of our rifles."

"Aye, aye; and he's in the right, too. For these three rifles of ours 'll do more to take the mischief out of the elephant than all their spears, axes, and arrows together," replied Bob.

But as he spoke, and we were entering a pathway in a thick thorny jungle, Fos said—

"Excellency, Missee, and Massa Bob Bosen, better now keep finger upon guns, for not know when rogue come." And adopting the lad's caution as we further advanced, we kept our pieces at half-cock, with fingers upon triggers.

Thus we marched for about half-an-hour, when the shrill sound of a whistle brought the party to a standstill.

"It am trackers," said Fos; and almost as he spoke a native burst through the jungle, and came running up to the headman.

"Hilloa, boy! what makes yonder nigger look so scared? Has he had a tussle with the enemy?" asked Bob, laughing.

"You make too light of our danger, Bob; for you know it is not a good soldier that underrates the strength of an unseen foe," said May.

"Aye, aye, may be all right enough; but still, d'ye see, Miss May, a man who has given three cheers at finding himself yardarm and yardarm, as it might be, with a whole fleet of Parlevous, aint exactly the sort of chap to be skeered by a four-footed dumb, beast like this lot of niggers, who arter all, every man jack on 'em, I b'lieve, 'd run if the creature was to show his trunk."

L.I.C.   T

Neither of us, however, paid much attention to the old man's boasting, for Fos, who had listened to the news brought by the tracker, said—

"Excellency, rogue 'bout here somewhere. Tracker found 'um foots."

"Found 'um foots," repeated the incorrigible Bob. "Is it the custom, then, of these here animals to shed their feet as they say they do their tusks?"

"A truce to this nonsense, Bob. And you, Fos, ask the headman whether we are to remain here at a dead halt, or to follow the brute's track into the jungle," said I.

And the boy having put the question, the headman, to my mortification, ordered the whole of us at once to encamp for the night, that by a night's rest we might be the better prepared for an encounter in the morning; an order, by the way, which by all but us Europeans and the man whose wife had been killed, was received with delight. As, however, to encamp we had to find fresh trees or open ground, we advanced into the jungle under the guidance of the tracker, who said he could lead us to an opening at some little distance. Well, onward we went for about another half-hour, when the whole party were brought to an involuntary halt by a loud whr-r-r-r, which, from the sound, seemed to come from no great distance in the front.

" Rogue's trumpet," said Fos.

" Then, forward !" I replied; and Bob and I, with our fingers upon the triggers, kept ahead, so as in the event of a sudden attack to cover May; but the trumpet ceased, and either from fright or indecision, the party stood silent, all but the murdered woman's husband, who with knife in hand darted madly forward in the direction of the sound, as if to cope single-handed with the brute assassin who had made desolate his hearth.

" Hilloa ! there goes the most plucky nigger in the fleet. Howsomdever, that aint no reason we should let him fight a giant with a toothpick." As Bob said this, he ran after the man, and having caught him by the waist-cloth, he added, " Come, mate, you get here under cover of our rifles."

The man submitted with a bad grace; and then for some minutes we stood still, listening with breathless anxiety, but neither sound nor movement did we hear that indicated the immediate neighbourhood of the enemy.

" I tell'e, Master Tom, it's my opinion we've jist been all skeered about nothing, and that mayhap the noise we heard was only a young monkey a-hailing his mother," said Bob.

" Hush ! Listen ! The brute is not far away," said I, hearing a noise, such as might be caused

by an elephant whisking his tail against his side
to brush away the flies.

"Aye, aye, it's the rogue now, no doubt; so
just you, boy, go and tell the skipper to extend his
two flanks, so that we may catch him in a circle."

Fos obeyed; but the headman, either out of
sheer obstinacy or for some especial reason of his
own, refused to comply.

"Then, Bob, we will advance without him,"
said I: adding, as I moved forward, "Follow,
old friend; but keep your charge ready, in case
both my barrels should miss."

"Aye, aye," he replied; and away we went
through the narrow path. I did not, however,
observe who had followed us, till feeling a light
hand upon my shoulder, I turned my head and
saw May.

"Is it you, May? For heaven's sake, then,
keep in the rear of both, or your danger may un-
nerve us."

"Nonsense, Tom; a rifle is a rifle, and as
telling in my hand as in yours. But," she added,
with alarm, and pointing to a thick bush near at
hand, "Look, Tom, look! Beware!"

I did look, and at once fell back a few paces,
saying—

"Silence! silence! for our lives! Speak not,
move not, and reserve your fire till I have
emptied both barrels."

What was it that had alarmed me ? I will tell you. From out of the thick thorny jungle just ahead, but through a mist, a network of twigs, branches, and brambles, flashed the glaring, glittering orbs of an elephant—possibly, nay, most probably, the rogue himself. I brought the rifle to my shoulder, yet did not dare to fire; for so thick was the network of branches in which the animal was, as it were, encased, that the ball might have been turned aside. No ; a miss was too serious a thing to risk; so I advanced step by step, till our eyes meeting pupil to pupil I trembled, for now I could see the brute's fore-head, aye, and the white spot which proclaimed him to be the assassin thief of which we were in search. I have said I trembled; but it was at the thought that May was behind, and that thought, by shaking my hand a little, lost me my line of fire ; for although I discharged both bar-rels one after the other, the beast threw his trunk upwards, and with a fearful shriek came rushing forward ; and nothing could have saved us had not brave May stopped his progress by a well-aimed ball.

" Hurrah ! the brute is dead," said I. A little too premature, however, was my rejoicing; for though perhaps scotched, he was not killed. Yet the animal must have been frightened at the reception he had met with, for instead of making further advance upon us, with a bellow of rage he forced his huge body through the dense jungle, and lashing it with his tail, and filling the air with the hideous screamings of his trumpet, he made off.

"Why, hang me, if the brute isn't like a British tar; he doesn't know when he's beaten," said Bob, not a little astonished at the small inconvenience the animal seemed to suffer from the contents of three barrels in his hide.

"Aye, aye, the brute is plucky enough, Bob; but that is no reason we should let him off so easily," I replied.

"Jist so, Master Tom, and that's my opinion, d'ye see; so while you reload and follow, I'll jist push a little ahead." And the next instant all three of us were running at full speed in the brute's track; and a very painful chase it was, for although the elephant had hewn out the pathway, the hooked thorns caught and scratched our limbs, and tore portions of our dresses to shreds. Yet scorning such difficulties, we continued onward, keeping the elephant in sight, but reserving our fire until he should present to us something like a penetrable portion of his body. Yes, still forward. Wh-r-r-r! sounded the monster's trumpet; crash, crash went the thorns and brambles beneath its huge feet; and although you may wonder at the agility of such a mountain of flesh, so fast did he run that we were at length compelled to halt to take breath, and strangely he stopped almost simultaneously.

" Hilloa ! he's going to give us a chance," said Bob, as he turned his head towards us.

"Aye, aye, we have him now, Bob," said I ; and bang, bang, bang went the three barrels ; but as our fingers touched the triggers the cunning rogue by a quick movement turned, and to our chagrin again the bullets fell harmlessly upon his tough hide.

" Now," said I to Bob and May, " load quickly ;" but as the smoke caused by the three discharges filled the jungle, from which it could but slowly escape, and the elephant might take advantage of this to attack, as it were, in the dark, I poised my rifle with its single loaded barrel before me, so that I might feel him with its muzzle.

" It is my opinion, Master Tom, that this chap thinks we are throwing cherry-stones at him," said Bob.

But, seeing that he had re-loaded, and beckoning him to follow, I passed onwards through the smoke, but, lo ! the rogue had disappeared ; and neither by sight nor sound could we tell that he was so near to us as he really must have been. We all stood speechless with astonishment.

" He must have passed through yon tall damp grass into his lair in the forest," said I.

"It's my opinion that he's gone through this ground to his own proper home," said Bob, stamping his foot, and adding, "for, d'ye see, it's my notion he wasn't an elephant at all."

"Why, how very queer, Tom; we have been running all this time in a circle," said May, as, passing out of the jungle track, we came upon our party, who were in the same position that we had left them.

"Golly, Massa Tom, den rogue come again soon, when not 'xpect 'um, 'cos 'um always go out same place, and in same place all round," said Fos, when I had explained to him our run.

Now, when the headman and some of his principal people, who had great faith in our rifles, heard of the rogue's escape, and how that he had resisted the bullets, they began a conference together.

"What's all the conflab about, boy," asked Bob.

"Excellency headman tink it no good try to kill rogue now, 'cos 'um tink God's angry 'cos 'um come hunt before ask wise man [an astrologer] for lucky day; and so 'um no more hunt to-day, but wait till morrow," answered Fos.

"The cowardly lubber," muttered Bob, adding, "it's my opinion, d'ye see, he intends to let us do the work, and take the credit to himself."

"Come, come, Bob; that was an ungenerous

speech, as to-morrow, perhaps, will show. Therefore, let us respect his prejudices for this day,"
said May.

"Maybe, maybe, Miss May; but still it's my
opinion, d'ye see, that all the morrows in the
world wont put pluck into the heart of a coward,"
replied Bob.

Now, during our short absence it had been
arranged that we should encamp for the night
upon an open space near the skirts of a forest
about half a mile to the north. Well, to that
place we proceeded, and upon our arrival I could
not help admiring the rapidity of the natives'
movements; for in less than an hour the tents
were up and the night-fires kindled. When Bob,
Fos, and I had, as usual, erected our tent near
a great tree, May gladly retired, leaving us together chatting about the prospect of falling in with
the rogue to-morrow.

"Rogue sometimes come in night, when not
'xpected," said Fos.

"The boy is right. Maybe he will," said Bob.

"Then suppose we anticipate his visit?" said I.

For although somewhat tired by the elephant-
chase, I felt too restless to sleep.

"Aye, aye," said Bob.

And in a minute or so, guns in hand, we had
gently stolen through the encampment and passed
the watch-fires.

"Excellency follow. Go to water where elephant come to drink at night," said Fos.

And we followed him for about the distance of a mile. The sun had long sunk. The moon had risen magnificently, shedding her silvery light upon the dark shadows of the trees; but before us the light fell upon what appeared a field of looking-glass, so brightly did it glisten.

"It is a lake," said I.

"Excellency, it am pool ob water, where rogue will come if 'um come at all," said Fos; adding, "but 'um better hide here little while."

And he crouched down behind some tree-stumps, Bob and I following his example.

For a time all was quiet. We could almost hear the stillness. By the way, have you, my reader, in the dead of night, when sleepless, pondering, thinking, never fancied that you could hear that mysterious stillness? Well, such did I fancy that night, and drinking in my ears the delicious sound, I almost fell asleep; however, I was soon awakened by the hoarse barking of the elk, the shrill mouthings of the spotted deer. I looked up above the tree stumps, then upon the other side of the pool. I could see the dark forms of the animals approach; then hear the splash, splash, splashing at different points of the pool, which, if I had not seen, would have told me that deer, dogs, and buffaloes, were bathing and drinking together.

"They are enjoying themselves, poor creatures! And well they may; for it's very little water that's to be got in these latitudes just now," said Bob; adding, "but where is our clever, plucky enemy, the rogue, boy?"

"May come now. Listen!" said Fos.

We did listen, and my heart bounded with joy, for crash, crash, went the branches and brambles.

"The enemy's in sight, Master Tom," said Bob, pointing his gun in the direction of an elephant just then pushing its way through the brushwood which covered that portion of the bank of the pool which it was approaching.

"Let me have first shot, Bob," said I, and my gun was to my shoulder; but, placing his hand upon the barrel, Bob said—

"Don't fire, it would be murder. See, it's only a poor creature with her babby!"

He was right; it was a mother bringing her young one down to the pool to teach it to drink, bathe, and play in the water, and I could not find it in my heart to disturb them; although, so disappointed was I at its not being the expected rogue, that I think I should have fired at the old male elephant—apparently the consort, and father of the little one in the pool, and who quietly followed them—had not Bob—who I dare say, by this time, you have found out was good at the main, though rough in speech and exterior—said:

"Don't hurt the poor beast; for, see, he is too attentive to his family to be a rogue. Besides, as we can neither eat him nor sell his carcass, we should only upset the happiness of yon lady and her big babby there, which, d'ye see, 'd be on-christian-like."

"Good, Bob, good. I will not harm the poor animals. But listen! I know that sound," said I, as the shrill trumpet of an elephant sounded through the night air.

"Excellency, stop moment," said Fos, falling upon his knees, and placing his ear upon the ground, but rising again, he said, "it is rogue; he has attacked the camp from the other side."

"For Heaven's sake think of May, Bob! Forward!" said I. And, following Fos, we sped backwards to the tents. "Onwards! onwards! for dear life's sake!" I exclaimed, as I then heard shoutings, and, I fancied, shriekings. We were in sight of the tents. A loud report fell upon our ears.

"Thank Heaven! she may yet be safe, for that was her rifle," answered Bob.

CHAPTER XV.

THE PLUCK OF THE NATIVES IS TRIED—MAY PER-
FORMS A GALLANT DEED, AND BOB TAKES A
PRISONER.

ONWARDS I ran, heeding not fallen tents, the half-
extinguished fires, or the questionably valiant
natives, who, with their still more terrified headman, ran to and fro, dancing and brandishing their
axes and spears at nothing, till I reached May's
tent, at the entrance of which she stood, laughing,
with the exploded rifle in her hand.

"Thank heaven! dear May, you are safe."

"Aye, Tom, never safer; though I think it
would have gone hard with us all here but for
this good gun; for you must know," she added,
"thinking it possible that our friend the rogue
might pay us a nocturnal visit, I rather dosed
than slept, and so far it was fortunate; for I
doubt whether I should have been so easily
awakened a short time since by the crashing of
yonder jungle. As to what that crashing might
mean, my day's experience had enlightened me;
so not doubting that the rogue was at hand, I
arose from my mat, seized my rifle, and went

directly to your tent to arouse you; but the
entrance being open, and you absent, for an
instant my courage failed, and gave place to fears
for your safety. There was, however, no time
for thought: action alone could save us; for even
before I could arouse these stupid natives, who
had permitted the fires to burn down too low to
be of any use, the rogue, the identical rogue of
this morning—for I knew him by the white spot
upon his forehead, which was clearly distinguishable by the light of the moon—came at a full trot,
nay, faster, down upon the encampment. He had
crushed beneath his huge feet three of the tents,
killing perhaps the poor fellows beneath.   The
noise aroused the people; they arose, shouted,
flourished their knives and axes, one even fired a
few arrows at him; but still down went the tents
one after the other, the beast walking leisurely
among them as if amused, and regardless of such
puny efforts to injure him.   At that moment
what would I not have given for your presence.
There was, however, one man of courage among
them.   The widower, having sent one well-
aimed arrow at the rogue, he threw his bow aside,
and with his axe attacked the beast with fearful
determination; but, alas! the man stumbled,
when, screaming and trumpeting with rage, the
rogue caught hold of the poor fellow with his trunk,
and the next instant would have been his last had

not a ball from my rifle told with such good effect, that it sent him back into the jungle screaming with pain or anger."

" It is a mercy he did not turn his vengeance upon thee, May," said I.

" Perhaps he would; but by that time there were so many of the natives aroused that I suppose he thought it unwise to continue the conflict."

" But," said I, " is it possible they have let him escape—that they did not follow him to his lair ?"

" The cowardly lubbers were glad to give him plenty of sea room. Hows'mdever that aint no reason why we shouldn't follow the brute up," said Bob.

" Aye, aye, Bob, follow it ; so, onwards !" said I. And with the widower for our guide, away went Fos, Bob, and I; but although our guide had watched the retreat of his enemy, so cleverly, so warily did the animal manage his escape, that after nearly three hours' search we had to return to the tents defeated, and so great had been our fatigue during the past twenty hours, that although it was broad daylight we threw ourselves upon our mats to seek a few hours' rest. When, however, I awoke and found that we had slept into the cool hours, I at once despatched Fos to the headman to ask if it were his intention to renew the search for the rogue that night.

Anent this rogue, my belief was that he was

mad; so cruel, so furious was he in comparison with the elephant tribe in general, who are proverbially gentle, and very rarely deserving of such epithets as savage, wary, bloodthirsty, and revengeful, as sportsmen who, to exalt their own prowess by misrepresenting the animal, term him.

"Such epithets as these," says one who knew more of the habits and nature of these noble creatures than any other writer, "may undoubtedly apply to the outcasts from the herd, the 'rogues,' or *hora allia;* but so small is the proportion of these, that there is not probably one *rogue* to be found for every five hundred of those in herds; and it is a manifest error, arising from imperfect information, to extend this censure to them generally, or to suppose the elephant to be an animal thirsting for blood, lying in wait in the jungle to rush on the unwary passer-by, and knowing no greater pleasure than the act of crushing his victim to a shapeless mass beneath his feet. At the same time the cruelties practised by the hunters have no doubt taught these sagacious creatures to be cautious and alert; but these precautions are simply defensive; and beyond the alarm and apprehension which they evince on the approach of men, they exhibit no indication of hostility or thirst for blood.

"An ordinary traveller seldom comes upon elephants, unless after sunset or towards daybreak, as they go or come from their nightly visits to the tanks; but when by accident a herd is disturbed by day, they show, if unattacked, no disposition to become assailants; and if the attitude of defence which they instinctively assume prove sufficient to check the approach of the intruder, no further demonstration is to be apprehended.

"Even the hunters who go in search of these animals find them in positions and occupations altogether inconsistent with the idea of their being savage, wary, or revengeful. Their demeanour when undisturbed is indicative of gentleness and timidity, and their actions bespeak lassitude and indolence, induced not alone by heat, but probably attributable in some degree to the fact that the night had been spent in watchfulness and amusement. A few are generally browsing listlessly on the trees and plants within reach; others fanning themselves with leafy branches; and a few are fast asleep; whilst the young run playfully among the herd, the emblems of innocence, as the older ones are of peacefulness and gravity."

Now, having read this certificate of the good character, noble nature, and amiable behaviour of the elephants, what will you think of English sportsmen, gentlemen who for mere amusement spend the whole of their spare hours in slaying these noble creatures? For, remember, it is not for profit, or to ensure the necessities of human life, for their bodies are left to decompose and defile the air. They are never used for food, for it is the tongue alone that is eatable. For profit they are not worth the trouble of killing, except it be, indeed, the tusks for their ivory; but, then, in Ceylon not one elephant in a hundred is found with this appendage, which alone makes the animal valuable as an article of commerce.

Now, having described to you the real character of the elephant as a species, and that of the rogue in particular, that you may not think my desire to destroy the terrible animal we were hunting arose out of a morbid love of mere brutal sport—for all sport is merely brutal that has not for its end the use or protection of man—I will resume my narrative.

" Upon what errand have you sent Fos ?" asked May, as she entered the tent, bringing in a mess of hot rice for our late breakfast.

" To ask the headman if he and his party intend to resume the hunt to-night."

" Then you will be disappointed with his answer, for the tents are lifted, and the whole party are about to return to the village."

" Nonsense, May ; you are joking."

" No, no ; Miss May aint the one to be a poking fun at us about such a matter as this," said Bob.

"Not I, indeed," she replied, seriously; adding, "strange things have happened while you have been sleeping : first, soon after your return this morning, an odd-looking, deformed little man made his appearance at the tent of the headman; and why or wherefore I know not, but his coming for some reason or other so frightened the whole party, that they at once began to lift their tents, at least those which had not already been destroyed by the rogue elephant."

"Maybe that little man was the rogue elephant in human form ; for, d'ye see, I don't half believe that beast *is* a elephant at all," said Bob.

"Come, come, Bob, no nonsense," said I, terribly vexed at May's intelligence.

"Nonsense, d'ye call it, Master Tom; to my thinking it's something more than nonsense to be dodged about after this fashion by a brute which, if so be he aint somebody else, and can change himself into a little man, big enough to frighten all these niggers—as Miss May says he has—can take bullets into his body as if they were plums, and then—great beast as he is—pop himself as easily out of sight as the demons do, through trap-doors and blue fire on the London play-boards."

At that moment Bob was interrupted by the return of Fos, who brought confirmation of all that May had told us.

" Headman had omen from gods, so wont hunt elephant rogue till get lucky day," said he.

" There," said Bob, " didn't I tell'ee that little man was more than he seemed ?"

" Little man on road to Kandy ; but when headman see him with big hump, like buffalo, on back, 'um wont go after rogue again, 'cos when gods send men with hump it not good go on, 'cos bad omen."

" Is that the cowardly fellow's only reason ?" I asked.

" Not dat only ; but headman say 'um got oder omens. Some of de people sneeze good bit— dat bad omen ; oder ob de people catch little lizard —dat bad omen. So headman put all omens in heap, an' it so frighten 'um dat 'um going back to village to wait for more lucky day."

" And a good riddance, too, the cowardly dog ; for if we have all the work, we shall have all the glory," replied Bob, adding, " for, d'ye see, Master Tom, I take it you aint a-going to turn tail."

" Not I, Bob, even if the destruction of this brute did not offer a chance of gaining the King's good offices for my father. But," I said to Fos, " get you, boy, to the headman, and say that without his aid we will kill the brute before another week is over our head ; but," I added, " if you can persuade him to let a few of the bravest and least frightened of his people remain as trackers, it may be better for us all."

"And mayhap it wont be any harm for me to go with the boy, and pick out the best-looking among 'em," said Bob, who, as I did not object to the suggestion, at once left the tent with Fos.

"I fear me this headman meditates some treachery, Tom," said May.

"Mere fancy, May; for to what purpose should he be treacherous?"

"I am not the keeper of his motives, Tom. But we shall see," she replied.

And then we entered into a conversation about the prospects of our again finding my father, the chances of her being restored to her own parent, about the past, the future, the present; indeed, about so many matters of interest, that I believe we had forgotten the very existence of Fos and Bob, till we heard a kind of whimpering in the native tongue, and the voice of the old sailor reply.

"Quick, you cowardly nigger, or I'll just give you your desarts by hauling you up to the yard-arm."

And almost at the same time he and Fos entered the tent, dragging a native with them.

"Hilloa! Bob, what have we here? Why, this is the fellow who robbed our friend the timber-cutter."

" Aye, aye, sir; caught the lubber at his tricks
again.   So this time I determined to be judge
and jury myself—that is, if so be it aint agin
orders. But," he added, " this is how it happened.
D'ye see, we had seen the headman, as they call
the fellow, and after the boy here had spun him
a long yarn in his own heathen lingo, he said as
how we might go and kill the elephant if we
liked ; but he didn't believe it possible no how,
seeing the gods had sent him so many omens ;
and he said also, that if we could persuade any of
his black fellows to go with us, he wouldn't
object.   Well, that being all we wanted of him,
we went to look after some of 'em. The only one,
howsumdever, that wasn't too frightened of the
little humpback, was the poor fellow whose wife
the brute killed ; but he promised to follow us
as soon as he had got his spears, ropes, and axe
ready.   As we were returning, who should cross
our path but this nigger, a-carrying in his arms a
young woman who was screaming herself into
fits ; but though I took him to be a land-pirate,
I wouldn't interfere in what didn't consarn me,
till I caught sight of our old shipmate the
timber-cutter in full chase.   Then, d'ye see, as
it struck me the rascal was running away with
t'other's daughter, I jist set my leg tackle in
order, and getting alongside, I gave him such a
broadside with my fists about midships, that he

hauled down his colours afore I could say Jack Robinson. Well, then, as I was a-coaxing the young woman to believe she was under safe convoy, and leave off crying, Fos comes alongside, and says he—

"'Massa Bosen wrong to take gal 'way from slave, 'cos headman say he may takee gal when can catch her.'

"When all at once remembering that lubber of a headman's judgment, I says—

"'Look you, boy, this here may be nigger law, but it aint British; so I shall jist hand the young woman over to her nataral parent.'

"And as by that time the father had come up, I clapped the young woman in his arms, and told Fos to tell him to sail out of these waters as fast as his legs would carry him, and that to give him all night to get clear, I'd keep this fellow under hatches till the morning; and that's why, d'ye see, Master Tom, I have brought the fellow here, where, with your leave, I intend keeping him till our shipmate has had time to get into another latitude."

"But did none of the headman's people see any portion of this affair?" I asked.

"Lor' bless you, no; most of 'em were too busy preparing to get away from the rogue elephant; besides, d'ye see, it all happened 'mid a clump of trees some distance from their tents."

"Well, well, Bob, as it's done it can't be helped; so just stow the fellow up in a corner out of the way," I replied, really vexed that such an awkward affair should have happened; for I well knew that should it reach the ear of the headman, it would place us in a very disagreeable position.

Bob obeyed my orders with such alacrity that in a minute or so the man, notwithstanding his appeals to me, and many offers to become our slave and assist in the capture of the rogue (for he was a noted tracker), was tied up in a bundle, and deposited in a corner behind a heap of baggage. But Bob exceeded his order, for he gagged the man; and well for us it was he did so, for very shortly afterwards we heard the sound of footsteps approaching the tent.

"Let us meet these people, whoever they are; for if they come in here, the fellow may make himself heard," said I; and we at once went forth.

CHAPTER XVI.

A TERRIBLE ENCOUNTER WITH THE ROGUE—THE
WIDOWER HAS A NARROW ESCAPE, AND MY LIFE
IS SAVED BY MAY, WHO PROVES HERSELF A
DIANA.

THE people we had quitted the tent to meet proved
to be the headman's contingent, *i.e.*, three men,
under the command of the widower, whose thirst
for revenge upon the assassin of his wife was so
great, that he not only refused to obey the omens,
but had persuaded the other fellows to join him;
but guess my vexation when, through Fos, I found
that he had witnessed Bob's late adventure; it
happened, however, to be but of small consequence; for he further told Fos that, as the
timber-cutter was one of his relations, and his
enemy a very bad man, and, moreover, we were
about destroying his ruthless enemy the "rogue,"
we might, as far as he was concerned, do our will
with the slave, and the headman be none the
wiser.

"May be all fair, square, and above board, but
it 'isn't a wise dog that bites his own tail;' so
we had better keep a sharp look out a-head for

treachery," said Bob, who had but small faith in humanity, at least in its Asiatic form.

"Massa Bosen tink ebery man bad as 'umself," said Fos.

"What d'ye mean by that, you mahogany-faced varmint?" replied Bob, laughing in spite of himself.

"Fos not mogany nor any oder wood, but 'ropean, and mean, dat s'pose rogue had killed Massa Bob's wife, Fos tink Massa Bob sell all 'um fader and moder before him (the boy meant ancestors) to people what help shoot beast what kill'd wife."

"The boy is right, Bob; this fellow will never betray those who are about to help him to revenge the death of his wife."

And as Bob had no reply, we began to discuss our plan of attack; after which, as it was all-important that we should before starting obtain some clue to the rogue's hiding-place, we sent out three trackers for that purpose.

My next difficulty was not a small one, for it was no less than how to provide for the safety of May. To take her with us seemed impossible; to leave her I dared not. The brave girl herself, however, soon settled the matter, by declaring that go with us she would, as she could keep near me with a loaded rifle to place in my hand in case of necessity.

Matters being thus arranged, we retired to our respective tents, there to hold ourselves ready for starting on the instant a tracker might return with the intelligence that the lair had been discovered; the night, however, passed without our receiving any such news; indeed, it was not till late the following morning that the trackers returned, then they said that at a distance of some five miles they had seen the rogue feeding and consorting with a large herd.

" Umpossible; rogue neber wid oder elephants," exclaimed Fos.

" Don't be forrard, boy, with your opinion, but just ask our mate here (pointing to the widower) what he thinks about it," said Bob.

Fos obeyed; and as I found the widower had every faith in the ability of his trackers, I gave the order for the start.

" Aye, aye, sir. But what's to be done with that land-crab of a pirate ?" said Bob, alluding to our prisoner the slave.

" Ask the fellow whether, if we give him his liberty, he will serve us faithfully during the hunt," I said to Fos; for I felt certain that, supposing (which, by the way, was very probable) he deserted us, the timber-cutter and his daughter had had so many hours start that he would not be able to overtake them.

" What says the man ?" I asked, as Fos came

out of the tent with a grin upon his countenance.

"So berry glad get 'um legs out ob ropes, dat slave say 'um use 'em anyhow Excellency like."

And the rogue really did appear to mean what he said, for finding himself free, and having shaken his legs and arms well, as if to get them in proper working order, he threw himself at my feet, and, with tears in his eyes, exhibited an amount of joy and gratitude that astonished me, until I discovered that Master Fos, taking advantage of our ignorance of the language, had practised upon the man a very grim joke, *i.e.*, he had persuaded the poor fellow that it had been our intention to carry him with us, and throw him beneath the merciless feet of the terrible rogue.

"You rascal! how dared you play such a joke upon the man?" said I.

"If Excellency angry, Fos berry much sorry; but de joke, as Excellency call 'um, not so bad as joke de rascal play timber-cutter," replied the boy with a grin.

And as there was some truth in what he said, I turned aside to look after our tents and packages, and seeing they were placed upon the horse, I helped May to mount; having placed a hunting-knife upon one side, an axe upon the other, and adjusted the rifle across the horse's neck, so that in the event of a sudden surprise it should be

ready ; and, for her further protection, told Bob
not to leave her side. I marshalled the little
line so that we could march as much at ease as the
nature of so rugged a country permitted, and thus
we proceeded for about three or four miles, till
we came to an extensive park-like opening, when
the widower, fixing his eyes upon a large patch
of jungle upon the opposite side, cried out ener-
getically—

"Alia ! hora !" [the elephant, the rogue.]

And our ears verified the accuracy of his quick
sight, for they were filled with the shrill soundings
of an elephant's trumpet.

The incident was exciting; the opportunity
was not to be lost; so leaving May and Bob
behind, the widower, Fos, and I, with the trackers
in our rear, ran forward towards the jungle, but
suddenly we came to a standstill, for a huge
elephant stood in our front, but quite motionless,
and gazing full in our faces, as if taking the measure of our capability to injure him.

"Hora ! hora !" cried the excited widower,
gnashing his teeth, and shaking his fist in its face.
But the brute as yet was not to be so moved;
indeed, his whole bearing seemed to be that of
contempt for such puny creatures.

"It am de rogue. See white forehead," said
Fos, levelling his rifle.

"Stay ; reserve your fire, boy," said I, preparing

for a good aim ; but at that moment the animal must have caught sight of the horse behind us (elephants have a great fear of, or perhaps dislike to, horses), for he turned round quickly and ran back into the forest. We followed in his track out of the jungle into the wood, there we suddenly lost him ; but a few minutes after, coming to the edge of a tract of high lemon grass, we again saw him ; this time he seemed greatly excited, for he lashed his tail, threw his trunk upward, and his feet forward, as if waiting for our advance. As we moved stealthily forward, reserving our fire until he should move his trunk from the only part at which it was of any use to aim, his forehead, the loudness of his trumpeting almost stunned us, and he pawed the ground, and paced backwards and forward, as if jealously guarding the entrance to some secret lair.

I continued to watch for a good mark for my bullet. To have fired until such an opportunity happened would have been madness ; for had I done so, and missed, the very smoke would have formed a cover under which he would have advanced ; but, oh ! how exciting had the scene now become. Advance we could not, recede we dared not, nay, we would not. Had we advanced we should have entangled our limbs in the tall grass, and so have found all quick movements impossible ; while if we had retreated, most assuredly the brute would have followed and overtaken us. For ten minutes we stood thus, watching each other, when suddenly the rogue, as if resolved to settle the transaction, and so get it off his mind, gave a fearful scream, threw his trunk in the air, so as to guard his forehead, and charged upon us. I had now no alternative. Bang went my piece full in his face, and he fell.

"Hurrah! it is all over with him," I cried, about to rush forward, but Fos caught my arm. It was well that he did, for almost simultaneously the great brute, who had only fallen forward upon his knees, arose with a loud roar, and thinking, I suppose, that sufficient for the time were the bullets thereof, turned tail and retreated into the thickest part of the jungle.

"Neber get him out more widout tom-toms," said Fos.

And the trackers were evidently of the same opinion; for seeing him retreat, they at once came up with the noisy little instruments, but before using them they went up to the widower, as if to receive his orders. While they spoke, I watched the man. His appearance made me shudder. The sight of his ruthless enemy seemed to have changed him into a being too fearful to look upon; every nerve was quivering with excitement, his eyeballs seemed starting from beneath his forehead, and while his right foot patted the ground, his fingers played nervously with the hilt of a long-bladed hunting-knife; nay, he appeared to be almost too much excited to speak. However, having spoken, the men at once began to beat their tom-toms. Deeming even the noise of these horrible little drums to be insufficient to provoke the beast to come forth once more, he ordered Fos to go a few yards to the right, and fire his rifle as often as possible. Well, for nearly an hour the men beat their tom-toms, Fos fired charge after charge, and the rest of us kept shouting till we had become hoarse; but still no elephant. The suspense was bearable no longer. I ran ahead, and was pushing my way through the tangled grass, when a shout from Fos made me aware that the beast had at length shown himself; nay, he was coming towards us at full charge, his trunk thrown high in the air, his ears cocked, his tail standing above his back as stiff as a poker, and screaming terrifically. I was too near to fire. I jumped aside, and fell in the grass. Fortunately he did not see me; unfortunately, however, for the widower, who blinded by rage at the sight of the monster, he picked him out. A human scream aroused me. I looked, and saw the poor fellow in the elephant's trunk high in the air. Another minute, he would be dashed to the ground, and trodden to death beneath the beast's huge feet. I fired; the bullet hit, but only annoyed him. Luckily, however, for

The enraged Elephant.—Page 305.

the widower, the brute quitted him and made at
once for me; but objecting to his visit, I fired the
other and only loaded barrel; and this time the
ball told, for the brute stopped, stunned and bleeding. My situation, however, was more terrible than
ever, for he now stood between me and the only
exit from the grass. For a few minutes the smoke
might protect me, at least till I had again loaded;
but imagine my horror—my ammunition-pouch had
fallen from my side! Never do I remember such
another moment. I was lost! May, my mother,
my father, Bob, all passed through my mind. I
mentally bade them farewell, and commended my
soul to heaven. Still there was a faint hope; he
might not find me. Alas! how vain such hope.
The smoke cleared away, he rushed towards me.
As a last chance, I lay hidden among the grass at
full length out of his track. But onward he came,
like a horse at full speed, screaming fearfully—
the grass flew to the right, to the left—and slash-
ing his trunk to and fro as if it had been whipcord.
But suddenly he stopped. Oh! that fearful instant. He was near me—he knew it; he was
about to put me to a slower death—to play with
before killing me. No; he had not found—he
was scenting; he was hunting me up, for he was
beating the grass with his trunk, searching. I
heard him close to where I was lying, still as death,
my last chance being that his sense of smell having

L. I. C. X

perhaps been injured, he might not find me.
Hush! hush! for now, as then, I can almost
hear the rustling of the grass as he approached.
Remember, it was seven feet high, and very
dense.   Well, at length I heard him beat the
grass above me with his trunk; I felt his breath,
and I held my own, shutting my eyes, expecting
every moment to be my last; but then I heard
the trampling of feet, the voices, the welcome
voices of Bob and May.   Crack went a rifle!
It must have hit the brute upon the spine; for
turning from me, he swung round rapidly, but
as he attempted to go forward, he screamed
aud tottered upon his legs.   Then I heard Bob
cry—

"Hurrah! my little Diana; that shot was
worth all the great guns in the ship."

Then came another sharp crack, and the unwieldy monster rolled over, dead.   But what were
my sensations at this sudden release from what
had appeared certain death?   I cannot describe
them.   It was not joy; no, but a kind of numb-
ness of the senses, a stupefaction that caused me
to stand gazing at my dead enemy as if under
some terrible fascination, from which, however,
I was aroused by the rough, manly voice of Bob,
who forcing his way through the grass, grasped
me by both hands, crying—

"God bless, you, Master Tom! you have had

a narrow escape; but," he added, as May followed,
" see your preserver."

" I know it," I replied, holding out my arms;
but I could say no more then, nor May either.
Her heart, large as it was, was too full. She
rested her head upon my shoulder, and Diana
changing into the affectionate sister, sobbed with
joy, gratitude, till her choking sensations being
relieved by tears, she exclaimed—

" Heaven be thanked ! you are not hurt."

" May," I said, solemnly, " you know not from
how fearful a death you have saved me." But placing
her hands upon my shoulders, and looking me full
in the face, she said—

" Tom, dear Tom, this is impiety; for the praise
is due to Him alone who at such a terrible
moment gave boldness to the heart, and nerve to
the hand of a poor weak girl."

" True, true, dear May, thou art right; still,
after Heaven, can I never forget to whom in this
world I am indebted for my life."

" But this is waste of time; it is cruel, it
is selfish; for even now the poor fellow first
attacked may be in the agonies of death," she
said : adding, " Come, come; let us search him
out."

" Aye, aye, May; I should have thought of
that."

But at that moment Fos came running through

x 2

the grass, and seeing me alive and unhurt he gave a leap, crying—

"Golly, golly! *Namo Bud-dhaya!* Golly, golly! Massa Excellency Tom not killed?"

"No, no, Fos; not this time," said I. "But the poor fellow, the widower?"

"Not dead, but berry bad; got 'um bones cracked," replied the boy, pointing to a spot a few yards from us.

We found the poor fellow lying upon the grass in the midst of his men, but unable to move, and groaning with pain.

"Tell these fellows to take him to the village at once," said I.

But perceiving me alive and unhurt, he compressed his lips together, as if endeavouring to subdue his agony, and asked Fos some question, the answer to which seemed to afford him so much delight that I desired to know what it was that had so pleased him.

"'Um so glad Excellency killed de rogue, dat 'um die happy; but say, s'pose do lib eber so long, 'um be slave to Excellency for eber and eber," said Fos.

Then hearing the wounded fellow mutter a few words and make some signs to his men, I desired to know what troubled him.

"'Um got somting to talkee, so 'um send men's ears away," said Fos, going close to the man, who

then and there began what seemed an address, for
it was delivered so earnestly ; but to my surprise,
every now and then Fos shook his fist in the poor
fellow's face.

" Why, what on airth are you at, you rascal?
Would you threaten a wounded man ?" said Bob.

" Golly, golly ! but 'um berry bad, Excellency.
Listen," replied the boy. But as the reader may
not so well comprehend the story if told in the
boy's broken English, I will relate it to him in
our own vernacular, leaving him to guess our
astonishment when we heard that when the
widower, who so earnestly desired the destruction
of the rogue, applied for permission to accompany
us, the headman granted it conditionally that he
would find some opportunity, while in the jungle,
to destroy both Bob and I.

" The rascally pirate !" exclaimed Bob.

" Did I not tell you there was danger of
treachery from this man ?" said May.

" The ungrateful villain !   But why does he
wish our death ?" said I.

And Fos told us the headman had further
desired that when the widower had slain us, he
should by force take May back to the village, that
he might send her to Kandy, or keep her himself
as a slave.   All of which the man had promised ;
but hearing we had slain the destroyer of his wife,
and, moreover, believing himself to be dying, he

had disclosed the plot, in order that we might now take any other road but the return path to the village.

"Oh! thou mahogany-faced, ebony-hearted land-shark!" said Bob, shaking his fist in the man's face.

"For shame, Bob! the poor fellow is dying," said May.

"Moreover, he repents, and has to a great extent repaired his error," said I: adding, "But ask him, Fos, if these fellows of his know of this plot."

"'Um say no, Massa Tom, and dat wont tell; so Excellency better tell men take 'um back to village, and tell 'um too, dat Excellency, Massa Bob, Missee May, and Fos come by-by," said the boy: adding, "Fos tink Excellency, Massa Bob, Missee, and Fos self better go away berry soon, 'cos debel headman will more wantee kill now rogue dead; 'cos he tell king 'um kill it 'umself, and so get reward."

"And it is my opinion, young scaramouch, that what you tink we all tink," replied Bob, mimicking the boy.

"And Fos tink, too," added the now justly irritated boy, "dat Massa Bob Bosen make berry good monkey, but 'um too old."

"Come, come, Bob, let the boy alone; you deserve the retort," said I, catching hold of the old sailor's arm just as he was about cuffing his ears.

"Bless my heart, so I do," replied Bob, good humouredly; adding, "Lord love you, Master Tom, I was only going to frighten the lad, by way of teaching him discipline. But, d'ye see, the sooner we begin our cruise the better."

And being myself of the same opinion, we assisted May upon the horse, from which she had descended in her anxiety to assist me, took farewell of the poor wounded fellow, and made way for the cool shade of the forest, where we pitched our tents; and having agreed to start very early the following morning, for fear of being pursued to that spot by the headman, we threw ourselves upon our mats to sleep.

To sleep, I said. Yes. But not for long; for during the night I was awakened by what I then thought the most terrible hurricane I had ever seen, heard, and felt. The lightning played among the trees with fearful vividness, and the thunder rolled in from the distant seas, till culminating, as it were, upon that spot, it burst with a sound, a violence that seemed to shake the earth to its centre. That explosion, however, was the herald of joy and happiness to many millions, for it ushered in the monsoon, which for many days had been threatening. The description, however, of the bursting forth of the monsoon in Ceylon, with all its attendant phenomena, is worthy of an abler pen than mine. Listen, therefore, to the words of Sir J. Tennent, who writes—

"It is difficult for any one who has not resided in the tropics to comprehend the feeling of enjoyment which accompanies these periodical commotions of the atmosphere. In Europe they would be fraught with annoyance; but in Ceylon they are welcomed with a relish proportionate to the monotony they dispel.

"Long before the wished-for period arrives, the verdure produced by the previous rains becomes almost obliterated by the burning droughts of March and April. The deciduous trees shed their foliage, the plants cease to put forth fresh leaves, and all vegetable life languishes under the unwholesome heat. The grass withers on the baked and cloven earth, and red dust settles on the branches and thirsty brushwood. The insects, deprived of their accustomed food, disappear underground, or hide beneath the decaying bark; the water-beetles bury themselves in the hardened mud of the pools; and the *helices* retire into the crevices of the stones, or the hollows amongst the roots of the trees, closing the apertures of their shells with the hybernating epiphragm. Butterflies are no longer seen hovering over the flowers, the birds appear fewer and less joyous, and the wild animals and crocodiles, driven by the drought from their accustomed retreats, wander through the jungle, and even--venture to approach the village wells in search of water. Man equally languishes under the general exhaustion, ordinary exertion becomes distasteful, and the native Sin- ghalese, although inured to the climate, move with lassitude and reluctance.

" Meanwhile, the air becomes loaded to satura- tion with aqueous vapour drawn up by the augmented force of evaporation acting vigorously over land and sea. The sky, instead of its bril- liant blue, assumes the sullen tint of lead, and not a breath disturbs the motionless rest of the clouds that hang on the lower range of hills. At length, generally about the middle of the month, but frequently earlier, the sultry suspense is broken by the arrival of the wished-for change. The sun has by this time nearly attained his greatest northern declination, and created a torrid heat throughout the lands of Southern Asia and the peninsula of India. The air, lightened by its high temperature and such watery vapour as it may contain, rises into loftier regions, and is re- placed by indraughts from the neighbouring sea, and thus a tendency is gradually given to the formation of a current bringing up from the south the warm humid air of the equator. The wind therefore which reaches Ceylon comes laden with moisture taken up in its passage across the great Indian Ocean. As the monsoon draws near, the days become more overcast and hot, banks of clouds rise over the ocean to the west; and in the peculiar twilight the eye is attracted by the unusual whiteness of the sea-birds that sweep along the strand to seize the objects flung on shore by the rising surf.

"At last the sudden lightnings flash among the hills and sheet through the clouds that overhang the sea, and with a crash of thunder the monsoon bursts over the thirsty land, not in showers or partial torrents, but in a wide deluge, that in the course of a few hours overtops the river-banks and spreads in inundations over every level plain.

"All the phenomena of this explosion are stupendous. Thunder, as we are accustomed to be awed by it in Europe, affords but the faintest idea of its overpowering grandeur in Ceylon, and its sublimity is infinitely increased as it is faintly heard from the shore resounding through night and darkness over the gloomy sea. The lightning, when it touches the earth where it is covered with the descending torrent, flashes into it and disappears instantaneously; but when it strikes a drier surface, in seeking better conductors, it often opens a hollow like that formed by the explosion of a shell, and frequently leaves behind it traces of vitrification. In Ceylon, however, occurrences of this kind are rare, and accidents a e seldom recorded from lightning, probably owing to the profusion of trees, and especially of cocoa-nut palms, which, when drenched with rain, intercept the discharge and conduct the electric matter to the earth. The rain at these periods excites the astonishment of a European. It descends in almost continuous streams, so close and so dense that the level ground, unable to absorb it sufficiently fast, is covered with one uniform sheet of water, and down the sides of acclivities it rushes in a volume that wears channels in the surface. For hours together, the noise of the torrent as it beats upon the trees and bursts upon the roofs, flowing thence in rivulets along the ground, occasions an uproar that drowns the ordinary voice, and renders sleep impossible.

"This violence, however, seldom lasts more than an hour or two, and gradually abates after intermittent paroxysms, and a serenely clear sky supervenes. For some days heavy showers continue to fall at intervals in the forenoon, and the evenings which follow are embellished by sunsets of the most gorgeous splendour, lighting the fragments of cloud that survive the recent storm.

" So instantaneous is the response of nature to the influence of returning moisture, that in a single day, and almost between sunset and dawn, the green hue of reviving vegetation begins to

tint the saturated ground.   In ponds from which
but a week before the wind blew clouds of sandy
dust, the peasantry are now to be seen catching
the reanimated fish, and tank-shells and water-
beetles revive and wander over the submerged
sedges.   The electricity of the air stimulates the
vegetation of the trees, and scarce a week will
elapse till the plants are covered with the larvæ
of butterflies, the forest murmuring with the hum
of insects, and the air harmonious with the voice
of birds."

CHAPTER XVII.

BOB MEETS SOME QUEER FISH, AND GETS INTO HOT
WATER, AND FOS MEETS WITH A RELATION.

ALTHOUGH the monsoon had expended its greatest
fury at its outbursting during the night, so frequent and heavy were the showers the next day,
that we were compelled to postpone our departure
till the succeeding morning; then, however, we
were so anxious to get away, for fear of being
pursued by the followers of the treacherous headman, that notwithstanding a drizzling rain, we
broke up our encampment, and again set forth—
but for where? Well, where chance alone might
direct; for as that part of the island was strange
to Fos, our guide, we were literally lost in the
woods and the wilds. In our perplexity as to
which point of the compass to direct our steps,
the boy said—

" Now rain falls fish come out, and many people
come catch 'um; so we not long 'fore meet people
to tell Excellency where find Kandy."

" That head o' yourn's too good for a mahogany
nigger; it's good enough for a Christian," said
Bob.

" Aye, aye," said I at once, to prevent an angry reply from Fos at being called a nigger. " So it matters but little which path we take; for doubtlessly we shall not be long without meeting some of the natives."

And so we penetrated through the jungle, till in about an hour we came upon a clearing, and by some groves of cocoa-trees in the distance, could tell that we were not far from a village; nay, I believe I could see the smoke arising from the huts; but, oh! how different, how delightful, by comparison with our previous journey, was this one. No burning sun or ground cracking with heat, and painful to the feet. The air was cool, deliciously refreshing. The earth, lately consuming to its last gasp, seemed moved; nay, called back to life, and was now swarming with fish. Never did I before or since see such multitudinous swarms of the finny creatures. The land had been deluged, every crack and cranny was full of water; and in these hollows—whether ponds, ditches, or little rucks—were alive with fish.

How singular, how wonderful, the phenomenon: full-grown fish alive, swimming, gambolling in places which, but a couple of days previously, had been encrusted with hardened clay. What would have been the astonishment, the surmises of the king, who wondered " how the apples got into the dumplings," at such a phenomenon. Yet Mr.

Yarrell, in his *History of British Fishes*, adverting to this phenomenon, gives it as his opinion that the eggs of the fish of one rainy season being left unhatched in the mud through the dry season, the vitality is preserved till the recurrence and contact of the rain and oxygen in the next wet season, when vivification takes place from their joint influence. This is the solution offered by one learned naturalist ; another, however, after combating it, and showing the improbability of such a theory, says :—

" Even admitting the soundness of Mr. Yarrell's theory, and the probability that, under favourable circumstances, the spawn in the tanks might be preserved during the dry season, so as to contribute to the perpetuation of their inhabitants, the fact is no longer doubtful that adult fish in Ceylon, like some of those that inhabit similar waters both in the New and Old World, have been endowed by the Creator with the singular faculty of providing against the periodical drought, either by *journeying overland* in search of still unexhausted water, or, on its utter disappearance, by burying themselves in the mud, to await the return of the rains."

" Now, look you, Master Tom, I believe these fishes must grow out of the mud, as mushrooms do in Old England, for otherways I don't see exactly how they could have got here," said the astonished Bob, as we stopped by the side of a small bubbling spring in which were gambolling some hundreds of fish.

" S'pose, Massa Bob Bosen try catchee some for eat," said Fos, defiantly, as if doubting the old sailor's ability to catch them.

" What! you mahogany lubber, d'ye think I can't ?" said Bob.

" S'pose 'um put hand in and try," was the reply.

" Aye, aye," said Bob; and in another instant he was upon his knees. No sooner, however, did he put his hand in the water than, pulling it out again and shaking it, much after the fashion of a cat its paws after stepping in water, he exclaimed, " Why, hang me if these fish aint a-boiling and a-growing at the same time !"

" Ho ! ho ! hi ! hi !" uttered Fos, laughing.

" Why, you young imp ! I believe you've been and done something to this here water."

" Bob, Bob, are you mad ?" said I, laughing at the way in which he continued to shake his hand.

" Now, look you, Master Tom, this aint to be laughed at, for the skin's coming off," said he, showing me his hand, when it was my turn to feel surprised; for the hand and fingers were as red as if they have been dipped in hot water.

" Aye, aye, Master Tom; you *may* look asto-

nished, for there is more in this here than is
nat'ral, and the sooner we steer out of a country
where even the fishes seem to be oh such good
terms with a certain personage that they can swim
about, quite happy and comfortable-like, in boiling water, why the better it'll be for us, maybe,"
said Bob, who although he had exaggerated by
stating the water to be at boiling heat, I found
it of about 115 degrees; which was sufficiently
wonderful, when you consider that the fish were
disporting in water at a temperature of at least
fifteen degrees higher than you could comfortably
bear a hot bath in this country. That, however, you
may not think I am now exaggerating, I must tell
you that it is not in Ceylon alone that fishes are
found alive in hot springs, for in Manilla they have
been discovered in water which raised the thermo-
meter to 187 degrees; again, in Bombay; while
Humboldt, when travelling in South America, saw
fishes thrown up alive from a volcano in water that
raised the temperature to 210 degrees—which, by
the way, is only two degrees beneath boiling-
point.

About an hour after Bob's adventure with the
fish, we came to the bend of a wide river, and
where, as Fos had promised, we saw a number of
men engaged catching fish, but by a process so
singular that we stopped to watch the movements
of one within a yard or two from us.

This man held in his hands a basket shaped like a funnel, but without either top or bottom. With this he waded through the shallow water, watching very intently, till seeing a shoal passing, down went the basket at once, securing some twenty or thirty fishes, which one by one he took out, and strung upon a string fastened round his waist. As, however, we were looking on, Fos startled us by running into the river, and hugging the fisher.

"Hilloa! what does the young lunatic mean by that?" said Bob.

"They are relations or friends. Do you not see they are embracing each other?" replied May.

And she was correct; for having held a short conversation, the boy, dragging the man out of the water and bringing him up to me, said—

"Excellency not lost now, 'cos know where 'um am. Dis place Bintenne; dis man Fos's moder's broder, what Excellency call uncle;" and almost in the same breath he added, "Moder's broder good man; will take all to village and give 'um half 'um house." Whereupon, looking upon this offer as very fortunate and opportune, and believing that half a house was better than none, we followed Fos and his uncle to the latter's residence, which, by the way, being one of the largest in the village, led us to believe that its owner was well to do in the world—that is, for his own part of it. And so it proved; for having first directed

Fos to take our horse and baggage into an out-building at the back, he led us into a large apartment, where shortly afterwards he set before us a large dish of lola—*i.e.*, a fish in appearance something between a trout and a carp, but delicious eating.

While we were pleasantly engaged in satisfying our appetites, Fos and his uncle were busily occupied conversing. When, however, we had concluded the meal, the boy told us he had been relating our adventures in Ceylon, but particularly the treachery of the headman, whom his relative said, was not only a bad man, but a great enemy of his own. Moreover, so pleased was our host that we had outwitted the knave, and so delighted at meeting again with his nephew, whom he had not seen for years, that the next day he would lend us a whole house instead of a half one, and that we might live in it as long as we pleased.

" But, Fos," said I, " tell thy worthy relative that although very grateful for his kindness, he will better serve us by helping us to reach Kandy with all possible speed."

" Did tell 'um, Excellency ; but say no good go Kandy; must not go, 'cos just come from Kandy 'umself, and know it bad to go dere."

"Just come from Kandy!" I repeated, anxiously; adding, " Does he, then, know aught of my father ?"

" Ess, Massa Tom ; dat is not ob Captain 'um-self, but say dat in Kandy dere many prisoners, Dutch, Portuguese, and oder white men."

" Then tell him that my father is among those prisoners, and we will not waste one day by remaining here."

" When one fish get in net, oder fish not get 'um out by getting in too," replied Fos.

" Bravo ! boy ; not a bad answer. That ma-hogany head o' yours is older than your legs by many years," said Bob. But the boy, noticing this only by an indignant look, added—

" S'pose Excellency want get fader 'way from Kandy, 'um stop here till find man go to Kandy, and tell Captain how to come away, and find son here living in house just like native, so nobody know 'um ;" and as there was really no resisting such an argument, it was arranged that we should the next day take up our abode in the offered house, and there remain till a trustworthy mes-senger could be found to perform the mission to my father, who watching his opportunity to escape, should, under his guidance, come direct to the village. So far so good. But for that night our host brought his sleeping-mat into the room appropriated to our use, and May was lodged with his wife and daughter in the other apartment or half of the house.

Delighted as I was at the mere possibility of

again meeting my father, nay, of rescuing him, I
could not sleep that night for thinking of the
indefinite period we might have to remain in that
village, and consequently the great burden that
the keeping of so many of us must be to our host.
The next morning, however, when we were all
assembled together, and I had explained this
difficulty, Fos said—

"If no like lib and do noting, s'pose Excellency
and Massa Bob go help fish, so catchee own food;
den while Excellency and Massa Bob Bosen go
fish, Fos stay here makee caps for head."

"Make what?" I asked, with surprise.

And the boy explained that his uncle and his
wife knitted caps for sale as one of their means
of existence.

"That will do; and a capital arrangement,
too," said I.

"And I," said May, "will help Fos to make
caps; and so we shall be all earning our living."

"And mayhap we shall make a fortin' out of
our airnings," replied Bob, laughing.

However, not caring for the old sailor's banter,
it was so arranged, and we were to begin the
next day. But we had "calculated without our
host;" for the following morning Bob, who had
been out of the house, returned, saying—

"The place is full of shaven-pated niggers."

"It am all de eye festival; last seven days," said Fos.

"All my eye festival? Do you mean that for impertinence, you young imp?" said Bob.

Fos did not mean to be impertinent. What, however, he did mean, I will tell you. But first —the shaven-pated individuals who had astonished Bob were priests. Of these there are vast numbers in Ceylon. Their dress consists of a yellow robe or cloth wrapped round their loins, and reaching down to their feet, and another yellow robe, several yards long, thrown over their left shoulder, which both before and behind reaches to the ground. They never wear stockings or shoes, seldom even sandals. Their heads are considered so sacred that no barber is allowed to shave them, that operation being performed by themselves upon each other.

They live by mendicity, though there are in almost all parts of the island lands belonging to the Wiharas (temples), which have in former times been left by the piety of individuals, or apportioned to them by the Singhalese kings. Every morning at daylight these priests take their dish, and, covering it with a piece of white cloth, go about from house to house through the village where they reside, to beg rice. They are seldom sent away empty-handed, for however poor the inhabitants may be, they generally in the course of the day put aside a little rice or fruit or money for the priest the next time he comes. It is considered a great sin to apply any of the rice thus consecrated to their own use. In towns, it is usual to see six or seven, or even more, of the priests thus begging from door to door. As soon as anything is put into their dish, the giver stands with hands placed together, in the attitude of worship, and receives the benediction of the priest, which benediction is generally an assurance to the donor of some good in a future state or birth as a recompence for the highly meritorious act that he performs in feeding the priests.

In the time of Was—that is, season of festivals —which, by the way, lasts three months, the priests leave their temples and live among the people in pansalas (*i.e.*, priests' houses) raised for them near a temporary building called the Bana Madama, and which is used by them in which to read the sacred book of Buddha.

During Was, or festival time, they employ themselves in teaching the children, for which they get no special pay, it being considered sufficient that they are altogether supported by the people and live upon the fat of the land. Now, as many festivals take place during Was, it is a time of great excitement among the people, who, as it arrives at a season of the year when they have not much to do in the fields—or even if they work in the days, they are at liberty in the evenings and nights, which they spend together, with their wives and children, in the Bana Madama (the temporary erection before named), listening to the reading of the priests; but to prevent the congregation from indulging in a natural inclination to sleep, instead of listening to what they cannot understand, at intervals men beat upon tom-toms.

Very holy are these priests in the eyes of the natives; and that they are held so sacred is a symptom that their hearts are not like those of the Chinese, quite steeled by egotistic materialism, and so sealed against the doctrines of Christianity which so many good and pious missionaries are even now toiling to plant in their bosoms. Yes, so sacred are these Buddhist priests held among this simple people, that whenever one, writes the Rev. James Selkirk, goes from his temple, or when he leaves it to keep Was, he is attended by one or more servants, who carry the Bana-book carefully wrapped up in a piece of white cloth on their shoulders, together with their clothes, umbrellas, or talipats. The priest has a small circular fan in his hand, which he must, according to the precepts of his religion, hold before him, so near his face that he cannot see more than "a bullock's length" of the road in which he is going. Moreover, a priest never bows to any person, considering himself superior to all human beings; and if a person stops to talk to one of them, he must stand with his hands together, held up close to his mouth, and speak in a whisper.

How truly different is the treatment of these mendicant priests of Buddha in materialistic, nay, atheistic China, where they are regarded as rogues and vagabonds.

Thus of the priests; of their temples I will only say that they are middling-sized buildings, with two apartments without windows, but on the walls of which are painted numberless gods and devils in red, yellow, and blue. The chief object, however, is a large figure of Buddha, before which stands an altar for the reception of oil and offerings. When families proceed in regular procession with their offerings, each person must hold the gift upon his head, and, both entering and leaving the temple, go straightways, neither looking to the right nor to the left, but keeping his face directed towards the image.

Now, the festival to which Fos alluded, and which lasted seven days, was the "Netra Pincama, or the Festival of the Eye," that is, painting of eyes in some twenty-four images about to be dedicated to their gods. It was a compound of piety and mountebankism. There were religious

services, but there were also processions, beatings
of tom-toms and other noisy instruments, wooden
figures of men upon horseback, figures of elephants,
people with offerings of oil and flowers and money;
then there were sweetmeat booths, dancing, singing, shouting, incessant tom-tom beating—in fact,
all the noise, bustle, and din of a fair, rather than
the dignified solemnity of a religious festival. So
we were heartily glad when the great discharge of
fireworks announced that *that* festival was over.

CHAPTER XVIII.

WE WITNESS SOME STRANGE DOCTORING, AND HAVE
A DAY'S SPORT AMONG THE FISHERMEN AND
CROCODILES.

ONE good resulted to us from the festival, for
among the musicians who had attended was one,
a near relation of our host, who had come from,
and was speedily to return to, Kandy. Well, from
this man we learned that some time before he had
quitted the capital, another white prisoner had
been brought to the King, who held him in a kind
of honourable durance—that is, although his
Majesty had watch and ward kept over him, he
allowed him a house and every other personal comfort but liberty.

Now, as from many inquiries made through Fos,
we had no remaining doubt that this prisoner was
my father, our minds became at ease—nay,
filled with hope and joy ; for the musician agreed
to find an opportunity of conveying to my father
a letter, in which I not only told him that we
were all well, but awaiting him at the village.
As, however, we knew not how long it might be
before my father could find an opportunity of

escape, we resolved to perform our self-assumed duties after the best of our abilities : May and Fos at their cap-knitting, Bob and I at fishing.

The day following the conclusion of the festival our messenger left for the capital, and we took up our quarters in the house appointed by our host, which, by the way, was a pretty little dwelling-hut, consisting of three apartments, and surrounded by a garden of trees, the chief of which were cocoas, tamarinds, and mangoes. Well, the day succeeding that upon which we moved, we had agreed—*i.e.*, Bob and I—to go with our host to the river ; but, alas ! in the morning he came, and with a woful face told us, through Fos, that during the night his wife had been seized with a severe illness.

" Poor woman ! But what is the matter with her ?" I asked.

" 'Um berry bad : got one, two, tree debils come to her ; and 'um going to fetch priest to drive 'um away," replied Fos.

" Now, look you, youngster, this is not a joking matter," said Bob, seriously indignant.

" Fos not joke, none at all. Massa Bosen can go see debil frightend away, and uncle's wife made well, if 'um like," replied the boy.

And so great was our curiosity to witness that common but still very remarkable ceremony that we accepted the invitation.

Near the house in which the patient resided were erected three enclosures of sticks, covered with white cloths and decorated with leaves of the cocoa-palm and flowers of the areka. Within each of these enclosures stood a small altar covered with plantain leaf, and having beneath it a dish of burning coals.

The priest wore a white cloth round his waist, a woman's jacket upon his back, a turban upon his head, and a number of small bells around his legs. This worthy personage having commenced the ceremony by placing offerings of sandal-wood and flowers upon the altar, which he sprinkled with consecrated water, muttered some cabalistic words of invocation while he slowly strewed powdered resin upon the burning coals. After this he took from the hand of an attendant a lighted torch, and for some time sang and danced as if frantic. This performance being concluded, the people presented him with a stick, to one end of which was tied a small bag of paddy, and at the other a cocoa-nut, and which he offered to the gods in the name of the sick person.

Then boiled rice and a curry made of seven different vegetables, sauce, fish, meat, and dried seeds, being placed upon the altar, the priest repeated more cabalistic words, and danced and sang as before. After this he fastened twelve small lighted torches (each intended to represent a god) to a piece of plantain-tree, which he again secured to a long pole fixed in the ground. Then, by the light of the torches having warmed three betel-leaves, he threw them thrice into the air, in the belief that if they fell on the glossy side it was a good omen, but if upon the reverse a bad one. After each throw, however, he went with the leaves to the sick person, and having declared that the illness would entirely leave, received a piece of money. The throwing being over, he put on a blue jacket, a lighted torch in each hand, painted his face, and began to dance more frantically than ever. Then, again, a mat was spread on the ground, upon which, with a torch in his mouth, lighted now at both ends, he laid down and put himself into different postures, after which, still remaining on his back, he threw powdered resin upon the lighted ends of the torch, believing, or pretending to believe, that, according to the direction the smoke took in ascending, he could decide from what quarter the devil came that was afflicting the sick person. Then again he took another handful of powdered resin, and having repeated several more charms, put it on live coals, and allowed the smoke to come in his face; then in a few minutes he began to stagger and run about the place as if mad; and when he came out again he was seized by two persons, who said to him, "We pray the gods to declare through this man what is the cause of this person's sickness, and by what means it may be cured." When thus asked, the priest said that such and such devils had occasioned the illness, and that it might be cured by such and such offerings and ceremonials. And thus ended this most miserable mockery of religion, and which has its origin in devil worship.

I must, however, tell you that the devil is regularly, systematically, and ceremoniously worshipped by a large majority of the native inhabitants of the island of Ceylon. Buddhism condemns and prohibits the worship of devils; but its principles make way for the introduction of this species of satanic adoration. Wherever Buddhism has been established, the inhabitants are left under the uncontrolled dominion of the devil. The writings of Buddha, which deny the existence of God, everywhere abound with accounts of the devil. In all the various transmigrations of Buddha, which amount to five hundred and fifty, the existence of the devil is recognised, and Buddha meets him at every turn. Under the chief is a succession of subordinate devils, of different sizes, dispositions, and colours, who all have to do with human affairs, all things in the world being under their control. They are all evil, exercising a most malicious influence over mankind, and the natives are under continual dread of them. Particular trees are supposed to be full of these devils, so that the natives are afraid to pass under them. This system of devil-worship has its priests and round of established ceremonies. To avoid the malignant interference of the devil in their concerns, they propitiate him by various offerings.

The Yakanduras (performers of devil cere-monies) are supposed to carry on continual inter-course with the evil one. They generally perform their ceremonies by night; and so deluded are the poor natives, that children at their birth are dedi-cated to him, or to one of these infernal beings. In hundreds of instances they are so anxious to place themselves and all they have under the care of the devil, that their children are dedicated to him before they are born. Now, can you fancy anything more shocking?

Terrible, however, as to my mind was this abject ignorance of the priests and people, a more hateful restorative ceremony is performed over the sick by the native astrologers or doctors, and which has thus been described by a worthy missionary who witnessed it. In the performance of his duties he visited a sick man, "when," says he, " I found the astrologer there who had been sent for by the sick man's relations, and who was beginning to make a large image of clay on a framework of bamboo. The next evening I found it completed, with four others, one of which was directly underneath, as if supporting the image first mentioned, and two of smaller size, one on each side. These were painted yellow, red, and black, and one of them had an immense tusk on each side of its mouth. The frame of bamboos which supported these figures was raised nearly perpendicular in a small cajan shed erected near the house. The intention of this was for a ceremony to be performed by the astrologer to see whether the stars under which the sick man was born were lucky or unlucky. On the night of the ceremony I went to see it. It commenced at nine o'clock, and would continue till sunrise next morning. The sick man was brought out of the house, and laid about two yards in front of the images, and was a long time supported by his wife. When she was tired, he was laid on his mat, with a pillow under his head. The ceremony then commenced, the astrologer repeating verses from some astrological books, in such high language that I could only understand a word here and there, and dancing to the sound of the tom-tom, which was beaten by the assistant. Half an hour after, a cocoa-nut which the astrologer had held all the time in his hand was put to the feet of the sick man; another half hour was spent in repeating verses and beating the tom-tom, then a piece of string, fastened to the head of the highest image

on the frame, descended over the whole length of
the body of the one underneath, and was put into
the sick man's hand. After a repetition of the
same verses, the man who had hitherto beaten the
tom-tom began to dance."

The worthy missionary, however, does not tell
us whether the patient lived or died. Of the
operators, however, he does say, " I know not a
more unconscionable and hardhearted set of men
than the Singhalese native doctors, most of whom
are also astrologers. When they are sent for to
a sick man, they generally say to the friends who
are near, " If you will give me so many rix-dollars
{a rix-dollar is eighteenpence) I will cure the sick
man." A promise is then made to him, and if
in a few days, when he has received half the sum
promised, any change for the worse takes place,
he then says, " This disease is of such a nature
that I shall not be able to cure it unless I receive
so much more money for medicines, and so much
for attendance." They are then obliged to promise a larger sum than the former, and I believe
it is a common thing for a native doctor to give
medicine which he knows will make the patient
worse, in order to extort from his ignorant
countrymen more money.

Now, as in spite of this (for her health) really
dangerous devil ceremony the wife recovered, our
host lost no time in resuming his business of

fishing; and in consequence of the recent rains, the river was full unto overflowing, whereby he anticipated a great draught. Upon the evening of her amendment in health he set out, attended by several of his men, and accompanied by Bob and me, for the purpose of planting the coral, an operation which answers the same purpose as the setting of nets of European fishermen. These " corals " are ingeniously constructed in the bed of the river, of strong stakes, protected by screens of rattan, which stretch diagonally across the river, so forming a series of enclosures of the shape of arrow-heads, into which the fish once swimming cannot easily escape.

Well, the following morning the party had nearly completed this arrangement for commencing their business. There was but one man in the river, and he was engaged securing the stakes, while his mates, having finished their portion of the labour, stood upon the banks waiting for him, when suddenly the lookers-on gave a shout of horror. The man in the water seemed to know its meaning, for instantaneously letting go his hold upon the stakes, he uttered one loud shriek, darted forward, and struck out for the shore; but, alas! when within but a couple of yards of his companions he sank to rise no more. He had been drawn under by a crocodile. The men upon the bank shouted, gesticulated; but as no earthly

z 2

power could aid the poor fellow, with threats of future vengeance they prepared to return to the village. Their sorrow for the fate of their companion was not unmixed with joy at their own escape: but a few minutes earlier, and either might have shared or anticipated his doom, for they had all of them been in the water. But however sudden and terrible was the man's fate, such events were of too common occurrence to make a very deep impression upon their minds. With Bob and me it was different. We stood in speechless horror lamenting the catastrophe, but regretful, angry that we had left our rifles behind; for at least, we thought, we might perchance have revenged the man's death.

"Only to think," said Bob, as we were returning to the village, " of coming to such an end, and in sight of so many people. Only to think we should have been such lubbers as to have come out at all in this onchristian land of savages and wild beasts without our pop-guns."

"Why, Bob, what would have been the use of our rifles?" But he made no answer, and I continued—"It was God's will the poor fellow should die by the teeth of that monster. But look you, Bob, I am resolved to watch for the brute to-morrow, and revenge this man's death."

" Give me your fist on it, give me your fist on it, Master Tom," he replied, shaking my hand ;

adding, "And it's hard if by this time to-morrow we don't give a good account of the scaly varmint."

When we returned to the village, we took our host to our own house, and then, when he and Fos had held a long conversation, the boy said, shaking his head—

" Berry drefful, berry drefful ! and uncle much sorry for poor fellow; berry good man, berry good fisher."

" Tell him that to-morrow his death shall be revenged, and the monster prevented from doing further mischief, if we are likely to entice him near shore," said I ; and the boy having imparted this to his uncle, the latter replied, with sparkling eyes.

" What says he, Fos?" I asked.

" Say crocodile sure come same place, and if Excellency kille 'um, all people, all village lub 'um and make big gifts; for must be de same crocodile kille gal last year."

Then, when Fos had reassured his uncle that we would accompany him in the morning with our rifles, he took his departure rejoicing.

At supper-time that evening, Fos repeated to us an account his uncle had related to him of the death of a girl by a crocodile. It was to the following effect.

The year before a number of women were engaged about mid-deep in the river cutting rushes, when suddenly the horny tail of a crocodile was seen above the water among them, and in another instant one of them was seized by the leg, and dragged into the deep of the stream. In vain the terrified creature shrieked for assistance; the horror-stricken group had rushed to the shore, and a crowd of spectators on the bank offered no aid beyond their cries. It was some distance before the water deepened, and the unfortunate creature was dragged for many yards, sometimes beneath the water, sometimes above the surface, rending the air with her screams, until at length the deep water hid her from their view.

The crocodiles which inhabit the rivers near the sea are of a far different kind from those found in the tanks. Of the more savage vermin, Mr. Baker, a great hunter in Ceylon, and who relates a story very similar to the foregoing, says some grow to a very large size, attaining the length of twenty feet, and eight feet in girth, but the common length is fourteen feet. They move slowly upon land, but are wonderfully fast and active in the water. They commonly lie in wait for their prey under some hollow bank in a deep pool; and when the unsuspecting deer, or even buffalo, stoops his head to drink, he is suddenly seized by the nose and dragged beneath the water, when he is speedily drowned, and afterwards consumed at leisure.

" But d'ye believe that the beast as killed the
fisherman is the same as killed that young woman?" said Bob, when Fos had finished his
story.

" 'Ess, Massa Bob, 'ess; 'cos when crocodile
once eat man or woman, tink 'um so nice dat
nebber forget, and always look out for anoder."

" That's civil of 'em, that is. Howsomdever,
we'll just put the two debts in one bill, and pay
'em off to-morrow," said Bob; adding, " But,
d'ye see, it would be as well to start pretty early
in the morning."

" Aye, aye, Bob; and so we will seek our mats
at once," I replied; and May, taking the hint,
retired to her own room; not, however, without
having first exacted a promise from us that we
would avoid getting into any useless danger.

When I awoke in the morning, the faintest tint
of grey streaked the sky. May was not stirring,
all was silent; and as I feared that, if awakened,
the brave girl might insist upon accompanying us,
I gently and quietly, without speaking, awoke Fos
and Bob. Then loading the three rifles, and
taking, moreover, a plentiful supply of ammunition,
we set off for the house of the boy's uncle, where,
finding that worthy and his men in readiness to
start, we made at once for the river. Scarcely,
however, had we reached its banks when Fos
alarmed us by crying out,

"Golly, golly, Massa Tom! 'um debel killee buffaloes."

The boy was right. The villagers had sustained another loss—two of their domestic buffaloes had been slain by the reptiles. The carcasses, which lay in the mud near the bank, presented a ghastly sight, the one being headless, the other half devoured. From the position of the headless carcass, it was evident that the voracious assassins had seized them by the snout while drinking, and drawn them into the water; where, having drowned the animals, they had commenced a gorge, from which in all probability they had only been driven by our arrival; and such being the case, it behoved us to be wary.

Our host's party had brought with them a couple of canoes, but such little trumpery things, they seemed incapable of bearing the weight even of a young monkey. Just imagine a boat so fragile that, although six feet in length, it was but one foot across, and alone secured from capsizing by an outrigger fixed to one side.

"Might as well go to sea in a butter-boat," said Bob.

"Aye, aye: maybe so, Bob; but as it is no time for grumbling, let us launch the craft," I replied. And having set them afloat, we pushed out the buffalo carcass further into the stream, and sat down silently to watch its movements.

After about ten minutes the carcass trembled on the water, bobbed down, and came up again.

" Crocodile just had bite," said Fos.

" Aye, aye. The brute's there, no doubt of it; so let us to the boats." And at once Bob and I got into our respective canoes, each with a native in the stern to steer and paddle, one gun (mine was the double-barrel), a rope, a hunting knife, and an axe. Thus armed and prepared, we pushed off from the shore, leaving there the natives with axes, spears, knives, and ropes, with Fos near them, to watch our movements, rifle in hand, so as in case of necessity and opportunity to assist us with an extra shot.

Bob and I were most perilously situated, for should our boats capsize there would be but a short space between us and the crocodile's jaws. Still, faint heart never earned a laurel; so keeping a dead silence, the steerers dropped their paddles in the water and held them loosely. Thus the canoes floated almost as they would. For nearly an hour we watched anxiously, but nought was to be seen; and our patience was becoming exhausted, when suddenly, at a distance of about one hundred yards, I observed several pieces of rough black wood upon the surface. There were seven, for I counted them; but oh! what a cold shiver ran through my frame as I recognised them to be the foreheads of as many crocodiles.

As action, however, was the best cure for shivering, I at once resolved to get near them. So, telling Bob to keep astern of my boat, and hold his rifle ready for an emergency, I beckoned to my steersman to paddle gently forward. He did so, and I saw that the seven brutes had the half-devoured carcass between them. Still more gently the canoe floated towards them. My hand was upon the trigger, ready to plant a bullet in the first head that ventured above water. A minute—a dread minute, the long snout and shoulders of one reptile projected from the water as he attempted to fix his claws into the flesh.

" Now is the time for a good shot," thought I ; so bang went the rifle, and although the whole seven heads instantly disappeared, one at least must have been told off as invalided and incapable of further mischief, for the water was crimsoned with blood. So far so good ; but remembering the story of the girl and the fate of the fisherman, it was to me but child's play, for I burned with impatience to rid the water of one dread assassin. But where was he? Not far off, certainly, I thought. It was not long after my first shot that, observing the buffalo beef had floated in-shore among the rushes, near the bank, I signified to the steersman to paddle into the shallow. When he had done this I jumped into the water for the

purpose of attaching the beast to the end of my
rope. Well, I had made the noose, and had even
thrown it so dexterously that it had encompassed
the meat; I had now only to draw it tight. This
I was doing when I was disturbed by the sound
of a low, prolonged whistle. I looked towards
Bob's canoe. The old man was bending forward
—that is, as forward as the cockleshell of a boat
would permit without capsizing—rifle in hand,
but with terror upon his face, and his finger
pointed to some object near me. The look, the
finger, evidently signified danger. I turned my
eyes to the spot indicated, when fancy my horror
at seeing projecting from a deep hole close to the
bank, and shaded slightly with rushes, the form
of a huge crocodile! Its eyes were fixed upon me;
and although the snout only was out of the water,
through its transparency I could trace the
reptile's immense length. The monster, I suppose, had been about to seize the buffalo beef
when I jumped out of the boat; but its attention
being diverted by my arrival, it now seemed undecided which morsel, myself or the beef, to
choose. It did not, however, remain long doubtful; for suddenly it ran forward, it had reached
within three yards of where I was standing, and
was between me and the shore. To retreat to
the boat was impossible, as the native, to avoid
any risk of his own safety by my jumping in and

so capsizing the little craft, had paddled it away. To swim across would have been madness, since I knew that there were at least a dozen of the same family in the water. I had but one chance; my one barrel was loaded, the weapon was to my shoulder. I pulled the trigger, but in the excitement, the terror of the moment, mistook my proper line of fire; the bullet whistled over him, ricochetting along the water. The brute saw his advantage; his whole body was now out of the water, and the next instant I should have been between its jaws, had not Bob also seen the advantage he had been waiting for—namely, the animal's exposing more of his head. He fired. It was the most timely shot I ever witnessed, for the monster, crawling back again towards his hole, had no sooner got into deeper water than, giving a convulsive slap with his tail that made the water foam, turned upon his back and sunk into the mud.

"Golly, golly! dat good," exclaimed Fos upon the other bank, jumping up with delight, while the natives by his side gave similar demonstrations of joy.

As for Bob, his fears seemed to have begun when the danger was over, for making his steersman paddle towards my boat, he caught hold of it, pushed it towards me, saying—

"Get in, Master Tom, for Heaven's sake! get

in with all speed; you have had a narrow escape, but get in, get in," he added, impatiently.

"Why, Bob, my friend, you are more scared now the danger's over than this nigger here when he pushed the boat out of my reach."

"Harkye, Master Tom; it's no time for fun—the danger is only begun. There is another and a larger brute about here somewhere—I have seen him."

"Then look you, Bob; just take hold of this while I load again," said I, tossing to him the end of the rope, which still remained around the beef.

Then when we had both loaded again, I took hold of the rope, and we paddled the boats just over the spot where Bob had seen, or fancied he had seen, the last-named crocodile. Well, there we stayed, at a distance of about ten yards from a large belt of rushes which were growing upon the shallow near the shore.

"Now," said I, "just hold your rifle ready, Bob, while I watch the bait."

So saying, I let go the rope, so that the beef could float at will, which it did among the rushes; and as by the time it reached them it had got to the length of its tether, I ordered my native to paddle the boat after it. The man obeyed, but with great reluctance. Well, onward went the beef among the rushes—so slowly, however, that it must have been from the force of the current;

but when it had passed about three yards in among the rushes, I ordered the native to hold fast, and to make sure of him, told Bob, who had followed us, to attach the two boats by a piece of cord, which he did with alacrity, saying—

"Aye, aye, Master Tom; the rascal shall play you no more tricks; but look," he added, suddenly.

I did, and saw the huge piece of carcass roll over as if clutched at by something beneath the water, and the next instant some reeds brushed against the side of our boats. The vibration caused the natives to tremble violently and look wistfully towards the shore.

"Look you; I'll have no tricks aboard this ship," said Bob, taking the paddles out of his steersman's hands, at the same time significantly signalling that his punishment for mutiny might be a cold bath, with a fair chance of a crocodile's jaws.

"The reptile is beneath our very boats," said I; but for nearly ten minutes I rested with my fingers upon the trigger, and my eyes resting upon the beef as fixedly as those of a devoted angler upon his float.

Suddenly it rolled over in the water, as if the crocodile had bitten at it, but missed its bite. In another minute the huge brute, as if to make sure, this time, thrust its head and shoulder above the

water, and snapped off a piece of some pounds'
weight. I fired ; but as the ball went through
its shoulder, I cried out—

" Push the boats astern !"

And well that I did so, for had I not, as the
wounded reptile came immediately beneath where
the boat had been, lashing its tail fearfully, we
should have been capsized.

A minute or two, and we saw the rushes
moving.

" Let us track him, Bob, he is among yon
reeds," said I.

But so alarmed were the natives, that it was
only by pointing our rifles at them we could
persuade the terrified fellows to move a paddle.
Then, however, having but little choice between a
bullet and a crocodile, they obeyed as if resigned
to fate.

Well, the rustling and trembling of the rushes
having ceased, we stood upon our paddles in their
very midst, awaiting the reappearance of the horny
head. Some time elapsed, and Bob, getting impatient, snatched a paddle from his steersman, and
poking with it among the rushes, cried out—

" Let's stir the fellow up."

I should have trembled for the consequences,
but I saw that we were now much nearer the
shore, and so under cover, as it were, of the rifle
of Fos, who was crouching down upon the bank,

with his piece levelled and his sparkling eye gleaming along the line of sight, looking terribly determined, and almost as ferocious as the reptile we were hunting.

Taking courage, therefore, I determined to follow Bob's example, but as I did so, and the paddle grazed (I felt it) against the reptile's scaly back, I must admit to feeling a very curious sensation.

" Pull astern—I can feel him !" I cried.

And scarcely had the men obeyed, when up to the surface came the monster—not to go down again, however, that time, as comfortably as he had come up, but with a present of a ball a-piece from Bob and me.

" Hurrah !" cried Bob.

" Golly, golly; but Massa Bob and Excellency make big generals, for 'um killed crocodile dat killee poor girl, poor man, and many people."

" If it be so, thank heaven ! for our time has not been wasted," I replied.

And at once we pulled for the shore, to the almost frantic delight of the two natives, who, having stayed to wipe the profuse sweat of fear from their foreheads, held their bodies erect and proudly, to receive their share of the plaudits with which their brethren were filling the air. And with reason did these poor people exhibit such frantic joy; for they believed—as, indeed, it afterwards proved—that the crocodile we had just slain was the identical reptile which had been so long their terror.

When these two trembling braves had freshened up their courage, and procured ropes and hooks, they got into their canoes, paddled back to the scene of their late terrors, and having dragged till they had found the body, brought it *to*, not *on*, the shore, for to accomplish the latter feat required the united strength of twenty men. When, however, the unwieldy but now harmless wretch lay stretched before them, the joy of the natives knew no bounds; and axe after axe fell upon its carcass as with savage delight they hewed it into a thousand pieces, all of which, by way of vengeance, they threw into the river again to be devoured by its own species.

As this part of the work was not to our taste, Bob and I, accompanied by Fos, left them at their labour, and returned to the village, much fatigued, but not a little pleased with the result of our toil.

CHAPTER XIX.

WE HEAR NEWS OF MY FATHER, AND SET OUT FOR
KANDY, BUT MEET WITH A WILD MAN ON THE
WAY.

How strange are the freaks of fortune; for
whereas we had arrived in that village not many
days before, strangers and beggars, the adventure
with the crocodiles had now rendered us so popular,
that there was not a soul in the place who did
not honour us with their regard, and what was more
substantial, some present, each according to his
means—some, small articles of jewellery, hunting
knives on spears, others fine cloths, but the greater
part brought gifts in kind, rice, fruits, and fish,
and knowing that we were Christians, so not
prevented, like themselves, from animal food, fowls
or venison ; and without exalting too highly our
own merits, I may say we deserved them all ; for
not only had we slain the two large crocodiles,
one of which they firmly believed, nay, positively
stated, to be the destroyer of their friends, and
so probably saved the lives of many others, but
we had set such an example of courage and fear-
lessness of the reptiles, that, for that season at

least, the river became cleared of the whole brood, and the neighbouring villagers enabled to carry on their fishing without molestation or even fear.

Thus for several months we lived a very happy life, tinctured, it was true, with much anxiety about my father; but then, of him we daily expected to hear good news; and indeed, about the fourth month, we did hear through the messenger sent by the uncle of Fos, that he was in good health, and although a prisoner, permitted by the King to take any amount of exercise, providing he did not attempt to escape from the guard set over him.

Now, this news gave us great pleasure, and much hope that he would soon find an opportunity of escaping, and making his way to our village. Here we resolved to await patiently that event; but, alas! twelve months elapsed without bringing us any better information; and anxiety becoming too great for patience, we had begun to think seriously of making a bold push for Kandy; indeed, to the presence of the King himself; when one evening—I remember it very well, for it was the night immediately preceding the outburst of the monsoon and the beginning of the rainy season—Bob, May, and myself were sitting together in our general apartment, arguing both for and against leaving the village, and venturing at once into the lion's den, when Fos entered with breathless haste, saying—

"Golly! golly! Massa Tom; messenger-man come again from Kandy."

"Well, Fos; what news of my father?" said I.

The news was speedily told.. The treacherous headman, whose niece we had saved from the Rodiyas, had discovered our residence at the village, and to curry favour at Court, had sent the intelligence to Kandy; the consequence of which was, that the King had despatched a party of soldiers to fetch us.

"But is my father in health?" I asked again.

"Captain Excellency all good in health," replied the boy.

"Well, then," I said to May and Bob, "as I would rather pay a voluntary visit to his Majesty than be taken to him by his slaves, we must find out if there be not a road leading to Kandy by which we can avoid meeting these people."

"Aye, aye, it's just my opinion; and the sooner we start, d'ye see, the better," replied Bob.

"Excellency go to-morrow daybreak. Fos talkee messenger, 'cos messenger not bad man, and know ebery where; know how get to Kandy widout meeting soldiers," said the boy; and so it came about that we left the hospitable village.

That night the monsoon burst forth in all its fury; the rain fell in deluge showers. As, however, the greater part fell during the night, we started at daybreak; and so popular had we become, that when we were ready to set out, we found the villagers had provided us with a horse, which they had laden with baggage. May mounted the animal we had brought with us, and bidding adieu to these simple, good-hearted people, we went on our way, led by the messenger of whom Fos had spoken so favourably.

"Mayhap I wouldn't like to have the keeping o' that land-shark of a headman," said Bob. As, however, he spoke we were just passing from a belt of forest upon an open plain. He stopped, saying, as he stumbled, "Here's a queer start, Master Tom; the whole country's covered with fishes;" but May and I having also at the same time observed that the ground was for some distance strewn with small silvery fishes, many dead, but numbers alive, we were standing still with astonishment at the sight. Fos, however, aroused us all by saying,

"S'pose Massa Tom, Missee May, Massa Bob Bosen neber see so many?"

"Never did, youngster. But, look you, how did they come here?" asked Bob.

"'Um rain berry bad, berry much bad, all night."

"Aye, aye, lad; but what has that to do with it?"

" It rain fishes all de night."

" Hilloa ! young impudence, you would try that yarn on me, would you ?" said Bob, and he would at the same time have pulled his ears had I not said—

" Shame, Bob ! shame ! let the boy have his joke. But come, Fos," I added, to the boy, " you must not play monkey tricks with us."

" Not joke, not monkey tricks ; it rain fishes all de night," he replied, sturdily.

And as I could obtain no other answer, nor indeed May either, we discontinued the subject, and made the best of our way through the fallen and in many instances floundering fish. But Fos was right. Fish showers, as I afterwards discovered, are no such uncommon things in Ceylon, or indeed in India generally. As a proof of this assertion, I must tell you, that in a newspaper called the *Bombay Times,* and which was published in 1856, a Dr. Buist says—"In the year 1824, fishes fell at Meerut on the men of her Majesty's 16th Regiment, then out at drill, and were caught in numbers. In July, 1826, live fish were seen to fall on the grass at Moradabad during a storm. On the 19th of February, at noon, a heavy fall of fish occurred in the Darrah Zillah, depositions on the subject being obtained from nine different parties. The fish were all dead ; most of them were large, some were fresh, others rotten and mutilated. They were seen at first in the sky, like a flock of birds descending rapidly to the ground. There was rain drizzling, but no storm. On the 16th and 17th of May, 1833, there occurred near Jumna a fall of fish, from a pound and a half to three pounds in weight, and of the same species as those found in the neighbouring tanks. On the 20th of September, 1839, after a smart shower of rain, a quantity of live fish, about three inches in length, and all of the same kind, fell about twenty miles south of Calcutta. On this occasion, it was remarked that the fish did not fall here and there irregularly on the ground, but in a continuous straight line, not more than a span in breadth."

Having adduced many other instances, the writer concludes thus—" One of the most remarkable phenomena of this kind occurred during a tremendous deluge of rain at Kattywar, in 1850, when the ground was found literally covered with fish ; some of them were found on the top of haystacks, where probably they had been drifted by the storm. At Poonah, after a very heavy fall of rain in August, 1852, multitudes of fish were caught in the ground in the cantonments, full half a mile from the nearest stream."

So well was the interior known to our guide, that for several days we continued our journey through a vast and apparently trackless forest without falling in with the king's troops ; but it being now the rainy season, we were enabled to travel by day. At night we bivouacked, as had been our custom in our former journey, beneath our tents, and surrounded by a cordon of fire. About the fifth night, however, we came to the ruins of an ancient city. Ruins, indeed ; for, once the palatial city of those monarchs who created the stupendous tanks of which I have told you, it was now a vast wilderness of mouldering walls, pillars, staircases, temples, and monuments, more melaucholy, by far more melancholy, than a city of tombs in the wildest desert, for it was all that was left of an extinct and nameless race, whose sole record are ruins—ruins so old that a vast and pathless forest has grown up and embedded them ; and the abodes of the once mighty, the beautiful of the earth, have become the lairs of savage beasts.

What a lesson to human pride and stately vanity ! Wherefore, to what purpose their centuries of greatness, of ambition, of wars and conquest ? No great convulsions of the globe, sufficient to uproot entirely from the earth the works of their hands and intellect, yet is the very name of this ancient and (judging from their ruined monuments) noble people erased from the tablets of human history. It is a melancholy retrospect, and bids us ask if the womb of the future has such a Lethe for the name of England: it is to be hoped not; nay, under Providence, without some mighty convulsion of nature, it is scarcely probable; for while the race of which I write were isolated in an island mid-Asia, we islanders of the Anglo-Saxon race aim to place our representatives, our name, our art, sciences, and that from which all have sprung, Christianity, in every nook and corner of the habitable globe.

Well, when we had stabled our two horses in the many-pillared but uncovered vestibules of the the greatest of these ruins—the palace; when we had pitched our tents in a vast but roofless apartment, which had probably once served the purpose of hall of audience; I could not help making some such reflections as above, and May, sympathizing with me, replied—

"Is it not sinful—is it not profanity—thus to use these ancient ruins?"

"All king and all people not care, 'cos been dead long time and can't see, so better sleep here den long ob wild beasts and snakes," said Fos.

"Now, look you, Master Tom and Miss May, to my thinking, it's all square and aboveboard; for, d'ye see, as the old skipper and his crew, who, may be, lived long afore I was born, have deserted the ship, I don't see as how we can be mustered among pirates for just putting our heads here for a night."

"Ah, Bob, Bob, you have no imagination," said May, laughing.

"Mayhap not, Miss May; but I've a good appetite, and d'ye see, I take it that that's a good deal more likely to keep life in this here old hulk of mine."

"You are right, Bob; after such a journey, and in such a place, fact must come before fancy," said I.

"And I take it, Master Tom, the facts you mean now are a good meal, and a long night's rest."

"Aye, aye, Bob," I replied.

And without further converse we set to work to make our bivouac perfect; after which, and having partaken of a good supper, we betook ourselves to our mats, upon which I believe we all slept, not only without a regret at making a rest-house and stable of the palace, but without our sleep being in the least disturbed by the ghosts or even dreams of the bygone monarchs, their race and splendour.

Now, as it was only the commencement of the rainy season, the weather was unsettled; and moreover, we were so much fatigued by our many days' journey, we resolved to rest for at least another day among the ruins. As to do this, however, necessitated that we should procure something in the shape of game—a buck, a fowl,

a hare, or, indeed, any eatable bird or animal
that chance might throw in our way—we had no
sooner partaken of our first meal than I fastened
my ammunition-pouch around my waist, snatched
up my rifle, and telling Fos to follow with his,
was about to depart into the forest, when May
insisted upon going with us, and as I could not
refuse, we all three started upon a half-rambling,
half-foraging expedition into the woods, leaving
Bob and the guide to take care of the tents and
baggage. Fos, however, who would never let an
opportunity of having a sly joke with Bob pass,
as we were leaving, turned back, saying—

"Massa Bob Bosen 'll be berry good man;
berry good man now all gone 'way but messenger
man."

"D'ye mean fun, you impudent lump of
mahogany?" asked Bob, laughing.

"Mean dat Massa Bob be berry good, 'cos
'bliged to hold 'um tongue, not speak."

"Not speak! what does the mahogany imp
mean?" again asked Bob.

"Fos not mogony imp, but white boy 'ropean;
and mean dat 'spose Massa Bob talkee, messenger man no understand 'um; 'spose messenger man talkee, Massa Bob no understand; so
'spose no good talkee at all," replied the boy, taking
care, however, as the words left his lips, to step
out of reach of the old sailor's hand.

Well, we had been wandering about the forest
some time without meeting with any game worth
the killing, when we came to the ruined wall of
an old temple.   Fos started suddenly; then
throwing himself down, and placing his ear upon
the ground, he said—

"Excellency, some man come dis way; 'spose
he no good; better hide by wall."

"A good suggestion, Fos," said I; and immediately we stepped behind the wall.   It was
about seven feet high, and riddled with holes,
before which were growing bushy, creeping
plants.   Pulling, however, the latter aside, we
could manage to see without being seen, *i.e.*, supposing the man, whoever he might be, did not
come behind the wall.

´ Now, the part of the forest out of which we
had just stepped and were now looking upon was
a kind of natural pathway; that is, for a long way
it was formed by an avenue of great extent,
but at such regular distances, and leaving the
path so equal in width nearly the whole of their
length, that it had the appearance of the planted
avenue of trees leading up to an English country-
house.   Well, we had not been upon the look-out
through the loopholes many minutes before I observed that which made me shudder, but caused
May to laugh aloud, saying,

"Fos, Fos, thou art but a sorry forest scout if

this be the enemy you '*s'posed*' we should not like to meet."

"Neber mind; Fos know what he knows. Guana come now, but man come after," replied the boy. May, however, did not notice his reply, for, observing my shudder, she laughingly said—

"Come, come, Tom; let me introduce you. This is an old friend whom I have not met since leaving Batavia."

And so saying, she took a noosed rope with a slip knot, which the boy had provided in case of requiring such a thing, and was about endeavouring to throw it over its body; but I caught her arm, saying—

"May, May, you shall not!"

"Tut, tut, Tom; it's only a poor guana," said she, slipping away; and the next minute she had so dexterously thrown the rope that the reptile was writhing and struggling in its coil. May, however, getting too near, received a blow from its tail that caused her to stagger. I caught her in my arms; but Fos, pulling out his hunting-knife, gave it a death-wound, saying,

"'Um pay for dat; neber hit Missee again."

"What have you done? Shame, boy, to kill the harmless creature!" said May.

The creature which May seemed so much inclined to pet was a loathsome-looking reptile, at least four and a half feet in length, with eruptive yellow blotches upon its scales; yet repulsive as is its species in appearance, its habits, history, and the uses to which it is applied, render some account of it interesting.

This lizard, called by the Singhalese Talla-goya, is the guana of the Europeans; and respecting it the great naturalist writer upon Ceylon whom I have before quoted, says:

"It may be seen at noonday, searching for ants and insects, in the middle of the highway and along the fences; when disturbed, but by no means alarmed, by the approach of man, it moves off to a safe distance, and the intrusion being over, returns again to the occupation in which it had been interrupted. Repulsive as it is in appearance, it is perfectly harmless, and is hunted down by dogs in the maritime provinces, where its delicate flesh is converted into curry, and its skin into shoes. When seized, it has the power of inflicting a smart blow with its tail. The Talla-goya lives in almost any convenient hollow, such as a hole in the ground, or the deserted nest of the ants, or the hearts of decayed trees."

Now, the Singhalese not only eat the flesh of this reptile, but use its fat for the cure of cutaneous diseases. At the same time, however, they believe that if taken inwardly it is a deadly poison; and this latter belief leads these barbarians to a practice so cruel, so inhuman, that

were it not, at least in my opinion, necessary that
I should picture the people of whom I write in
their cruelties as well as their pleasantries, the
animals of their land, and its natural history, I
would forego relating it.

First, I must inform you that there is a terrible and deadly poison known among the Singhalese as the Cobra-tel. This poison is the horror
of all the natives; but the ceremony of its composition is as fearful as the caldron scene of the
witches in *Macbeth*—worse, far worse; because,
while the latter is fiction, the former is fact, and
fact, too, that is well vouched for by a leading
English official, in whose district the mysterious
compound was commonly manufactured, and who
gives for its composition the following receipt:

" Before commencing the operation of preparing the poison, a cock is first sacrificed to the
Yakkos, or demons. The ingredients are extracted from venomous snakes—the cobra de
capello (from which it takes its name), the cara-
mella, and the tic polonga, by making an incision
in the head, and suspending the reptiles over a
chattie to collect the poison. To this arsenic and
other drugs are added, and the whole is to be
boiled in a human skull, with the aid of the three
Talla-goyas, which are tied on three sides of the
fire, with their heads directed towards it, and tor-
mented by whips to make them hiss, so that the

fire may blaze. The froth from their lips is then added to the boiling mixture, and so soon as an oily scum rises to the surface, the cobra-tel is completed."

Now it is scarcely a consolation to know that, after all this unnecessary torture of the poor reptiles, the only positive poisonous ingredient of the whole compound is the arsenic. Now, supposing that these people had been guilty of no other and worse cruelties or miserable supersti- tions, such practices as these being common among them, must not the usurpation of the government by the English (for usurpation it was), or indeed of any other Christian people, be a blessing that, when their eyes become opened to civilization, must fill their hearts with gratitude for the past and hope for the future?

But to return to May's lizard. When Fos had killed it, he took up the body by the tail, saying—

" Take talla to Massa Bob, for cook; it berry good eat."

" Throw it down, boy, and let us hide again, for some hunter is at hand," said I, hearing the barking of dogs and a rustling among the under- wood; and no sooner had we resumed our former positions at the loophole than there came the twang of a bow. A small monkey fell dead in the path, and directly afterwards two small cur- dogs and a man burst through the bushes; but

perceiving the guana in addition to the poor little
animal he had just killed, he danced about it joyfully, and the dogs seemed to participate in their
master's pleasurable sensations, for they sniffed,
wagged their tails, and barked as they ran several
times round the dead carcasses.

At the sight of the new comer May shuddered,
and exclaimed, in a low voice—

" Gracious Heaven ! Tom, is it a man ?"

" A very fair imitation, at all events, May," I
replied, laughing.

" It am savage man, Rock Veddah, 'um come
hunt guanas ; but 'spose not find one, 'um shoot
monkey," said Fos.

Well might May have asked whether the object
who now stood contemplating his game was a
man, as you will admit, reader, when I tell you
that he was about four feet in height, slightly
humped on the back, immense head upon a long
thin neck, with legs, arms, hands, and feet so
badly matched in shape and size that they looked
as if they had been promiscuously chosen from a
heap and thrown upon the rest of his body at
odd times and at random.   His eyes were small,
black, and piercing, and shone like those of a wild
cat at night, through a mass of black, rugged,
uncombed hair, which hung in matted lumps to
his waist ; his beard, of the same colour and in
similar order, reached his middle.   His dress was

as scant, but not so clean even as those india-rubber-jointed gentlemen with boneless backs who twist themselves out of shape at theatres for the amusement of the British public; that is, he had but a dirty cloth around his waist, which reached to his knees. But repulsive as was his appearance, he was evidently a mighty hunter, for he was armed with a six-feet bow of light supple wood, with strings made of the fibrous bark of some tree greased and twisted. The ammunition for the bow consisted of a quiver of arrows about three feet long, the heads of which were seven inches in length, but flat like a dinner-knife, brought to a sharp point, and feathered at the other end by a handful of peacock's pinions. These, with an iron-headed sharp axe stuck in his girdle, completed his arms of offence and defence.

"Shall we go forth and accost him?" said I, being anxious to be relieved from our uncomfortable position.

"Nay, Tom, it were unwise; for as we may perhaps be no less strange to him than he to us, the poor creature may attack us before we have time to make him comprehend that our intentions are peaceable," said May.

"Aye, aye, May, right again; but," I added to Fos, "can you understand his language?"

"'Ess, Excellency, Fos can talkee leetle; but Veddah got monkey, will cook and eat 'um, so better not talkee till done eating, 'cos hungry savage more savage. Let him feed first, den he good-tempered, savage and talkee," replied Fos.

" By which you mean, if we would have him good-tempered, we must feed the beast. Bravo! Fos. I believe you must have been brought up in a menagerie."

" Fos not know what menagy am; but 'um know all beasts, men, women, little child too, all berry savage if hungry."

" This venerable sage of the East gives good advice, May."

" True, Tom; Fos is a shrewd observer of human nature," replied May; adding, " But look, see; the creature is about to prepare his meal."

I did look, and that, too, for some time intently, for his actions were curious.

First, his mode of making a fire surprised me. Having broken one of his arrows, he sharpened one of the pieces to a thin point, and made a hole in the other to receive it; then placing the latter on the ground, and holding it down firmly with his toes, he whirled the pointed one round the hole, rolling it rapidly between the palms of his hands. In a few moments it began to smoke; a little charcoal then fell into powder, and shortly a spark jumped out, kindled the charcoal-dust, then blowing it gently with his breath, he lighted a dry leaf by its heat, and piling up small chips and dry twigs upon the flame, raised in a few minutes a good blaze.

Having thus kindled the fire, the Veddah cut down three nearly straight branches from the nearest tree, two of these he stuck in the ground on either side of the fire, one end of the other he shaped into a sharp point, and having run it through the monkey, he placed it over the fire, having first cut hollows in the tops of the posts or supports, so that the horizontal piece would turn after the fashion of a spit. Scarcely, however, had he so far perfected his culinary arrangement, when we heard a loud grunting : this aroused the dogs, who began to sniff and bark, and ran into the bushes from which we had first seen the man make his appearance. The dogs having disappeared, the Veddah left the fire, and sitting down, he caught up his bow, and to my astonishment, in that position, with the toe of his right foot against the bow, he placed an arrow, then drawing the string to its greatest extent with his right thumb and finger, he sat awaiting the enemy, whatever it might be.

" It wild pig ; Veddah man can see 'um," said Fos ; and he was right. The dogs had hunted out of the bush a huge wild boar, who, attracted either by the savoury scent of the roasting monkey or the defiant attitude of the Veddah, came at

full charge down the path, snorting and grunting.
The man waited till the animal was within a few
yards of him; twang went the string, but the
arrow, striking the brute only in the shoulder, he
stopped for an instant as if to draw it with his
mouth. The Veddah had his hand upon another
arrow. Before, however, he had time to place it,
the infuriated boar stood over him; nay, he had
gored his right leg, which bled profusely. So,
without an instant's thought, I brought my rifle to
my shoulder and gave piggy its contents.

"Dat save Veddah man's life," said Fos, as
the animal rolled over dead. But the astonishment of the savage—how can I describe it? He
turned round and gazed about him like one
thunderstruck; and seeing us come from behind
the wall, he endeavoured to get up as if to run
away, but his leg was so severely gored by the
tusks of the boar that he could not stand. However, Fos soon removed his fears by making him
understand that we did not mean to harm him;
when the poor fellow, in a wild, guttural tongue,
endeavoured to explain his gratitude for the timely
aid which had saved his life.

"What does he say, Fos?" I asked.

"'Um say 'um tank Excellency for killing pig,
and dat we shall have all his roast monkey."

"Roast monkey!—pah!" I exclaimed, with
disgust; adding, "But let us look to his wound,

or it is not many more roast monkeys he will have the chance of eating."

And so we set to work—May, Fos, and myself —and by tightly bandaging the poor fellow's leg with handkerchiefs, we stopped the bleeding ; and having succeeded so far, we helped him to walk with us to our tents.

CHAPTER XX.

WE MAKE A SENSATION AMONG THE WILD PEOPLE
OF THE WOODS, BUT ARE KINDLY RECEIVED.

CAN I picture to you Bob's astonishment when
he met us helping along the Veddah? He stood
with his arms akimbo for a minute, then with a
loud laugh he exclaimed—

" What, Master Tom ! is this here the kind of
game you are going to treat us to? What
animal is it, for it aint a man and it aint a
monkey, d'ye see?"

" Shame, shame, Bob ! to joke at the appearance of a fellow-creature. Are you a Christian,
that you can laugh at a wounded man ?"

" Wounded ?" said Bob, for the good-natured
old fellow had not noticed the bandage ; " aye,
aye, I ought to have known he hadn't his sea-
legs, or, d'ye see, you wouldn't be towing him
along this fashion."

" Aye, aye, Bob," I replied, " the poor fellow
has been gored by a boar, and I fear we have
made but sorry surgeons ; so look you to his
wounds."

Whereupon my old friend uttered not another

word; but lifting the little savage in his arms, carried him to the tent, untied the bandage, dressed the wound, and laid his patient at ease upon his own mat. This being done, he helped to dress the guana (which, by the way, I omitted to tell you, Fos had dragged along with him by means of the rope coil, and which he had fastened around his waist). But did you really make a supper of this lizard? perhaps asks my reader; to which I answer, Indeed we did, and found it very good eating. But then it must be remembered that we had that best of sauces—a keen appetite. After such a confession, you will perhaps think us a little too squeamish about the roast monkey. But no; for although the latter animal may be no flattering likeness, it bears *too* near a resemblance to the form of humanity to be eaten by—at least Europeans. Fos and the guide were, however, of very different opinion, for they more than once expressed regret at not having brought the dainty with us.

During that night the Veddah suffered a great deal of pain; but the next morning, although he could not stand, the anguish had sufficiently subsided for him to enter into a long conversation with Fos and the guide, both of whom managed, although with some difficulty, to hold converse with him.. Upon asking Fos the subject of their discourse, he told me that the poor fellow was

profuse in his expressions of gratitude for saving
his life from the boar, but further prayed that we
would carry him to his own village, a distance of
some ten miles from the ruins.

"Ask the guide if this village is in our road,"
said I.

"Now, look you, Master Tom; I don't see that
question's of any use, for, d'ye see, if so be it isn't
in our way, why, we must go out of our way, for
though, poor fellow, a savage-like, he's got his
feelings, and maybe wouldn't thank us for saving
his life only to leave it, maybe, at the mercy of
one of that big pig's relations who might be
passing."

"Fie, Tom, fie; to hesitate for an instant.
What is ten miles more or less to us; for have
we not two horses, upon one of which the man
can ride; while, if need be, I can walk?" said
May.

Whereupon, really feeling ashamed at having
even *seemed* to hesitate as to my duty when the
life of a fellow-creature was at stake, I complied,
nay, there and then, without another word, assisted Bob to lift him upon the baggage-horse.
And that God never permits a good action to go
unrewarded will be proved very shortly.

Well, it was near dusk when, under the instructions of the Veddah, the guide led us to the
village. The spot dignified by such a title was

nothing more than a clearing of some hundred square yards in the forest; the only semblance of human habitations being some four or five little huts made of mud and bark. As for the inhabitants—well, I cannot better describe them than by telling you they were all (some fifty), men, women, and children, in personal appearance, dress, and style, very like the wounded man, except that the women and girls were even more repulsive to gaze upon.

Now, as we approached this village, the first signs of which were a number of wretched little dogs, which came snapping, snarling, and yelping at our heels, the Veddah made a sign that he wished to speak to Fos, and the boy having gone up to him, said—

"Veddah man say better let 'um go first, 'cos Veddah people not knowe Excellency, Missee, and Massee Bob am friends, will shoot arrows."

"Aye, aye; and a very necessary precaution too," said I.

So, having lifted the wounded man from the horse, the guide and Fos took him between them, went on in advance; and in that order we marched among the Veddahs, who no sooner set their eyes upon their friend or relation, than one and all jumped about, and chattered like so many monkeys, in doubt as to whether they should be joyful or angry. A few words, however, spoken by our friend to a man who seemed to be the chief or headman, turned the scale so decidedly for joy, that its very exuberance became a sad nuisance.

Now, in all lands, whether savage or civilized, it seems that the first token of gratitude and welcome to strangers, is the offering of eatables and drinkables. So with these Veddahs; for arriving at the first of the huts, the chief ran in, and in a minute returned, holding before us a kind of wicker-basket full of pieces of dried venison, roots, fish, honey, and rice. The offer was embarrassing, for we had no relish for the food, at least, in the form before us; while to refuse would be to give serious offence; but as I was pondering how to meet the difficulty, Bob said—

" Look you, Fos, just tell this under-dressed skipper that we'll take it mortal kind on him just to put that mess out of sight; but if so be he'll just order some of these monkeys to leave off chattering their teeth, and grinning at us, as if we were clowns at Bartlemy Fair, and help us up with our tents, we'll take it kind. But look you," he added, "ask him civil-like, d'ye see, so that the nigger wont be offended."

" 'Ess; but no good tell 'um all dat, 'cos it make 'um angry. He tink you refuse presents," replied Fos.

"Then tell him we can't eat except beneath our own tents," said I, thinking thus to meet the difficulty.

And it did; for the chief, no doubt believing our objection arose from religious scruples (for, you know, there are many castes in the East who will not eat in company with certain other castes), at once ordered the men to help Bob erect our tents. While, however, they were being prepared, Fos, I, and the guide kept very close to May's horse, for the women, children, and even some of the men, coming around the horse, sadly distressed her by their curiosity; for not only did they continue to stare with wonder, as if she had been some animal compounded of half-woman, half-horse, but chattered and examined her white skin, her dress, her hat; the latter they even took off, and one after the other placed it upon their own heads; and lastly, two of the women, taking hold of her feet, were about to pull off her shoes, had I not somewhat rudely driven them away. This I for a moment feared would embroil us with the men, but when they ran, screeching and howling, to their male friends who were erecting the tents, the latter, to my regret rather than satisfaction, drove them back with what I *supposed* (not knowing their language) to be hard words, but *knew* were hard blows—a custom which in the East, I may remark par parenthesis, is not uncommon.

When the tents were prepared for our reception, and we had taken possession, we duly received the eatables, a portion only of which we partook —viz., the rice, cocoa-nuts, and water, which, indeed, was all we required to satisfy nature; after which, May retired to her own tent; and for her better security, Bob and I resolved to sit upon the ground opposite the entrance, rifle in hand, sleeping and watching by turns—a precaution which, by the way, we adopted more for our satisfaction than that we believed she would meet with harm.

Now, as I took first turn at the watch, I obtained an insight into the natural habits of these people. It was a beautiful moonlight night, and the moon, at least to my seeing, never shone upon so curious a scene. The people had gone to rest —to roost would be as good a term, for the majority of them slept upon small wooden stages erected among the branches of the trees; the huts seemed to be only for the aged, the sick, or the wounded, for our travelling companion was carried into one of them. As for the chief, after having placed his bow and arrows so as to be at hand in case of necessity, he stretched himself at full length upon the ground, and with his axe clutched in his right hand, went to sleep. The children and younger members of his family laid down around him, rolling close together for the sake of warmth, while the rest of the tribe stretched themselves in similar position, with bows near and axes in hand, so as to form one large circle.

A solemn silence reigned around. The moon shone brightly upon the forms of these savages, who, if guilt causes restlessness and sleepless nights, must have been, as indeed I do not doubt they were, simplicity and innocence itself; for not a murmur came from their lips, not a limb did they move. Well, this strange scene set me pondering as to who and what this strange tribe were, their origin, their history. The result of these ponderings will not interest you. Some facts, however, about them may at least much interest you.

I have pictured their personal appearance, their dress, arms, and village, from which you will doubtlessly term them savages. It is wrong, however, to apply that epithet; for although a simple, untaught, and, from deficiency of intellect, probably, an unteachable race, at least for generations to come, they are without those vices and dispositions generally associated with those tribes we name savages. In height and human beauty they rank below the unfortunate and miserable Rodiyas, yet by the Singhalese they are held as belonging to the highest caste, and for this reason :—

Once upon a time a Veddah being chased by a

wild animal, took refuge in a tree, whence all night
he threw down flowers to drive away his pursuer;
but in the morning, instead of a wild beast, he
found an idol under the tree, who addressed him
with the announcement, that as he had passed the
night in worshipping and offering flowers, the race
of the Veddahs should ever after take the highest
place in the caste of the Vellales, or cultivators,
the most exalted of all. Now, although the Veddahs affect ignorance of this legend and unbelief
in its truth, yet they would not upon any consi-
deration touch meat with a civilized man from
Kandy itself if he were of a lower caste. This
pride, however, may have had its origin in the
fact that they are the descendants of the Yakkos,
or aboriginal inhabitants, who upwards of two
thousand years ago were driven into the wilds of
the east and south by a great conqueror.

It is said there are three classes or divisions of
these people. The Rock Veddahs, the Village
Veddahs, and the Coast Veddahs. The habits and
customs of all three are, however, so very similar,
that to classify them would be to make a distinction without a difference. The Rock Veddahs
remain concealed in the forests, subsisting on roots,
fish, honey, and the produce of the chase; lodging
in caves, or under the shelter of overhanging
rocks, and sometimes sleeping on stages which
they construct in the trees. In the choice of

their food, all are almost omnivorous; no carrion or vermin being too repulsive for their appetite. They subsist upon roots, grain, and fruit, when they can procure them, and upon birds, bats, crows, owls, and kites, which they bring down with the bow; but for some unexplained reason they will not touch the bear, the elephant, or buffalo, although the latter are abundant in their hunting grounds. The flesh of deer and other animals they dry on stages in the sun, and store away in hollow trees for future use, closing the apertures with clay. They invariably cook their meat with fire, and their greatest luxuries are guanas and roasted monkeys.

The Rock Veddahs are divided into small clans or families, who agree in dividing the forest among themselves for hunting grounds, the limits of each family's possession being marked by streams, hills, rocks, or some well-known trees; and these conventional allotments are always honourably recognised and mutually preserved from violation. Each party has a headman, the most energetic senior of his tribe, but who exercises no authority beyond distributing at a particular season the honey captured by the various members of the clan. The produce of the chase they dry and collect for barter, carrying it to the border of the inhabited country, whither the ubiquitous Moor men bring cloths, arrow-heads, to be exchanged for deer flesh, elephants' tusks, and bees'-wax; but in these transactions the Veddahs are seldom seen by those with whom they come to deal. They deposit in the night the articles which they are disposed to part with, indicating by some mutually understood signals the description of those they wish in return; and these being brought on the following morning to the appointed place, disappear during the ensuing night. Money to them is worthless; but cocoa-nuts, salt, hatchets, iron arrow-heads, and dyed cloths, or cooking chatties, are valuables much in request.

In their domestic lives they are simple in the extreme, marriages amongst them are settled by the parents of the contracting parties; the father of the bride presents his son-in-law with a bone; his own father assigns him a right of chase in a portion of his hunting-grounds; the bridegroom then presents the lady with a cloth and some rude ornaments, and she follows him into the forest as his wife. As for their dead, so rude are they, that they do not even bury them, but cover the bodies with leaves and brushwood in the jungle. Rarer, however, even among the wildest of savages, they have no knowledge of a God, nor of a future state; no temples, no idols, no altars, prayers, or charms; and, in short, no instinct of worship, except, it is reported, some addiction to cere-monies analogous to devil worship, in order to

L.I.C.   C C

avert storms and lightning; and when they are sick, they send for devil-dancers to drive away the evil spirit who is believed to inflict the disease.

Their dance is executed in front of an offering of something eatable, placed on a tripod of sticks, the dancer having his head and girdle decorated with green leaves. At first he shuffles with his feet, to a plaintive air, but by degrees he works himself into a state of great excitement and action, accompanied by moans and screams, and during this paroxysm he professes to be inspired with instruction for the cure of the patient.

The Village Veddahs, like those, for instance, among whom we bivouacked, are but in a very slight degree more civilized. They wear a larger cloth around their waists, the women ornament themselves with necklaces of brass beads, and bangles cut from the chank-shell. The ears of the children, when seven or eight years old, are bored with a thorn, by the father, and decorated with rings. But they have no idea of time, or distance; no names for hours, days, or years. They have no doctors, and no knowledge of medicine, beyond the practice of applying bark and leaves to a wound. They have no games, no amusements, no music; and as to education, it is so utterly unknown, that they are unable to count beyond five on their own fingers. Then, as for their means of living, they accept wages in kind for driving away wild elephants from the paddy-fields. The women plait mats from the palm-leaf, and the men make bows, the strings of which are prepared from the bark of the rittagha or upas tree. Such was the state of these strange people at the time of which I write, and to a great extent *is* now; but for the future there is great hopes; the British Government have taken them in hand, offered them settlements, cottages, agricultural implements and seeds for themselves, school-houses and instructors for their children, and although of the many who accepted these offers, numbers were unable to subdue the wild habits which from birth had belonged to them, and returned to their savage lives, future generations must reap a harvest from the seeds now sown.

CHAPTER XXI.

WE TAKE LEAVE OF THE VEDDAHS, BUT ARE
PRESENTED WITH A CHARM THAT LEADS TO
THE DISCOVERY OF MY FATHER.

THE next morning, after regaling ourselves upon
dried venison, fish, and rice, I told Fos to signify
to the chief that we wished to take our departure.
This intelligence he received with visible regret.
When, however, he was told that we could upon no
account remain there longer, he and his people
helped us to take down our tents and pack the
baggage. This being done, he and some of his
people brought, one an axe, another a bow and
arrows, others, pieces of venison ; and the women,
beads and shells, begging that the good white
men who had behaved so kindly to their relation would deign to accept them ; and great was
their distress when they were made to understand
that for want of carrying power alone, we could
but accept of a few of the beads, a bow, an axe,
and some arrows, each of which we would
manage to carry with us in remembrance of their
simple but most hearty hospitality.

Then, as May was about to mount her horse,

the chief spoke a few words to Fos, and, accompanied by two of his people, scampered away in the direction of their wounded relation's tent.

"What says the good man ?" I asked.

"Chief good man, berry grateful ; say Excellency and Massa Bob not go away till 'um broder wid bad leg come bring present ; say good-bye."

"Now, look you, Master Tom," said Bob, " I take it it'll be all the better for our shipmate's game leg if we were just to go and see him, and so save the poor fellow the trouble of a hop upon one leg, to the injury perhaps of t'other."

"True, Bob ; we should have thought of that before," said May.

But as she spoke the invalid came out of the tent, supported between the chief and another man ; and having made a short speech to Fos, ended by placing in his hands—guess how much to our surprise—a small object wrapped in a piece of talipat-leaf.   Fos taking the parcel, said—

"Veddah man say 'um nebber forget good white men, which mean Excellency, Missee May, Massa Bob, and Fos."

"You a white man, you mahogany monkey !" said Bob, interrupting him.

"'Ess, Massa Bob ; if Fos not born toder side ob sea, 'um white boy 'ropean for all dat."

"Come, come, boy ; we are keeping this poor man standing.   Tell us what he said," added I.

"'Ess, Excellency, 'cos Fos know how 'bey orders much as Massa Bob; all white boys 'ropean good at dat, 'specially when 'um paid dollars," replied Fos; adding, " Veddah man so berry glad for what Excellency do for 'um, dat he make present ob charm, which will keep debels away, and help 'um to find 'um fader; dat is, Excellency, de Captain."

" A charm! let me see it," said May, laughing, and holding out her hand.

Fos gave her the parcel, but having opened it, she fell backwards a few steps, placed her hand over her eyes as if to strengthen her vision, saying, " Gracious goodness! this is a charm indeed. Ask him, boy—ask him how it came in his possession."

" Great Heaven!" I exclaimed, taking it from her hand, almost stunned with astonishment.

" Golly, golly, what 'um de matter?" said Fos, absolutely frightened at our surprise, and no doubt believing that the Veddah had given us a small cobra or something equally terrible.

" Pepper and pumpkins, here's a breeze! Why, I'll eat my old head if that aint the Captain's Bible," said Bob.

And, reader, you will not be surprised at the effect that present had upon us, when I tell you that it was my father's portable Bible, a present on their marriage from my dear mother, and without which he had never put to sea; nay, which scarcely ever was absent from his bedside—a book, apart from its holy and intrinsic value, he would never have parted with by fair means. Yet there it was, or rather had been, in the possession of literally a wild man of the woods, and, moreover, strangely regarded by even him as a charm to help us on our journey. Indeed, it would have been a charm; for though I believe neither of us omitted either the last thing at night or upon opening our eyes of a morning, to offer up prayers to God, yet had we often and bitterly regretted the want of that book of books, that "charm" indeed, as the Veddah believed it; the only "charm" which God has given and man needs to help him upon even a longer and more dangerous journey than ours had been—even the journey through life.

But that book!—how did it leave my father's possession?—how could the Veddah have obtained it? I burned to know, yet feared to ask, for truly I thought it must have been a strange accident that would have caused my father to give, sell, or even lose it. My agitation, however, subsiding, through Fos I asked and learned the following story:—

Some weeks before, while a party of the Veddahs, led by the man we had saved from the boar, were in the forest hunting, they fell in with two white men, one tall, the other short, when the latter, seeing himself and companion surrounded, and, I suppose, thinking by enemies, pulled a pistol from his breast and fired it among them.   Now, although fortunately no person was hurt—for the weapon missed fire—the hostile act so enraged the Veddahs that they at once fell upon the strangers, and would have slain them with their axes, but the tall white, believing his last moment to have arrived, took this book from his pocket, opened and kissed the page—an act so mysterious or so curious to these simple and superstitious people, that for some unaccountable reason or other (what, I know not) they took it into their heads the tall stranger was an astrologer or doctor, which in their belief being a person on intimate terms with their devils, they refrained from hurting either; nay, at once endeavoured to cultivate the mysterious stranger's friendship and goodwill by offering him dried venison, water, and rice.   Well, the tall white man, seeing his advantage, endeavoured to improve it by all manner of gestures, and succeeded so well that the chief took both of them home with him to his village.

When, however, the white men reached the chief's hut, they saw at once the reason of this sudden change from hostility to friendship.   A little girl, the chief's only child, lay there ill with a fever, and, notwithstanding the devil dancers had been called in and performed, she was dying.   In fact, as I have said, the white man was believed to be an astrologer or doctor, and his book was thought to be the charm that would cure the child; and for that reason had they been brought to the village.

Now, the tall white man being unable, from ignorance of their language, either to accept or to refuse the office, remained by the side of the child. Indeed, it was the intention of the chief that he should do so; for, having brought him provisions, he left him alone. The curious part of the story is to come. The chief had quitted the tent, believing that, without being alone with the child, the white Doctor could work no good; still, curiosity leading him to peep through a crevice, he saw him open the book, and kneeling near the patient, read aloud from its pages. If, I thought, that white man was my father —and I could not doubt it—he was seeking consolation from that holy book; he was praying for succour in his difficulties; for the welfare of myself and mother. Tears came into my eyes at the thought, for it had been his common practice at sea. That attitude of prayer, that reading aloud, the chief believed to be the charm that was to cure his daughter!—oh! how little did my good father at that moment imagine by what means Providence was working out his deliverance. Shall I tell you the strange coincidence?—the child was better the next morning. The chief was delighted, and by every possible gesture endeavoured, and at last succeeded, in making the white Doctor comprehend that he wished him to repeat the charm—pray again—read again. And then—for my father often told me of it afterwards —he did read, he did pray, and that too from the bottom of his heart; and it was the Lord's will that the child should recover. She did, and the gratitude of the people towards my parent and his companion knew no bounds.

"But look you, mate," said Bob, at this point of the relation, "can't you tell us what's become of the skipper, for that's the part of the yarn we want to get at?"

"S'pose Massa Bob not in such big hurry, Fos tell him dat Veddah man found out white men had run away from Kandy, and dat after 'um stop here two, tree week, tink King's soldiers come after 'um; so 'um make Veddah man know dey want to go to sea and get big ship. Den Veddah man find out dat, he go 'long wid white men and show 'um sea, where leave 'um."

"When did they leave here? Did the Veddah see them go on board a ship?" I asked, anxiously. And Fos, replying to both questions, made answer—

"White men leave here week ago, but Veddah man ony go as far as forest, near sea, when 'um say good-bye and come back."

Now making out from this long story that my father and his companion had not left the spot upon which we then stood more than a week, and thinking that even then he might be wandering in the woods near the sea, where the Veddah had left them, I said—

"Now, Fos, tell this Veddah man that if he would really repay us for saving his life, that he must send with us, at once, the same guide who accompanied my father;" for that this tall white man and he were one and the same person I could not doubt.

"But the Bible, Tom, the Bible; how did this man get that from your father?" said May.

"Dat berry bad part," replied Fos; adding, "Veddah man tink book berry fine charm to cure little child, and big man, and women—all, ebery ting, debels and all,—so 'um watch Captain till see book fall; den Veddah man not able to keep 'umself from pickin' it up and keeping it. But 'um berry sorry now, so gib 'um back."

That the Veddah had stolen the Bible was very clear. As, however, he had returned it voluntarily, and his having done so seemed so likely to lead to my meeting my parent, I pardoned the offence; and the man who had guided my father and his companion to the sea-coast being found, we bade these simple people a hearty farewell, and set out in the same direction.

CHAPTER XXII. AND LAST.

WHICH DISCOVERS MY FATHER, AND MAKES EVERY-
BODY AS COMFORTABLE AS THEY DESIRE TO BE.

AGAIN were we wending our way through the
woods and the wilds, but this time avoiding instead
of seeking Kandy; and moreover, with hearts
rendered so buoyant by our recently excited hopes
of soon meeting my father, and heads so full of
all we had to tell and hear when fortune again
brought us together, that days flew with the
seeming speed of hours, and hours with that of
minutes.

Encamping at night, as usual, beneath our
talipat tents, and by day trusting to our rifles or
our skill as fishermen for our meals; fording
rivers; traversing one day a dense jungle, another
a dense forest, or another a vast plain; then at
times through ruins of great cities, amid the
sculptured monuments and mouldering palaces of
the long since dead, and who were now sleeping
by thousands, nay, millions, beneath our footsteps,
we continued for more than a week—nay, it was
not until the ninth day that, leaving the deep
shades of a great forest, our eyes were gratified

and our hearts gladdened by the sight of the sea as it heaves, rolls, and gambols in the great Gulf of Manaar, which separates the island of Ceylon from the continent of India.

I said we left the forest. Even so; but observing at no great distance a Singhalese town, we thought it more prudent to avoid than throw ourselves in the way of the natives, for we could not forget the adage that tells of the many chances of a slip between the cup and the lip. The cup of joy was near, but only near; and to escape all hazard of a slip which might dash it from our lips ere we had time to taste, we determined to return to the forest, there to pitch our tents, as we hoped, for the last time in Ceylon. But fortunately we were saved even that trouble; for our Veddah led us to one of those large but isolated rocks so common in the scenery of that island. And this afforded both a shelter and a hiding-place; for although now deserted and buried among huge trees, it had once been a Buddhist temple, proofs of which remained in the many sculptured images of Buddha still in good preservation, hewn from the solid rock, which formed the walls of its cavernous interior. The rock had another advantage. It served the purpose of an observatory; for the pinnacle, which was an immense height, was easily reached by a series of rude steps cut out of the solid sandstone.

And the use of this "look-out" was soon put to the test; for upon the morning after our reaching this retreat, Fos, who had been to the sea to catch fish for our morning's meal, returned with the joyful intelligence that he had seen a big ship.

"A big ship!" exclaimed Bob and I, simultaneously.

"'Ess," returned the boy, "and s'pose Excellency and Massa Bob go top ob rock, 'um see for 'umself."

"Bravo! little mahogany; you'll live to be an admiral yet," said Bob.

And in a very few minutes he and I were standing side by side at the top of the rock, having tried hard to make out the nation of a great ship nearly a mile out in the gulf.

"Well, Bob," said I, "what do you make of her? Is it a company's ship?"

"No, no, Master Tom; that craft never came out of the port of London—no, nor out of a king's dockyard either."

"Then what do you make of her?" I again asked, impatiently; and Bob, having taken time to consider, said—

"Now, look you, Master Tom; it's my opinion she's a Dutchman."

"Aye, aye, maybe, Bob, and bound for Batavia. But look you, friend, she is at anchor."

"Aye, aye, at anchor she is, there's no doubt;

and that'll just serve our turn, if we can only hail her."

"True; but how is that to be done?" I replied.

And Bob, having scratched his head and strained his eyes, replied, as he pointed to a dark mass floating upon the water, apparently within a few yards of the shore—

"Easy enough; for I take it that's a lot of timber logs; and if they be, d'ye see, it's only to rig out a raft and just go out to her."

Bob's plan admitting of no argument, we at once went together down to the shore; and as fortunately not a living soul seemed nearer than the town, we closely examined the logs, the result being our full belief that they had floated round the coast, and were the property of some native merchant in the town who had thus temporarily secured them by stakes until he had an opportunity of selling them.

"These will do, and will make a capital raft; but then, how shall we get ropes with which to lash them together?"

"Now, look you, Master Tom; it's best not to make mountains of molehills, for, d'ye see, Fos is cunning enough to get anything we may want, if so be he only makes up his mind."

And when we got back to the cavern, the readiness with which the boy undertook the dangerous office of venturing into the town, and also pressed the guide into the same service, fully justified Bob's eulogium.

Well, having dispatched the two messengers upon one horse, we sat down to await their return; but some misgivings coming over my mind as to my father's having got safe away from the island, and expressing a doubt as to whether we should ourselves quit Ceylon until we had obtained a better clue to his whereabouts, we argued the matter *pro* and *con*, and that, too, without being able to make up our minds as to which would be the better. In the midst of our conversation we were interrupted by the return of the guide and Fos, and the latter with such a load in his arms that May exclaimed—

"Why, gracious, boy, how did you manage to obtain that quantity of rope?"

"Fos got no dollar, but got horse; and as horse no more good now, 'um gib 'um to rope-maker for all dis," he replied.

"And a capital exchange too, just now," said I.

"'Ess, 'ess, and so Excellency say, once, twice, good many times, when 'um hear what Fos got to say."

"Have you, then, news of my father?" I asked, anxiously.

"Excellency open 'um ears, and Fos tell," was the reply, and then he gave us an account of his adventures, which was to the following effect.

Upon reaching the town, he had gone at once to the house of a dealer in implements used by the fishers and other seafaring people. Of this man he begged the loan of a coil of rope, which he said was for the use of his master, who was at that time near the town with some timber which had broken its lashings, offering at the same time to leave the horse as a security; that his employer upon coming to the town would return the rope, and pay for the loan. Now the dealer did not believe this statement; but being a rogue, and thinking the boy had stolen the horse, readily agreed to make the exchange. Well, Fos having delivered the horse and taken the rope, was about to return, when suddenly he saw pass the door the son-in-law of the treacherous headman, the same, in fact, who had promised that, upon reaching Kandy, he would do his best to assist my father to escape.

For a minute the sight of this man made him tremble; but believing the latter had not seen him, and resuming his presence of mind, he asked, as if from mere curiosity, "Who that person was that had just passed the house?" when the dealer replied—

"That, Excellency, is an officer of the Lion King, who has sent him with a large party of soldiers down to the coast in search of two white prisoners who some time since made their escape from Kandy."

This news alarmed the boy, and again losing his presence of mind, he inquired " If the white men had been found?" when the dealer replied, that some weeks before, two white men had come to that town selling knitted caps, and as the articles were good, in great request, and the white men were themselves so harmless, the governor and the people begged of them to settle there. Well, they complied, and prospered so well in their business, that in a few weeks they took into their service a Moor man who had recently arrived from the great seaport Dutch town, some twenty miles further along the coast.

Two mornings, however, after the Moor man had entered their service and gone into their house to live, the white men were missing; they had disappeared in the night. Now, the governor hearing of this, and suspecting some foul play upon the part of the Moor man, commanded that person to be tortured into a confession; but there was no need for the torture, for the man admitted that, upon coming to the town, and recognising the two white men as being two of the prisoners who, while in Kandy, had done him some good service, he gave them the joyful information that a large Dutch ship was at that very time being laden at the Hollanders' seaport from which he had come; and as it was in the hope of meeting some such ship that the white men had come to that town, they no sooner heard the news than they in the middle of the night departed; "And," added the dealer, "it must have been one of the lucky days of the beef-eating slaves, for not many hours after there came to this town in search of them this officer of the Lion King, who had orders to take them or their heads to Kandy."

"Thank Heaven, they are safe!" I exclaimed, as the boy concluded.

"Aye, aye, Master Tom; I take it they are in yon Dutchman out in the Gulf," said Bob.

"'Ess; tink so too. But Excellency better 'scape; for Fos tink dealer am rogue, and watchee de way 'um come, so tell king's soldiers to follow," said Fos.

Need I tell you how our movements were expedited by this intelligence? how that, leaving bag and baggage, we made our way to the logs of timber? or how that, in less than an hour by our united exertions we had lashed the smaller logs together, taken leave of the grateful Veddah, shipped ourselves on board, and by the aid of large branches, which with our axes we had hewn from the trees, had pushed the temporary bark far off from the shore? But with all our exertions and activity we were not on board an instant too soon. We were not fifty yards out before the shore was lined by a party of half-naked soldiers, headed by our somewhile friend, the headman's son-in-law. Fortunately, the fellows were not armed with the bow, which in their hands might have been deadly, but with old Dutch or Portuguese firelocks. Seeing, however, they were about to fire, we all fell flat upon our faces; the balls whistled by us, and before they had time to reload (a tedious operation with such gentry), we had the advantage; for while we were out of reach of such gun-shots as they could send, they were at the mercy of our rifles, and I believe some half-dozen of the fellows would have fallen by the hands of Bob and Fos had I not commanded them to desist; for now that we were beyond range of their weapons, I did not wish to harm them, although had they followed us in boats it would have been a difficult affair. Well, turning our backs to them, with Bob at the helm, myself and May holding up a pole, upon which was fastened a long white cloth, so as to attract the attention of the crew of the Dutchman, and Fos and the guide tugging at the primitive oars, we made what way we could towards the ship, and every inch made was by sheer exertion, for it was almost a dead calm; and thus were we toiling, when May, starting back with fright, exclaimed—

" Great Heaven, what a monster ! Your rifle, Bob ! your rifle, Tom !"

Bob and I were alike startled ; and we should have fired, had not Fos cried out—

" Nebber be frighten ; it am only poor dugong, what you call mermaid, wid 'um leetle baby."

And as the animal which had so frightened us, in no less terror disappeared again beneath the water, we could not help laughing at the affectionate tones in which Fos had interceded for the poor creature. But, my reader, I believe you would have been no less startled ; for the object which so alarmed us by coming up just a few yards before our raft was a huge fish—I suppose I must call it a fish—with a head almost human, and which, as it sat or floated perfectly upright, with one arm or flipper it supported itself, and with the other clutched to its breast a young one.

" A mermaid do ye call the thing? Then if it is, where's its long hair, its comb, and looking-glass? No, no. I tell 'ee, Master Tom, the sooner we get aboard that ship the better; for this here aint a nat'ral country where fishes boil themselves in hot water by way of a bit of fun, and creatures as might be Mrs. Neptune and her last baby out for a airing is to be found."

This animal, named the dugong, is, and has been for many, many centuries, the most remarkable creature to be found in or near this most wonderful island ; and there is little doubt that as it is the only mermaid or merman that exists throughout nature, it is from the dugong the ancients took their notion of the beautiful but fabulous creature so called. This opinion, by the way, is not my own, but that of Sir J. Tennent, who says :—" The rude approach to the human outline observed in the shape of the head of this creature, and the attitude of the mother while suckling her young, holding it to her breast with one flipper while swimming with the other, holding the heads of both above water, and when disturbed, suddenly diving, and displaying her fishlike tail—these, together with her habitual demonstrations of strong maternal affection, probably gave rise to the fable of the ' mermaid ;' and thus that earliest invention of mythical physiology may be traced to the Arab seamen and the Greeks, who had watched the movements of the dugong in the waters of Manaar."

But to return to my narrative. Scarcely had Bob concluded his opinion upon the necessity of getting out of Ceylon, than May exclaimed,

" Thank Heaven! they see us."

And looking towards the ship, I saw a boat being let down her side; speedily it was manned, and in a short time they were alongside the raft, when guess our surprise, our heartfelt joy, at seeing in the stern-sheets my father—alive—safe—well. In a few minutes more we were on board the ship, and after our mutual joy had a little subsided, and May, Bob, and I had related our adventures, he told us how, that on

arriving at Kandy the King sent for, and told
him that he must remain a prisoner for the rest
of his days; but that his captivity would be an
easy one if he would promise not to attempt
an escape; and how, that not giving such a
promise, he was placed among several other
Europeans, with the exception of himself all
Hollanders, and there for many weary months
he remained, until one day he and one of the
Dutchmen managed to evade the watchfulness of
their guards, and escape into the forest.

What the difficulties of my father and his
companion were in traversing the wilds between
the capital and the sea-coast, without arms or
ammunition, the reader may judge from those
which we, under more favourable circumstances,
had to encounter.

"Now," concluded my father, "we have surmounted so many difficulties, let us never forget
that it is both wicked and useless to repine at
any calamity, however great, for few indeed are the
difficulties that cannot be overcome by will and
patience, and fewer the troubles which may not be
regarded as the germs of blessings which but remain hidden till it suits God in his wisdom to
develop them."

And my father's words cannot be controverted;
for who can doubt that aught but Providence
could have conducted us all safely through so
many dangers, in such a wilderness of savage

beasts, and more savage men, only to bring about such a reunion as that day had happened. Thus we all thought, and that night our thanksgiving mingled together.

My task is nearly concluded, for I have only to tell you, that a breeze springing up the next morning, we sailed for Madras, where we were hospitably and joyfully received by the governor, who had long given us up as lost. But as my father's ship had long since left India for England, we took a passage in the Dutchman for Bantam, in Batavia, where May was once more restored to her parent, and Bob and my father intended to remain till an English ship should touch at the island; we took Fos with us, and as I could not find it in my heart to leave May, I remained with her father in the capacity of chief clerk, afterwards to become partner; I kept the boy with me, and together we went through many adventures in that island; so many, indeed, that they would require another volume for their relation; but whether that will ever be written, will greatly depend upon the interest my readers may show in this narrative of the adventures of a boy, a girl, and a bosen lost in the wilds.

THE END.

Original Juvenile Library.

A CATALOGUE

OF

NEW AND POPULAR WORKS,

PRINCIPALLY FOR YOUNG PERSONS.

Goldsmith introduced to Newbery by Dr. Johnson

PUBLISHED BY

GRIFFITH AND FARRAN,

SUCCESSORS TO

NEWBERY AND HARRIS,
CORNER OF ST. PAUL'S CHURCHYARD, LONDON.

MDCCCLX.

ILLUMINATED GIFT BOOKS.

Every page printed in gold and colours, from designs by
MR. STANESBY.

SHAKESPEARE'S HOUSEHOLD WORDS;

With a Photographic Portrait taken from the Monument at
Stratford-on-Avon. Elegantly bound in Illuminated cloth,
richly gilt, 9s. ; morocco antique, 14s.

LIGHT FOR THE PATH OF LIFE;

From the Holy Scriptures. Small 4to, price 10s. 6d. extra
cloth ; 14s. calf, gilt edges ; 18s. Turkey morocco antique.

"Charmingly designed and beautifully printed."—*Art Journal.*

THE BRIDAL SOUVENIR;

Containing the choicest Thoughts of the Best Authors, in
prose and verse. Elegantly bound in white, price 21s. gilt
edges.

" A splendid specimen of decorative art, and well suited for a bridal gift."
—*Literary Gazette.*
" The binding in gold and white, with moresque ornamentations, is very
appropriate."—*Illustrated London News.*
" One of the most attractive of modern publications."—*Art Journal.*

ELEGANT GIFT FOR A LADY.

TREES, PLANTS, AND FLOWERS ;

THEIR BEAUTIES, USES, AND INFLUENCES. By MRS. R.
LEE (formerly Mrs. Bowdich), Author of "The African Wan-
derers," &c. With beautiful coloured Illustrations, by J.
ANDREWS. 8vo, cloth elegant, gilt edges, price 10s. 6d.

" The volume is at once useful as a botanical work, and exquisite as the
ornament of a boudoir table."—*Britannia.*
" As full of interest as of beauty."—*Art Journal.*

BEAUTIFUL LIBRARY EDITION.

THE VICAR OF WAKEFIELD;

A Tale. By OLIVER GOLDSMITH. Printed by Whittingham.
With Eight Illustrations, by J. ABSOLON. Square fcap. 8vo,
price 5s. extra cloth ; 10s. 6d. antique morocco, gilt edges.

"Mr. Absolon's graphic sketches add greatly to the interest of the volume.
Altogether, it is as pretty an edition of the 'Vicar' as we have seen. Mrs.
Primrose herself would consider it 'well-dressed.'"—*Art Journal.*
" A delightful edition of one of the most delightful of works. The fine
old type and thick paper make this volume attractive to any lover of books."
—*Edinburgh Guardian.*

NEW AND POPULAR WORKS FOR THE YOUNG.

WILL WEATHERHELM;

Or, the Yarn of an Old Sailor about his Early Life and Adventures. By W. H. G. KINGSTON, Author of " Peter the Whaler," &c. Illustrated by G. H. THOMAS. Fcap. 8vo, price 5s. cloth ; 5s. 6d. gilt edges.

THE WHITE ELEPHANT;

Or, the Hunters of Ava, and the King of the Golden Foot. By WILLIAM DALTON, Author of the "War Tiger," &c. Illustrated by HARRISON WEIR. Fcap. 8vo, price 5s. cloth ; 5s. 6d. gilt edges.

FRANK AND ANDREA;

Or, Forest Life in the Island of Sardinia. By ALFRED ELWES, Author of " Paul Blake," &c. Illustrated by ROBERT DUDLEY. Fcap. 8vo, price 5s. cloth ; 5s. 6d. gilt edges.

THE NINE LIVES OF A CAT:

A Tale of Wonder. Written and Illustrated by C. H. BENNETT. Twenty-four Engravings. Imperial 16mo, price 2s. 6d. cloth ; 3s. 6d. coloured.

THE GIRL'S OWN TOY MAKER,

And Book of Recreation. By E. LANDELLS, Author of " The Boy's Own Toy Maker," " Home Pastime," &c. With 200 Illustrations. Royal 16mo, price 2s. 6d. cloth.

BLIND MAN'S HOLIDAY;

Short Tales for the Nursery. By the Author of " Mia and Charlie," " Sidney Grey," &c. Illustrated by JOHN ABSOLON. Super-royal 16mo, price 3s. 6d. cloth ; 4s. 6d. coloured, gilt edges.

TUPPY;

Or, the Autobiography of a Donkey. By the Author of " The Triumphs of Steam," &c. &c. Illustrated by HARRISON WEIR. Super-royal 16mo, price 2s. 6d. cloth ; 3s. 6d. coloured, gilt edges.

FUNNY FABLES FOR LITTLE FOLKS.

By FRANCES FREELING BRODERIP (Daughter of the late THOMAS HOOD). Illustrated by her Brother. Super-royal 16mo, price 2s. 6d. cloth ; 3s. 6d. coloured, gilt edges.

THE HISTORY OF A QUARTERN LOAF.

Rhymes and Pictures. By WILLIAM NEWMAN. 12 Illustrations. Price 1s.

A WOMAN'S SECRET;

Or, How to Make Home Happy. 18mo, with Frontispiece. Price 6d.

*** This little work is admirably adapted for circulation among the working classes, being written in a pleasing and attractive style, and containing useful receipts for preparing plain, cheap, and nutritious food.

HAND SHADOWS,

To be thrown upon the Wall. A Series of Novel and Original Designs. By HENRY BURSILL. 4to, price 2s. 6d. plain ; 3s. 6d. coloured.

" Uncommonly clever—some wonderful effects are produced."—*The Press.*

A SECOND SERIES OF HAND SHADOWS;

With Eighteen New Subjects. By H. BURSILL. Price 2s. 6d. plain ; 3s. 6d. coloured.

THE TRIUMPHS OF STEAM;

Or, STORIES FROM THE LIVES OF WATT, ARKWRIGHT, AND STEPHENSON. By the Author of "Might not Right," "Our Eastern Empire," &c. With Illustrations by J. GILBERT. Dedicated by permission to Robert Stephenson, Esq., M.P. Royal 16mo, price 3s. 6d. cloth ; 4s. 6d. coloured, gilt edges.

" A most delicious volume of examples."—*Art Journal.*

THE WAR TIGER;

Or, ADVENTURES AND WONDERFUL FORTUNES OF THE YOUNG SEA-CHIEF AND HIS LAD CHOW. By WILLIAM DALTON, Author of "The Wolf Boy of China," Illustrated by H. S. MELVILLE. Fcap. 8vo, price 5s. cloth extra.

" A tale of lively adventure, vigorously told, and embodying much curious information."—*Illustrated News.*

THE BOY'S OWN TOY MAKER:

A Practical Illustrated Guide to the useful employment of Leisure Hours. By E. LANDELLS. Second Edition. With upwards of 150 Cuts. Royal 16mo, price 2s. 6d. cloth.

" A new and valuable form of endless amusement."—*Nonconformist.*
" We recommend it to all who have children to be instructed and amused."
—*Economist.*

BY THE LATE THOMAS HOOD.

THE HEADLONG CAREER AND WOFUL ENDING OF
PRECOCIOUS PIGGY. Written for his Children, by the
late THOMAS HOOD. With a Preface by his Daughter ; and
Illustrated by his Son. Post 4to, price 2s. 6d. coloured.

" The Illustrations are intensely humorous."—*The Critic.*

THE FAIRY TALES OF SCIENCE ;
A Book for Youth. By J. C. BROUGH. With 16 beautiful
Illustrations by C. H. BENNETT. Fcap. 8vo, price 5s. cloth.

CONTENTS : 1. The Age of Monsters.—2. The Amber
Spirit.—3. The Four Elements.—4. The Life of an Atom.—
5. A Little Bit.—6. Modern Alchemy.—7. Magic of a Sun-
beam.—8. Two Eyes Better than One.—9. The Mermaid's
Home.—10. Animated Flowers.—11. Metamorphoses.—12.
The Invisible World.—13. Wonderful Plants.—14. Water
Bewitched.—15. Pluto's Kingdom.—16. Moving Lands.—
17. The Gnomes.—18. A Flight through Space.—19. The
Tale of a Comet.—20. The Wonderful Lamp.

" Science, perhaps, was never made more attractive and easy of entrance
into the youthful mind."—*The Builder.*

" Altogether the volume is one of the most original, as well as one of the
most useful, books of the season."—*Gentleman's Magazine.*

PAUL BLAKE ;
Or, The STORY of a BOY'S PERILS in the ISLANDS of CORSICA
and MONTE CRISTO. By ALFRED ELWES, Author of " Ocean
and her Rulers." Illustrated by ANELAY. Fcap. 8vo, 5s. cloth.

" This spirited and engaging story will lead our young friends to a very
intimate acquaintance with the island of Corsica."—*Art Journal.*

SUNDAY EVENINGS WITH SOPHIA ;
Or, LITTLE TALKS ON GREAT SUBJECTS. A Book for Girls.
By LEONORA G. BELL. With Frontispiece by J. ABSOLON.
Fcap. 8vo, price 2s. 6d. cloth.

" A very suitable gift for a thoughtful girl."—*Bell's Messenger.*

SCENES OF ANIMAL LIFE AND CHARACTER ;
FROM NATURE AND RECOLLECTION. In Twenty Plates. By
J. B. 4to, price 2s. 6d. plain ; 3s. 6d. coloured, fancy
boards.

" Truer, heartier, more playful, or more enjoyable sketches of animal life
could scarcely be found anywhere."—*Spectator.*

THREE CHRISTMAS PLAYS FOR CHILDREN;

THE SLEEPER AWAKENED. THE WONDERFUL BIRD. CRINOLINE. By THERESA PULSZKY. With Original Music, by JANSA; and Three Illustrations by ARMITAGE, coloured. Price 3s. 6d. cloth, gilt edges.

DER SCHWÄTZER;

Or, THE PRATTLER. An amusing Introduction to the German Language, on the Plan of "Le Babillard." With 16 Illustrations. 16mo, price 2s. cloth.

TABULAR VIEWS OF THE GEOGRAPHY AND SACRED HISTORY OF PALESTINE, & OF THE TRAVELS OF ST. PAUL.

Intended for Pupil Teachers, and others engaged in Class Teaching. By A. T. WHITE. Oblong 8vo, price 1s. sewed.

MIGHT NOT RIGHT;

Or, STORIES OF THE DISCOVERY AND CONQUEST OF AMERICA. By the Author of "Our Eastern Empire," &c. Illustrated by J. GILBERT. Royal 16mo, price 3s. 6d. cloth; 4s. 6d. coloured, and gilt edges.

"With the fortunes of Columbus, Cortes, and Pizarro, for the staple of these stories, the writer has succeeded in producing a very interesting volume."—*Illustrated News.*

JACK FROST AND BETTY SNOW;

WITH OTHER TALES FOR WINTRY NIGHTS AND RAINY DAYS. Illustrated by H. WEIR. 2s. 6d. cloth; 3s. 6d. coloured, gilt edges.

"The dedication of these pretty tales proves by whom they are written; they are indelibly stamped with that natural and graceful method of amusing while instructing, which only persons of genius possess."—*Art Journal.*

OLD NURSE'S BOOK OF RHYMES, JINGLES, AND DITTIES.

Edited and Illustrated by C. H. BENNETT, Author of "Shadows." With Ninety Engravings. Fcap. 4to, price 3s. 6d. cloth, plain, or 6s. coloured.

"The illustrations are all so replete with fun and imagination, that we scarcely know who will be most pleased with the book, the good-natured grandfather who gives it, or the chubby grandchild who gets it, for a Christmas-Box."—*Notes and Queries.*

MAUD SUMMERS THE SIGHTLESS;

A NARRATIVE FOR THE YOUNG. Illustrated by Absolon. 3s. 6d. cloth; 4s. 6d. coloured, gilt edges.

"A touching and beautiful story."—*Christian Treasury.*

CLARA HOPE;

Or, THE BLADE AND THE EAR. By MISS MILNER. With Frontispiece by BIRKET FOSTER. Fcap. 8vo, price 3s. 6d. cloth ; 4s. 6d. cloth elegant, gilt edges.

" A beautiful narrative, showing how bad habits may be eradicated, and evil tempers subdued."—*British Mother's Journal.*

THE ADVENTURES AND EXPERIENCES OF BIDDY

DORKING, AND OF THE FAT FROG. Edited by MRS. S. C. HALL. Illustrated by H. WEIR. 2s. 6d. cloth ; 3s. 6d. coloured, gilt edges.

" Most amusingly and wittily told."—*Morning Herald.*

ATTRACTIVE AND INSTRUCTIVE AMUSEMENT FOR THE YOUNG.

HOME PASTIME;

Or, THE CHILD'S OWN TOY MAKER. With practical instructions. By E. LANDELLS. Price 5s. complete, with the Cards and Descriptive Letterpress.

*** By this novel and ingenious " Pastime," beautiful Models can be made by Children from the Cards, by attending to the Plain and Simple Instructions in the Book.

CONTENTS : 1. Wheelbarrow.—2. Cab.—3. Omnibus.— 4. Nursery Yacht.—5. French Bedstead.—6. Perambulator.—7. Railway Engine.—8. Railway Tender.—9. Railway Carriage.—10. Prince Albert's Model Cottage.—11. Windmill.—12. Sledge.

" As a delightful exercise of ingenuity, and a most sensible mode of passing a winter's evening, we commend the Child's own Toy Maker."—*Illustrated News.*

" Should be in every house blessed with the presence of children."—*The Field.*

HISTORICAL ACTING CHARADES;

Or, AMUSEMENTS FOR WINTER EVENINGS. By the Author of "Cat and Dog," &c. New Edition. Fcap. 8vo, price 3s. 6d. cloth ; 4s. gilt edges.

"A rare book for Christmas parties, and of practical value."—*Illustrated News.*

THE STORY OF JACK AND THE GIANTS;

With Thirty-five Illustrations by RICHARD DOYLE. Beautifully printed. New and Cheaper Edition. Fcap. 4to, price 2s. 6d. in fancy bds. ; 4s. 6d. coloured, extra cloth, gilt edges.

" In Doyle's drawings we have wonderful conceptions, which will secure the book a place amongst the treasures of collectors, as well as excite the imaginations of children."—*Illustrated Times.*

HISTORY OF INDIA FOR THE YOUNG.

OUR EASTERN EMPIRE;

Or, STORIES FROM THE HISTORY OF BRITISH INDIA. By the Author of "The Martyr Land," "Might not Right," &c. With Four Illustrations. Second Edition, with continuation to the Proclamation of Queen Victoria. Royal 16mo, cloth, 3s. 6d. ; 4s. 6d. coloured.

"These stories are charming, and convey a general view of the progress of our Empire in the East. The tales are told with admirable clearness."—*Athenæum.*

THE MARTYR LAND;

Or, TALES OF THE VAUDOIS. By the Author of "Our Eastern Empire," &c. Frontispiece by J. GILBERT. Royal 16mo, price 3s. 6d. cloth.

"While practical lessons run throughout, they are never obtruded; the whole tone is refined without affectation, religious and cheerful."—*English Churchman.*

JULIA MAITLAND;

Or, PRIDE GOES BEFORE A FALL. By M. and E. KIRBY, Authors of "The Talking Bird," &c. Illustrated by JOHN ABSOLON. Price 2s. 6d. cloth ; 3s. 6d. coloured, gilt edges.

"It is nearly such a story as Miss Edgeworth might have written on the same theme."—*The Press.*

PICTURES FROM THE PYRENEES;

Or, AGNES' AND KATE'S TRAVELS. By CAROLINE BELL. With numerous Illustrations. Small 4to, price 3s. 6d. cloth ; 4s. 6d. coloured, gilt edges.

"With admirable simplicity of manner it notices the towns, the scenery, the people, and the natural phenomena of this grand mountain region."—*The Press.*

THE EARLY DAWN;

Or, STORIES TO THINK ABOUT. By a COUNTRY CLERGYMAN. Illustrated by H. WEIR, &c. Small 4to, price 2s. 6d. cloth ; 3s. 6d. coloured, gilt edges.

"The matter is both wholesome and instructive, and must fascinate as well as benefit the young."—*Literarium.*

ANGELO;

Or, THE PINE FOREST AMONG THE ALPS. By GERALDINE E. JEWSBURY, Author of "The Adopted Child," &c. With Illustrations by JOHN ABSOLON. Small 4to, price 2s. 6d. cloth ; 3s. 6d. coloured, gilt edges.

"As pretty a child's story as one might look for on a winter's day."—*Examiner.*

GRANNY'S WONDERFUL CHAIR;

AND ITS TALES OF FAIRY TIMES. By FRANCES BROWNE. With Illustrations by KENNY MEADOWS. Small 4to, 3s. 6d. cloth ; 4s. 6d. coloured, gilt edges.

"One of the happiest blendings of marvel and moral we have ever seen." —*Literary Gazette.*

ALFRED CROWQUILL.

TALES OF MAGIC AND MEANING;

Written and Illustrated by ALFRED CROWQUILL, Author of "Funny Leaves for the Younger Branches," "The Careless Chicken," "Picture Fables," &c. Small 4to, price 3s. 6d. cloth ; 4s. 6d. coloured, gilt edges.

"Cleverly written and abounding in frolic and pathos, and inculcate so pure a moral, that we must pronounce him a very fortunate little fellow who catches these 'Tales of Magic' from a Christmas-tree."—*Athenæum.*

FAGGOTS FOR THE FIRESIDE;

Or, TALES OF FACT AND FANCY. By PETER PARLEY. With Twelve Tinted Illustrations. Fcap. 8vo, 3s. 6d. cloth.

CONTENTS : The Boy Captive ; or, Jumping Rabbit's Story—The White Owl—Tom Titmouse—The Wolf and Fox—Bob Link—Autobiography of a Sparrow—The Children of the Sun : a Tale of the Incas—The Soldier and Musician—The Rich Man and his Son—The Avalanche—Flint and Steel—Songs of the Seasons, &c.

"A new work by Peter Parley is a pleasant greeting for all boys and girls, wherever the English language is spoken or read. He has a happy method of conveying information, while seeming to address himself to the imagination."—*The Critic.*

THE DISCONTENTED CHILDREN;

AND HOW THEY WERE CURED. By MARY and ELIZABETH KIRBY, Authors of "The Talking Bird," &c. Illustrated by H. K. BROWNE (Phiz). Second Edition, price 2s. 6d. cloth ; 3s. 6d. coloured, gilt edges.

"We know no better method of banishing 'discontent' from school-room and nursery than by introducing this wise and clever story to their inmates." —*Art Journal.*

THE TALKING BIRD;

Or, THE LITTLE GIRL WHO KNEW WHAT WAS GOING TO HAPPEN. By M. and E. KIRBY, Authors of "The Discontented Children," &c. With Illustrations by HABLOT K. BROWNE (Phiz). Price 2s. 6d. cloth ; 3s. 6d. coloured.

"The story is ingeniously told, and the moral clearly shown."—*Athenæum.*

THE MERRY WEDDING;

Dedicated without permission to the Brides of England. In Six Plates, with verses. Oblong 4to, price 2s. 6d. plain ; 3s. 6d. coloured.

WORDS BY THE WAYSIDE;

Or, THE CHILDREN AND THE FLOWERS. By EMILY AYTON. With Illustrations by H. ANELAY. Small 4to, price 3s. 6d. cloth ; 4s. 6d. coloured, gilt edges.

"Seldom have we opened a book designed for young people which has afforded us greater satisfaction. It has our most cordial commendation."— *British Mother's Magazine.*

"The simple and quiet manner in which the beauties of nature are gradually unfolded is so fascinating, and the manner in which everything is associated with the Creator is so natural and charming, that we strongly recommend the book."—*Bell's Messenger.*

PLAYING AT SETTLERS;

Or, THE FAGGOT HOUSE. By MRS. R. LEE, Author of "The African Wanderers," "Adventures in Australia," &c. Price 2s. 6d. cloth ; 3s. 6d. coloured, gilt edges.

"A pleasant story, drawn from the reminiscences of the author's own child-life."—*The Press.*

THE REMARKABLE HISTORY OF THE HOUSE THAT

JACK BUILT. Splendidly Illustrated and magnificently Illuminated by THE SON OF A GENIUS. Price 2s., *in fancy cover.*

"Magnificent in suggestion, and most comical in expression."— *Athenæum.*

LAUGH AND GROW WISE;

By the Senior Owl of Ivy Hall. With Sixteen Large Coloured Plates. Quarto. Price 2s. 6d. fancy boards.

LETTERS FROM SARAWAK,

Addressed to a Child. Embracing an Account of the Manners, Customs, and Religion of the Inhabitants of Borneo, with Incidents of Missionary Life among the Natives. By MRS. M'DOUGALL. Fourth Thousand, enlarged in size, with Illustrations. 3s. 6d. cloth.

" All is new, interesting, and admirably told."—*Church and State Gazette.*

ALFRED CROWQUILL'S COMICAL BOOKS,
Uniform in size with "The Strawwelpeter."

PICTURE FABLES.

Written and Illustrated with Sixteen large coloured Plates, by ALFRED CROWQUILL. Price 2s. 6d.

THE CARELESS CHICKEN.

By the BARON KRAKEMSIDES. With Sixteen large coloured Plates, by ALFRED CROWQUILL. 4to, 2s. 6d.

FUNNY LEAVES FOR THE YOUNGER BRANCHES.

By the BARON KRAKEMSIDES of Burstenoudelafen Castle. Illustrated by ALFRED CROWQUILL. Coloured Plates. 2s. 6d.

BY MRS BRAY.

A PEEP AT THE PIXIES;

Or, LEGENDS OF THE WEST. By MRS. BRAY, Author of "The Borders of the Tamar and the Tavy," "Life of Stothard," "Trelawny," &c. &c. With Illustrations by HABLOT K. BROWNE (Phiz). Super-royal 16mo, price 3s. 6d. cloth ; 4s. 6d. coloured, gilt edges.

" A peep at the actual Pixies of Devonshire, faithfully described by Mrs. Bray, is a treat. Her knowledge of the locality, her affection for her subject, her exquisite feeling for nature, and her real delight in fairy lore, have given a freshness to the little volume we did not expect. The notes at the end contain matter of interest for all who feel a desire to know the origin of such tales and legends."—*Art Journal.*

OCEAN AND HER RULERS;

A Narrative of the Nations who have from the Earliest Ages held dominion over the Sea ; comprising a brief History of Navigation, from the remotest Periods to the Present Time. By ALFRED ELWES. With Frontispiece by SCOTT. Fcap. 8vo, 5s. cloth.

" The volume is replete with valuable and interesting information; and we cordially recommend it as a useful auxiliary in the school-room, and entertaining companion in the library."—*Morning Post.*

THE FAVOURITE PICTURE-BOOK;

A Gallery of Delights, designed for the Amusement and Instruction of the Young. With several hundred Illustrations from Drawings by J. ABSOLON, H. K. BROWNE (Phiz), J. GILBERT, T. LANDSEER, J. LEECH, J. S. PROUT, H. WEIR, &c. Royal 4to, price 3s. 6d. bound in an elegant cover; 7s. 6d. coloured, or mounted on cloth.

THE DAY OF A BABY-BOY;

A Story for a Little Child. By E. BERGER, with Illustrations by JOHN ABSOLON. Second Edition. Super-royal 16mo, price 2s. 6d. cloth; 3s. 6d. coloured, gilt edges.

"A sweet little book for the nursery."—*Christian Times.*

CAT AND DOG;

Or, MEMOIRS OF PUSS AND THE CAPTAIN. A Story founded on Fact. Illustrated by HARRISON WEIR. Fifth Edition. Super-royal 16mo, 2s. 6d. cloth; 3s. 6d. coloured, gilt edges.

"The author of this amusing little tale is evidently a keen observer of nature. The illustrations are well executed; and the moral which points the tale is conveyed in the most attractive form."—*Britannia.*

THE DOLL AND HER FRIENDS;

Or, MEMOIRS OF THE LADY SERAPHINA. Third Edition. With Four Illustrations by H. K. BROWNE (Phiz). Small 4to, 2s. 6d. cloth; 3s. 6d. coloured, gilt edges.

"Evidently written by one who has brought great powers to bear upon a small matter."—*Morning Herald.*

CLARISSA DONNELLY;

Or, THE HISTORY OF AN ADOPTED CHILD. By MISS GERALDINE E. JEWSBURY. With an Illustration by JOHN ABSOLON. Fcap. 8vo, 3s. 6d. cloth; 4s. gilt edges.

"With wonderful power, only to be matched by as admirable a simplicity, Miss Jewsbury has narrated the history of a child. For nobility of purpose, for simple, nervous writing, and for artistic construction, it is one of the most valuable works of the day."—*Lady's Companion.*

WORKS BY THE LATE MRS. R. LEE.

ANECDOTES OF THE HABITS AND INSTINCTS OF
BIRDS, FISHES, AND REPTILES. With Six Illustrations by HARRISON WEIR. Fcap. 8vo, 5s. cloth.

ANECDOTES OF THE HABITS AND INSTINCTS OF
ANIMALS. Second Edition. With Six Illustrations by HARRISON WEIR. Fcap. 8vo, 5s. cloth.

"Amusing, instructive, and ably written."—*Literary Gazette.*
"Mrs. Lee's authorities—to name only one, Professor. Owen—are, for the most part, first-rate."—*Athenæum.*

TWELVE STORIES OF THE SAYINGS AND DOINGS OF
ANIMALS. With Illustrations by J. W. ARCHER. Super-royal 16mo, 2s. 6d. cloth; 3s. 6d. coloured, gilt edges.

"It is just such books as this that educate the imagination of children, and enlist their sympathies for the brute creation."—*Nonconformist.*

ADVENTURES IN AUSTRALIA;
Or, THE WANDERINGS OF CAPTAIN SPENCER IN THE BUSH AND THE WILDS. Second Edition. Illustrated by PROUT. Fcap. 8vo, 5s. cloth; 5s. 6d. gilt edges.

"The work cannot fail to achieve an extensive popularity."—*Art Journal.*
"This volume should find a place in every school library, and it will, we are sure, be a very welcome and useful prize."—*Educational Times.*

THE AFRICAN WANDERERS;
Or, THE ADVENTURES OF CARLOS AND ANTONIO; embracing interesting Descriptions of the Manners and Customs of the Western Tribes. Third Edition. With Eight Engravings. Fcap. 8vo, 5s. cloth; 5s. 6d. gilt edges.

"For fascinating adventure and rapid succession of incident, the volume is equal to any relation of travel we ever read. It exhibits marked ability as well as extensive knowledge, and deserves perusal from all ages."—*Britannia.*
"In strongly recommending this admirable work to the attention of young readers, we feel that we are rendering a real service to the cause of African civilization."—*Patriot.*

SIR THOMAS;
Or, THE ADVENTURES OF A CORNISH BARONET IN WESTERN AFRICA. With Illustrations by J. GILBERT. Fcap. 8vo, cloth, price 3s. 6d.

"The tale gives a faithful picture of the manners and customs of the people of Fanti."—*Morning Post.*

FAMILIAR NATURAL HISTORY.

With Forty-two Illustrations from Original Drawings by
HARRISON WEIR. Super-royal 16mo, 3s. 6d. cloth, plain;
6s. coloured, gilt edges.

HARRY HAWKINS'S H-BOOK;

. SHOWING HOW HE LEARNED TO ASPIRATE HIS H's. Frontispiece by H. WEIR. Super-royal 16mo, price 6d.

" No family or schoolroom within, or indeed beyond, the sound of Bow
bells, should be without this merry manual."—*Art Journal.*

THE FAMILY BIBLE NEWLY OPENED;

' WITH UNCLE GOODWIN'S ACCOUNT OF IT. By JEFFERYS
TAYLOR, Author of "A Glance at the Globe," &c. Frontispiece by J. GILBERT. Fcap. 8vo, 3s. 6d. cloth.

"A very good account of the Sacred Writings, adapted to the taste,
feelings, and intelligence of young people."—*Educational Times.*

. "Parents will also find it a great aid in the religious teaching of their
families."—*Edinburgh Witness.*

KATE AND ROSALIND;

OR, EARLY EXPERIENCES. By the Author of "Quicksands
. on Foreign Shores," &c. Fcap. 8vo, 3s. 6d. cloth; 4s. gilt
edges.

"A book of unusual merit. The story is exceedingly well told, and the
characters are drawn with a freedom and boldness seldom met with."—
Church of England Quarterly.

"We have not room to exemplify the skill with which Puseyism is tracked
and detected. The Irish scenes are of an excellence that has not been sur-
passed since the best days of Miss Edgeworth."—*Fraser's Magazine.*

GOOD IN EVERYTHING;

OR, THE EARLY HISTORY OF GILBERT HARLAND. By MRS.
BARWELL, Author of "Little Lessons for Little Learners,"
&c. Second Edition. With Illustrations by JOHN GILBERT.
Royal 16mo, 3s. 6d. cloth; 4s. 6d. coloured, gilt edges.

"The moral of this exquisite little tale will do more good than a thousand
set tasks abounding with dry and uninteresting truisms."—*Bell's Messenger.*

WORKS BY W. H. G. KINGSTON.

RED MARKHAM IN RUSSIA;

Or, THE BOY TRAVELLERS IN THE LAND OF THE CZAR. With Illustrations by R. T. LANDELLS. Fcap. 8vo, price 5s. cloth ; 5s. 6d. gilt edges.

" Most admirably does this book unite a capital narrative with the communication of valuable information respecting Russia."—*Nonconformist.*

SALT WATER;

Or, NEIL D'ARCY'S SEA LIFE AND ADVENTURES (a Book for Boys). With Eight Illustrations. Fcap. 8vo, price 5s. cloth ; 5s. 6d. gilt edges.

" With the exception of Captain Marryat, we know of no English author who will compare with Mr. Kingston as a writer of books of nautical adventure."—*Illustrated News.*

BLUE JACKETS;

Or, CHIPS OF THE OLD BLOCK. A Narrative of the Gallant Exploits of British Seamen, and of the principal Events in the Naval Service during the Reign of Her Most Gracious Majesty QUEEN VICTORIA. Post 8vo, price 7s. 6d. cloth.

" A more acceptable testimonial than this to the valour and enterprise of the British Navy has not issued from the press for many years."—*The Critic.*

MANCO, THE PERUVIAN CHIEF.

With Illustrations by CARL SCHMOLZE. Fcap. 8vo, 5s. cloth ; 5s. 6d. gilt edges.

" A capital book ; the story being one of much interest, and presenting a good account of the history and institutions, the customs and manners of the country."—*Literary Gazette.*

MARK SEAWORTH;

A Tale of the Indian Ocean. By the Author of "Peter the Whaler," &c. With Illustrations by J. ABSOLON. Second Edition. Fcap. 8vo, 5s. cloth; 5s. 6d. gilt edges.

" No more interesting, nor more safe book, can be put into the hands of youth; and to boys especially ' Mark Seaworth' will be a treasure of delight."—*Art Journal.*

PETER THE WHALER;

His Early Life and Adventures in the Arctic Regions. Second Edition. With Illustrations by E. DUNCAN. Fcap. 8vo, 5s. cloth ; 5s. 6d. gilt edges.

" A better present for a boy of an active turn of mind could not be found. The tone of the book is manly, healthful, and vigorous."—*Weekly News.*

" In short, a book which the old may, but which the young must, read when they have once begun it."—*Athenæum.*

WORKS BY MRS. LOUDON.

DOMESTIC PETS;

Their Habits and Management ; with Illustrative Anecdotes. By MRS. LOUDON, Author of " Facts from the World of Nature," &c. With Engravings from Drawings by HARRISON WEIR. Second Thousand. Fcap 8vo, 2s. 6d. cloth.

CONTENTS :—The Dog, Cat, Squirrel, Rabbit, Guinea-Pig, White Mice, the Parrot and other Talking-Birds, Singing-Birds, Doves and Pigeons, Gold and Silver Fish.

"A most attractive and instructive little work. All who study Mrs. Loudon's pages will be able to treat their pets with certainty and wisdom." —*Standard of Freedom.*

FACTS FROM THE WORLD OF NATURE,

ANIMATE AND INANIMATE. Part 1. THE EARTH. Part 2. THE WATERS. Part 3. ATMOSPHERIC PHENOMENA. Part 4. ANIMAL LIFE. By MRS. LOUDON. With numerous Illustrations on Wood, and Steel Frontispiece. Third Thousand. Fcap. 8vo, 5s. cloth, gilt edges.

" The rare merit of this volume is its comprehensive selection of prominent features and striking facts."—*Literary Gazette.*

"It abounds with adventure and lively narrative, vivid description, and poetic truth."—*Illustrated News.*

" A volume as charming as it is useful. The illustrations are numerous and well executed."—*Church and State Gazette.*

TALES OF SCHOOL LIFE.

By AGNES LOUDON, Author of " Tales for Young People." With Illustrations by JOHN ABSOLON. Second Edition. Royal 16mo, 2s. 6d. plain ; 3s. 6d. coloured, gilt edges.

"These reminiscences of school-days will be recognised as truthful pictures of every-day occurrence. The style is colloquial and pleasant, and therefore well suited to those for whose perusal it is intended."—*Athenæum.*

TALES FROM CATLAND.

Dedicated to the Young Kittens of England. By an OLD TABBY. Illustrated by H. WEIR. Third Edition. Small 4to, 2s. 6d. plain ; 3s. 6d. coloured.

"The combination of quiet humour and sound sense has made this one o f the pleasantest little books of the season."—*Lady's Newspaper.*

THE WONDERS OF HOME, IN ELEVEN STORIES.

By GRANDFATHER GREY. With Illustrations. 2nd Edit.
roy. 16mo, 3s. 6d. cloth; 4s. 6d. coloured.—*Contents :*—

Story of—1. A CUP OF TEA.   2. A PIECE OF SUGAR.
    3. A MILK-JUG.   4. A LUMP OF COAL.
    5. SOME HOT WATER.   6. A PIN.
    7. JENNY'S SASH.   8. HARRY'S JACKET.
    9. A TUMBLER.   10. A KNIFE.
         11. THIS BOOK.

"The idea is excellent, and its execution equally commendable. The subjects are very happily told in a light yet sensible manner."—*Weekly News.*

EVERY-DAY THINGS;

Or, USEFUL KNOWLEDGE respecting the PRINCIPAL ANIMAL, VEGETABLE, and MINERAL SUBSTANCES in COMMON USE. Written for Young Persons, by a LADY. 18mo, 2s. cloth.

"A little encyclopædia of useful knowledge; deserving a place in every juvenile library."—*Evangelical Magazine.*

PRICE SIXPENCE EACH, PLAIN; ONE SHILLING, COLOURED.

In super-royal 16mo, beautifully printed, each with Seven Illus-trations by HARRISON WEIR, *and Descriptions by* MRS. LEE.

    1. BRITISH ANIMALS.   First Series.
    2. BRITISH ANIMALS.   Second Series.
    3. BRITISH BIRDS.
    4. FOREIGN ANIMALS.   First Series.
    5. FOREIGN ANIMALS.   Second Series.
    6. FOREIGN BIRDS.

₊ Or bound in One Vol. under the title of "Familiar Natural History," *see page* 14.

Uniform in size and price with the above.

THE FARM AND ITS SCENES. With Six Pictures from Drawings by HARRISON WEIR.

THE DIVERTING HISTORY OF JOHN GILPIN. With Six Illustrations by WATTS PHILLIPS.

THE PEACOCK AT HOME AND THE BUTTERFLY'S BALL. With Four Illustrations by HARRISON WEIR.

A WORD TO THE WISE;

Or, HINTS ON THE CURRENT IMPROPRIETY OF EXPRESSION IN WRITING AND SPEAKING. By PARRY GWYNNE. Fifth Edition. 18mo, price 6d. sewed, or 1s. cloth, gilt edges.

"All who wish to mind their *p's* and *q's* should consult this little volume." —*Gentleman's Magazine.*
"May be advantageously consulted by even the well-educated."— *Athenæum.*

THE FAVOURITE LIBRARY.

A Series of Works for the Young; each Volume with an Illustration by a well-known Artist. Price ONE SHILLING.

1. THE ESKDALE HERD-BOY. By LADY STODDART.

2. MRS. LEICESTER'S SCHOOL. By CHARLES and MARY LAMB.

3. HISTORY OF THE ROBINS. By MRS. TRIMMER.

4. MEMOIRS OF BOB THE SPOTTED TERRIER.

5. KEEPER'S TRAVELS IN SEARCH OF HIS MASTER.

6. THE SCOTTISH ORPHANS. By LADY STODDART.

7. NEVER WRONG; or, THE YOUNG DISPUTANT; and "IT WAS ONLY IN FUN."

8. THE LIFE AND PERAMBULATIONS OF A MOUSE.

9. EASY INTRODUCTION TO THE KNOWLEDGE OF NATURE. By MRS. TRIMMER.

10. RIGHT AND WRONG. By the Author of "Always Happy."

11. HARRY'S HOLIDAY. By JEFFERYS TAYLOR.

12. SHORT POEMS AND HYMNS FOR CHILDREN.

The above may be had, Two Volumes bound in one, at Two Shillings cloth; or 2s. 6d. gilt edges, as follows:—

1. LADY STODDART'S SCOTTISH TALES.

2. ANIMAL HISTORIES. THE DOG.

3. ANIMAL HISTORIES. THE ROBINS and MOUSE.

4. TALES FOR BOYS. HARRY'S HOLIDAY and NEVER WRONG.

5. TALES FOR GIRLS. MRS. LEICESTER'S SCHOOL and RIGHT AND WRONG.

6. POETRY AND NATURE. SHORT POEMS and TRIMMER'S INTRODUCTION.

STORIES OF JULIAN AND HIS PLAYFELLOWS.

Written by his Mamma. With Four Illustrations by JOHN ABSOLON. Second Edition. Small 4to, 2s. 6d. plain ; 3s. 6d. coloured, gilt edges.

" The lessons taught by Julian's mamma are each fraught with an excellent moral."—*Morning Advertiser.*

BLADES AND FLOWERS;

Poems for Children. Frontispiece by H. ANELAY. Fcap. 8vo, price 2s. cloth.

" Breathing the same spirit as the nursery poems of Jane Taylor."—*Literary Gazette.*

AUNT JANE'S VERSES FOR CHILDREN.

By Mrs. T. D. CREWDSON. Illustrated with twelve beautiful Engravings. Fcap. 8vo, 3s. 6d. cloth.

" A charming little volume of excellent moral and religious tendency."—*Evangelical Magazine.*

HINTS TO A CLERGYMAN'S WIFE;

Or, FEMALE PAROCHIAL DUTIES PRACTICALLY ILLUSTRATED. Dedicated to the Rev. C. BRIDGES. Third Edition. Fcap. 8vo, 3s. cloth.

CONTENTS: Part 1. Hints relative to Personal Character. Part 2. Hints relative to active exertion among the Poor—Cottage Visits—The Sick—Schools—Religious Instruction of the Young—Cottage Reading—Parochial Library—Suggestions for the Employment of the Poor, &c.

" This very useful book is evidently the work of an author practically conversant with her subject in all its bearings and details. We cordially recommend the work to the careful study of all Christian ladies, whose position in life gives them influence among the poor of their parish."—*Englishwoman's Magazine.*

ILLUSTRATED BY GEORGE CRUIKSHANK.

KIT BAM, THE BRITISH SINBAD;

Or, THE YARNS OF AN OLD MARINER. By MARY COWDEN CLARKE, Author of "The Concordance to Shakspeare," &c. Fcap. 8vo, price 3s. 6d. cloth ; 4s. gilt edges.

" A more captivating volume for juvenile recreative reading we never remember to have seen. It is as wonderful as the ' Arabian Nights,' while it is free from the objectionable matter which characterises the Eastern fiction."—*Standard of Freedom.*

" Cruikshank's plates are worthy of his genius."—*Examiner.*

THE HISTORY OF A FAMILY;

Or, RELIGION OUR BEST SUPPORT. With an Illustration on Steel by JOHN ABSOLON. Fcap. 8vo, 2s. 6d. cloth.

" A natural and gracefully written story, pervaded by a tone of scriptural piety, and well calculated to foster just views of life and duty. We hope it will find its way into many English homes."—*Englishwoman's Magazine.*

RHYMES OF ROYALTY.

THE HISTORY OF ENGLAND in Verse, from the Norman Conquest to the reign of QUEEN VICTORIA; with an Appendix, comprising a Summary of the leading events in each reign. By S. BLEWETT. Fcap. 8vo, with Frontispiece. 2s. 6d. cloth.

NEW AND CHEAPER EDITION.

THE LADY'S ALBUM OF FANCY WORK,

Consisting of Novel, Elegant, and Useful Patterns in Knitting, Netting, Crochet, and Embroidery, printed in colours. Bound in a beautiful cover. New Edit. Post 4to, 3s. 6d. gilt edges.

HANS CHRISTIAN ANDERSEN.

THE DREAM OF LITTLE TUK,

AND OTHER TALES, by H. C. ANDERSEN. Translated and dedicated to the Author by CHARLES BONER. Illustrated by COUNT POCCI. Fcap. 8vo, 2s. plain; 3s. coloured.

" Full of charming passages of prose, poetry, and such tiny dramatic scenes as will make the pulses of young readers throb with delight."—*Atlas.*

VISITS TO BEECHWOOD FARM;

Or, COUNTRY PLEASURES AND HINTS FOR HAPPINESS, ADDRESSED TO THE YOUNG. By CATHARINE M. A. COUPER. Illustrations by ABSOLON. Small 4to, 3s. 6d. plain; 4s. 6d. col.

" The work is well calculated to impress upon the minds of the young the superiority of simple and natural pleasures over those which are artificial." —*Englishwoman's Magazine.*

MARIN DE LA VOYE'S ELEMENTARY FRENCH WORKS.

LES JEUNES NARRATEURS;

Ou, PETITS CONTES MORAUX. With a Key to the difficult
Words and Phrases. Frontispiece. 18mo, 2s. cloth. ·

"Written in pure and easy French."—*Morning Post.*

THE PICTORIAL FRENCH GRAMMAR,

FOR THE USE OF CHILDREN. With Eighty Engravings.
Royal 16mo ; price 1s. 6d. cloth; 1s. sewed.

"The publication has greater than mechanical merit; it contains the
principal elements of the French language, exhibited in a plain and expressive manner."—*Spectator.*

THE FIRST BOOK OF GEOGRAPHY,

Specially adapted as a Text Book for Beginners, and as a
Guide to the Young Teacher. By HUGO REID, Author of
"Elements of Astronomy," &c. Third Edition, carefully
revised. 18mo, 1s. sewed.

"One of the most sensible little books on the subject of Geography we
have met with."—*Educational Times.* "As a lesson-book it will charm the
pupil by its brief, natural style."—*Episcopalian.*

INSECT CHANGES.

With richly Illuminated Borders, composed of Flowers and
Insects, in the highly-wrought style of the celebrated
"Hours of Anne of Brittany," and forming a First Lesson
in Entomology. Small 4to, 5s. in elegant binding.

"One of the richest gifts ever offered, even in this improving age, to child-
hood. Nothing can be more perfect in illumination than the embellishments
of this charming little volume."—*Art Union.*

THE MODERN BRITISH PLUTARCH;

Or, LIVES OF MEN DISTINGUISHED IN THE RECENT HIS-
TORY OF OUR COUNTRY FOR THEIR TALENTS, VIRTUES,
AND ACHIEVEMENTS. By W. C. TAYLOR, LL.D., Author
of "A Manual of Ancient and Modern History," &c.
12mo. Second Thousand, with a new Frontispiece. 4s. 6d.
cloth; 5s. gilt edges.

CONTENTS: Arkwright—Burke—Burns—Byron—Canning—Earl of Chat-
ham—Adam Clarke—Clive—Captain Cook—Cowper—Crabbe—Davy—Eldon
—Erskine—Fox—Franklin—Goldsmith—Earl Grey—Warren Hastings—
Heber—Howard—Jenner—Sir W. Jones—Mackintosh—H. Martyn—Sir J.
Moore—Nelson—Pitt—Romilly—Sir W. Scott—Sheridan—Smeaton—Watt
—Marquis of Wellesley—Wilberforce—Wilkie—Wellington.

"A work which will be welcomed in any circle of intelligent young persons."—*British Quarterly Review.*

HOME AMUSEMENTS:

A Choice Collection of Riddles, Charades, Conundrums, Parlour Games, and Forfeits. By PETER PUZZLEWELL, Esq., of Rebus Hall. New Edition, revised and enlarged, with Frontispiece by H. K. BROWNE (Phiz). 16mo, 2s. 6d. cloth.

EARLY DAYS OF ENGLISH PRINCES.

By MRS. RUSSELL GREY. Dedicated, by permission, to the Duchess of Roxburghe. With Illustrations by JOHN FRANKLIN. Small 4to, 3s. 6d. cloth ; 4s. 6d. coloured, gilt edges.

"Just the book for giving children some first notions of English history, as the personages it speaks about are themselves young."—*Manchester Examiner.*

FIRST STEPS TO SCOTTISH HISTORY.

By MISS RODWELL, Author of "First Steps to English History." With Ten Illustrations by WEIGALL. 16mo, 3s. 6d. cloth ; 4s. 6d. coloured.

"It is the first popular book in which we have seen the outlines of the early history of the Scottish tribes exhibited with anything like accuracy." —*Glasgow Constitutional.*

"The work is throughout agreeably and lucidly written."—*Midland Counties Herald.*

LONDON CRIES AND PUBLIC EDIFICES,

Illustrated in Twenty-four Engravings by LUKE LIMNER; with descriptive Letter-press. Square 12mo, 2s. 6d. plain ; 5s. coloured. Bound in emblematic cover.

Originally published under the Superintendence of the Society for the Diffusion of Useful Knowledge.

ARITHMETIC FOR YOUNG CHILDREN,

in a Series of Exercises, exhibiting the manner in which it should be taught. By H. GRANT, Author of "Drawing for Young Children," &c. New Edition. 1s. 6d. cloth.

"This work will be found effectual for its purpose, and interesting to children."—*Educational Times.*

"The plan is admirably conceived, and we have tested its efficacy."—*Church of England Quarterly.*

MRS. TRIMMER'S HISTORY OF ENGLAND.

Revised and brought down to the present time by MRS. MILNER. With Portraits of the Sovereigns in their proper costume, and Frontispiece by HARVEY. New Edition in One Volume. 5s. cloth.

"The editing has been very judiciously done. The work has an established reputation for the clearness of its genealogical and chronological tables, and for its pervading tone of Christian piety."—*Church and State Gazette.*

THE CELESTIAL EMPIRE;

Or, POINTS AND PICKINGS OF INFORMATION ABOUT CHINA AND THE CHINESE. By the late "OLD HUMPHREY." With Twenty Engravings from Drawings by W. H. PRIOR. Fcap. 8vo, 3s. 6d. cloth ; 4s. gilt edges.

"This very handsome volume contains an almost incredible amount of information."—*Church and State Gazette.*

"The book is exactly what the author proposed it should be, full of good information, good feeling, and good temper."—*Allen's Indian Mail.*

"Even well-known topics are treated with a graceful air of novelty."—*Athenæum.*

TALES FROM THE COURT OF OBERON;

Containing the favourite Histories of TOM THUMB, GRACIOSA AND PERCINET, VALENTINE AND ORSON, and CHILDREN IN THE WOOD. With Sixteen Illustrations by ALFRED CROW-QUILL. Small 4to, 2s. 6d. plain ; 3s. 6d. coloured.

GLIMPSES OF NATURE,

AND OBJECTS OF INTEREST DESCRIBED, DURING A VISIT TO THE ISLE OF WIGHT. Designed to assist and encourage Young Persons in forming habits of Observation. By MRS. LOUDON. Second Edition, enlarged. With Forty-one Illustrations. 3s. 6d. cloth.

"We could not recommend a more valuable little volume. It is full of information, conveyed in the most agreeable manner."—*Literary Gazette.*

"A more fitting present, or one more adapted to stimulate the faculties of 'little people,' could not be published."—*Bath and Cheltenham Gazette.*

THE SILVER SWAN:

A Fairy Tale. By MADAME DE CHATELAIN. Illustrated by JOHN LEECH. Small 4to, 2s. 6d. plain ; 3s. 6d. coloured cloth.

"The moral is in the good, broad, unmistakeable style of the best fairy period."—*Athenæum.*

"The story is written with excellent taste and sly humour."—*Atlas.*

THE YOUNG JEWESS AND HER CHRISTIAN SCHOOL-

FELLOWS. By the Author of "Rhoda," &c. With a Frontispiece by J. GILBERT. 16mo, 1s. cloth.

"The story is beautifully conceived and beautifully told, and is peculiarly adapted to impress upon the minds of young persons the powerful efficacy of example."—*Englishwoman's Magazine.*

RHODA;

Or, THE EXCELLENCE OF CHARITY. Fourth Edition. With Illustrations. 16mo, 2s. cloth.

"Not only adapted for children, but many parents might derive great advantage from studying its simple truths."—*Church and State Gazette.*

WORKS BY THE AUTHOR OF MAMMA'S BIBLE STORIES.

FANNY AND HER MAMMA;

Or, EASY LESSONS FOR CHILDREN. In which it is attempted to bring Scriptural Principles into daily practice. Illustrated by J. GILBERT. Second Edition. 16mo, 2s. 6d. cloth; 3s. 6d. coloured, gilt edges.

"A little book in beautiful large clear type, to suit the capacity of infant readers, which we can with pleasure recommend."—*Christian Lady's Mag.*

SHORT AND SIMPLE PRAYERS

FOR THE USE OF YOUNG CHILDREN, WITH HYMNS. Fourth Edition. Square 16mo, 1s. 6d. cloth.

"Well adapted to the capacities of children,—beginning with the simplest forms which the youngest child may lisp at its mother's knee, and proceeding with those suited to its gradually advancing age. Special prayers, designed for particular circumstances and occasions, are added. We cordially recommend the book."—*Christian Guardian.*

MAMMA'S BIBLE STORIES

FOR HER LITTLE BOYS AND GIRLS, adapted to the capacities of very young children. Tenth Edition, with Twelve Engravings. 2s. 6d. cloth; 3s. 6d. coloured, gilt edges.

A SEQUEL TO MAMMA'S BIBLE STORIES.

Fifth and Cheaper Edition. With Twelve Illustrations. 2s. 6d. cloth; 3s. 6d. coloured, gilt edges.

SCRIPTURE HISTORIES FOR LITTLE CHILDREN.

With Sixteen Illustrations by JOHN GILBERT. Super-royal 16mo, price 3s. cloth; 4s. 6d. coloured, gilt edges.

CONTENTS:

The History of Joseph.	History of our Saviour.
History of Moses.	The Miracles of Christ.

_{*} *Sold separately: 6d. each, plain; 1s. coloured.*

BIBLE SCENES;

Or, SUNDAY EMPLOYMENT FOR VERY YOUNG CHILDREN. Consisting of Twelve Coloured Illustrations on Cards, and the History written in Simple Language. In a neat Box, 3s. 6d.; or dissected as a Puzzle, 6s. 6d.

First Series: History of Joseph.	Third Series: History of Moses.
Second Series: History of our Saviour.	Fourth Series: The Miracles of Christ.

"It is hoped that these 'Scenes' may form a useful and interesting addition to the Sabbath occupations of the Nursery. From their very earliest infancy little children will listen with interest and delight to stories brought thus palpably before their eyes by means of illustration."—*Preface.*

TRUE STORIES FROM ANCIENT HISTORY,

Chronologically arranged from the Creation of the World to the Death of Charlemagne. Eleventh Edition. With 24 Steel Engravings. 12mo, 5s. cloth.

TRUE STORIES FROM MODERN HISTORY,

Chronologically arranged from the Death of Charlemagne to the Present Time. Eighth Edition. With 24 Steel Engravings. 12mo, 5s. cloth.

TRUE STORIES FROM ENGLISH HISTORY,

Chronologically arranged from the Invasion of the Romans to the Present Time. Sixth Edition. With 36 Steel Engravings. 12mo, 5s. cloth.

STORIES FROM THE OLD AND NEW TESTAMENTS,

on an improved plan. By the Rev. BOURNE HALL DRAPER. With 48 Engravings. Fifth Edition. 12mo, 5s. cloth.

THE WARS OF THE JEWS,

as related by JOSEPHUS ; adapted to the capacities of Young Persons. With 24 Engravings. Sixth Edit. 4s. 6d. cloth.

THE PRINCE OF WALES'S PRIMER.

With 300 Illustrations by J. GILBERT. Dedicated to Her Majesty. New Edition, price 6d. ; with title and cover printed in gold and colours, 1s.

HOW TO BE HAPPY;

Or, FAIRY GIFTS : to which is added, A SELECTION OF MORAL ALLEGORIES, from the best English Writers. Second Edition. With 8 Engravings. 12mo, 3s. 6d. cloth.

THE ABBE GAULTIER'S GEOGRAPHICAL WORKS.

I. FAMILIAR GEOGRAPHY,

With a concise Treatise on the Artificial Sphere, and two coloured Maps, illustrative of the principal Geographical Terms. Fourteenth Edition. 16mo, 3s. cloth.

II. AN ATLAS,

Adapted to the Abbé Gaultier's Geographical Games, consisting of 8 Maps, coloured, and 7 in Outline, &c. Folio, 15s. half-bound.

BUTLER'S OUTLINE MAPS, AND KEY;

Or, Geographical and Biographical Exercises; with a Set of Coloured Outline Maps; designed for the Use of Young Persons. By the late WILLIAM BUTLER. Enlarged by the Author's Son, J. O. BUTLER. Thirtieth Edition, revised. 4s.

BATTLE-FIELDS.

A graphic Guide to the Places described in the History of England as the scenes of such Events; with the situation of the principal Naval Engagements fought on the Coast of the British Empire. By Mr. WAUTHIER, Geographer. On a large sheet, 3s. 6d.; in case, 6s.; or mounted on oak, varnished, 10s. 6d.

THE CHILD'S GRAMMAR.

By the late Lady FENN, under the assumed name of Mrs. Lovechild. Forty-seventh Edition. 18mo, 9d. cloth.

ROWBOTHAM'S NEW AND EASY METHOD OF LEARN-

ING the FRENCH GENDERS. New Edition. 6d.

BELLENGER'S FRENCH WORD AND PHRASE-BOOK;

Containing a select Vocabulary and Dialogues, for the Use of Beginners. New Edition, 1s. sewed.

ALWAYS HAPPY;

Or, Anecdotes of Felix and his Sister Serena. By the Author of "Claudine," &c. Eighteenth Edition, with new Illustrations. Royal 18mo, price 2s. 6d. cloth.

ANDERSEN'S (H. C.) NIGHTINGALE AND OTHER TALES.

2s. 6d. plain; 3s. 6d. coloured.

ANECDOTES OF KINGS,

selected from History; or, Gertrude's Stories for Children. With Engravings. 2s. 6d. plain; 3s. 6d. coloured.

BIBLE ILLUSTRATIONS;

Or, a Description of Manners and Customs peculiar to the East, and especially explanatory of the Holy Scriptures. By the Rev. B. H. DRAPER. With Engravings. Fourth Edition. Revised by J. KITTO, Editor of "The Pictorial Bible," &c. 3s. 6d. cloth.

"This volume will be found unusually rich in the species of information so much needed by young readers of the Scriptures."—Christian Mother's Mag.

THE BRITISH HISTORY BRIEFLY TOLD,

and a Description of the Ancient Customs, Sports, and Pastimes of the English. Embellished with full-length Portraits of the Sovereigns of England in their proper Costumes, and 18 other Engravings. 3s. 6d. cloth.

CHIT-CHAT;

Or, Short Tales in Short Words. By a MOTHER, Author of "Always Happy." New and Cheaper Edition. With New Engravings. 2s. 6d. cloth; 3s. 6d. coloured, gilt edges.

CLAUDINE;

Or, Humility the Basis of all the Virtues. A Swiss Tale. By the Author of "Always Happy," &c. Ninth Edition. 18mo, price 3s. cloth.

CONVERSATIONS ON THE LIFE OF JESUS CHRIST,

For the use of Children. By a MOTHER. A New Edition. With 12 Engravings. 2s. 6d. plain; 3s. 6d. coloured.

COSMORAMA.

The Manners, Customs, and Costumes of all Nations of the World described. By J. ASPIN. New Edition, with numerous Illustrations. 3s. 6d. plain; and 4s. 6d. coloured.

INFANTINE KNOWLEDGE;

A Spelling and Reading Book, on a Popular Plan, combining much Useful Information with the Rudiments of Learning. By the Author of "The Child's Grammar." With numerous Engravings. Ninth Edit. 2s. 6d. plain; 3s. 6d. col.

FACTS TO CORRECT FANCIES;

Or, Short Narratives compiled from the Biography of Remarkable Women. By a MOTHER. With Engravings. 3s. 6d. plain; 4s. 6d. coloured.

FRUITS OF ENTERPRISE,

Exhibited in the Travels of Belzoni in Egypt and Nubia. Thirteenth Edition, with six Engravings. 18mo, price 3s. cloth.

THE GARDEN;

Or, Frederick's Monthly Instructions for the Management and Formation of a Flower-Garden. Fourth Edition. With Engravings of the Flowers in Bloom for each Month in the Year, &c. 3s. 6d. plain; or 6s. with the Flowers col.

EASY LESSONS;

Or, Leading-Strings to Knowledge. New Edition, with 8 Engravings. 2s. 6d. plain; 3s. 6d. coloured.

KEY TO KNOWLEDGE;

Or, Things in Common Use simply and shortly explained. By a MOTHER, Author of "Always Happy," &c. Thirteenth Edition. With sixty Illustrations. 3s. 6d. cloth.

THE LADDER TO LEARNING:

A Collection of Fables, Original and Select, arranged progressively in words of One, Two, and Three Syllables. Edited and improved by the late MRS. TRIMMER. With 79 Cuts. Nineteenth Edition. 3s. 6d. cloth.

LITTLE LESSONS FOR LITTLE LEARNERS,

In Words of One Syllable. By MRS. BARWELL. Eighth Edit., with numerous Illustrations. 2s. 6d. plain; 3s. 6d. col.

THE LITTLE READER;

A Progressive Step to Knowledge. New Edition, with sixteen Plates. Price 2s. 6d. cloth.

MAMMA'S LESSONS

For her Little Boys and Girls. Twelfth Edition, with eight Engravings. Price 2s. 6d. cloth; 3s. 6d. coloured, gilt edges.

THE MINE;

Or, Subterranean Wonders. An Account of the Operations of the Miner, and the Products of his Labours; with a Description of the most important in all parts of the World. By the late Rev. ISAAC TAYLOR. Sixth Edition, with numerous corrections and additions, by MRS. LOUDON. With 45 new Woodcuts and 16 Steel Engravings. 3s. 6d. cl.

THE OCEAN;

a Description of Wonders and important Products of the Sea. Second Edition. With Illustrations of 37 Genera of Shells, by SOWERBY; and 4 Steel and 50 Wood Engravings. 3s. 6d. cloth.

THE RIVAL CRUSOES,

And other Tales. By AGNES STRICKLAND, Author of "The Queens of England." Sixth Edition. 18mo, price 2s. 6d. cloth.

SHORT TALES,

Written for Children. By DAME TRUELOVE and her Friends. A new Edition, with 20 Engravings. 3s. 6d. cloth.

THE STUDENTS;

Or, Biographies of the Grecian Philosophers. 12mo, price 2s. 6d. cloth.

THE SHIP;

a Description of different kinds of Vessels, with the Distinctive Flags of Different Nations, and numerous Engravings. By the late REV. ISAAC TAYLOR. Sixth Edition, revised by M. H. BARKER, the Old Sailor. 3s. 6d. cloth.

STORIES OF EDWARD AND HIS LITTLE FRIENDS.

With 12 Illustrations. Second Edit. 3s. 6d. plain ; 4s. 6d. col.

SUNDAY LESSONS FOR LITTLE CHILDREN.

By MRS. BARWELL. Third Edition. 2s. 6d. plain ; 3s. col.

THE TWIN SISTERS;

Or, the Advantages of Religion. By Miss SANDHAM. Twenty-second Edition. 18mo, price 3s. cloth.

A VISIT TO GROVE COTTAGE,

And the India Cabinet Opened. By the Author of " Fruits of Enterprise." New Edition. 18mo, price 3s. cloth.

DISSECTIONS FOR YOUNG CHILDREN.

In a Neat Box. Price 6s. each.

1. Scenes from the Lives of Joseph and Moses.
2. Scenes from the History of Our Saviour.
3. Old Mother Hubbard and her Dog.
4. The Life and Death of Cock Robin.

TWO SHILLINGS EACH, CLOTH.

With Frontispiece, &c.

DER SCHWÄTZER : an amusing Introduction to the German Language. 16 plates.

LE BABILLARD ; an amusing Introduction to the French Language. 16 plates.

COUNSELS AT HOME ; with Anecdotes, Tales, &c.

MORAL TALES. By a FATHER. With 2 Engravings.

ANECDOTES OF PETER THE GREAT, Emperor of Russia. 18mo.

ONE SHILLING AND SIXPENCE EACH, CLOTH.

THE DAUGHTER OF A GENIUS. A Tale. By MRS. HOFLAND. Sixth Edition.

ELLEN THE TEACHER. By MRS. HOFLAND. New Edition.

THE SON OF A GENIUS. By MRS. HOFLAND. New Edition.

THEODORE ; or, the Crusaders. By MRS. HOFLAND.

THE HISTORY OF PRINCE LEE BOO. New Edition.

TRIMMER'S (MRS.) OLD TESTAMENT LESSONS. With 40 Engravings.

TRIMMER'S (MRS.) NEW TESTAMENT LESSONS. With 40 Engravings.

ONE SHILLING EACH, CLOTH.

WELCOME VISITOR ; a Collection of Original Stories,

NINA, an Icelandic Tale. By the Author of "Always Happy."

SPRING FLOWERS and the MONTHLY MONITOR.

LESSONS of WISDOM for the YOUNG. By the REV. W. FLETCHER.

YOUNG JEWESS and her CHRISTIAN SCHOOLFELLOWS. By the Author of "Rhoda."

THE CHILD'S DUTY. Dedicated by a Mother to her Children. Second Edition.

DECEPTION and FREDERICK MARSDEN, the Faithful Friend.

DURABLE NURSERY BOOKS,

MOUNTED ON CLOTH, WITH COLOURED PLATES,

ONE SHILLING EACH.

1 Alphabet of Goody Two-Shoes.
2 Cinderella.
3 Cock Robin.
4 Courtship of Jenny Wren.
5 Dame Trot and her Cat.
6 History of an Apple Pie.
7 House that Jack built.
8 Little Rhymes for Little Folks.
9 Mother Hubbard.
10 Monkey's Frolic.
11 Old Woman and her Pig.
12 Puss in Boots.
13 Tommy Trip's Museum of Birds, Part I.
14 ——————— Part II.

DURABLE BOOKS FOR SUNDAY READING.

SCENES FROM THE LIVES OF JOSEPH AND MOSES.
With Illustrations by JOHN GILBERT. Printed on Linen.
Price 1s.

SCENES FROM THE HISTORY OF OUR SAVIOUR.
With Illustrations by JOHN GILBERT. Printed on Linen.
Price 1s.

DARNELL'S EDUCATIONAL WORKS.

The attention of all interested in the subject of Education is
invited to these Works, now in extensive use throughout the
Kingdom, prepared by Mr. DARNELL, a Schoolmaster of many
years' experience.

1. COPY BOOKS.—A SURE AND CERTAIN ROAD TO A GOOD
   HAND WRITING, gradually advancing from the Simple
   Stroke to a superior Small-hand.

   LARGE POST, Sixteen Numbers, 6d. each.

   FOOLSCAP, Twenty Numbers, to which are added three Sup-
   plementary Numbers of Angular Writing for Ladies, and one
   of Ornamental Hands. Price 3d. each.

   ₄ This series may also be had on very superior paper, marble covers,
   4d. each.

   "For teaching writing I would recommend the use of Darnell's Copy
   Books. I have noticed a marked improvement wherever they have been
   used."—*Report of Mr. Mayo (National School Organizer of Schools) to the
   Worcester Diocesan Board of Education.*

2. GRAMMAR, made intelligible to Children, 1s. cloth.'

3. ARITHMETIC, made intelligible to Children, 1s. 6d. cloth.

   ₄ Key to Parts 2 and 3, price 1s. cloth.

4. READING, a Short and Certain Road to, price 6d. cloth.

GRIFFITH AND FARRAN,

CORNER OF ST. PAUL'S CHURCHYARD.

www.ingramcontent.com/pod-product-compliance
Lightning Source LLC
Chambersburg PA
CBHW022021110726
47901CB00006B/1609